**Omaima Al-Khamis** was born in Riy
She holds a BA in Arabic literature from
a diploma in English from Washington
career as a teacher of literature before spending ten years as director
of educational media in the Ministry of Education in Saudi Arabia.

A prolific writer, she began writing for newspapers at an early
age. She has published novels, short-story collections, opinion pieces, and children's books, and has been translated into English, Ital-
ian, and other languages. Her first novel, *al-Bahriyat* (Sailors), was a
popular success and her second novel, *al-Warifa* (The Leafy Tree),
was longlisted for the International Prize for Arabic Fiction in 2010.

*The Book Smuggler* (titled *Masra al-Gharaniq fi Mudun al-'Aqiq* in the
original Arabic) was published in 2017 and is her fourth novel. It
won the Naguib Mahfouz Medal for Literature in 2018.

She lives in Riyadh with her husband, two sons, and daughter.

**Sarah Enany** is a literary translator and a professor in the English
Department of Cairo University, Egypt.

# The Book Smuggler

Omaima Al-Khamis

Translated by
Sarah Enany

hoopoe
AN IMPRINT OF AUC PRESS

First published in 2021 by
Hoopoe
113 Sharia Kasr el Aini, Cairo, Egypt
One Rockefeller Plaza, 10th Floor, New York, NY 10020
www.hoopoefiction.com

Hoopoe is an imprint of The American University in Cairo Press
www.aucpress.com

ISBN 978 1 61797 998 9

Library of Congress Cataloging-in-Publication Data

Names: Khamīs, Umaymah, author. | Enany, Sarah, translator.
Title: The book smuggler / Omaima Al-Khamis ; translated by Sarah Enany.
Other titles: Masrá al-gharānīq fī mudun al-ʿaqīq. English
Identifiers: LCCN 2020043854 | ISBN 9781617979989 (paperback) | ISBN
9781649030597 (epub) | ISBN 9781649030603 (adobe pdf)
Subjects: LCSH: Smugglers--Islamic Empire--Fiction. | Booksellers and
bookselling--Islamic Empire--Fiction. | Scribes--Islamic
Empire--Fiction. | Voyages and travels--Fiction. | Historical fiction.
Classification: LCC PJ7842.H3213 M3713 2021 | DDC 892.7/37--dc23

2 3 4 5    25 24 23 22 21

Designed by Adam el-Sehemy
Printed in the United States of America

To the Voyagers, the Cranes, from Wasil ibn Ataa to Muhammad Abid al-Jabri: Voices of the Fettered Mind

# Historical figures

| | |
|---|---|
| **Abu al-Alaa al-Maari** | Renowned, blind ancient Arab poet. |
| **Abu Bakr** | The first of the First Four Caliphs of Islam, who ruled after the Prophet's death. |
| **Abu Hayan al-Tawhidi** | Renowned tenth-century Arab intellectual and philosopher. |
| **Abu Nawas** | Famous ancient Arab poet, known for his verses on the love of boys among others. |
| **Ahmad ibn Tulun** | Founder of the Tulunid dynasty in Egypt, best remembered for his great mosque. |
| **Amr ibn al-Aas** | Arab commander who led the Muslim conquest of Egypt and Egypt's first Islamic ruler. |
| **Caliph Abd al-Malik** | Fifth Umayyad caliph. Revived Umayyad authority, quelling Kharijite rebellion. |
| **Caliph Adud al-Dawla al-Bouhi** | "Pillar of the Dynasty," a Buyid caliph whose empire stretched from Yemen to the Mediterranean. |
| **Caliph al-Hakim bi-Amr Allah** | Sixth Fatimid caliph of Egypt, best known for his arbitrary and bizarre laws, such as prohibiting the sale of women's footwear and the eating of *mulukhiya*. |
| **Caliph Mamoun** | Seventh Abbasid caliph, Baghdad. Known for supporting Mutazilism and imprisoning the strict Imam Ahmad ibn Hanbal. |

| | |
|---|---|
| **Caliph Muawiya** | Founder and first caliph of the Umayyad Caliphate. Ascended to the caliphate after conflict with Ali ibn Abu Taleb, ending with Ali's assassination by a Kharijite. |
| **Caliph al-Muizz (li-Din Allah)** | Fourth Fatimid caliph of Egypt, best known for constructing the walled city of what is now Old Cairo as the new capital of the Fatimid Caliphate. |
| **Caliph al-Muqtadir bi-Allah** | Eighteenth Abbasid caliph, Baghdad. |
| **Caliph al-Mustansir** | First caliph of Cairo for the Mamluk Sultanate. |
| **Caliph al-Mutasim** | Eighth Abbasid caliph, Baghdad. |
| **Caliph al-Qadir** | Abbasid caliph in Baghdad best known for supporting the Sunnis against the Shiites. |
| **al-Farabi** | Famous Persian philosopher of early Islamic times. Said to have preserved the ancient Greek texts in the Middle Ages. |
| **Harut and Marut** | Two angels mentioned in the Qur'an (2:102), said to have tested the people with sorcery. |
| **Hisham ibn al-Hakam of the Umayyads, also known as al-Muayyad** | Shiite scholar of the second century AH, a defender of the doctrine of imams being selected on the basis of wisdom and logic. |
| **Ibn Hanbal** | One of the four Great Sunni Imams, known for his strictness. |
| **Ibn al-Haytham** | Famous Arab polymath, astronomer, and physicist, known as "the father of modern optics." |
| **Ibn Hisham** | Editor of the ancient biography of Prophet Muhammad written by Ibn Ishaq. |
| **Ibn al-Muqaffa** | Renowned ancient Arab poet. |

| | |
|---|---|
| **Imam Ali ibn Abu Talib** | The fourth of the Four Caliphs of Islam, who ruled after the Prophet's death. Shiite Muslims believe that Ali should have been First Caliph rather than Abu Bakr and Umar after him, which caused a schism between them and Sunni Muslims. He was assassinated by a member of the Khawarij sect in 661. |
| **Imam al-Husayn** | Son of Ali ibn Abu Taleb and grandson of Prophet Muhammad, third Shiite Imam. Rejected the claim to the Caliphate of Yazid, son of Muawiya, and consequently was killed in the famous battle of Karbala. Hussein's death became the catalyst for the Umayyad Caliphate's eventual Abbasid overthrow. |
| **Imam al-Shafei** | One of the four Great Sunni Imams, known for his leniency. |
| **Imru al-Qays** | Renowned ancient Arab poet. |
| **al-Jahiz** | Renowned ancient Arab prose author and Mutazilite. |
| **al-Kindi** | Famous Iraqi Muslim philosopher, mathematician, physician, and musician, known as "the father of Arab philosophy." |
| **al-Mutanabbi** | Renowned ancient Arab poet. |
| **Umar (ibn al-Khattab)** | The second of the First Four Caliphs of Islam, who ruled after the Prophet's death. |
| **Uthman ibn Affan** | The third of the First Four Caliphs of Islam, who ruled after the Prophet's death. |
| **Yazid ibn Muawiya** | Second Umayyad Caliph; attained power after the beheading of al-Husayn in the Battle of Karbala. Understandably, bad blood between the supporters of Ali and those of Yazid and Muawiya ensued. |

# Dynasties

| | |
|---|---|
| **Abbasids** | Arab clan descended from Abbas ibn Abd al-Muttalib, 750–1517 with the exception of the years 1259–60. |
| **Buyids** | Ancient Shiite Iranian dynasty of Daylamite origin, ruled Iraq and southern Iran 934–1062. |
| **Byzantines** | The Byzantine Empire was the continuation of the Roman Empire in the Middle Ages. Its capital city was Constantinople; it fell to the Ottoman Empire in 1453, and until then was the most powerful empire in Europe. |
| **Umayyads** | Ruling family of the Muslim Caliphate 661–750; overthrown in 750 by the Abbasids. |

# Peoples

| | |
|---|---|
| **Ayyarin** | Criminal gangs. |
| **Berbers** | Old name for people of the Maghreb. |
| **Daylamites** | An Iranian people of the Daylam, which refers to the mountainous regions of northern Iran on the southwest coast of the Caspian Sea. |
| **Hanbalites** | Followers of the principles of Imam Ibn Hanbal. |
| **Hanafites** | Followers of the principles of Imam Abu Hanifa. |
| **Hashimite** | Member of the clan of Hashim. |
| **Ishmaelites** | Muslim Arabs descended from Ishmael, the elder son of Abraham. |
| **Jahmis** | Followers of the thinking of Jahm ibn Safwan, who denied all the names and attributes of Allah considered sacred by orthodox Muslims. The word came to be a pejorative term among early Hanbalites, with a connotation of heresy. |

| | |
|---|---|
| **Khawarij, aka Kharijites** | Sect in the first century of Islam who revolted against Caliph Ali after he agreed to arbitration with his rival Muawiya I for succession to the caliphate, and later assassinated him. |
| **Mushabbiha** | Those who compare God to human form—considered blasphemous by some Muslims. |
| **Mutazilites** | Rationalist school of Islamic theology based on justice and monotheism. Considered blasphemous by some. |
| **Nasibi (pl. Nawasib)** | A Shiite slur for Salafi (Sunni) Muslims, literally meaning "hater." |
| **Qarmatians** | Branch of Shiite Islam, notorious for sacking Mecca in AD 930. |
| **Rafida** | Derogatory Sunni term for Shiite Muslims, meaning "those who reject" since Shiites view Ali as the Prophet's first successor. |
| **Rajilat al-Hanabila** | Civilian militia intent on establishing the strictest principles of Imam Ibn Hanbal by force. |
| *saqaliba* (**sing.** *saqlabi*) | Muslim Slavs from Central and Eastern Europe, originally brought to the Arab world as slaves. |
| **Shiites and Sunnis** | Shiite Muslims do not recognize the first three caliphs—Abu Bakr, Umar, and Uthman—as the legitimate successors of Muhammad. Shiites believe Ali to be the first successor. This is why Shiite worship is centered around Ali as a descendant of the Prophet Muhammad, and drives some Sunni Muslims to brand them as heretics. |

## Terms

| | |
|---|---|
| *bimaristan* | Hospital. |
| *fitna* | *Fitna* is a catchall term literally meaning "sedition," but can also mean "temptation" or "civil war" depending on the context. |

| | |
|---|---|
| **The Fitna of Cordoba / of the Umayyads** | The Fitna of Cordoba, aka the Fitna of al-Andalus, resulted in the collapse of Umayyad and Amari rule, the fragmentation of Muslim Andalusia into *taifa*s, or factions, and the end of the Islamic Caliphate in that region. |
| | The Umayyad Fitna is a period of unrest in the Islamic community following the death of Muawiya I, whose throne was claimed by Husayn ibn Ali and then by Abdallah ibn al-Zubayr. Umayyad rule was ultimately restored, but the rift between Shiite and Sunni widened. |
| **House of Wisdom** | Another name for the (ancient) Great Library of Baghdad. |
| *jizya* | An ancient tax levied on non-Muslims living in an Islamic state. |
| **the Mahdi (the Fatimid Mahdi)** | The Mahdi is the prophesied redeemer of Islam. Mostly Shiites (and relatively few Sunnis) believe that the long-awaited Mahdi will appear at the end of the world to bring about a perfect and just Islamic society. |
| **Quraysh** | The ancient Arabian tribe from which the Prophet first hailed. |
| **zakat** | Islam-mandated annual charitable sum. It was enforced by law under caliphs of early Islamic dynasties and paid into the state treasury. |

# 1

# Caravans Pursued by Longing, Exiled by Drought
## Shaaban 4, AH 402; March 1, AD 1012

I TURN MY FACE TO the city of Jerusalem, and I am neither prophet nor saint nor missionary.

I am no disciple in the first stages of reaching up to attain knowledge, excavating for answers in the discussion circles of mosques and the loneliness of monks' cells; I am but a book-seller in the era of sedition, or, as it is known, *fitna*: conflict and quarrel, the lust for burning records and manuscripts, and purging sins with blazing coals.

Behind us is the town of Ayn al-Tamr, giving way in the west to Basra in the Levant. The land slopes gently into flat plains, except for a few hills, and passages through valleys. Sand dunes part and rejoin; suddenly, from between them, there appear breathtaking towers of rock, sharpened like great djinn standing in rows in preparation for some monumental task. Around the bases of these great pinnacles and among their curves, mirrored streams twine, shining with pebbles and filled with sweet water. The branches of palms and acacias interlock around them, flocks of wary partridges followed by their chicks filling the spaces between their rocks, like beads in a tightly strung rosary.

We pause to sleep beneath the shoulder of the mountain. We cook our food and feed our beasts of burden. When evening comes, some of us retire to the caves for shelter from the bite of the cold wind. In the cave, we light a small fire that makes our shadows flicker on the rocky walls; when we stare into the dark, we know they are not our shadows, but folk we cannot see, taking their supper in grim silence. We call to them in greeting, but they make no answer; instead, a cold wind blows in from the mouth of the cave, making us cry out the Lord's name. We sleep like a pack of wolves, with one eye open, before we go out again at dawn, down the treacherous mountain paths to the caravan preparing to set off.

I stopped sleeping in caves after that. I preferred to remain close to my crate of books, for fear it might pique someone's curiosity enough to steal a glance inside.

Before sunrise, a freezing wind from the Levant blows over us, nipping at my extremities and rustling the dried evening primrose bushes on our path, making them tremble and whine. I wait for the sun to rise into the sky for a little warmth: a sky of such deep blue that even the flies would not think of buzzing there. The caravan leader commands the camel driver to raise his voice in song, in hopes of revitalizing the beasts. We approach an oasis where some of the clansmen of the tribe of Kalb ibn Wabara are wintering.

The camels rest on the outskirts of the tribe's winter grounds for a number of days. Before we resume our journey, the caravan leader asks them for a tracker to accompany us, to guide us to a shorter path through the Sarhan Valley, leading down to Basra and thus saving us four days of travel.

Numb with cold, I wrap my turban more securely about my head and bow my head to protect the bridge of my nose. From my sleeve, I withdraw Galen of Pergamon's book of medicine. It is the only book I have dared to keep outside the crate. I sink into endless recipes: the imbalance of humors in the body, earth, water, heat, cold, pulled this way and that by the forces of attraction and stability, digestion and impulse, and all that Galen believed to be the cause of disease. I fear for the balance of my own humors now that my extremities feel frozen. I wrap my merino-lined Nabatean abaya of thick wool more closely about me, its edges embroidered with curlicues resembling the crest of a hoopoe. When the healing *saba* breezes come from the southeast, it is as though the air is gentle hands caressing my frozen limbs. Perhaps if I listen closely to the southern breezes, I will hear the rattle and clatter of the caravans of the *mustariba*, the Adnanite Arabs, who have left their ruins in the Arabian Peninsula and moved on to the paths of flooding in the north.

Hundreds of caravans, lost, pursued by longing, exiled by drought, seeking out fertile lands where rivers once flowed, hills were verdant, and fields bore fruit, in the depths of every one of them a Bedouin melancholy with the dream of return.

A bookseller: perhaps it is my true occupation, or perhaps I use it to hide from the suspicions and doubts of the travelers on this caravan, bearing perfumes from Baghdad to Jerusalem. I avoid their evening gatherings; I ignore the lines they throw me, hoping to reel me in to their conversation. I am terse and monosyllabic, my motions quick and darting. Will they notice that I am a terrified fugitive, transporting not only philosophical and heretical tomes, but also the commandments of the Just Monotheists, not knowing to which of these groups he belongs? For I am still a spirit suspended somewhere between the two, between two statuses manifested in this era they call the Cream of Ages. I am Mazid al-Hanafi, son of Abdullah Thaqib al-Hanafi and Shammaa of the House of Wael, and what I possess is little indeed, down to the scant layer of fat under the skin of my old she-camel, Shubra. I named her so on the advice of al-Fazzari, the Bedouin who sold her to me under the southern wall of Baghdad. He told me that Shubra was the name of a great she-demon who lived in the desert, whose powers would be summoned if my camel were named after her, making the camel light of foot and energetic, flying like the wind as her namesake does. She would then cross the deserts and the dunes, he said, and obey my every command.

However, the she-demon did not seem to find my camel's hairy, bony body an agreeable home for her presence, what with her pendulous lips and cracked pads. The poor creature walked with difficulty, lagging behind the caravan, straining under the crate of books her puny legs were ill-equipped to carry, the distances she walked eating away at them. Was her weariness due to the books of philosophy and heresy she carried on her back?

More than two years before, when we had passed by the tomb of Abu Taher al-Janabi al-Qarmati in the region of Ihsaa, the keepers of the mausoleum told us that the she-camel who had carried upon her back the famous Black Rock, which was ripped from the Holy Kaaba and brought to Ihsaa, had grown fat and healthy and put on flesh, and was blessed every year with twins. What odd tales the keepers told us! One was that the body of Hamdan al-Qarmati did not decompose in its grave because the maggots were kept miraculously from his sacred body, and that tall men in green robes circumambulated the mausoleum nightly, singing God's praises. Meanwhile, the philosophers' weight upon Shubra's frame caused her to wither away mile after mile.

I had determined that Damascus would be my next stop after Baghdad: its mosques, its imams, its libraries, all held much in store for me. Damascus was the home of Muawiya ibn Abu Sufyan, whom I always imagined with a crown befitting a caesar and not the turban of an Islamic leader. In my mind, he swaggered along wearing a robe of scarlet silk swirling proudly about him, with bright eyes that brought together intelligence and the lusts of a tyrannical monarch.

My grandfather was a sheikh and the imam of a mosque in the Citadel of Bani Ukhaydar in the region of Hijr al-Yamama in the central Arabian Peninsula. After each prayer, he would say prayers atop the minaret for long life and power and eventual rise to the caliphate for the descendants of Imam

Ali ibn Abu Talib, as the Shiites do, after which all the inhabitants of al-Yamama would say "Amen!" But he never cursed the imam Muawiya, merely saying, "The Shiite descendants of the Prophet have a dispute with the people of the Levant rooted in conflict over who should rule, and Muawiya is the aggressor in that dispute. However," he would continue, "when power settled upon Muawiya and his rivals were done away with, he became a just caliph, with an army and conquests that shine upon the pages of his good deeds." When I was born, he named me Mazid after his own grandfather, whereupon the men of Bani Ukhaydar all remonstrated with him, saying, "Mazid is but an anagram of the name of Yazid ibn Muawiya, Lord damn him! How could you name your grandson such a name?" But he ignored them and kept my name unchanged. Since my name means "more," he prayed to the Lord to give me more years of life, more earnings in this world, and more knowledge and education.

According to Damascenes, the only remaining copy of the definitive version of the Holy Qur'an created by Uthman ibn Affan, which he distributed among the different lands, is in the Umayyad Mosque. They say that its pages are still stained with his blood. The paper traders at the Baghdad Market still repeat this story to one another in wonder, saying that those who believe it are heretics: Uthman was murdered in Medina, while his copy of the Qur'an remained in the Levant. Yet the tale is still told in Iraq.

I ached for the libraries of the Syriac Catholic priests in Damascus, who left no book by the Greeks they encountered untranslated. However, all the caravans that left Baghdad for Jerusalem refused to pass by Damascus that year. There was news that, despite the Byzantine emperor Basil's ten-year pact of peace with the Fatimids, some mercenaries from his armies were disguising themselves in the garb of Arab traders, or as pilgrims headed for Jerusalem; once in this guise, they approached the caravans of the Silk Road on their way from Persia laden with saffron and jasper, or from Iraq and Oman laden with perfumes and gum arabic. They set upon them and robbed them of everything, even the traders' garments, then heated a piece of metal in the shape of a crucifix, branded their backs with it, and fled.

The Fatimid wali in Damascus turned a blind eye to their doings, with the excuse that the handful of soldiers in his province were ill equipped to face the gangs of the Normans. In truth, he cared nothing, nor did he listen to the complaints that reached his ears, so long as the caravans arriving from Byzantium and their lands had paid him the pilgrimage tax for Jerusalem.

Free will, not predestination. There are burning coals of longing in my heart that are not yet ash. Baghdad kicked me out; I did not leave it willingly. Baghdad is a savage seductress, like a beauty into whose tent I had crept, and had drunk of her springs and plucked her fruits, but who then viciously told me to leave at dawn. It was that city that revealed to me the greatest secret, where the Just Monotheists breathed their message into my heart. My departure from Baghdad left me disturbed and flustered, as though beneath me were only the wind.

Predestination or free will? On that day, when I fully resolved to leave Baghdad, at midday I was still walking around this and that caravan, where the camels slept, in search of one to join. Some advised me to direct my steps to al-Anbar, where I should find a great many caravans whose camel drivers were the best at tracking and knew all the desert paths: the caravans arriving in Baghdad, it was explained to me, had avaricious leaders—so avaricious, some swore, that they split up the booty collected from the traders' caravans with the robbers who ambushed them along the way. I looked into people's faces and examined their features: it was not as though a thief would approach me and say, "Honorable brother Mazid, I am a robber, so please do not choose my caravan."

It was the habit of caravan leaders to call out their destination. But my arrival at the market coincided with the arrival of caravans from the desert, laden with its bounty: grouse, sparrows, desert truffles, and the bitter apples that the people of Baghdad regularly ingested to purify their insides. Everyone in the marketplace clustered around the caravans, and no one paid me any mind.

I kept walking until I reached the riverbank. I began to hear the cries of the boatmen and the dinghy skippers, reaching me together with the braying of camels and the moist perfume of river silt mixed with the ashes of burnt palm fronds.

A man caught my attention. He was standing by an immense white she-camel, sitting like a hillock, with tiered wooden shelves atop her hump. Upon these shelves, in neat rows, the man was carefully placing small glass bottles, each of a different color. I had never seen anything as beautiful as the colors of these bottles, the charm of their ornamentation, or the intricacy of the miniatures painted upon them. One was the color of saffron, the next azure, the next turquoise. Their stoppers were all of petaled crimson, ornamented with the same color as the bottle they were placed in. Some were inscribed with names such as "water lily, narcissus, bay laurel"; others with "iris, lily, myrtle"; others "sage, henbane, bitter orange"; and still others with "cadaba, sweet basil, rhubarb." When the man had finished arranging them in their boxes, he covered them with a linen cloth, a thin boy behind him sewing the edges of the linen into the edges of the boxes with great skill, as though he had been born with that great sewing needle in his hands. My avid stare eventually caused the man to turn and smile quizzically at me. He had sharp features and a deeply lined face. His neatly trimmed beard had white hairs in it, but his shoulders were wide, and his body was muscular and built like a soldier's, incongruous with his elderly and tired features. He appeared unperturbed at my intense scrutiny. Indeed, he spoke to me in the accent of a Daylamite, as though continuing a long conversation: "That's the way of perfumes, like a virgin's lips or butterfly wings. Air and light ruin them—especially ambergris. That's why they must be protected on this long journey."

His pleasant demeanor encouraged me to ask eagerly, "Where to?"

The Daylamite responded unhesitatingly, "To Basra in the Levant."

"Perhaps you will pass by Damascus on the way?" I said beseechingly.

"And perhaps you are eager for a brand in the back," he retorted in a mocking tone. He then began to repeat the tales everyone was telling about the Byzantine marauders disguised as caravan drivers. When he arrived at the part of the story about the red-hot brand they applied to traders' backs, he called out to a man feeding his camels a short way away from us. "Hilal! Come over here!"

Hilal's name means "crescent," and he was like the waning crescent moon: tall, skinny, hollow-cheeked, carrying ropes bundled around his arm. "Show us your brand," the Daylamite sneered.

After a moment's hesitation, Hilal, wretched and humiliated, turned and opened the neck of his tunic, showing his shoulder blade. "God damn them," he said. "They tied me up after I killed three of them!" We could see it clearly: the brand of a cross, the scar gouged deep into the flesh of his back, not yet fully healed; its edges were still suppurating. Before I could so much as wince in sympathy, the Daylamite gave Hilal a kick in the buttocks. "Go!" he guffawed lewdly. "Let's hope it's just your shoulder the Byzantines branded, and not some other place!"

I was stricken at his cruelty in the face of the man's age and his brokenness. Still, the Daylamite was my last hope for leaving this day. He was one of those men whose caravan you want to join: he had an air of competence and power about him, like the last and best resort after an exhausting journey. The deep timbre of his voice, the scent of perfumes in his abaya, the delicacy of his hands, and the awe in which his underlings held him, all bespoke a trader who could loosen the purse strings of barter and lubricate the long journey with the salve of stories; a skilled broker who could so side with the buyer that the latter felt they were buying the goods together.

He charged me a sum greater than that usually asked by caravan leaders. It was, later, he who recommended Farrazi, that camel dealer who saddled me with Shubra. But my mind was set at rest by his presence. It was the whisper in my breast that said, "Do not pretend that you have free will; do not fight destiny. It will surely be the death of you. Pass along the road set forth for you by Fate alone."

Only then did I know that God intended me to stay away from Damascus, and that I would be accompanying this caravan to Basra; from there, I should certainly find passage to the City of Prophets. I hurried to my Hashimite teacher to inform him that there was no way to reach Damascus, and that my next stop after Baghdad would be Jerusalem.

## Bajkam's Chests

It would not be long now until we reached Basra in the Levant. Whenever we stopped, the Daylamite leader of our caravan always warned us away from the chests eroded by the desert sand, which we thought were treasure chests. "They are," he said, "the chests of Bajkam, the minister of Caliph al-Radi, who was said to have embezzled a great fortune from the treasury and was afraid the money would be taken back after al-Radi's death. He collected it in chests and went out to the desert with a slave of his. He would have the slave dig a deep hole and mark the spot; then he would bury the chest, murder the slave so that he would not divulge the secret of the treasure, bury the slave in another chest by the side of the first, and go home." It is said that in this desert wilderness, there are nearly forty chests. And because the caravan robbers have already taken all that was in the chests over the years, there is nothing left but the chests with the betrayed slaves, whose souls would surely destroy anyone who dared open them.

My turban was only three arm spans long; I unfurled it and covered myself with it when I slept, including most of my face, so no member of the caravan could stare at my sleeping face and identify me. Or perhaps I simply desired the security I had known since I was a child of having my face masked. Only the chest of books, large and full, burdened the poor she-camel; I walked by her side at times, and sat at her right thigh at others, armed with nothing but my victuals, my collection of various acquisitions, and the wisdom of the ancients. The superlative craftsmanship of the chest and its expensive wood led me to sprinkle a layer of dust over it whenever we stopped, for its noble appearance was incongruous with my modest—almost mean—attire.

I would get rid of much of the contents of this chest in Jerusalem. I had been told that the scientists of Jerusalem, and especially its priests, were eager for knowledge and informa- tion, and took pride in their church libraries. They took care of these books, which contained the wisdom of the Greeks and the secrets of transforming base into precious metals, and would pay a month's salary for the privilege of adding a valu- able book to the libraries and treasure troves of the churches of Jerusalem. If I told them these were the books that were sold for their weight in gold immediately upon their translation in the House of Wisdom, the Grand Library of Baghdad, they would no doubt eagerly purchase them, whereupon I would have spread the books of wisdom and philosophy throughout libraries and theological circles, not to mention the high prices that would not only cover the costs of my journey, but place some gold dinars in the purse at my waist. I did not know in truth whether these books were actually the ones whose pages were exchanged for gold at the House of Wisdom, or merely copies. I was only a simple trader: a few little lies were well within my right to purvey my wares, like the lies the Bedouin told when he sold me Shubra.

## A Veil Scented Like the Hills in Springtime

I am Mazid al-Najdi al-Hanafi, born in Hijr al-Yamama; my mother was Shammaa, of the House of Wael. Shammaa had long braids, and you could hear the jingling of her silver jewelry wherever she went. Her veil smelled like the hills in springtime.

I was her only child: in my childhood, she thought me so fair-skinned and beautiful that she not only covered my face for fear of the evil eye, but planted a demon in every corner of our house and neighborhood to frighten me, so that I would not play too far from the house with the other children and allow them to, as she said, "pluck the roses from my cheeks." She followed me from room to room, or stood at the doorstep watching me climb the stairs, hand in hand with my grandfather, up to the Citadel of Bani Ukhaydar. Or perhaps she merely made the excuse for her constant movement from corridor to hallway to passageway so that she would not have to sit in the same room with my father. I rarely saw them speaking with affection or familiarity. He would stand at the door and call her: "You, woman from the House of Wael!" then proceed to upbraid her for mysterious matters between them. She would go to the farthest corner of the house and burst into heaving sobs, crying out the names of her family in al-Aflaj, who were four days' and nights' journey from Hijr al-Yamama.

My father was a camel trader, with broad shoulders, towering height, and a thick black beard down to the middle of his chest. One of his eyes was always red and teary, and in his final years, this eye melted from its socket out into his hand so that he only had one eye. My grandfather was from

Khadrama, but then moved to al-Yamama and settled there, having become the imam of the mosque of the rulers of Bani Ukhaydar Citadel, who were descendants of Imam Hassan, the Prophet's grandson, peace be upon him. The sheikhs of al-Yamama say of their ancestors that, when they intermingled with the best of all lineages, that of the Prophet, the lands of al-Yamama became green, their springs welled with water, plants burst forth, and the beasts became fruitful ever since they arrived, for they are the ones that the Lord promised springs when they arrive "shining of face and limbs from ablutions on the Judgment Day."

Hijr al-Yamama is the heart of al-Yamama and a destination for the neighboring towns and estates. The caravans on pilgrimage pass through it, and it is the market where my father set up shop, buying, selling, lending, and borrowing on credit. His coffers filled with dirhams, and his belt grew heavy with dinars; his flocks multiplied, and he bought estates, each with a well of its own, watering the date palms, vineyards, and fields of wheat. His silos, his crops, and his herds meant he could take his pick of any bride whose beauty was spoken about in al-Yamama, even if she was four days' journey away in the village of al-Aflaj.

My mother, Shammaa, was a delicate and blooming beauty. She had the features of a pampered little girl, and her cheeks were as round as the half-moon. Women called her "the quail" because of her tripping, pretty steps. Her voice was pliant and soft, which usually annoyed my father, who constantly complained about how slow she was to get to the point, how she was raising me "like a girl," and how she avoided him under the guise of following me around. I would run away from their skirmishes and go to my grandfather instead.

My shyness and tenderhearted nature led me to stick close to my grandfather. I followed him as he went from our house to the mosque, and we passed together through its great gate.

I sat next to him in the high pulpit as he recited the Qur'an at dawn, waiting for prayer time to arrive, watching the light spilling through the triangles and circles cut into the dome of the mosque roof, until the muezzin would call worshippers to prayer: "*God is Most Great, God is Most Great,*" ending with the unusual phrase, "Come to the best of all works!" After this, my grandfather would lead the men in prayer. "Come to prayer," he would say, and then, in an uncommon mixture of Sunni and Shiite, "Muhammad and Ali are the best of all men!" Then he would ask me to move back in the ranks and not look up at the ceiling or around at the faithful, but rather bow my head in respect at the presence of the Almighty, and look at the spot where one prostrated oneself. But I ignored him, spending prayer time watching the birds that looked in on us through the triangular and circular openings in the dome, wondering if they were praying along with us or watching us so as to betray our secrets to the desert robbers.

The mosque was the most impressive structure in al-Yamama. It was built of stone, not mud brick. Its inner walls were faced in gypsum, with blue leaf on top. Its pillars were topped with ornaments of white gesso. The prayer hall and the pulpit were covered with Persian carpets that tickled the soles of my feet, filling me with delight when I walked barefoot upon them. Next to the pulpit were wooden shelves set into the walls, inlaid with mother-of-pearl and framed with engraved wood, bearing copies of the Qur'an and some prayer books. Against the sides of the mosque were chambers and private boxes furnished with Persian carpets and woolen cushions for those spending time there in contemplation and prayer. Next to these were straw-stuffed silken cushions for discussion circles, in addition to brass urns with water for ablutions set out by the entrance. All this had been brought in by a great caravan by order of a Byzantine woman, Qout al-Quloub, mother to Prince Yusuf, and a favorite of His Majesty Ahmad. Not long after her son was born, he fell victim to an illness that strikes down many of the infants of Bani Ukhaydar and kills them speedily. The infant was at death's door; Qout al-Quloub made a sacred vow that if her son lived, she would furnish the Mosque of Our Lord. She fell asleep that night, her son hanging between life and death, his every breath dropping out onto his pillow. It was still misty at dawn, the mosques giving the call to prayer, when she glimpsed the Prophet Muhammad, prayers and peace be upon him, the babe's great-great-great-grandfather, bearing a piece of white silk dripping with water. "It is the water of the River Kawthar in Paradise, for the apple of my eye," he said, and passed the silken cloth over Yusuf's brow, cheek, and breast. The fever was extinguished with the sunrise. With the afternoon prayers, Yusuf was sitting up in bed, recovered, and asking for something to eat. She did not give him anything to eat; instead, she rushed to the mosque, spread out a prayer mat, and prostrated herself with great sobs, so that her slave girls could barely tear her away. From that day on, it is said, the mosque received special treatment from her.

Vultures nest on the towering eastern spires, five stories high, of the mighty Citadel of Bani Ukhaydar. The towers have two gates that open onto the palm groves. On the right side of these are the soldiers' barracks and the guardhouses, while the left side, overlooking the plains of Bani Hanifa, is inhabited by His Majesty Sayyid Ahmad ibn Ukhaydar, his womenfolk and family and servants. On feast days at prayer time, we saw the womenfolk descending draped in wools, silks, and satins, and heard the susurrations of their clothing rustling through the hallways and the whispers of their anklets as they walked. On the breeze wafted the perfumes of rose and safflower, thickening the air on the way to the mosque. Ornamental wooden screens were set up for them at the back of the prayer hall, and some of the little princesses rushed out from behind the barriers with faces as radiant as the full moon, chased by slave girls, their delicate hands adorned with henna and the chirping of their high voices filling the space of the mosque.

The Citadel is a tremendous castle overlooking al-Yamama from a great height. The people of al-Yamama look up at it in awe. An astounding stone staircase ascends to the castle, carved into the mountainside, each step exactly the same size. It is said that it is the wind that carved out the staircase, commanded by the prophet Sulayman for the extinct tribes of Tasm and Jadis, the bygone inhabitants of al-Yamama. I always accompanied my grandfather up the staircase to arrive at the mosque and commence prayer. In the middle, we began to hear the soldiers singing and the clatter of their weapons as they leapt about and yelled and took their exercise before the noon prayers: "There is no real man but Imam Ali ibn Abu Talib, and there is no real sword but Ali's sword, Dhu al-Faqqar, which the Prophet gifted to him!"

The wife of My Lord Ahmad, Qout al-Quloub, bless her, gave my grandfather a generous salary. Not only did he lead the prayers at the mosque, but he also owned a large ledger bound in precious leather and trimmed in brass, with a lock, where he set down the contracts of sale, debt, wills, and marriage. Then he locked the ledger up with a key he wore around his neck.

The lower square of Hijr al-Yamama is surrounded by passageways filled with stores: blacksmiths, tailors, spice traders, and other tradesmen and craftsmen. The northern side of the square is devoted to caravans, and from there the tradesmen who owed debts, the craftsmen in dispute, and the cheated laborers all climbed up to see my grandfather. They would stand at his door, crying out loudly, "Abu Abdullah! Wise man!" whereupon my grandfather would grant them an audience, hearing their complaints from morning till the noon prayers. After the noon prayers was the time for quarreling spouses, orphans whose inheritance had been unjustly taken, and brothers in disputes over inheritance. Between the afternoon and sundown prayers was time for the discussion circle: he went up to the mosque again, under his arm either a copy of the Qur'an with a thick leather cover inlaid with mother-of-pearl, or two large volumes bound in deerskin—the first was *The Classes of Poets* by Abu Sallam al-Jamihi, in which he classifies Islamic and pre-Islamic poets according to early critical criteria, and the other Ibn Hisham's *Life of the Prophet Muhammad*. He always said that these were the books that had cost him two years' savings on his lone journey to Baghdad. If it rained, he kept them inside a wooden box, then took them out and smoked them over acacia wood to dry them out as protection against mice, finally storing them in a silken bag. But my passion for such books was enough to keep the mice away: they were barely ever out of my hands. If not for my fear of my grandfather's displeasure, I would have pillowed my head on them as I slept. The other books in his library he had bought from the caravans en route to Mecca, which usually spent three nights in al-Yamama. Sometimes, years would go by without a single caravan, for fear of desert bandits who kidnapped pilgrims and sold them into slavery, or bands of marauding Qarmatians.

To my good fortune, that year—AH 400, the year I resolved to set off for Baghdad—there arrived at al-Yamama great numbers of caravans returning from Mecca, who arrived safely and informed us that the speech at the hajj pilgrimage that year had been given by the Shiite Fatimid ruler, a descendant of the Noble House of the Prophet, peace be upon him. The Citadel of Bani Ukhaydar, also Shiite, could barely contain the chorus of "*God is Most Great!*" and "Praise the Lord!"

## A Pen Next to the Throne

When my grandfather was teaching me how to hold a pen, my small hands were always stained with date syrup. My grandfather, not content with merely washing them, would make me perform ablutions "because the pen is next to God's throne, above all impurities; we must cleanse ourselves before taking it up." He would say: "The *alif* is tall and proud like a palm tree; the *baa* is like a pot with a small fire burning underneath," but I liked the *raa* best of all, because it was like the crescent moon that signals the start of Ramadan and the start of Eid.

In my grandfather's room, there were always loaves made from flour, soft dates, and jars of sweet water flavored with date pollen. My mother used to say that when she came from al-Aflaj as a young bride, she was afraid and weeping, so he placed a sweetmeat in her hand of the type they call *al-mann wa-l-salwa*, or manna. "Suck on it slowly," he said, "for it heals the wounds in the heart."

"I never asked him where he obtained it," my mother would say. "His room was always full of good food, and you could get soft dates in winter from there if you but asked him." His noble presence and his room both always smelled sweet, the latter filled with those we could see and those we could not. I remember sticking even closer to my grandfather during that time, never leaving him, coming and going, waking and sleeping.

At night, I would fight sleep so as to see who brought him his essentials while he was busy praying, kneeling and prostrating himself. When sleep rained down heavy on my eyelids, I heard clearly the rustle of wings; then I would hurriedly close my eyes, for fear of seeing some strange creature fluttering in the darkness of the room, even if it were an angel. "Grandfather," I remembered asking him, "who brings you fresh dates in the dead of winter?"

Pensively, he would answer from the Qur'an's Sura of Saad, staring at a mysterious point in front of him: "*Truly, such will be Our Bounty; it will never fail.*"

A road winding up through the palm groves and the water-wheels separated the center of Hijr al-Yamama from the Citadel and our homes. My closeness to my grandfather set me apart from the other boys my age, who were impulsive and mischievous. I did not leap around between the waterwheels and climb palm trees as they did, or fill the farmers' water troughs in exchange for a handful of dates or a piece of meat cooked in milk. On feast days I did not push and shove with the other boys to be allowed to restrain the sheep's heads and tails while the older men slaughtered them, garnering a piece of fat or liver as their prize.

This last was the cruelest thing and the most painful to my heart. Because I was the son of Abdullah al-Thaqib, I was obliged to watch the scene—the butcher's knife slicing through the animal's carotid artery, the bleating that tore at your heartstrings—without flinching: it was dishonorable to turn my face away or close my eyes against the sight. I was taught this by a slap in the face from my father's massive hand when he asked me at six years old to hold tightly a small billy goat for the slaughter. The goat was my friend Shaqran, which means "blond": he had shining golden fur and a bright forelock. His mother had died after he was born, and his twin brother as well, leaving only Shaqran. I stayed with him, soaked a rag in goat's milk, and let him nurse at it, and gave him water to drink with my own hand. I let him sleep by my side until he revived, found his feet, and gamboled about me all over the house. As he grew older, he became playful and butted you with his head, but I never stopped letting him nurse at the rag while we played and kept each other company. Little did I know that my father's weeping red eye was watching all this with a plan in mind.

I took hold of Shaqran and twisted his neck. His eyes were pleading, a little surprised at this rough play. I wept and refused. But the slap in the face brought me back to the slaughter: I twisted Shaqran's head and the butcher slit his throat, guffawing. My brother skinned him while the other boys laughed at my tears. The next day, I awoke with a fever, shivering at the nightmares that crowded in on me. My grief lay upon the ground as long as my shadow.

*

This was not enough for my father. He chose me, out of all his sons by other women, to put out the eye of the stud of a herd of camels. It was a tradition among the Arabs of al-Yamama, upon their herd reaching one hundred, to put out the eye of the stud to keep the evil eye from afflicting the herd. From that day on, I learned the trick of the black curtain. My eyes would be open, but my sight would be absent. Thanks to the curtain I pulled down over my soul, my heart and my faculties would allow my eyes to remain open without injury or nightmares. I would rush away from all this to a spring among the date palms of al-Yamama, plunging into it and remaining there until my body ceased its trembling. After that, I would emerge and take refuge in my grandfather's garden, reciting the Qur'an and chanting its verses. "The Qur'an is like a necklace of pearls slipping out of memory," Grandfather used to say, "so you must recite it every day to allow it to settle in the heart." Sometimes we would recite poetry together; to memorize the poem, Grandfather would ask me to write it out in gypsum chalk on a blackboard he had set aside for me. He particularly loved the poetry of al-Asha al-Hanafi, reciting the verses and asking me to repeat them after him. When he came to certain verses, he was overcome by nostalgia, and his voice would grow loud with sobs.

> Have you not seen the cities of Iram
> And Aad, gone in a day and night?
>  And others before them gone and buried,
> Not spared by precaution or fight?
>  And all who lived in Tasm and Jadis
> Who suffered days of affliction and blight?

I read the books and wanted more; I devoured the dates at harvest season and steadily outgrew the bounds that circumscribed me in Hijr al-Yamama. I learned that the stars that

19

shine upon us have shone upon many other peoples, and that before yawning disasters come to us, they first feel the need to sleep. My grandfather's books shaped who I was and influenced my nature. It was here that I started out, with these books tattered from too much reading, which Grandfather placed in rows on the shelves of his small reception area.

This reception area took up an entire wing of our house. Light came in through the cracks in its door. It opened out onto a palm grove. In the middle of the door hung a metal ring from which hung a small, veined hand that I imagined to belong to a midget demon. The naughty boys always knocked at the door and ran away.

In this reception area, Grandfather received those who came to consult him, his friends, and some of his students; it was here that he kept his famous ledger that constituted the memory of al-Yamama.

During the season of hajj pilgrimage, many pilgrims passed through our town, as well as people headed to Mecca in search of knowledge and proximity to the home of the Prophet. They were not all awe-inspiring or dignified men of learning; most of them were foreigners or fools. I remember one of them saying he had come from Mosul, wearing a bizarre red abaya with letters and numbers on it. He told many stories and anecdotes, claiming that God Himself had privileged him with his knowledge and learning, that he knew the name of the golden calf that people had worshipped and the name of the wolf that had eaten Joseph. "But Joseph wasn't eaten by wolves!" Grandfather interrupted mockingly.

"I mean the one that *would have* eaten him!" the other worthy stammered.

Grandfather refused to accept payment or gifts for his services. He placed a jar in his window alcove into which his visitors could drop whatever they wished to pay on their way out: most contented themselves with prayers for my grandfather's good health, so the jar remained vacant but for what My Lady Qout al-Quloub, mother to the little prince Yusuf, placed in it. When the jar was full, Grandfather would go out into the marketplace of al-Yamama. I went with him. Wending our way around the palm trees and wells, we arrived at the center of the square, where we would buy a measure of flour, a sack of raisins, and a small lamp. Then, passing by other tradesmen, we bought a skillfully carved wooden bowl for *tharid*, our traditional dish of meat and rice. At the women's stores, we bought a carpet or a woolen abaya. Before we went back up to the summit of the Citadel, Grandfather would hand out his purchases as gifts and charity to the beggars and mendicants who had been waiting for his return from the market. Thus we returned empty-handed and with an empty jar. Meanwhile, Shammaa of the House of Wael stood at the head of the stone stairs, wringing her hands in worry at our tardiness.

Our house was one of the few in al-Yamama built on foundations of stone. It was three stories high, ending in a top floor of spacious wings for the womenfolk. Its nooks and crannies pulled me hither and thither; I was never bored when I was there. In abandoned corners of the house, I might find a cat with a litter of kittens, a slave girl embroidering the sleeves of a garment, or, in a nook high up on the roof, a bird's nest with two eggs in it, next to which I sat waiting to see the bird that felt so safe in our house until Grandfather started the afternoon prayers in the town mosque and I rushed to join him.

I push my face into the deerskin sheets and distance myself from those around me. From Jamhi Saqr al-Asha Hanifa to *The Highest Level of the Great Poets*: what a magnificent pillar of Arab song! Blind, worn away by the love of wine and women, but his verse still sung in al-Yamama, his name passed from town to town and carried on the wind, chanted by slave girls and repeated by tellers of tales! Even my mother I heard whispering:

I set my heart on her by chance;
She loved another at a glance.
Her sweetheart had another lover;
And so we each pine for another.

She was always whispering of love and the pains of parting, but my father was definitely not the protagonist of her stories.

My grandfather's rooms were an Aladdin's cave. He insisted that the best way to memorize poetry was by reciting it. "A head full of music is like the parched earth: it soaks up all you pour into it." No sooner did he say this than he launched into a recital of some epic poem by his beloved al-Asha Hanifa.

Take your leave of Hurayra, watch the receding caravan.
Can you bear to say goodbye to her, you loving man?
Her hair is long, her smile is bright, and oh, she walks
    so slow,
As barefoot in a mud puddle, so leisurely she goes.

The barnyard animals would fall silent, listening to our voices, ceasing their neighing, lowing, and buzzing. The bees would hover closer and start to build honeycombs by the window, while the date palms would wave their fronds in time to the music.

Our voices would bring our father to us: he would stand at the door to the room, blocking the light for a long time. With his thick black beard and massive turban, he was an imposing figure. He had conquests, heroic deeds, herds of camels, acres of crops, and herds of cattle to his name, and a group of women and children of whom it is said he had only ever loved Shammaa of the House of Wael, who never loved him. He shook his head scornfully, disparagingly. "He who has missed his chance at fighting and heroism consoles himself with religion and poetry."

My grandfather would retort, without raising his eyes from his ledger, "We leave those to you." And he would motion to me to come with him, and leave my father's presence.

## Lower Najd and Upper Najd

I am Mazid al-Hanafi, and I come from Najd. It is a land of plenty, filled with lush vegetation, rich herds, populous villages, bubbling springs, and generous abundance. Now there are many deserts, plains, hills, and mountains between me and al-Yamama; the melancholy songs of the Arabian lands, and the scents of the Daylamite trader's perfumes. Whenever the fabric covering them dried out, the trader gently, tenderly rewetted it; whenever we passed by chests covered in sand, he repeated his warning against going anywhere near Bajkam's chests. "The sand around them," he cautioned, "is haunted, shifting, ferocious." But still the songs filled my breast: I hummed them under my breath.

> Now rescue comes after your clan's accusation.
> Tears, help me with parting from Najd and privation.

On the back of my she-camel, Shubra, are some coins, as few as the years I have lived in this world, and the sack of my clothes that keeps me company. The Great Secret has been breathed into my breast, and the wisdom of the ancients lies beneath my sleeve. I do not dine with my companions in the caravan, preferring to eat alone. It is only a few days to Ramadan. I stealthily slip out Galen of Pergamon's book and leaf through it with careful eagerness. I take some dates from my sack and a piece of meat cooked in milk, and nibble on them quietly like a terrified desert mouse. I run a hand over the crate of books. I open its lid carefully, stealing a glance: I see *al-Muqaba-sat* and *al-Imta' wa-l-mu'anasa* by Abu Hayman al-Tawhidi, and the *Aghani* of al-Isfahani, with which I have paved the face of the box: the gossip and babble of the courtiers and companions of sultans arouse no suspicion, although my solitary nature and curt speech earn me suspicious looks from the caravan guards.

Once, at the start of our journey, the Daylamite leader of the caravan invited me to share his meal, but I refused on the pretext that I was fasting; he did not repeat the invitation. I gave him to understand that I was a seeker of knowledge headed for Jerusalem, and other words calculated to stopper the cracks through which curious eyes might seek to learn the secret of the heavy chest that so exhausts my camel.

Tonight marks the twenty-ninth night since I left Baghdad. I kept looking back at it when we left with the caravan. Its lights gathered on the horizon, steeped in the scarlet glow of a city whose air was filled with low-hanging dates, the yearning of lovers, the bickering of clerics, and the arguments of discussion circles in mosques. Its pathways were so muddied with blood that it appeared on the horizon like a ruby.

The outskirts of Jerusalem and the Mount of Olives beckon.

Baghdad has turned me, Mazid, a seeker of knowledge with a fragile heart, who frequents discussion circles in mosques and peruses the wares of sellers of books, into a heretic fleeing Baghdad, a crate of the works of philosophers, logicians, and questioners in my possession. Still, this journey of mine was not as painful as my first journey, the one that took me away from al-Yamama at the outset of Muharram in the year AH 400.

# 2

## Following the Big Dipper
## Muharram 4, AH 400; August 28, AD 1009

WE WERE THREE COMPANIONS, BROUGHT together by the caravan that accompanied those returning from Mecca, leaving for Basra after a brief sojourn in Hijr al-Yamama. The caravan leader told me that it was a long way from Hijr al-Yamama to Basra: two hundred parasangs. It was a long and costly journey, and payment must be made in advance. It devoured most of the coins in my possession, and an *ardab* of dates besides, which I plucked from our date palms with my own hands and presented to him.

We left al-Yamama in the evening to avoid the blistering heat of noon. The caravan followed the stars of Banat Naash, also known as the Big Dipper, along flat pathways where mountains and elevations were rare. The sobs of the daughter of the House of Wael tore at my innards: my loneliness at the thought of what was to come and my fear of the dark path we were on made me cling to Musallama and Sakhr, who hailed from the tribe of Tamim. They were two young men who were traveling with the caravan to rejoin their cousin in Iraq, and they were exactly alike, although one was taller than the other. Both wore their hair in long braids and looked at you with the same fleeting glances; both had the same loud voice and light, graceful step. Although their clothing was somewhat modest, and their demeanor somewhat rough, they were skilled at lighting a fire and preparing food in mere moments, and they could catch a rabbit, skin it, and prepare it with bread to make an excellent *tharid* soup for dinner. I shared their meals, feeling that they were shields for me against the arrows of being alone in a strange land. By the third day of our journey, I and Musallama of Tamim and his cousin Sakhr counted each other as traveling companions, brought together by our youth, the harsh unfamiliar path, and the songs we sang to the camels to make them walk on.

The two young men from Tamim were affiliated marginally with the great tribes that had quit Najd and the small towns in the embrace of the mountains of Tuwaiq, heading for the lands of Iraq, seduced by the promise of Caliph al-Muizz li-Din Allah al-Bouhi to grant them what plots they could settle in and cultivate in that country, for ownership or lifelong use, depending on how close each of them was to the clerks of the Diwan or the treasurers. There were two forms of this: a *qatia* was a gift outright, granted to a man to live in and cultivate, with one-tenth of its crops going to the treasury, and passed on to his children after him. The second was a *tuma*, or lifelong right to use the land, which the treasury would reclaim after a man's death. The Tamim boys' uncle had a *tuma*, which he had been given by the Diwan of Bakhtiyar, son of Muizz al-Dawla al-Bouhi, ruler of Baghdad.

The voice of the camel driver from al-Yamama to Basra was a yowl, pouring yet more blackness into the pit of my soul. I availed myself of every opportunity when he was silent to raise my voice in one of the poems I used to sing with Grandfather among the date palms of al-Yamama. Afterward, the owner of the caravan hurried to me and begged me to walk in the lead, so that I could recite poetry and sing to the camels to make them walk on. The caravan poured out slowly over the sand dunes of the al-Dahna Desert that led to Iraq. Musallama and Sakhr were glad of the new, privileged position I had attained, and joined me at the forefront of the caravan. When I ceased my camel song, exhausted, they took turns reciting some short verses of the Qur'an, and occasionally the Sura of al-Rahman, which would motivate the camels to resume their trotting over the dunes, our way lit by the distant glimmer of some feeble stars or a newborn moon that never strayed too far from the horizon.

## The Mausoleum of al-Qarmati

The caravans were uneasy and apprehensive when we reached the outskirts of the land of Hajjar, inhabited by the clan of al-Qaramita: it was said that they contaminated their wells with bitter melon to afflict passing caravans with thirst and exhaustion, whereupon the tribes people would attack them, capture the pilgrims, and sell them into slavery or force them into servitude as shepherds until such time as they could ransom themselves after long years of hard labor, returning to their homeland only to find their inheritance divided up and their women remarried.

The leader of the caravan issued various commands to us: first, that we only enter Hajjar in groups; second, that we not display any sign of riches; and third, that we not engage with any of them in argument. We arrived on a Friday night, the horizon cloying with the scent of date palms, and the air filled with the susurration of waterwheels. The camels were rested and fed, fires were lit, and dinner cooked. The next day, we went to the town marketplace, the doves easing the sweltering afternoon heat with their cooing. We performed Friday prayers in the great mosque of the town.

On our way back to the caravan, we took a path that passed by a walled garden, lush and flourishing. We glimpsed a great dome in its center, ornamented with mosaic tiles and surrounded by a low wall, inlaid with stones carefully set in the likeness of palm fronds, and with pots of mint and sweet basil set atop it. The windows of the dome were made of green-painted wood, decorated with rings of iron. Outside the gate to the low wall stood a magnificent black stallion, whickering and shaking its head violently against the flies.

We dared not broach the wall or draw too near the dome, so awe-inspiring was it, and because the people of Hajjar appeared to look upon it with great favor: everyone leaving the mosque raised a hand and saluted the structure, which remained mysterious until we reached the outskirts of the city and asked a date seller about it. Tradesmen are the best source of secrets; every tradesman hopes to unburden himself of his wares all in the folds of conversation. "That dome," he whispered to us, "is built upon the tomb of Our Lord and Master Hamdan al-Qarmati. The stallion, with bit and bridle and saddle, never leaves that spot, day or night; he is waiting for him to be born again, surge out of his grave, and ride him once again, setting out to fill the land with justice after long unfairness."

Musallama's and Sakhr's eyes gleamed with derision and they began to make uncharitable jests. Chasing one another around the date stall, they lurched drunkenly and yelled, "I am the sainted Hamdan!" and bellowed boisterously in the date seller's face. They quite disrupted the air of reverence with which the poor tradesman had been telling the tale of al-Qarmati's grave. I gave him a few coins and comforted him by sending up a loud prayer to Master al-Qarmati for his benediction and forgiveness, then chased Sakhr and Musallama off.

We all shared the dates, which melted in the mouth, so sweet were they. I turned a blind eye to Sakhr's and Musallama's harsh and ill-mannered demeanor. Their preferred method of waking me for dawn prayers was poking me in the shoulder with a stick. They stared long and openly at the women in the caravan with overwhelming lust, and gobbled their food greedily, provoking the mockery of the caravan owner, who said, "When will you be satisfied?"

Sakhr would mutter back with his mouth full, "When I fall on my face fast asleep!"

But "the companion is your light on the way," as the proverb goes; I made no attempt to disembarrass myself of them at that time.

# Eye of the World

We set the sun at our right hand and journeyed until we arrived at a place only a parasang from Mirbad, three miles from Basra. Although it was nearly sundown when we arrived, no sooner had we settled the camels and sat down than the horizon filled with the dust of carriages drawn by donkeys and mules, driven by the tradesmen of Basra. They eyed us like vultures circling their prey. I could not see anything about their clothing that set them apart from the people of al-Yamama, except that their turbans were more carefully wrapped about their heads and in colors that matched their abayas. They craned their necks to see the best wares we had brought from the depths of the desert: thick woolen camel-hair abayas, colorful carpets, fat preserved in pots made of dried pumpkins, and hard, dry pellets of yogurt called *jamid*. There were some gourds that the pilgrims from Mecca had been careful not to touch throughout our journey, and these they now hawked with calls of "Water from the sacred well of Zamzam, for those who would drink it!"

A group of camels now split from the caravan and continued on to Kufa. I saw their procession heading north, and wished I could have gone with them to visit the tomb of Imam Ali, peace be upon him. Musallama called to me, "Hold your tongue! It's only those who want to die martyred that go to Watermelon Land," by which he meant Kufa. "If you call for prayers and peace upon Prophet Muhammad like a Sunni, and pray for his companions, you'll be chopped into little pieces by the Shiites who live there! Sunnis have only one job there, and that's as street sweepers."

Musallama and Sakhr's words sobered and shocked me: how had they known that I was not a Shiite descendant of the Prophet? Was it only because I was their friend? When the caravans to Mecca passed us by in al-Yamama, those in the caravans would ask us, "Have the descendants of Hanifa turned Shiite now that they are ruled by the clan of Ukhaydar? People follow the religion of their monarchs, after all."

29

My grandfather would respond with verse twenty of the Sura of al-Imran: "*So if they dispute with thee, say, 'I have submitted my whole self to Allah and so have those who follow me.'*" This only mystified me more: were we Shiite or Sunni? Grandfather would lead the men in prayer; we fasted in Ramadan; when he came back from Iraq, he added his prayers for the descendants of the Prophet, traditionally Shiite, to his Sunni prayers, and asked God to return their rights to them and vindicate them against their enemies. But he was incensed by the clan of al-Qaramita's actions, their arguments, and their theft of the Black Rock in Mecca and placing it in the region of Ihsaa. He always said, "They are nothing but thieves, heretics, and social climbers."

When Grandfather died, a great many things changed. His Majesty Ahmad ibn Ukhaydar rejected everyone who applied to replace him, and brought in an imam from Basra, a thin man with a narrow brow and a hooked nose, a piercing glare and an irascible demeanor. He arrived in al-Yamama on a Friday, and spent a week in bed with a fever. The Friday after, he glimpsed a nitraria bush in a square adjoining the palace. He ordered it to be cut down at once, for the End of Days was nigh, when the Muslims, it was said, would vanquish the Jews, and if a Jew hid behind a tree branch it would betray him and say, "There is a Jew behind me"—all but the nitraria bush! Besides, he went on, the nitraria bush came to Yazid in his sleep and said to him, "Take vengeance on the people of Medina, who murdered Uthman!" leading to the Battle of Hurra.

At the time, I thought the imam's resentment of Muawiya and Yazid was part and parcel of his cantankerous nature and a means of flattering the Shiite lord of the Citadel; I had not yet heard the imams of Karkh hurling vile insults at these two personages every Friday from their pulpits.

Ah, Basra. They call it "The Eye of the World." "Mother of Iraq," they say, too, and "the Tigris's favorite daughter." They say if you take a handful of its soil in your hand, a date palm will grow out of it. Together we went forward,

Musallama, Sakhr, and I; the tradesmen of Basra passed by us and we were devoured by their eyes, with our humble clothing and unkempt hair. We had nothing to barter with them, for our supplies were exhausted; we only had a few dirhams left, and were unsure if these would be enough to secure us passage to Baghdad with another caravan.

I suggested that we spend some time in Basra, working for a wage at some inn or another, or in harvesting crops in estates or farms, until we scraped together the money to continue on our journey; it was a valuable opportunity to explore its mosques, discussion circles, and theological discussion groups before going on to Baghdad. My companions fell silent. Instead of responding, sly expressions formed on their faces. Since we were some distance from the marketplace and far into the palm groves, I feared that we might appear suspicious. "Let's go back," I said.

"You go back," said Musallama. "We'll catch up."

I know not what alerted me to the fact that they had some plot in store for me. I was exhausted and alone, filled with dark thoughts. The scent of palm pollen surged through my veins. Still hearing the waterwheels of al-Yamama, I let the sound of the wind calm me as it wended its way through the cracks in the dry earth. I went to sleep for a while in a mud-brick mosque I had glimpsed at the start of our path.

The windows of the little mosque were set high, close to the ceiling. I curled up in a dark, cool corner. The faithful performing the evening prayers had started to leave the mosque, leaving only an imam in a black turban inside, with some farmers and young boys clustered around him in a semicircle as he told them the Story of the Owl.

As I lingered between sleep and wakefulness, I heard him preaching, repeating in bored tones, as though he had given this sermon hundreds of times, "That bird insisted that Imam al-Husayn must die a martyr, and like all birds, it sang in the morning, sought its daily sustenance, and returned to its nest to sleep every night. But after the lord of all young men in Paradise, Imam al-Husayn, died, the owl repented by fasting all day and weeping all night, so it fasts by day and laments by night, wishing peace and prayers on the Prophet's grandson and the members of his family."

I do not know whether the story was being told to preach or to entertain, but my eyes began to drift shut as I listened, and I knew not when they left. I remained, listening to the hooting of the owl coming in through the high windows of the mosque all night long.

The poke of a stick in my shoulder woke me from a deep sleep and a dream that had captivated all my senses: white skies, the scent of rain. I was soaring with a flock of cranes. Our eyes were fixed on the pinnacle of a shining mountain, toward which we were flying. Another poke in my shoulder, harsher. Although I was still half asleep, I could make out in the predawn mist the face of Musallama of Tamim, with his unkempt braids, thick beard, and prominent cheekbones. He whispered roughly, "Wake up for the dawn prayers!"

"The imam hasn't announced the start of prayers yet," I slurred.

He poked me again. "Get up! I want you for something. It's important. I'll wait for you at the door to the mosque."

I dragged myself up heavily, shuffled over to the place set aside for ablutions, and washed to rid myself of the fogginess of sleep. When I came out, Musallama and Sakhr were standing at an angle next to the doorway on the eastern side, waiting for me, their woolen abayas wrapped around them, glancing about apprehensively. The outlines of the farmers were beginning to appear from among the shadows of the date palms, hurrying toward the mosque.

They motioned to me to follow them. I did so with difficulty; it was all I could do to keep pace with their hurried footsteps. We walked for a long while by the fence until morning had broken completely, although misty; finally, we reached an abandoned wall at the edge of a thick grove of palm trees. In this mist, I saw the head of a slaughtered animal, severed and cast aside by the wall, its skinned hide and mounds of its meat cut up next to a pool of blood.

All the sleepiness left me and my eyes widened. "What's this?" I asked them.

"We found it, a stray," Musallama said. "And a stray is a find, and a find is a gift. We slaughtered it and ate our fill of its flesh." He added, "We shall light a fire to cook the meat, and you will eat your fill as well."

"Are we going to eat all this meat?" I asked, slack-jawed.

"The rest of the meat and hide we will put in these baskets and cover them with palm fronds, and slip into the Basra market to sell them," said Sakhr. "We can buy new clothes and a lively mount to ride in turns, and accompany a caravan to Baghdad. We have no wish to go into Baghdad and enter our uncle's house with such mean attire and looking so unkempt."

Stunned, watching the morning's flies swarming the carcass's head, I said, "But how do you know it was a stray? The custom is to go calling throughout the marketplace for a number of days, three at the least, calling out for its owner, and only then, if no one responds, is it a find."

"It's a find!" Sakhr yelled out.

"The rule for a stray is three days!" I cried back heatedly. "And you only arrived in Basra yesterday!"

Mocking, Musallama said, "We don't know about your religion, you who lived all your life in al-Yamama, how you misinterpret it and twist the meanings of the sacred texts."

Sakhr was usually a man of few words, leaving the talking to his cousin Musallama, but he suddenly called out with a passion betrayed by the tremor in his voice and his fist, which he shook in my face, "It's a find! Don't you understand? Come near and eat of its delicious grilled liver! When it's in your stomach, cover it up with some of these delicious Basra dates we plucked from the abandoned wall behind us."

"And are those stray dates, too?" I said dryly.

"No," they said, uncaring. "But the wall's abandoned and unguarded. It's probably a charity field for passersby and travelers like ourselves. We have heard much about the people of Basra and their generous nature: they do not even pick up the dates that fall from the trees when the wind blows. If the winds are strong, they know that the dates will go to the poor and needy, and to lone travelers."

Musallama turned to the west and called out "*Allahu akbar*," then added: "Let us perform the dawn prayers here before it is too late."

We stood behind Musallama, who led us in prayer. The buzzing of the flies grew louder around the head of the animal. The stench of blood was all around us. Some sparrows and other birds alighted, pecking at the remains. I snatched a glimpse of the birds. The owl was not among them: it was fasting, readying itself to mourn all night, lamenting al-Husayn. What a life, frittered away between fasting and grieving!

We knelt and prostrated ourselves, led by Musallama, who recited the Sura of al-Kawthar sweetly. We arranged to meet the following day, when I would tell them what I had decided with regard to accompanying them to Baghdad.

All the way, I walked with my head down, full of suspicion, for fear someone would realize my stomach was full of stolen meat. The afternoon sun shone down on the date palms and the birds in the branches called out with joy. How I wished I could spend the day cooling myself among the waterwheels, washing my soul clean of the slaughtered animal's blood. I had thought that strangers in a new place would be extra careful, timid and timorous, asking permission almost for the very air they breathed. But Musallama and Sakhr had transformed it into a land of conquest, battles, and booty.

The walls of the mud-brick mosque appeared before me, with its high windows beneath which I had spent the previous night. When I arrived there, I met the imam at the door, the teller of the Story of the Owl. In the morning light, his face looked fresher; he was short and stout, with a large paunch. "Which clan of Arabs are you from?" he asked, friendly.

"I am a Hanafite Sunni from al-Yamama," I replied.

"May the clan of Bani Ukhaydar always prosper, proud descendants of the Prophet Muhammad!" he said genially. "What was rightfully theirs was wrested from them, but God is all-knowing. I saw you yesterday, coming to the mosque to sleep. I didn't like to wake you; you seemed tired. I am Sheikh Zakir, the imam of this mosque."

"Two hundred parasangs between al-Yamama and Basra, and it has taken all I have to get here," I said. "My destination is Baghdad, but I mean to stay awhile in Basra before I journey on to Baghdad."

I did not tell him that I was penniless and without resources, but he appeared to divine it, for immediately he asked me, "You are of the clan of al-Yamama, which must mean you can climb palms and collect dates and prune the trunks and cut off the dried fronds, in exchange for a dirham and a handful of the dates of each palm?"

I agreed at once; Sheikh Zakir's offer was a valuable gift indeed, especially as it would rid me of Musallama and Sakhr.

I met them the next morning near the mosque; they had changed their clothing and bought abayas like those brought in by the caravans, although they were still barefoot and wild-haired. They urged me to accompany them to their uncle's house; he was a camel trader, they told me, between the desert of Samawa and Baghdad, and was a close friend of the Persian clerk who managed the treasury. Proudly, they told me that the clerk would place them on the list of those who would receive gifts and bequests from the caliphate, allowing them to remain in Baghdad and enjoy the rivers, buildings, bridges, and gardens that city boasted, filling their ears with the music of the anklets of its wanton slave girls. They had no need to go forty parasangs northward in order to cultivate desert land bequeathed to them for five years and confiscated once more if they were to fail to make it bloom. "We will only need to visit those bequests of land once a year, or else hire someone to cultivate them," they said slyly.

I made excuses, telling them I was still exhausted from the journey and needed a few days in Basra. I also said I planned to attend some discussion circles held by the imams, and to visit the libraries in the city. I made sure to say farewell to them well away from the mud-brick mosque, and slipped away wondering at how gentle, even vulnerable, they seemed at our goodbye. Tears sprang to Sakhr's eyes, and I could not recognize them as the men who had decapitated the animal in the predawn mist and eaten its liver raw.

They left, waving and insisting that we must meet as soon as I arrived in Baghdad. Their uncle, they told me, was named Qutayba al-Tamimi, well known to all the traders of Baghdad. "But I have no desire to know him," I muttered under my breath. I turned and made my way back to the mosque, to retrieve the rest of my things I had left there. I looked for Sheikh Zakir, the imam who had promised me a job and a boat to carry me to Baghdad.

The afternoon prayers had just ended and the men were leaving the mosque and spreading throughout the fields. I entered the mosque to find a foreign boy who spoke broken Arabic. He was collecting the reed mats after prayers and humming a song whose words were a mystery to me. Sheikh Zakir was sitting behind the pulpit turning a book over in his hands. He glimpsed me out of the corner of his eye as I approached him, so he closed his book and turned toward me, saying, "Warmest greetings to the Hanafite traveler!"

I sat near him, cracking my knuckles nervously. "I can start work today," I said.

He tilted his head and stared at me doubtfully. "Have you ever trimmed date palms before?" He added mockingly, "Mind the climbing ropes; they'll give you calluses. Besides," he went on more seriously, "the ropes they give hired hands aren't always the strongest. They've caused many a man to fall off the top of a tree. That field behind you"—he gestured—"has swallowed up seven men. That's why they call this orchard 'the Man-eater.' But, after it claimed the lives of seven men," he explained, "its owner devoted its earnings to charity, to support the discussion circles of Basra, including its slave boys and girls and all its cattle and beasts of burden."

I held my breath. How did this man know that I had never trimmed a date palm in my life? I had no wish to be dissuaded from continuing on to Baghdad by the superstitious nonsense of this sheikh. I had been up all night making my plans and budgeting for the hundred dirhams I planned to earn from working on the date palms, even if I was a failure in these orchards—as I had been in al-Yamama. My father's hired farmhands had always done this job in my stead.

"Never fear," I said. "I will do the work as it should be done."

He nodded, visibly unconvinced. "Are you good at anything else?"

I was speechless, not only because of this sheikh's stubbornness, but because I realized that I was not good at anything—or, at any rate, nothing of any use in a date-palm orchard by the riverside. Even slaughtering lambs had been a bitter experience that had permanantly turned me against my father. Without waiting for my answer, he said, "What did you do in al-Yamama? How did you pass the time?"

After some hesitation, I said, "I assisted my father, who was a camel trader." Then I whispered, "And most of my time I spent reading."

His eyes, narrowed in ridicule throughout our conversation, suddenly widened. I discovered on the spot that they were bright green, like a cat's. He passed me the book in his hand and said, "Then read: let's hear you do it."

I opened it to a page and read. "And know, my son, that there are two types of fortune: fortune that you seek out, and fortune that seeks you out; the latter will come to you even if you do not go to it. How bitter is submission when you are needy, and cruelty when you are wealthy!"

Shocked, he shook his head. "I swear, my boy," he whispered, "it is your own fortune that you have read. What is all the world but signs and omens? Here is your fortune: it has found you."

Not long after, I found myself seated at a low, round wooden table, holding a sheepskin-bound ledger with pens, ink, and several sheets of parchment at my side, setting down the name of every man who was due to work that day in the farm of the Man-eater, north of Basra: the name of every one of those I had been going to stand alongside as a day laborer. But every man's fortune is predestined, you see.

Great numbers of men poured into the Man-eater orchard. Most of them were strangers to the city who had asked around in the marketplace for a means of earning money. There were Bedouins from Yemen, Hijaz, Amman, and Upper Najd whom fortune had brought to Basra, eyes fixed on Baghdad. I spent some time after the dawn prayers setting down the names of the men who had arrived that day and separating them by task: some collected dates, some trimmed the roots and cut off the dry fronds. These earned two dirhams a day, while those who cut the grass and cut canals for waterwheels earned one. When that task was done, I made out another copy of their names, and gave it to a peasant who was slight of build, with repulsive features and copper-colored skin, and who wore a wide-legged *sirwal* and a short shirt with no garment over them. He carried a whip everywhere, but he only ever lashed at the flies. However, he seemed to like brandishing it to fortify his image and make up for his short-ness of stature and slightness of build. The first of these copies I would rush to the owner of the orchard, who lived in one of the mud-brick houses next to the barns. He asked me to help him set out the dirhams next to each man's name; when we were done, he put them in a cloth sack, which he placed in a leather belt around his stomach.

Then we heard the call to the noon prayers from sev-eral minarets; we would pray together, whereupon he would invite me to share his meal. The only time I was able to find a moment to go into Basra and make the rounds of its mar-ketplaces and stores was after the afternoon prayers; when sunset came near, I hurried back to the orchard to supervise the handing out of payment to the men and match the names to the faces, as a long line of men may always be infiltrated by sly freeloaders claiming to have done a day's labor in the orchard. At that time, a few servants would come out of the mud-brick houses adjoining the orchard, bearing parcels and utensils, and helping each other carry gigantic baskets full of puffy, hot wheat bread, just out of the oven. They spread out reed mats beneath the palm trees and placed the loaves on them, along with bowls of date syrup and milk, around which the laborers gathered, exhausted and ravenous; they did not leave until they had all but eaten the utensils and mats as well.

I would stride back to the mosque, filled with unaccus-tomed pride: that of a man upon whose shoulders weighty burdens are placed and upon whose every word people hang—a man who comes home in the evening with dinars singing in his pocket. In al-Yamama, I had been always under someone's wing: the wing of Shammaa from the House of Wael, the wing of Grandfather, the wing of the overarch-ing fame of my father, the wing of the great Citadel of Bani Ukhaydar. Beneath that shadow, I could see but remained unseeing; my eyes had merely widened at the boundless won-der of this world.

Despite the sultry evening air and the fatigue in my limbs, my longing for books remained as strong as ever, nagging at me persistently enough to make me break the bounds of guest etiquette, and I approached the imam before he began the evening sermon. Defying his vigilant green eyes, I took small steps toward him. He had taken off his turban and placed it next to him, revealing his pointy bald head, and stretched his legs out, leaning on the wall and lost in thought. I whispered in trepidation, "May I read some of the books on the shelves?"

He looked at me silently for a while, and I almost retreated. Soon, however, he gathered in his legs and stood. I reached out a helping hand, but he ignored it. I muttered, "I'll just take a quick look at them," as if to apologize for the trouble I was causing him. Then, as though to assure him of my good intentions, I added, "Just . . . I'll just stand at the shelf for a moment."

He made his feeble way to the wooden closet where he stored his books, and pulled out the key he kept hanging around his neck. Then he pulled the doors fully open for me. Hurriedly, I reached out and snatched the first book my hand could reach: I was afraid he would change his mind or forbid me from reading something or other. Unfortunately for me, it was a short manuscript, just a few pages long. He gripped my wrist and read the title: *The Influence of Melodies on the Souls of Animals* by al-Hassan ibn al-Haytham. "Ah, Ibn al-Haytham!" he cried out. "But be careful of old Hassan's words; they may drive you mad and fill your head with bizarre imaginings. "Why, they say that once he was in a mosque in Baghdad and was stopped by a man by the name of Ibn al-Marsataniya, right hand raised high with a copy of the book *On the Configuration of the World*—which is a book Ibn al-Haytham wrote, in case you didn't know—and started accusing him of heresy and sacrilege!" He chuckled. "The man pointed out the circles and symbols in the book and said they were spells and magical talismans, and that 'These are the circles penned by a man who claims to know the mysteries of the Unseen! What a travesty, what a disaster!' Meanwhile, the common people and the rabble around him were yelling God's praises and getting all worked up. Then he set the book on fire in the central square of the mosque." The sheikh shook his head regretfully. "Hordes of people were always following Ibn al-Haytham around. They almost killed him before the Fatimid caliph rescued him and invited him to Egypt, saving his life."

I arranged my features in an expression of interest and sympathy for Ibn al-Haytham, just waiting for the sheikh to finish speaking so I could be alone with my short manuscript. I looked at the title again: *The Influence of Melodies on the Souls of Animals.* I found that someone had written on the cover of the book, below the title:

I have always searched for knowledge and the truth. I believe that to draw nearer to God, there is no better way than to search for knowledge and the truth.
—Ibn al-Haytham.

I rushed to the place where I made my bed: a dark corner, two pillars separating it from the rest of the mosque, where the extra mats and pillows for Friday prayers were stored. I lay down there with a lantern whose flame was almost extinguished, but I leapt energetically among the book's lines, despite the poor quality of the paper and the worn pages. Those only increased my ardor, like a beauty withholding her charms. I caught some lines saying that singing affects camels, making them go faster or slower, and that music fills sheep's udders with milk, and brings chameleons out into the sunshine, and increases the yield of date palms, and makes goats more fertile.

Sleep claimed me before the lantern could go out; in my dreams, I saw a short man with dark skin and a sparse mustache and neatly trimmed beard. He had visited us once at my grandfather's guest rooms in al-Yamama, bearing a book in his sleeve, and he had joined us in reciting the poetry of his beloved al-Asha, the poet of all poets: the horses and birds had fallen silent, listening to us, while the owl above my windowsill never ceased its lamenting of al-Husayn.

## Fliers

I had swum beside the waterwheels of al-Yamama. I had plunged into its pools, searching for fish and frogs. I had splashed water on the other boys and been splashed in turn. Still, for all that, the thought of a journey by boat filled me with terror.

The harvest-season labor lasted three weeks. On the day the work concluded in the Man-eater orchards, the supervisor gave me a gold dinar over and above my pay, and prayed for my safe journey and success. Before this, he had been urging me to stay: "There are many people who will want a silent accountant, who eats little and gossips less, with a neat and beautiful hand." But his offer did not interest me; it was, besides, clear that he was making it by way of apology for the paucity of my recompense. He did not insist, nor did I take it seriously. Perhaps Basra was only a way station for me on my journey to Baghdad, also known as the Home of Peace. It was he who had advised me to take a riverboat to Baghdad. "Getting to Baghdad by river will save you several days compared to traveling by caravan," he advised me. "If you wish, I will give you the name of a man who is known for his skill in riding the river and controlling his boats, and has a reputation as a good man, besides." It was clear that he was trying to palm off the ignorant traveler onto a friend of his, but why not? I would go to where he had directed me, and he who feigns ignorance is the winner, as they say.

I went to Bata'ih, the location he had described to me. There were not many people there. I told one of the dockworkers that I wished to register among the travelers leaving the next day. "Oh, there's no need to register," they said.

"Every day there are quite a few boats leaving, although the water's low this time of year. Just come out here tomorrow after the dawn prayers, and you shall definitely find a boat to take you aboard."

My heart trembled. Was it from fear of riding the river, or being near Baghdad? I told Imam Zakir that I planned to leave the next day. He nodded soberly. After the evening prayers, he brought me Ibn al-Haytham's book as a gift. I thanked him and rushed forward, meaning to kiss his brow, but he fended me off, laughing. "Not to worry! I have placed this book in the most honorable location: instead of it being eaten by moths, it fell into your lap. It shall not crumble to dust now! Take it and copy it. This, I swear, is the original copy from the pen of Ibn al-Haytham."

I did not know back then that one day I should play the game of light and shadow with Ibn al-Haytham himself.

With the morning mist, steam still rising from the river reeds, we boarded a narrow dinghy, twenty arms' lengths long, of the type called a flier, to take us to the ship, which could not make it as far inland as Basra. The river route from Basra to the city of Wasit, which we would pass by, branches into three, and the water coming from upriver all empties out before arriving at Basra into marshlands and swamps called al-Bata'ih. When ships arrive, they unload their cargo onto small boats that can traverse this portion, which splinters into narrow channels choked with interlaced reeds. Among these channels were huts for the guards, their windowless shapes like beehives. I did not search for the man recommended to me by the supervisor at the orchard. I took a boat whose boat-man seemed to have sprung up among the river reeds, short and thin and wiry, with sprightly movements, leaping and bounding over the surface of the boat with the effortless skill of a dragonfly building a nest. But his boat was narrow, barely enough for my size: I placed my things in the bottom of the boat beneath my feet. The boatman gave an oar to each of the ten men who had boarded the boat. "Row calmly and gently," he advised us, "so you do not tire yourselves out. Keep calm even if we meet thieves or bandits: row fast and cry out loudly, 'God damn all infidels!' so that the guards will hear you and come to our rescue."

As we slipped through the reeds, he never stopped chattering praise for the sturdiness of his boat and the strength of its construction, using papyrus stalks harvested in the heat of August, the craft being a family secret handed down for generations since the dawn of time, and so on and so forth, until we reached the sailboat that was to carry us to Baghdad.

The sailboat was roosting on the edge of the marshlands, imposing as a clan leader's tent. Next to it was a small boat bearing two boys as identical as two peas in a pod. Or perhaps I should say two pumpkins: they had huge heads and were uncouth, demanding the full fare, first to Wasit, then to Baghdad, before the craft so much as set sail. The man boarding the boat ahead of me was coming from Yemen, and I could hear him insulting them under his breath. "Damn them! They want their fee in advance, even if they let us fall into a whirlpool or become food for the fish on the journey." His ire, however, did not show on his face: his narrow lips were carefully clamped together in a feeble smile he aimed at them when they helped him up on deck.

We sat in a corner of the deck: the breeze was cool and refreshing, as though we had ascended to a higher plane of the atmosphere, quite different from the sticky heat that had buffeted our faces when we were closer to the surface of the river among the reeds. The ship delayed its departure until it was almost evening. Although the boatmen were uncouth, we were pleasantly surprised to find a little boy handing out stalks of sugarcane and some cucumbers by way of hospitality. The captain finally told us that he would not be able to set sail by night, and that we would commence our journey at first light. Some of the passengers berated him angrily, quoting Khalid ibn al-Walid's famous saying, "Travel by night, morning's delight."

"That, my dear fellows," the captain said, "is all very well in the desert, when we travel in the nighttime to avoid the heat and the harsh hot winds; but it is different on the river. We must be able to see our path and watch out for whirlpools and clumps of reeds."

I was undisturbed by this, unlike my companion from Yemen, who began to show the symptoms of seasickness. His name was Hezekiel. I thought his name strange until he told me he was Jewish, a follower of Moses. His destination, he told me, was Wasit, to join his family there and work at minting coins, now that there was little demand for such work in Yemen: in that land, he told me, they now mixed gold and silver with mercury when minting coins, so that their weight would not change despite the loss of precious metal replaced by mercury. Wise traders recognized these coins, he told me, and called them "mercury-laced" or "counterfeit." You could only tell such a coin by biting it and bending it with your teeth. The trade caravans had stopped accepting gold and silver coins from Yemen, because the path was rocky and treacherous and the sea full of pirates, and now the money was counterfeit as well. The market for such coins had slumped in Yemen, but flourished in Wasit.

I remembered then the uncle of Shammaa of the House of Wael, who had left for Iraq and lived in Lower Wasit, and worked in a farm given to him that was called al-Yamama of the Foreigners. Should I stop in Wasit, the City of Pilgrims, and spend some days there? Should I do my religious duty to visit my mother's family, and visit my great-uncle? But it appeared that the dirhams in my possession would not allow for such a luxury.

On the evening of the second day, we glimpsed Wasit at a distance. "There it is!" called the boatman. "We shall drop anchor on the western side. If you want the eastern bank, you'll need to take a dinghy."

The port was crowded with ships and boats carrying dates, pumpkins, and pomegranates northward toward Baghdad or back south to Basra. Hezekiel took his leave after extracting a promise from me to visit him in Wasit. The pumpkin twins resumed their uncouth demanding of the full fare in advance of the passengers embarking at Wasit, before the latter could so much as catch their breath and put down their traveling chests.

## The Home of Peace Is Theirs

That night, I left the Karkh market behind me and left for the place they call the Circular City, having secured a tiny room that I rented at the Khan al-Hashimi boardinghouse a few days after I arrived in Baghdad—a rare achievement for a stranger to the city. But the bird of good luck, who is not a frequent visitor to me, was flying in my skies and dropped the room into my lap. The fabric of Fate weaves its threads in secret. I was led to this room by a chain of events that could not possibly have been coincidence: they had shaped my life up to this point and would continue to shape what was left of it, all my tomorrows, causing me to doubt once again whether one is predestined or the possessor of free will. The answer still slips through my grasp, and I do not think that I shall ever manage to reach it until I am laid in the earth.

Baghdad, the Circular City, boasts a perfect circular shape that would be the envy of any heavenly body, and glitters like a garment of light. If you wish for glory or seek to capture power, find it here, on its streets and among its mosques and paper traders, for whatever bounty you do not avail yourself of, you shall not find in any other city. It is a place that orbits around itself, its heart a cluster of caliphs' palaces separated by three walls from the rest of the city. Crowded, noisy, bustling, where shoulders rub in its streets, it was overwhelming for me; I was accustomed to limitless open spaces and a desert horizon that unfurled broad and lonely, where anyone approaching could be glimpsed from afar. It is the destination of those who seek knowledge and the final stop on the path of caravans: it was hard to find a place that offered shelter to a studious man who would venture far to seek knowledge but does not have the warmth of a sack of dinars on his belt. The places available for my lodging were limited. But the muezzin of the Great Mosque directed me to this boardinghouse: perhaps it was a discreet dismissal, to rid himself of my presence, sleeping every night in a corner of the hall or under the stairs of the pulpit.

I had always heard from my grandfather that the best sanctuary for a stranger to any city was the House of God, the Great Mosque. "It is the center of any city," he said, "and the location of its treasure, and its affairs ultimately come together there. Its laws have their origins there." But the muezzin of the mosque appeared not to have heard my grandfather, and he was not friendly to strangers. During my nights at the mosque, I made the acquaintance of four brothers from Baluchistan, who had performed the hajj pilgrimage that year and were now on their way home. They had a fifth brother, they said, who had opted to remain in Mecca as a neighbor to the Holy Kaaba. We slept beneath the steps of the minaret, and every night they would tell me the strange and wonderful story of the brother they had left behind. He was a skilled horseman, they said, and an avid hunter, and he spent most of his time in that activity, giving all his attention to it; he left the shepherding, the keeping of cattle, and the planting of fields to them, and occupied himself with chasing prey. One day, on a hunting trip, on a high mountain with serpentine rocky paths, he had glimpsed a white deer, finely formed, with gold rings around its hooves and thick black lashes that feathered upward from bright eyes. Its delicate nose was extended to a spring of water, about to drink. "What did our brother do but loose an arrow that pierced it to the heart?" they told me, "It fell, dead. Then the entire mountainside was filled with screams of grief and wails of despair. The leaves of the trees and the rocks on the mountainside fell. The deer was none other but the daughter of the sheikh of the mountain, and she had taken the form of a deer to drink from the spring away from her bodyguards."

Another took up the tale. "This was in defiance of the prophecy of her old nurse, who told her, 'An arrow will pierce your heart. I hope it is the arrow of love, not of death.' Our brother managed to escape the vengeance of the ruler of the mountain, the fearsome sheikh who made the wind, rocks, and caves of the mountain do his bidding, for killing his favorite daughter, Jilayn. But he returned to us distracted, his eyes wandering every which way. His sprightly nature was gone; he took to staring at us and then bursting into loud weeping, or else he would wake up in the middle of the night, sit bolt upright, and scream out, 'Jilayn!'"

"The doctors and physicians tried to cure him, but to no avail," another brother said, "and so we resolved to take him on a pilgrimage to the Holy Lands. When we arrived in Mecca, he clung to the curtains of the Kaaba and would not let go. He just kept weeping, day and night, without ceasing, until a patch of the fabric fell into his hand, upon which was written: 'From the Almighty and All-Forgiving to My truehearted believer: Go, for you are forgiven for all your sins, before and since.' And this was the very heart of the reason he had performed the pilgrimage: to be forgiven for his sins! Before that, we had asked him to leave the holy place and return to where we had pitched our tents, and he had refused. But after the piece of fabric fell upon him, he came back to us, his color improved, and his eyes no longer wandered. 'I was waiting for permission to go from my Lord God,' he said, 'and here He has given it to me.' He showed us the piece of fabric, and after that, he decided to remain in Mecca, close to the Holy Kaaba, for God only knows how long, now that his health and peace of mind have been restored after long confusion."

The Baluchistanis told the story of their brother over and over again, recalling it with wonder and admiration. Then they would take to muttering, "If He wills a thing to happen, he has but to say 'Let it be' and it shall come to pass." I did not interrogate them as to the details of their story, although it changed every day in the retelling, and they corrected one another or reminded each other of the events in their own tongue. Eventually I, too, began to remind them of some of the details they had forgotten—the valorous exploits of their brother; his sharp, lethal arrows; and the leaves falling all at once from the trees as the sheikh of the mountain wailed in grief.

The Baluchistanis were absent from the mosque for most of the day seeking gainful employment and the dirhams I had earned at the Man-eater orchard allowed me some space to explore the city. I wandered for long distances through its alleys, allowing my feet to lead me. I wanted to drink in the city: its mosques, its discussion circles, the paper markets, the flirtations of its girls taking the air on the riverbanks. In the evenings I took care to return to the mosque, because the policemen and the informants were always to be found in the alleyways and the squares after evening prayers time. They had flashing eyes, belts bearing long knives called *tabrazin* at their waists, and green turbans on their heads adorned with a piece of brass stamped with the caliph's seal. I did this for a few days before the muezzin came rushing to me, bearing the good news that he had found a room for me in at the khan of Abu al-Hassan al-Hashimi.

## The Khan of Abu al-Hassan al-Hashimi

Abu al-Hassan al-Hashimi was one of the notables of Baghdad. He was well known as a lover of science and knowledge; he spent most of the days of the year journeying between Baghdad, Sindh, and the northern borders that adjoined Byzantium. He built a great boardinghouse on the eastern side of the River Tigris, close to its banks, and hired the most skillful craftsmen and the best builders and fabricants to build it. Roofed and three stories high, it was a magnificent architectural achievement, far grander than the surrounding houses and dwellings. When it was perfect, he set it aside as a religious endowment for scholars and students of theology. This information was all given to me by Abu Qandil, the muezzin who secured me the room. I knew it was prudent to ignore half of what he said, on account of his earnest wish to get me out of his mosque, but the other half still sounded good enough for me to direct my steps there. After all, just the availability of an empty place was a blessing for which I should be thankful.

Abu Qandil held forth on how Khan al-Hashimi had a section devoted to craftsmen and a section for tradesmen, while the second floor held stalls, paper traders, and calligraphers. Some of the rooms in the boardinghouse, he said, were set aside for students of theology coming to Baghdad from all over the world in exchange for small services performed by the students— assistance in running the boardinghouse in Abu al-Hassan al-Hashimi's absence, as he was away for many months. "Go there," the muezzin said, "and tell them you were sent by the muezzin Abu Qandil. That should, God willing, be enough to guarantee you a room." Ignoring my openmouthed stare, he patted me on the shoulder and exited through the eastern gate to the mosque. As he went, he gestured to an aqueduct, a stream of water paved with stones. "Walk next to this canal," he instructed. "They call it the Chicken Canal. Go east toward the river. You'll find it there. If you get lost, ask somebody. Everyone knows where it is."

The muezzin's enthusiasm was almost like an eviction: I felt a little insulted. I collected my things, resolving never to darken his door again. But soon enough I found myself muttering under my breath, "That's probably just what he wants. It's never a bad thing to get used to the rudeness of those you meet on your travels, where there's no protection from your mother's reputation, nor from your grandfather's prayers, all intertwined with the scent of the date palms of al-Yamama."

I went eastward, alongside the Chicken Canal. There were some leaves and straw floating in it, and dried windfall fruit. On my left was the round wall of the city, tall and imposing, said to be thirty-five arms' lengths high, with square stones interlaced like the tight knit of fabric. Entry was only permitted to travelers. No beasts of burden were allowed in the circular inner sanctum of the caliphate except those belonging to the caliph and his retinue and the palace courtiers.

The smell of the river led me to my destination. Here, in Baghdad, the river smelled different from Basra. The river gives every city a different air, mood, and scent, and while in Basra the river breezes come to you mingled with the thick scent of reeds, here they come to you laden with sounds like cooing, chuckling, and neighing. The cries of birds grow louder by the riverbank, and the paths are crowded with walkers, passersby, and folk hurrying on their way. The closer you get to the river, the thicker the date palms around it.

Suddenly I came out onto a great round plaza, into which a number of narrow paths led. A wooden platform was erected in its center and everyone crowded around it. I stood watching them curiously as they whispered among themselves and looked around, directing their attention to one of the alleyways.

Before long a group of guards appeared at the mouth of the alleyway, shoving a man with a bowed head, who was crying out and trying to get away from them. When they passed by me, I could see that their captive appeared to be wealthy, his features showing the soft living of palaces: he wore a luxurious garment and expensive leather slippers, and when they pushed him up onto the scaffold, they made him kneel and pulled his turban off, whereupon his well-groomed hair spilled over his shoulders like a shining curtain. From where I stood, I could see the beads of sweat on his broad noble brow. They bound his hands behind his back with hempen ropes, then tied him to a pillar on the scaffold. Suddenly, I saw him surge up and spit in the face of one of the guards. The guard slapped his face and kicked him between the legs; he fell forward, retching.

My bones trembled. I began to feel nauseated myself. Around me, the assembled throng took to clapping and whistling, and some shouted, "Yes, slap him! He hoards money! He doesn't pay his zakat and give his rightful due to charity!"

One of the guards brought a bucket filled with a sticky black liquid, a ladle floating at the top, and started to pour it over the man's long, glossy hair and his expensive garment to the cheering and whistling of the crowd, who pelted him with pebbles. The bound man cried out, "Merchants of Baghdad! Lend me money to give to these demons! You all know who Abu Muhammad ibn Umar is! You all know my integrity in the marketplace! Lend me money, or tell these demons to give me five days to sell one of my holdings and pay the amount they claim I owe the treasury! But know that it is unjustly demanded, making its way into the stomachs of the Persians!"

When he said his last line, the soldier upended the bucket over his head: he floundered around, gasping, half dead, as the onlookers called out, "Have you such need, then, keep the sum of your zakat?" And they took to pelting him with orange peels and cow pies.

It was as though Baghdad was stealing my joy from me, the joy that had filled me as I was walking alongside its aqueducts and enjoying the river breezes filling my lungs. It had shown me one of its darker faces—of which many were yet to be revealed.

Abu Qandil had been right: I had no need to inquire of any passerby the location of Khan al-Hashimi, for it dominated the riverbank, towering over it with the solidity of a mountain. Only about a hundred arm spans from the Tigris, it was bustling with folk coming in and out, chimneys emitting smoke dotted about the corners of the building. The northern outer face was devoted to craftsmen's workshops, heads bent everywhere to their carving, tapping and ornamenting the edges of various things. Despite the press of faces and tongues, they quickly spotted a stranger, and turned to stare at the man loitering by the boardinghouse. To conceal my embarrassment, I approached a blacksmith standing at the door of his stall. His face was smudged with soot, and his thick, fleshy features softened to see me. "What is the name of the person responsible for the khan?" I asked.

"Over there." He pointed out the entrance to me. "At the far end of the khan, by the stairs that take you up to the second floor. His office has a green wooden door. It's the only one that color in the whole place. You'll find the man you're looking for there."

I could tell from his accent that he was a foreigner. Before he could press me for more detail, I thanked him, feeling that his eyes were glued to my back.

The khan's ceiling towered high above me, its cylindrical central hallway so vast you could scarcely glimpse the other exit: to my left, like a far-off light, was the ground floor, surrounded with archways and close-set wooden pillars with bases of green marble. A stinging spicy scent and a thick perfume suffused the entire place.

I pushed in toward the right-hand side: to my left were spice stores, perfumers, potters, and sellers of fabrics and carpets. By the time I arrived at the room with the green wooden door the blacksmith had described, I was overwhelmed by the colors, smells, and sounds, as though I had been transported to a magical market.

I knocked on the door, and waited for a while before knocking a second time. There was no response. I had already turned to go when I heard a muffled voice from inside. "Who is it?"

I hurried back and pushed the door open, poking my head inside. Inside were thick shadows, the smell of paper and inks that concealed the interior from me. I pushed the door open wide to let in enough light for me to identify the owner of the voice. He was a slight little man, like some poisonous creature that never leaves its hole. He had slender fingers, red eyes, and a pale face. He was sitting at a table piled high with papers, inks, files, and sheets of inscribed leather. My boldness in opening the door wide appeared to have disgruntled him. "What's the matter?" he squeaked snappishly. "What do you want?"

I was taken aback by the hostility in his tone, despite his squeaky voice. "Peace be upon you," I said. "I come recommended by Abu Qandil the muezzin—"

"Damn that fellow!" he burst out. "He never stops sending riffraff and idle trash our way!" Not waiting for an answer, he growled, "Look here, young man. This khan wasn't set up by my lord al-Hashimi to provide shelter for every stray mendicant. It's for brilliant students only—those who have the ability and talent that can serve and receive service in return. A man's value lies in his skills. Where are you from, and what is your skill?"

My experience in Basra seemed to have been a preparation for this moment, making me better equipped to withstand his boorish response. I took a step in his direction and plucked his quill from the inkwell. Upon a piece of leather that lay before him, I wrote in my best handwriting, "I am from the land of the poet who wrote: 'He who headbutts a rock to soften it, / Does it no harm, but his skull's often hit.'"

"Isn't that a verse by al-Asha?" he said. Then he recited: "'Still you remain swaggering and arrogant; / Sunnis of al-Yamama; what do you want?'"

He went on: "You would speak of skulls, you who are related to the lying false prophet Musaylima? No wonder, for it's among your folk that the horns of the Devil will appear!"

By now I was red in the face, and quite ready to come to blows. Perceiving this, he surged up from his seat and quickly opened a wooden box that lay in the corner of the room. From this he produced a key. "Maysara!" he called out. The little boy who had been at the door to the room came in. "Take this gentleman to room seven." Turning his attention to me, he said, "Close the door behind you on the way out. Tomorrow, come to me after noon prayer to receive the list of your duties."

## The Spirits of Room Seven

Although the room was small and sparsely furnished with a threadbare carpet and a cotton mattress rolled up in one corner, with a small high window, little more than a porthole, it was a palace compared to the space I had occupied beneath the pulpit in the mosque. It was friendly, devoid of the cold, abandoned air of some long-empty houses, where the walls stare at you with chilly suspicion. In fact, some small creepers growing outside had pushed their buds into the room and were curling about the corners of my casement. I said the traditional greeting, "Peace be upon you," by way of hello to the room when I came in, which made the boy, Maysara, look at me oddly as he handed me the key.

It soon became clear that Khan al-Hashimi was one of the prominent landmarks of Baghdad. It was close to the wall of the Circular City, in a neighborhood overlooking the Tigris called Bab al-Hadid, ornamented with estates and date-palm orchards. The close-set stalls in the khan wall meant the streets around it were packed at every time of day, and guaranteed custom from the denizens of the Circular City. In fact, they had clients from every neighborhood in Baghdad, as their wares were of a high quality that was rare indeed.

The rooms of Khan al-Hashimi were not an outright endowment; in other words, living there was not free. It was said that al-Hashimi had established the boardinghouse to protect students from the humiliations of want, hoping that they might become accustomed to a proud life of labor by means of providing accommodation in exchange for services provided. One of these was helping rebuild the outside of the building, especially the eastern wall, which faced the river and sustained regular damage from the flooding of its waters. The Tigris was prone to flooding, and could flood up to twenty-one arm spans on occasion, quite high enough for the waters to reach the floors of the stalls. The playful creatures of the river would swim up to the walls of the khan, climbing plants would grow upon the walls, birds would nest in the cracks, and all this needed continual restoration. The students who lived in the khan would come together under the supervision of a group of Nabatean builders, and soon the walls would be restored, the path to the river repaved, and some of the windows of the façade stained with tar and then decorated with colored gesso. The students might also take part in the harvest season, plucking dates for the estates owned by Abu al-Hassan al-Hashimi in their spare time. Some of those who could read and write kept the accounts for the stores of the khan in his absence. This was my allotted task, which I performed diligently and with a devotion to duty so palpable that it eventually made me share the fate of the cranes. It was indeed a shocking tale, filled with wonder, terror, and cunning.

There was a slave girl whose task it was to take care of the rooms, by the name of Jamra. She gave us food every morning: bread as dry as her veined hands, which we dipped in date syrup. Although her face was half obscured by tattoos, and her eyebrows as hairy as a scarecrow's, some of the students who lived in the rooms winked and nodded that she could also be prevailed upon to perform other services in the night. But her manners were as unpleasant as her looks, and I had no inkling how any of them could bring themselves to know her. But for all that, sometimes she would give me a pomegranate or an apple; I would find it on the windowsill of my room.

My neighbor in the next room of the khan was a young Egyptian named Hassan. He had a round, smiling face, with a light smattering of beard on his cheeks. His large head was always moving and turning this way and that. He was a merchant fallen on hard times, here from Egypt to sell his wares—namely, papyrus. He had brought large quantities of it, polished and shining, and was trying to sell it in Baghdad, but it was not as popular as he had hoped: the paper traders only used it for book covers, and for drawing and ornamentation to hang on walls. Papyrus was no longer in demand, having been replaced by thin sheets of paper made by the Barmakid factory in Baghdad, or manufactured in Fergana, China, or Khorasan, the last of which was currently taking over the paper trade. The thin sheets of leather that used to be written on were now reserved for bookbinding, not the pages of books; leather is dry, heavy, and unwieldy, and if damp should touch it, it softens and renders the text upon it unreadable, then dries wrinkly and malodorous, tempting the mice to it as a meal.

Due to the lack of interest in Hassan's wares, he now worked as a boys' schoolteacher. One of the corners of the khan was endowed as a small school for two groups of folk: the poor boys of Karkh in the morning, and foreigners who wished to learn Arabic, the language of the Qur'an, in the evening. The school was noisy at all times: the reprimands and shouts of the teachers, the games and mischief of the pupils. My neighbor's good-natured and friendly demeanor made me even fonder of the khan and those who lived in it, for Hassan the Egyptian was a pleasant companion with a keen memory who knew by heart many verses by al-Mutanabbi, and recited them fluently. When Jamra reproached him for lingering in his room of a morning, keeping her from cleaning it, and punished him by withholding his breakfast, he chuckled, laying a hand on his breast and bowing before her in mock contrition. "What shall I do with you, Jamra? You whose lips are like wine, whose commands are ours to obey, yet you have a harsh tongue!" Then he recited: "'Each man to what he is accustomed, O my word; / To strike the enemy's the custom of the sword.'"

He was not only conversant in al-Mutanabbi; he knew a great many works of grammar and theology by heart, or so he said. When I asked him to recite them together so I could learn them, or to dictate them to me so I could write them down and learn them later, he shook his head and avoided me, parroting an old proverb, "He who learns texts knows all that's best!"

I had no wish to tell Hassan much about my life, not only because he was garrulous, but because his behavior was strange: sometimes he was filled with jokes and good cheer, generously handing out sweetmeats and fruit to the other students; at other times, however, he would plunge into moods of despondency and resentment so black that he barely returned my morning or evening greetings. Curled up outside his door was a pretty Persian cat. She came to see him, meowing, whereupon he would pet her and feed her. She disappeared into his room and slept there all day. She remained resistant to my efforts to coax her into my room or offer her some food, waiting for Hassan to come and feed her. He named her Morgana, and said, joking, "Morgana is my lady friend; she turns into a ravishing fairy at night, and stays in my bed until dawn, when she jumps back into her cat skin."

"Why don't you have her knock on our doors, then?" I asked, grinning. "Instead of leaving us to flirt with dry, withered old Jamra."

Slyly, he would quote to me: "'None shall know her but the patient; / None shall know her but the reverent.'"

I recall waking once at dawn and going out to relieve myself. I seemed to glimpse a coat of calico fur hanging at Hassan's door. My mind was half-addled with the idea that perhaps Morgana was indeed with Hassan.

The name "al-Hashimi" was often mentioned in the khan, until it became immense in my head. I could not manage to form a clear image of him in my mind's eye. The only time I could see him closely was when I glimpsed him sailing through the library of the khan, surrounded by his men and those who wished to speak with him. Hassan told me that he had tried many times to get a small plot of land by the river from al-Hashimi, to plant papyrus and then use it to make paper, but, according to Hassan, "He seems always pensive and distracted, thinking of this and that. He has no idea of the importance of this project! Or," he mused, "maybe he's afraid that by supporting my endeavor he will make me a favorite, which will arouse the suspicion that he is close to the Egyptians or to the throne of Egypt—and that would mean he is tacitly supporting the Shiite Fatimid Dynasty against the Sunni Abbasids. Especially since the Abbasid caliph, al-Muqtadir bi-Allah, never managed to beat back the Fatimid Dynasty or stop it from forming. All he could do was put out a message casting doubt on the heritage of the Fatimid Mahdi, who claims, as you know, to be the grandson of Muhammad, son of Ishmael, son of Jaafar the Truthful! His message affirms that the Fatimids who now rule Egypt are not the descendants of the Prophet Muhammad after all, but of a man named Disan ibn Said al-Kharmi; in other words, that their claim is false and they are not the descendants of Imam Ali ibn Abu Talib, the grandson of the Prophet."

Hassan went on, head bowed as though he were imparting some great news: "No matter what they say about their heritage, the Fatimids have managed to build glory, to found a civilization and raise the light of Islam high!"

Everyone who frequented the Paper Traders' Street in Baghdad also visited the Library of Abu al-Hassan al-Hashimi. He had devoted a broad expanse of the khan to it: it was not for buying or selling but only for seekers of knowledge. He moved some of the books there that his personal library could not house, or that he did not need at his home, a great palace in Rusafa on the other side of the Tigris, which Hassan described as "like the sultans' palaces." I recall, back home in al-Yamama, that the Prophet's descendants considered it beneath them to work in trade or craft: according to them, they ought to live off *al-khums*, or the fifth of any sum collected as the spoils of war (in Sunni tradition) or according to a number of complex tax laws (in Shiite tradition), the honor of their ancestry, and the income from their estates. They should be above jostling with the common folk in trade and taking a portion of the poor man's lot.

Perhaps this was why al-Hashimi had established this endowment, along with its library, which drove me mad, so many books did it hold and so varied were their titles. The library took up the entire eastern corner of the khan, some of its windows overlooking the river. I crept into it on the second day I stayed at the khan. I could not wait to become accustomed to the place, or earn its denizens' trust: even the blacksmith at the front of the khan stared at me as I headed with quick strides to the door of the library, a mysterious deep look in his eye that I was unable to interpret at the time, and only learned the meaning of much later.

There was a door inside the khan leading to the library, but it was closed; that was why I used the outer door with access to the street. Outside, I paused for a moment by a magnificent elm, with a thick trunk and lush branches, some touching the windows of the khan. Birdcages of varying sizes hung on its branches. One held several yellow-bellied bulbuls that sang and hopped around inside; the other held a single sullen nightingale. Three of them held large colorful birds that looked rather like eagles; they returned my scrutiny with their own silent gaze. One of them tilted its head and squawked out a strange sentence: I staggered back in shock. It was the first time I had heard talking birds. I looked about me questioningly. The boy, Maysara, who had led me to my room the previous day, was sweeping up the bird droppings and cleaning out the cages. "What is it saying?" I asked him avidly.

With a cunning smile, he said, "A status between two statuses."

"What does that mean?" I asked.

Instead of answering my question, he said, "These birds were put here by my lord al-Hashimi. Whenever a student finishes reading a set of books specified by the librarian, and passes a test on them, he gives him a gift by setting one of the caged birds free, as a sign that the student has been liberated from the cage of ignorance."

I smiled, entranced by the charming conceit. "What further wonders, Baghdad, do you have in store for me?"

Leading into the library was a short passageway with a few wooden seats on either side and a breathtakingly high ceiling topped with a glass dome. This led into a large circular room that was rather dim, with shelves of gesso up to the ceiling, all covered with books and manuscripts and ledgers that were numbered and arranged by subject. A strong smell of leather mingled with the heaviness of smoke and the perfume of tree leaves that the librarians burned incessantly to keep moths and rodents out.

I completed my tour of the library, a deep delight spilling through my veins. How I yearned to devour the pages of these books! I was like one of the faithful touring the dwellings of his nymphs in Paradise for the first time.

Something at the farthest corner of the library caught my eye. It was a room without a door, within which a scribe and a number of copyists sat at neighboring tables. Around them, the floor was paved with boxfuls of all kinds of paper, ink, and writing utensils. They were so engrossed in their work that they barely spared a glance for my arrival, then bent their heads once more over their texts. They were writing upon polished, glossy paper that their pens slipped over with ease. This must be, I thought, Fergani paper. They were not only rearranging and rebinding books and replacing ruined pages, but copying and correcting as well. Three of the copyists had long, delicate fingers holding dainty pointed pens. They were numbering the pages, ornamenting the margins and covers, and applying gold leaf. When they were done with each book, they handed it to a man sitting in the corner of the room with a crucible of melted wax bubbling before him. He waited for it to cool and painted the front of each page with a thin layer of wax to protect it.

Seeing my fascination with and constant frequenting of al-Hashimi's library, Hassan said to me, "The scribes are the grandsons of those brought in by the vizier al-Fadhl al-Barmaki when they founded the papermaking industry in Baghdad, and it's become an inherited family business." I had no real interest in this information: I had acquired the skill of filtering through the mountains of anecdotes that Hassan deposited in the laps of his interlocutors. However, it did give me pause when he put his head close to mine and whispered, "Al-Hashimi owns priceless copies of the translations that were in the House of Wisdom, which they now sell in secret for fear that they will be burned for heresy." He went on, "It is said that the Surianese and their priests pay high prices to have them in their church collections. And that's nothing to the prices they pay if you take them to Andalusia, and especially Cordoba! They're mad for them there." After a moment's silence, he resumed. "I don't know now, of course, what's become of Cordoba after the Fitna. Does it still have its old passion for books and libraries, of which they say that the Fitna of the Umayyads has burned so many?"

I listened to Hassan with profound regret that these translations were now scattered throughout different lands, depriving me of the chance to read them. He whispered, "Abu al-Hassan is a lover of science. His home in Rusafa is a Mecca for poets and men of letters. But he does not stay in Baghdad long; he is always journeying hither and yon, for fear of arousing the suspicion of the caliph that he is hiding some wish to rise to power because he has so many visitors to his home."

"But this caliph is weak!" I burst out. "He wasn't even able to keep the Fatimids out of the Hijaz! And the sermon at this year's hajj was given by Egyptians, and the Buyid Dynasty controls the region!"

"Do you think that anyone needs him, or listens to him?" Hassan whispered. "He's a puppet caliph. The Persian Buyids have already got all his power. He does not sound the bugles of battle or send armies out, or even choose a wali for his throne. They coin money in his name and theirs; it is only for fear that the people will rise against them that they pray for him on Fridays. Other than that, his hands are tied. If he was not a descendant of the Abbasids, and were it not for the Persians' fear of a popular uprising, they would have unseated him already. Last year, there was a strong rumor that they would remove him and instate the Fatimid caliph in his stead, but they hesitated for fear that there might be a descendant of the Prophet with a claim to the throne, someone who would command their obedience and they would end up sharing power."

## Ishaq al-Wasati's Tavern
My days in Baghdad began to take on a certain order. I divided my time between the discussion circles and the library and, in the evenings, the welcome and friendly company of Hassan's varied and neverending chatter. My silence stretched in his presence: there was no need for me to keep up my end of the conversation.

Ten days after I settled in the khan, Hassan told me that a relative of his, a trader coming from Egypt, was on his way to Basra, and that he wished to invite him out to dinner. With a sly wink, he said, "We're going to Ishaq al-Wasati's bar! I know my relative—he likes a bit of fun. He sways in time to the music and the dancing lovelies!"

I was not about to turn down such an offer. It was a side of the city I had been awaiting my whole life long. I had never tasted alcohol, for no other reason than that it was unavailable in al-Yamama—at least in our house, although there was a certain fabric trader in al-Yamama who brewed it and sold it in secret. When he died, the people of al-Yamama were perplexed: should they bury him with the Muslims, or had he committed a cardinal sin? My grandfather settled it, not bothering to argue with them: he went to his house, washed and prepared the corpse with his sons, who were still young, then ordered him borne in his coffin to the mosque. Only some paupers followed him, hungry men whom my grandfather promised the customary meal after burial.

Hassan's relative did not resemble him at all; he had nothing like that brightness and alertness that Hassan's large head contained. Hassan was always looking about like a hawk watching a hunter; his relative was a bent-backed older man, wearing an almost threadbare abaya and sandals so intertwined with his toes that he seemed to have been born in them. He had nothing of the elegance and good humor of a rake about him. Why had Hassan chosen to entertain him at al-Wasati's bar? Apparently, the one who wanted to drink and sway with dancing lovelies was Hassan, not his broken-down old relative.

Ishaq al-Wasati's tavern was some distance from the khan, so we took one of the small boats clustered around the riverbank for two dirhams each. The boatman took us to the bar, also on the river, discreetly situated behind fruit trees and date palms which shielded it from passersby to a great extent, so that only would-be patrons could divine its existence.

I had never been to a tavern in my life. Therefore, I stepped into it with my left foot forward, as one does when entering an outhouse. Later, I would look back on this behavior as naïve and childish: a man is firm of purpose, after all; either you wish to enter, or you do not. The tavern was a building like any other; not, as I had imagined, a gloomy cavern. It had a red-tiled roof and good stone walls: it might have been a renovated monastery. Its outer door opened onto a long rectangular room with a back door leading out into a rear garden whose walls were covered with climbing jasmine. There was a fountain in the center, a lady of stone pouring water into it from a sculpted urn. Around it, the patrons sat at tables with short wooden legs inlaid with mother-of-pearl, and drinks were being handed around that did not make them, as I had supposed, lose their minds; they did, however, talk loudly and burst into guffaws of laughter. To one side was a man with a lute who played a mournful, melancholy tune. Everyone was occupied with their own companions. I was astonished to see white-bearded old men wetting their mustaches in the silvery tankards of beer and licking them in delight.

Everyone there seemed to know Hassan. As soon as we walked in, we were approached by a young waiter with a smiling black face and in clean, elegant clothing. Hassan said haughtily, faking a noble mien, "Muhammad, take me to Ibn Hani's trellis." Muhammad bowed his head with a smile and led the way with quick strides that had us running after him. We went down a colonnade overlooking the garden, roofed with palm thatch and surrounded with pots of Persian jasmine, two steps elevated from the ground, furnished with colorful rugs and couches adorned with paintings of hunters chasing gazelles. As we were sitting down, Hassan called out to the waiter, "Bring us some of what Abu Nawas speaks about in his poetry—'Give me the medicine that is itself my sickness!'"

Muhammad, the waiter, strutted about, pleased that the patrons knew him by name. We had followed him like barnyard hens following a crowing rooster. I studiously refrained from saying to him, "Being famous among tavern patrons is hardly cause for vainglory."

A low brass table was set before us. The smiling, dark-skinned young man left and returned at once, bearing a tray laden with dishes: greens, fried unripe dates, salted hazelnuts, peeled pistachios, and pieces of sugarcane washed with rosewater. Hassan poured our drinks from a jug. "Have a taste of this," he said. "They ferment it from Tawhidi dates. It's delicious."

"Does it make you drunk?" I asked naïvely.

"Give me strength to deal with you desert Arabs!" said Hassan, already starting to lean back, smiling and humming along with the lute player. "Forever in your tents debating how to find the Good Lord Almighty with what you can deduce from your senses! You quote the likes of al-Jahiz's apocryphal Arab who, when asked how he knows God, answered, 'The baby camel indicates the camel's existence, and the tracks indicate the traveler's persistence,' and so on and so forth! Mazid of al-Yamama, use your head! The Lord has said only 'Avoid.' He says, 'Intoxicants are an abomination of Satan's handiwork, so avoid them.' He has not said that they are prohibited. He has only said that of pork." He sat up straighter and assumed a more serious tone. "Whatever has become of Imam Abu Hanifa's fatwa that strong drink is permissible in small amounts? And Sufyan al-Thawri, who issued his own fatwa that the only drink that is prohibited is wine made from grapes, and of course drunkenness itself, but not alcohol? What is prohibited, he says, is that which will make you drunk if you, once you have started, are on the verge of inebriation."

In a deep bass voice like a bull's, our guest bellowed, "Hassan! Don't press our guest in matters of religion! Let him choose as he pleases!" He grinned broadly, showing yellowed teeth. "Or else he'll end up like the judge in the story. They say that a judge went knocking on the door of a nobleman, being thirsty, and asked the servant for a drink to quench his thirst.

It was a cunning waiter who answered the door, so he brought him wine, and the judge asked him, suspicious of the flavor, 'Is this alcohol?' 'No,' the waiter said, 'it's liquor.' And he kept on telling him different names for it: raisin juice, then booze, then sauce, then sozzle swill, and the judge kept on drinking glass after glass until he fell flat on his face, and had to be wrapped in his garment and carried home."

Hassan threw back his head and laughed until his turban fell off, pointing at me. "We'll see tonight whether we're going to have to wrap this son of the desert in his robes and carry him home!"

Music filled the air. Breezes from the river wafted over us. And the imam Abu Hanifa had permitted a glass of wine in these surroundings, after all, as long as it didn't make one drunk. But how was I to know how drunk is drunk enough for a sin? Should I measure it with the span of my hand? I was an innocent, but at the same time I had a great thirst for experience. I gave myself over to the ecstasy running through my veins.

The smell and taste were too sharp for me: I brought the cup near to my lips, only to move it away again. After a short while, Hassan's guest slurred, "Where are the fat geese?" He too had taken off his turban, and was starting to watch the people around him. I realized then that, since we left home, we had not spoken to him or made any pleasantries as hospitality dictated. He spoke again like a grunting bull, "Is there some place where a man can take his pleasure with a wild young deer or gazelle next to this house of wine? I hear that they only cost two dirhams a night."

"Ishaq al-Wasati's tavern is for gentlefolk only!" Hassan snapped. "It isn't for lowlifes or men who call for gazelles or geese! Sit in your corner. If a goose, as you say, comes to you or beckons, then that's allowed tonight. Otherwise, stay put, or they'll throw you out and your shoes after you."

I was not accustomed to hear such reproachful and harsh tones from Hassan, but clearly alcohol brought out sides of him that he normally kept hidden. To lighten the atmosphere, I said, "How goes it for the paper traders of Egypt? Is the market flourishing?"

He turned to me with his entire body, putting his back to Hassan in an attempt to avoid another argument. "The book trade is not very strong with that mad boy on the throne of Egypt," he said. "He is full of doubt and suspicion, and is a burner of books. Therefore, people occupy themselves with their own affairs and calamities rather than writing books. Although I have heard that al-Azhar University has a great library." He bowed his head, shaking it sorrowfully. "A few days before I left Egypt, Cairo of the caliph al-Muizz was abuzz with what its ruler had done. He was riding through the market and passed by a women's bathhouse, and heard the women within singing and laughing loudly in a manner he deemed debauched. He commanded that the gates be shut and locked and bricked up, so that the women all suffocated inside the bathhouse."

When he saw my jaw drop in shock and my stricken face, he caught himself, perhaps not wishing to sully the image of his homeland. " Slow down," he said. "There is no longer anything in Egypt worth visiting. And if the very name of Egypt is mud in Baghdad these days, it's because Caliph al-Qadir of Baghdad never ceases to stir up public sentiment against the ruler of Egypt. Everyone who comes and goes from Egypt is classed as a spy." His voice rose. "They even charged me extra for an entry tax! I'm no trader! All I have are a few valuable embroidered cotton caftans that I do plan to sell, but they wouldn't believe that they're part of the clothing I plan to wear. The guards all but devoured me with their eyes, as if to say, 'How can a man so ill-dressed be carrying such rich Egyptian cotton caftans?'"

Hassan sighed. "At the head of this nation are three caliphs. Each has set aside minarets to sing his praises: one in Baghdad, one in Cairo, and one in Cordoba. We do not know which prayer will reach the ears of the sky first, that we may join ranks beneath it. In any case, if they fall out, they will trample us like elephants, and it is we who will pay the price dearly, from our daily bread and our livelihoods. See how the prices are rising in Baghdad now that the trade routes are beset by bandits and the taxes high!"

It was true; all trade was going through a slump, even the book trade. Many old manuscripts were in the possession of my lord Abu al-Hassan al-Hashimi, for instance, carefully preserved in his home at his estate in Rusafa, hidden away in a secure place, only viewed by his family. Due to their content, he could never convey them to the sellers of books and papers.

I took to poking fun at the sudden wisdom that had come over Hassan. At that moment, I seemed as far from that library as Canopus from the Pleiades.

## Rajilat al-Hanabila
## 2/3/ AH 401, AD 14/10/1010

I trod carefully on the shores of the discussion circles in the mosques, watching closely. I listened to what the imams said before selecting a number of them to frequent studiously so as to be accepted as a student there. I feared being captivated or enthralled by any single one of them, and thus unable to break free. In Baghdad, many wonders awaited me. In the first week after I arrived, the brothers from Baluchistan and I had been out looking for a place to stay when the call to the sunset prayer sounded from the minarets, and soon after, the imams announced the start of the prayer. Hurrying to the gate of the nearest mosque, which was on my right, I found myself pulled back sharply by a hand grabbing my tunic. "Hold, hold!" one of them said. "Go not into that mosque. They are suspicious characters."

I wriggled free. "What of it?" I said. "How know you this?"

"Soft you, young friend," he cried, "and beware the followers of Imam ibn Hanbal!"

"Why? What is their fault?" I asked.

He came closer. "We know them," he whispered. "We pass through Baghdad frequently as we come and go from the pilgrimage to Mecca, so we know enough to avoid them now. Look around you! Not one man in Karkh is going into their mosque. Just praying with them is enough to call down suspicion on you. They think nothing of depicting the God they worship as an image, with limbs and dimensions, spiritual or physical! They think He may move about, descend, and ascend into the heavens, and"—he lowered his voice—"that He can *manifest* and take *tangible form*." He straightened. "Ask the muezzin of our mosque about them; he knows their blasphemy well."

Their urgings and the looks on their faces forced me to acquiesce, resolving to ask further about matters of which I knew nothing. I prayed with them at a mosque of their choosing. I refrained from telling them that when I pray to God, I picture Him on His throne surrounded by light and angels. His hand is white and veined, and it is like that of my grandfather. Sometimes he rests it on the arm of his throne; at other times he is holding a pen with which he writes our fates. My perplexity and the winks and whispers among the people of Karkh at the *mushabbiha*—that is, those who envision the Lord God as a personage—did not dissuade me from joining the discussion circle of the sheikh, the follower of Imam ibn Hanbal, Muhammad al-Tamimi. His fame had reached al-Yamama; I recalled that Musallama and Sakhr of Tamim waxed lyrical about him and his vast knowledge. For all that, I knew they were only praising him because he was a member of the clan of Tamim, not out of experience or awareness or any real desire for learning.

In his discussion circle, Sheikh Muhammad al-Tamimi appeared awe-inspiring and imposing, with a great many followers. He had the expression of a father preaching to his sons, although his two lower front teeth were missing, making his lower jaw jut out slightly. But this did not affect his mellifluous voice, the freshness of his imagery, or his fluid and well-turned phrases. The whiteness of his beard connected with the whiteness of his turban, forming a halo around his face that made it light up. His abaya was of the fine wool worn by most of the notables of al-Yamama. The discussion circle around him was wide enough for several rows, and his followers listened to him reverently, holding their breath like hunters lying in wait for an unapproachable herd of deer. I did hear some of them whispering and nudging one another about the fact that he had married a young girl from Yemen in recent years: when he spent the night with her, he would come to them the next morning smiling from ear to ear and in a very cheerful mood, the wellspring of inspiration would open, and he would chatter and digress and fill the circle with talk. On the other hand, if he spent the night with his first wife, he would arrive in a dark mood, scowling and impatient: on those mornings, beware of asking him for a favor or for clarification of anything that seemed unclear. I did not become a regular there, for reasons I knew not. Was it because the Tamim cousins had spoken of him? Or was it because the night I decided to join his circle, I had seen in a dream a great eagle come to my window, with a face like Sheikh al-Tamimi? Had it only been his accent, tripping off his tongue like that of my grandfather, that first drew me to him?

With the early signs of spring, the sky may lour over Baghdad. Strong winds spring up and the roads are clogged with thick red mud. Cold winds laden with sand and dust veil the sky with a color like saffron. The mosque I was going to was opposite the Kufa Gate of the Circular City. I emerged from the gate and walked along the city wall. I was worried and confused. I had been told that the discussion circles of the mosque were filled with arguments and even insults, all but telling the other party, "Leave me alone." I had laid out the cups of my soul to fill with the knowledge of Baghdad: with interpretations of holy texts, biographies of important personages, well-formed arguments, and the charm of poetry, all the while searching in the desert for the poets of Najd and Tamim, whose poems, my grandfather said, formed the basis for all the rules of grammar and language, set out by Sibawayh in his *Excursion of the Thirsty Soul*; yet I had found naught but the discussion circles of the mosques, which had become a forum for exchanging insults.

I left the circle, feeling the red dust between my teeth. I wondered whether to pass by the market to buy food for myself or go back to the khan, perhaps for Jamra to give me something to eat.

Suddenly I heard a hubbub and the footsteps of a crowd approaching. I drew back, afraid. It was not yet time for evening prayers, but the red dust had brought on an early darkness against which even the streetlamps struggled. The smell of the Chicken Canal was stifling, as it had been since the flooding of the Tigris, clogged with manure and the remains of spoiled food. In the tight space between the wall of the Circular City and the canal, a few arm's lengths away, a crowd of perhaps eight men thundered, yelling and cheering. They were mightily built, with great beards ending in unkempt braids that looked not to have seen balm or care for a year or more. They were barefoot, brandishing thick sticks. When they passed, they looked at me suspiciously. "Peace be upon you," I said.

They all muttered a greeting under their breaths. One of them came up to me, so close that his nose was almost touching my face. I could smell him: he smelled like a billy goat getting ready to mount a nanny goat. Then he drew back. He had been *sniffing* me. Why should he do that? Had he been seeking the scent of alcohol on my breath?

I caught snatches of their conversation as they retreated. They were saying that the red dust that covered Baghdad was the wrath of God because ministers had been appointed from among the Rafida, or rejectionists, and clerks from among the Christians and Sabians to work in the ministries of the state. I slowed my steps, stealing glances at them. They stopped again and encircled a young man walking with a small boy beneath one of the streetlamps of the Circular City. In the faint light, I could see the young man scream at them, the cords of his neck standing out: "This boy is my brother, you disgusting, filthy boors! How dare you!"

"How shall we know that he is?" one of the men said. "Perhaps you are leading him astray for vile purposes that, as they say, shake the throne of the Almighty, thus bringing down more of God's wrath upon us."

Passersby had started to congregate, drawn by the commotion. The young man looked hither and thither, crying out, "Police! Guards! These riffraff would abduct my brother!"

At this, the men dispersed, muttering rebelliously. The young man kept calling, "Chief of police! Captain of the watch! Where are you?"

My chest was tight as I went into the khan. There was a fine layer of red dust over my bed and my books; but this had not kept Jamra from placing three pomegranates on my windowsill once more. I devoured one and took the other to Hassan, the light from under his door betraying that he was still awake.

Thank the Lord, Hassan was in a pleasant mood. He had just bathed, and was robed in a new silk caftan, which I guessed was a gift from his relative, the merchant. He greeted me, wreathed in smiles, and invited me in. When I told him about the ruffians causing a to-do in the streets, he turned his head to the right and spat. "Ah," he muttered. "Those are probably Rajilat al-Hanabila."

"What on earth are Rajilat al-Hanabila?" I asked.

"They are followers of Sheikh al-Birbihari of the School of Imam Ibn Hanbal. They call themselves Rajilat al-Hanabila, or the Foot Soldiers of Ibn Hanbal. They walk around the marketplaces as though they were debt collectors or keepers of accounts. They spy on store owners buying and selling, block the path of men walking with women or young boys, and attack bars, spilling the wine they find, attacking the singers, and smashing musical instruments. Ishaq al-Wasati's tavern used to be a favorite place for their conquests, before Ishaq made a secret agreement with the chief of police and a group of guards, who now defend him in exchange for protection money. The chief of police has many times made an example of these self-styled foot soldiers, prohibiting them to meet even in twos, forbidding discussion of their creed, and also forbidding their imams from starting group prayers without saying '*In the name of God, the Merciful, the Compassionate,*' at morning prayers and the two evening prayers, since it is their blasphemous habit not to say it out loud." Resentfully, Hassan went on, "But it was no use. It didn't stop their evil; in fact, it made them more seditious."

Hassan's words were a balm for the lonely heart, calmed the troubled soul, and leached the blackness from one's breast. We devoured our pomegranates, and the trouble in me receded. I took my leave of him and returned to the shelter of my room. As my hand was on the door, he said, "Where do you get these good pomegranates?"

"I don't know," I said, "but Jamra puts them on my windowsill."

"*Jamra?*" He gave me a look, eyes full of mischief. "*She* puts them? Or do *they* put them for her?"

I froze. "Who are 'they'?"

"The ghosts of the room," he responded carelessly.

"I'll leave it up to God to give you the punishment you deserve!" I burst out. "You just urinated in the pool of rose-water you gave me with your own hands."

My sleep that night was disturbed. Every time I startled awake, I glimpsed a group of men, perhaps eight in number, in a line against the wall facing me.

## A Sentinel, Ready

Toward the end of Ramadan, there are fewer students around the sheikh, and during the feast they all but disappear. Most of them go on excursions, taking boats out on the river and heading north. I was alone in the discussion circle, so near to Sheikh al-Tamimi that he observed how carefully I bent over my papers. I was trying to follow what he was saying about the sum of the zakat for breaking one's Ramadan fast. Perhaps it was my good handwriting or how close I was to him, and how careful I was to take down everything he said, but the students were teasing me and making fun of my assiduous note-taking. "*Not a word does he utter*," they joked, quoting verse eighteen of the Sura of Qaf, "*but there is a sentinel by him, ready to note it.*" In any case, Sheikh Muhammad asked me to sit by his side and take down everything he said. He would like, he said, to compile it into a book in the future.

A discussion circle dictated by Sheikh Muhammad Zayd al-Tamimi at the Mosque of the Mother of Sultan al-Mutawakkil, may she rest in peace, Tuesday 4/10/ AH 401, 11/5/ AD 1001. I write as my Sheikh Zayd al-Tamimi says, anger in the depths of his voice, "Shiites claim to follow the Prophet's descendants, yet they insult every one of the Prophet's followers. They believe in *raj'a*, that the Prophets will rise again, and in *bida'*, meaning that it is possible to change what is divinely ordained by human deed, although the sacred texts are clear as day before them and cannot be changed, as *ijtihad*, or interpretation, in the texts is forbidden.

I was writing silently with my head down, until such time as I could find out who Mazid al-Hanafi was.

I had no time to spend alone to "consult my heart," as Islam says; Baghdad's marketplaces are filled with argumentation, and no sooner does a black cloud lift off the discussion circle in the mosque than another takes its place. At the circle of Sheikh al-Tamimi the day before, three young men I did not recognize had arrived. They walked about the assembly, bristling with ill intent. They wore silk and fine wool, and their hands were smooth and soft like those of pampered slave girls, hands that had never held hammer or hoe. Their gazes were insolent and they seemed to be spoiling for a fight.

A few of the sheikh's disciples whispered among themselves that they were Persian merchants from Rusafa, their bellies full and their hours empty, so they filled them with blasphemous arguments that amounted to casuistry, empty talk, and remnants of the heresies preached by the fire-worshipping Persians. Thus, they came to make trouble at the Sunni discussion circles, picking fights with the congregation, the venerable sheikhs, and the theologians. Some of them claimed to be descendants of the Prophet's disciples, but they were all cursed with casuistry and heresy. Thus, they secretly became adherents and disciples of the school of rationalism, the Mutazilites. They remained, however, loyal to taqiya, which means they show outward piety while hiding their true intentions. I had no idea who they really were: Baghdad showed me a strange new face every day, and from its numerous neighborhoods one surprise after another dawned, leaving me startled and pensive. I had a constant premonition that something significant would befall me here, but I did not know at that time that it was behind the door of my own room.

Why do enemies of Sheikh Muhammad al-Tamimi spring up from every nook and cranny? Even that gecko of a supervisor of the khan! He was now friendly enough and returned my greeting—especially when he observed how studious I was and how keen I was on spending time in the library. He called me over as I passed by to write out the cover of a book of notes he had compiled, and gave me papers on occasion to copy out for him. This day, he called me to him as I was hurrying out. I wished he had not called! Sheikh al-Tamimi was accustomed to preaching his sermon the minute the afternoon prayers concluded, and I did not want him to finish his prayers before I had prepared my pens and paper and tools for note-taking. "At your service," I said, perforce, breathing hard.

"Mazid," he said, like a father advising a son. "I am glad you have found employment."

I looked at him, taken aback. "I have not, but am still seeking it."

The right-hand corner of his mouth turned up in what might have been a smile, making him look even more like a lizard. "What about your note-taking for Sheikh al-Tamimi?"

"He asked me to." I tried to be curt, hoping to avoid extending the conversation. "I couldn't say no. But he only gives me two dirhams."

"What?" he shouted. "Don't be naïve, boy! Don't let the followers of al-Birbihari exploit your naiveté and your fine handwriting. May the Lord punish them for what they have done! They are but ignoramuses of ill breeding and filthy origin. They devoured their books when hungry, thinking them bread. They are many, breeding like flies in Baghdad, since the era of their *mushabbiha*. it is said that Sheikh al-Birbihari crossed the Tigris to the western side and sneezed, and when his companions blessed him, they made such a noise that the caliph heard it all the way in his palace. The caliph asked after them, and, from what he heard, he came to fear them." He nodded. "See? Even caliphs fear them."

I raised an eyebrow in surprise, wanting nothing more than to pick up the inkwell and upend it over his head for his rudeness and boorishness, but I had neither the time nor the courage. Instead, I feigned great interest and surprise: this gecko fellow must, after all, feel that his advice was well received and that he had done me a favor. The ground between us must remain green and fertile, for it was he who was giving me free accommodation in the khan. "May God protect us from their evil!" I said, nodding. "Heaven preserve us from the *mushabbihah*! Prayers and peace upon the Prophet Muhammad and his pure descendants!"

I had imagined that this prayer for the Prophet's descendants would appease him. I only found out that he was a Sabian, a believer in Noah as his prophet, a few days before my departure from Baghdad.

## The Sedition of Strangers

The season of pilgrimage to Mecca was upon us. The hajj caravans from India and foreign lands began to arrive in Baghdad. But this year, none of them went on to Mecca, so treacherous was the road and so full of bandits and Qarmatians. The hajj season they spent in Baghdad, which caused the markets to fill up and flourish, and anyone with stock brought it out and displayed it: jars of oils, crates of dried dates, small dolls of wood and cloth, old pots and pans, little statuettes found in the ruins of bygone nations and presented as people who followed the magic spells of Harut and Marut and were cursed thus by God, metamorphosed into stone. Even Ishaq al-Wasati's tavern was livelier in the hajj season: pilgrims from China poured in, drinking raisin wine and listening to the music. Their eyes would narrow in delight until you could barely make them out, all the while keeping their wits about them and remaining alert; then they would leave, in groups, looking down and always on guard, having left the waiter a generous tip.

My heart was heavy and I was preoccupied at that time. It had been a year since I left al-Yamama. How had the days slipped through my fingers so fast? An entire year since my breast had filled with the breezes of al-Yamama, the perfume of its date palms, the spray of its waterwheels. A year since I had watched our star, Suhayl of al-Yamama, rise; a year since I had felt the cold of the late night, a year since I had seen Shammaa of the House of Wael and heard the rustle and swish of her clothing. I sent two letters to her with caravans headed there; I had also met her uncle when he was visiting Baghdad, the one whom the Bouhis had given land in Wasit. He told me that they were well, but that my mother missed me and asked me to return: she had, he said, found me a young and stunningly beautiful bride. Heaven forgive you, Shammaa of the House of Wael! Still tempting her little boy so he would listen to her, just as she used to tempt me with dates soaked in syrup.

The strange young men still hovered around the discussion circles of al-Tamimi, their flowing silken abayas dragging behind them. I did not know who they were; what I did know was that they could not stand my Sheikh al-Tamimi, always dragging him into disputation. Because my ears still retained the clarity and sensitivity born of the desert sands, I heard them one day as they whispered, drawing near our circle: "We'll see what that senile old fool and his men do today."

I was struck by the hate in their voices. As they came nearer, I recited the verse: "Not a word does he utter but there is a sentinel by him, ready to note it." But they paid me no heed. One of them scrutinized me closely, then turned up his nose and looked away. The others ignored me completely, although I sat at the sheikh's side. As we were preparing for the lesson, the mosque attendant, whom I often saw filling the pitchers for ablutions, hurried toward us. In the center of our circle, he threw down two leather scrolls carefully wrapped, crying out, "Pray for them!"

Every day, one or two of these scrolls, bearing names of the sick or dead, arrived, that we might pray for them. We passed the scrolls to our Sheikh al-Tamimi, who opened them up and turned to face Mecca. "Heal all sickness, Lord of All, You who heal all. There is no recovery but through You, a healing after which there is no illness. In Your hands is all healing, and there is none who may reveal it but You, Lord of both worlds. I ask You, of Your limitless compassion and generosity, and Your protection, to heal"—he looked at the scroll to assure himself of the name of the sick person—"to heal Fatima, daughter of Hammad, and to grant her health and vitality."

"Amen," the murmur went through the circle. I remembered the "Bless you" in the story that reached the palace of the caliph. Only an "Amen" from the lips of the faithful fills the abayas of the imams, and puffs up their turbans, and reassures them as to the submission of their followers. Sheikh al-Tamimi unfurled the second scroll hurriedly. "Lord, ensure that Yusuf ibn Nour is in a better place, with better folk, and admit him to Paradise, and protect him from the torments of the grave, and the torments of Hellfire. Lord, treat Yusuf ibn Nour according to Your worth and not according to his worth. Repay his charity with charity, and his injuries with forgiveness. Amen."

The entire mosque reverberated with such a hearty "Amen" that I half fancied Yusuf ibn Nour would emerge from his grave reborn. The circle complete, we began, hearing murmurs from other discussion circles in the mosque whose sheikhs had started to give their sermons. Our sheikh, al-Tamimi, adjusted his turban, then began in a mellifluous voice. It appeared he had taken note of the young men lying in wait for him and seeking to make trouble. In my hand was my pen; on my right was my inkwell, and I attempted to keep pace with the words issuing from his mouth and set down some of what he said about the signs of polytheism and how to rid oneself of it and pray sincerely to the face of God Almighty. Suddenly, someone called out, interrupting: "Venerable Sheikh! I wish to inquire about a lesson I am told you gave yesterday."

My sheikh frowned. Everyone's necks craned toward the owner of the voice. It was one of the strange young men. He had a sparse mustache and no beard, and his white silk turban had slipped back to reveal half his head. His wide, long-lashed brown eyes had dark circles around them, like one who is up reading half the night; but his fresh complexion betrayed the featherbeds of luxury he hailed from. He spoke loudly, mockery concealed deep in his tones. "Sheikh Muhammad. You insist that the Lord is seated upon His throne, and insist upon describing an embodiment of the Lord. Therefore, would you tell us what form He took when he manifested in the final third of last night?" He went on: "When He manifests, He is not one. There are many of Him, spreading far and wide in every land. Imam Ali, in his *Nahj al-Balagha*, says, 'He who describes the Lord limits Him; and he who limits Him places Him among the number of things that can be counted,' which is a clear instance of polytheism and blasphemy against the creed of monotheism."

This question was received with dead silence. A ponderous hush fell over the discussion circle where my sheikh's students and adherents sat. I could tell the difference between the students and the adherents: a student always has an inkwell by his side, while an adherent merely listens closely. Despite his disgruntlement and the ire that sparked in his eyes, my sheikh lowered his head and clapped his hands for silence, swallowing with difficulty.

That night, when I went back to my room, I went quietly over the notes I had taken at that moment, when hands had been raised bearing inkwells with the desire to split open the strangers' heads. I found that I had written, by way of introduction to my sheikh's response to the would-be rationalist:

> The curse of the People of the Book is contentiousness and sophistry. Ibn Hanbal has written that the Lord created Adam in His image: sixty arm spans tall. When He created him, he said, "Go, and greet such and such a number of angels seated there."

Then there was a blank line. He must have fallen silent; then, I found that I had written:

81

One of Sheikh al-Tamimi's students said, "He who turns rationalist turns heretic."

I had left another line blank. Then I had written:

Sheikh al-Tamimi said, "Sophistry is sin; in creating a fatwa, one must judge by the general intent of the text, not by the specific occasion. Whoever delves too deeply into the books of philosophy and follows the Mutazilites in being rationalist, follows them into their conflict with the pillars of religious law. Nothing they have said comes of a clear conscience, but of ill intent and weak faith. We come now to the response to your question. Sheikh al-Birbihari, may he rest in peace, mentions that the Lord seats the Prophet, peace be upon him, next to Him on the throne, and that the seat is where the feet of Almighty God are placed. That said," he added in the standard conclusion of every imam explaining a matter of religion, "only God is all-knowing.

The reader will note that I neglected to close the quotation marks on the above speech: this is because the mosque suddenly erupted around us into an uproar. The questioner yelled, "*Allahu akbar!*"—a cry taken up by his companions, who added, "Blasphemy! They say that God has feet! The Holy Qur'an says, 'There is nothing whatever like unto Him!' Death to the Hanbalites!"

Then another of them roared, "Wasil ibn Ataa, the founder of the Mutazilites, has said, 'He who proves that the Lord hath a meaning or an old description hath proved that there are two gods!' Remember, according to the Mutazilites, the changeable forms of Earth cannot be applied to an unchanging God!" Then a third bellowed, "The Lord is above any image or likeness!"

Then one of the men ran up to the pulpit. He climbed up it as though he were about to call out to prayer and yelled, "There is only one God, and there is nothing whatever like unto Him! He has neither body nor spirit nor corpse nor form nor flesh nor blood nor personage nor essence nor breadth nor length nor color nor taste nor smell!" From around the circle, his friends yelled the name of God and screamed out, "No coldness! No dryness! No height! No width! No right, no left, no front, no back! He does not beget, nor is He begotten! Anything that can come to mind or be pictured by imagination is nothing His like!"

The sheikh of the neighboring discussion circle rushed over to us, barefoot, staring as if to ask what was going on, craning his neck behind us, his students gathered behind him. When they heard the verbal battle and saw the inkwells being brandished, I heard him saying as he moved away, "Damn them all! The Hanbalite *mushabbih* who would give the Lord dimensions is describing a graven idol! And the Mutazilites who place the Lord above meanings and descriptions are but describing nothingness!"

One of his students asked him, "Which of them is in the right? Who has escaped damnation, my imam?"

"Heaven preserve us!" His sheikh called down the blessings of the Lord, shaking his head. "I cannot but think that they are both headed for Hellfire."

I had written no more beyond this point. What I wrote down thus far was from memory. Sheikh al-Tamimi yelled, "*Allahu akbar!*" followed by a great number of those around him, and craned his neck high, two greenish veins standing out in it, which I had only seen before on the pulpit at his Friday prayers. He recited in a voice shaken to the core, "'Fain would they extinguish Allah's light with their mouths!' That is what the heretics and blasphemers have done! The Prophet of this nation has come to show us the shining white path, from which none stray but the damned. . . . Sophistry and contentiousness on the pretext of using one's mind is a deviation from the Prophet's tradition. Every deviation and suspicious behavior is rooted in using one's mind. The sin of Iblis, the Devil, was allowing his opinion to rule him instead of the text, and his choice of his personal desires in defiance of God's command."

I remember that at that moment, one of the young strangers grabbed a hand armed with an inkwell on its way to split his head open. I leapt up then and ran out of the mosque, hoping to find some soldier or captain of the guard to break up the quarrel. Someone had already done so, I found, for I had barely gained the doorway when the guards thundered into the mosque. Their leader entered the mosque on horseback, followed by four foot soldiers with their swords drawn, followed by two others armed with slingshots. The horse neighed loudly, making the walls of the mosque vibrate. Everyone fell silent. The captain of the guard, mounted on his horse, yelled fit to shake the walls of the mosque, "Who would defile the House of God with contentiousness and sophistry? Have you returned to your old ways of rationalization and contention? May the Lord curse you all!" Then he quoted,

> Our religion was well and good until
> The rationalists, with their logic bottomless.
> Whene'er they meet, they shout and yell
> Like foxes howling at a sarcophagus.

I was astonished at the education of the captain of the guard: my sojourn in Baghdad had only shown me foreign, boorish guards. He cried out, "My Lord Abu Ghalib ibn Khalaf, the best leader and the commander of the armies, has commanded us to preserve the land and cut off the heads of evildoers and hang all those who would spread *fitna* among the Muslims. And you are the imams of *fitna*! You are the root of all evil! You never cease your temptations but continue on!

And I swear to God, I shall not leave this spot unless I take the fomenters of unrest with me, leading them with a rope around their necks like beasts!"

My bones quaked. I was astonished to observe that none of the combatants said a word or made a move to report any of the others. They knew full well that he meant what he said: that a severed head hanging in a public square would guarantee peace in Karkh for at least a month. He returned to roaring at them. "Who is stirring up the rabble in the House of God?" Then he turned around to find the one who had rushed to call them in from the square. It was one of the mosque attendants, fearing that the expensive carpets of his mosque would be stained with ink; but now he found himself in great trouble. He tottered forth, his legs barely able to support him. He wore an odd turban with a tall cap. It made him look like the *majazib*, one of the softheaded religious fanatics who ran around in the squares. He spoke clearly, but I could not hear it from where I stood: I gathered that he had made up some story, I know not how he managed it that fast. "The people in the mosque are upset," he said, "because beardless boys are allowed into the discussion circles, tempting men to sin and lust, and distracting seekers of knowledge."

The captain of the guard's voice was suspicious. "Where are they?"

The attendant pointed out a young man sitting in a nearby circle. The boy fell onto his face, prostrating himself, sobbing so hard that he choked. I thought that he would die from weeping. "Bring him," said the captain to one of his guards.

The guard went to him and dragged him by his ankle, facedown, still in a crouching position, screaming like my pet goat, Shaqran, being dragged to the slaughter. The guard lifted him by his ankle and struck him across the face. "Silence," he said, preparing to throw him under the hooves of the captain's horse.

"No! No! No!" screamed the boy. "I don't want to die!"

It was evident that the captain of the guard had not been taken in by the trick or the answer: he could see that the boy was only a scapegoat. "What's your name?" he bellowed.

The boy made no answer, prostrating himself and crying. "Take him outside," the captain said to another guard. "If I see you again in the circles of men, I'll string you up by the ankle on the gate to the city!"

The captain looked over everyone again, staring into the terrified, lowered faces. With a tug on the reins of his horse, he wheeled about and exited. The guards remained in place, looking after him, the rear end of his horse scattering dung here and there to tell them what its master thought of them.

Sheikh Muhammad crept out, holding his turban and his shoes, having lost them in the fracas. He headed for the small door of the mosque set next to the place for ablutions, followed by two of his students who feared for his safety. I followed, bringing his books and papers. We sat in a safe corner underneath the stairs leading up to the minaret.

We sat there for a long time. The guards stayed for a while in the mosque. There was a window opening onto where they were standing, and we could hear them saying, "Where are they? Where are the whoresons? Where are the ones who stir up foment in the House of God?"

My sheikh muttered, eyebrows raised, "Heaven repay you with everything you deserve, you fire-worshipper."

That night, I volunteered to accompany our sheikh to his home in the outer courtyard of the mosque. There were few people passing, but we had barely slipped into the alley where he lived when, from the shadows, a group of men burst out, bellowing, "God grant you victory over your enemies, our sheikh!"

I stilled. The blood froze in my veins. I had not recognized them at the beginning: they were barefoot, with thick beards, and brandished thick sticks. A group of Rajilat al-Hanabila.

They surrounded the sheikh and insisted on accompanying us for his protection. My sheikh shook his head, refusing adamantly. "Bless you, gentlemen," he said smoothly, "but we would prefer not to attract attention or provoke passersby or the guards or, worse yet, the Ayyarin gangs. Go on your way, God be with you."

They looked into each other's faces in perplexity. After much hesitation and lingering and whispering between Sheikh al-Tamimi and their leader—who had a truly extraordinary beard, which carpeted his chest like those of the monarchs of bygone kingdoms I used to see adorning the maps of Baghdad—while the rest of his companions thumped their staffs against the ground and incessantly called down God's understanding and His forgiveness, they finally disappeared into one of the houses behind the mosque.

I slowed my steps, trying to keep pace with my sheikh's heavy, exhausted tread. "What happened?" I asked him.

"They have gone astray," he said, "and seek to lead others astray with them. They would extinguish the light of the Lord with their mouths. God damn the Rafida and the atheists!"

"But how do you know that they are Rafida?" I said, perplexed. "Where did they come from? They surrounded us in the mosque, crowded around us, and then disappeared in a flash."

My sheikh answered despondently, drooping like a wet chick: "Be not dismayed, my son. This has long been their custom. Now hand me what you have taken down."

I excused myself, telling him I had not written everything down due to the chaos that had descended upon us. He made no reply. I felt uncomfortable asking more, so we walked slowly toward his house, which was luckily (or possibly unluckily) quite a distance from the mosque. He seemed much older, and very tired. I had no desire to add to his burdens. When we arrived at the door to his house, he reminded me again of his papers and notes, and how important it was that I bring them tomorrow.

In addition to taking notes for him, my sheikh, al-Tamimi, required me to copy out ten pages every night, which he then sold as though they were his, at two dirhams a page. Meanwhile, I got nothing but two dirhams for everything. He explained it away by saying that he had a large family and two wives to support. "What will it harm you," he said, mocking me, "if the rats in your room go hungry? But I have a thousand mouths to feed alongside my rats, not to mention two she-wolves who compete with one another for my money."

How hard it would be, after all this, to bend my knees at your discussion circle, Sheikh al-Tamimi! I should finish the copy of *Sahih Muslim*, Sheikh Muslim's well-known compilation of the Prophet's sayings, that I was currently working on, then take my leave of him. If he wished, he might grant me a degree in the science of hadith; if not, I had no need of his degree.

On my way back to the khan, with my sheikh's voice ringing in my ears—"Be glad; the Lord is with us"—I muttered, "Is the Lord really with us? Is He on our side? Those strange young men with their soft hands quoted God and the Prophet too!"

## Graven Idols and Nothingness

The strangers' *fitna* did not cease. That night, it made its way into my breast. It remained there like chaff stirred up by the winds, howling madly, keeping me awake and making me easy prey to thoughts of graven idols and nothingness. I could scarcely wait for morning to come, so I could become something other than what I had been the night before, like a snake that sheds its skin and goes forth enjoying a different taste of the air and sunlight on its new hide.

But that night, the argument started by the strange young men with Sheikh al-Tamimi remained in my ears like the buzzing of a beehive, and clung to the hem of my garment. My eyes remained open, fixed on the rafters of my room. A spider, wispy but diligent, was spinning its home. What form had God taken in His descent to the lowest heaven in the final third of the night?

I rose from my bed and commenced the *tahajjud* prayer, placing my requests and my abject need in the hands of my Creator. "I am Mazid al-Hanafi, seeking Your blessing and forgiveness."

When dawn broke, I approached the soul-stealing gates that separate the moment of death from the isthmus that links this world to the next. I glimpsed great crimson curtains falling from the sky into my skull. They were of costly silk, with gold ornamentation, the Qur'an verse "*There is nothing whatever like unto Him*" embroidered on them. I drew near to them and buried my face in them. I felt their softness against my cheek like the velvet cushions that the mother of my lord Yusuf had brought in to decorate the mosque at al-Yamama. I pressed my face against their smoothness. They parted to reveal an awe-inspiring man with an imposing build, seated with a bowed head that stretched from east to west, contemplating what lay beneath his feet. I trembled all over; I heard the beating of my heart in my ears; it looked like my grandfather, with some of the features of Sheikh al-Tamimi, a pen in His mighty hand.

At that moment, I felt I was upon the isthmus, and that I had been dreaming. I opened my eyes and tore up the picture, erasing it from my mind. Curse the heretics who had sown doubt in my heart and banished sleep from my eyes. But was it they who had sown the seed of doubt? Or was it my fate that challenged my will? What was I but a vigilant jerboa that spends its time chasing a chance to gnaw and nibble on books and yet more books? I had become the joke of everyone who worked at the library, who told me I might as well use the books for pillows and make my bed there.

The next morning I woke heavyhearted and drained. Had I forgotten to recite the verses of the Qur'an that morning to bless my day? Or had I eaten too much yesterday of the lamb shank soup that the people of Karkh make so well? Was it the soup that stole the lightness from my spirit, robbed my movements of their grace, and dragged me down to the level of the common folk who care for nothing but their base urges?

I had come to Baghdad only to find that it was not the city I had constructed in my mind during my childhood in al-Yamama, envisioning it as built of bricks of gold and silver. It was a cold and heartless place that cared nothing for those who visited it. I had wished to pluck the fruits of its glory, and to be blessed with an education at the hands of clerics and learned men and good friends; but Baghdad is an angry, forbidding city, visited by every nation; people from all lands pour into it like a river. There is little to be earned, and there are so many learned men and poets that they number more than the civil servants of the caliph; they are so unfortunate that they envy one another their daily bread, snatching it out of each other's hands like goshawks and kites.

Nevertheless, on many occasions, the manservants of the caliph al-Qadir would emerge from the gateways of the Circular City, coming from the kitchens of the caliph's palace, bearing upon their heads trays with breakfast for all the mosques close to the wall.

Baghdad's alleyways clamored and flourished with chatter; it had no time to listen to me. When I arrived there, its people were still speaking of a star that appeared in its sky the Friday night that was the first of the month of Shaaban, like Venus in size and luminescence. It bobbed up and down, with a light like that of the moon; it remained there until the middle of the month of Dhi Qidah, three months later. The people of that city considered it an ill omen and went around expecting a disaster; stars always bring disaster.

Back home in al-Yamama, after Grandfather's death, my announcement of my wish to leave for Iraq was akin to another funeral coming out of our house. My mother wept; she refused to sit with me or talk with me any more. She would place my meals before me, then jump up and swish out, the only sounds the whisper of the silver jewelry at her hands and in her braids. Our talk was limited to my request for her blessing at my departure. I laid siege to her with that request for months, closing my eyes to the tears that gathered beneath her eyelashes; when I insisted, tears would spill from both her eyes at once.

I had decided to go, but not when; should I wait for wintertime, or accompany the caravans going to Mecca? It was forty parasangs from al-Yamama to Ihsaa, a hard distance to cross unless it was winter, when the rainwater collected in streams that people could drink from. Upon my arrival in Ihsaa, I would be close to Basra; but I decided to accompany the hajj caravans despite the broiling heat, as these were better equipped and more securely guarded. Shammaa of the house of Wael was, at that time, still reciting a list of suitable brides for me, finding them the best traps for a boy of twenty to keep him in al-Yamama. "If a boy reaches twenty and remains unmarried," she always said, "the men of al-Yamama will cast doubt on his manhood. Your cousin, who is your age, is married and has started a family already: his first son recites the Sura of Ikhlas whenever he comes to visit!" Then the list started: "Salma, Jazla, Wadhaa . . ." How pretty they looked in my mother's list! There they stood in her words, all lined up, smiling, like pampered narcissus blossoms by a stream. Anklets, bracelets, henna-painted hands, flirtatious smiles . . . but if I should point, lay my finger on a name, and meet the owner of that name at our house as a prospective bride, well then, she would become like all the other women who visited my mother, bony and dusty, complaining of their boorish husbands and the unfairness of Fate.

My grandfather had had an unfinished dream in Baghdad that he had never managed to fulfill; thus, he returned to al-Yamama. This was why my cries to be permitted to go there grew louder after his death. Al-Yamama appeared to shrink, its houses becoming smaller and its streets narrower, like an old garment I had outgrown. My soul mounted higher, reaching for the stars: I was visited by strange dreams, filled with the voices of women singing poems about waiting that sounded more like mourning, songs I had never heard before. Was there someone waiting for me in Baghdad?

## The Ashmuni Festival

The Christians of Baghdad have a festival they call the Ashmuni Festival, held at the Monastery of Ashmuni in a region west of the Tigris they call Qurtubl, not far from Khan al-Hashimi. The sound of their hullabaloo and the clangor of the celebrants' utensils and the preparations rang out as far as the khan. "Come home early from the circle of that sheikh of yours who speaks of what he does not know," Hassan said, and winked at me as we headed out that morning. "We must go and celebrate with the Christians of Baghdad at their festival; it is a joy that cleanses the soul!"

It was not only for Christians; the entire populace of Baghdad seemed to have moved there, to the banks of the Tigris, while others were still arriving from nearby towns, mooring their boats and small craft by the monastery. They strolled around and took the air, making their way down the pathways to reach the wall of the Circular City. They stared astonished at the regularity and solidity of the stones that made it up, reading al-Jahiz's verses carved into a polished stone by some students:

> I never saw such circular regularity,
> As though poured from a mold of singularity!

Then they would go back for a stroll on the banks of the river.

Some of the celebrants had pitched tents and thatched shelters around the monastery and a branch of the river they called Batatya, where there were also rest houses and marquees. Unveiled girls came out of these, walking about, their eyes taking in with pride the hearts that broke under their feet. A few paces behind them walked boys with silver daggers in their belts and whips in their hands, which they cracked in the air to defend the girls against anyone who might disturb them. Despite their come-hither looks, the girls' shaved faces betrayed that they were naught but eunuchs.

The monastery flung open its doors and the bells rang. There was a bar in the corner of the monastery, which had set out a great many jugs and massive jars of wine and fermented dates, which were doled out in scoops, poured into brass cups, and sold to the revelers. "The best wine in Baghdad is here," Hassan whispered to me. "That is why the clerics ask the caliph to confine Christians to their homes and force them to wear tan tunics with a patch in the front and rear, and don wooden clogs if they are riding a beast of burden." He shook his head. "How terrible that the caliph grants their request when he has two Christian physicians in his palace, one of whom attended his own mother, Sultana Tamani, may she rest in peace." He warmed to his subject. "Last year, the common people revolted against the Christians' presence in Baghdad: they attacked the church in the neighborhood of Daqiq and set it alight. It collapsed upon some people and killed them. They are hardly different from that insane boy currently on the throne of Egypt! He had the Church of the Resurrection in Jerusalem, site of the Holy Sepulcher, burned to the ground."

"And in spite of the persecution," I said wonderingly, "here they are, celebrating. The balm of time and the will to live heal many wounds."

He gave me an unreadable glance. Then he tugged at my sleeve and quickened his pace. "Let's eat some of that fish I promised you."

I was not a great lover of fish: I was, after all, an Arab of Najd, who had never known the taste of it. Hassan always told

me that the folk of Baghdad had their own strange and delicious recipe, wrapping it in sweet basil. He hurried around,
looking for the places where fish was being grilled. He was
wide-eyed and impressed, his big head darting with more
gusto than usual as he watched the bold beauties walking
about; he flirted with them with one eye and glued the other
to the smoke ascending from the barbecues, constructed of
carefully set stones on the banks of the Tigris. Atop them were
great slabs of river fish, as long as your arm, and everyone
jostled and crowded the cooks.

Hassan shouldered his way through the throng. Abandoning the reticent, almost dainty stride he normally affected and
the way he wrapped his abaya about him with the dignity of a
teacher, he thrust his way into the crowd and took to pushing
and shoving to get a share of the fish.

I stood waiting for Hassan to return with his prize of two
fish for us: I had no stomach for jostling. I watched the people
passing by. My curiosity was piqued by a great crowd around
a marquee, kept at bay by guards. When I approached, I
glimpsed through the heads and necks of the crowd a group
of stunning girls, unveiled, sitting cross-legged on cushions
and playing musical instruments. In the center was a singer
with her face veiled, a great brass bowl of water before her
with flower petals floating in it. She played passionately on the
lute and bent her head to the bowl like a mother protecting
her infant. Her lady friends took up her song and poured it
over the tambours, shaking them seductively.

I could not take my eyes off the songstress. Despite the
transparent green veil draped over her face, adorned with
precious stones about her brow, her distance from me, and
the heads of the spectators, I could still divine the light that
surrounded her.

We selected a spot under a tree to take our meal. However, I was so captivated and enthralled that, for the first time
ever, I could not taste it. The voice of the girl was still running

through my ears. I recalled having heard that singing when I traveled to Baghdad in my mind with my grandfather, the nymphs of Baghdad calling to me.

"It is the marquee of Zahira," Hassan said with his mouth full. He held out a grilled fish spread out on hot loaves of flatbread atop a plate of banana leaves. Then he saw that I had gone quite pale. "Be consoled, Arab of the desert! This is Zahira of whom we speak: she is a star that you may look upon but never reach, the loveliest songstress in all of Baghdad. She only sings in the marquees of the ministers, or at the gatherings of the elite." He did not appear preoccupied with her, and seemed more interested in moving to a quieter location away from the crowds watching Zahira.

Suddenly, the crowd dissipated from around the tent and rushed off to the left-hand side. The servants were calling out, I found, that the marquee of the caliph's late mother, Tamani, had just opened, with a great banquet free for all. At last we settled beneath two palms sharing the same pot, the ants industriously crawling over the palm debris scattered about us. "What on earth?" I remonstrated. "Would you have us eat by the roadside in full view of everyone?"

Hassan was hungry and short-tempered with it. Raising his eyebrows, his meal still in his hands, he said, "Tell me—if we were in a barn, and cattle instead of people all around you, would you still feel ashamed to eat in their presence?"

I blinked in surprise without speaking. He put his meal down and stood up, adjusting his turban and abaya, brushing the grass stalks and straw from the latter. Then he started declaiming at the top of his voice. "Thanks be to the Lord who alone is beauty and perfection! I swear there is no God but Allah, alone with no other gods, with nothing his like or his equal, the Blessed Names and the highest attributes are all His, and He is the greatest and the most proud and jealous God! I swear that our prophet Muhammad is His loyal servant and His messenger, of splendid character and good manners and a kindly nature, and the best of all who have ever been beloved of the Lord God by approaching Him with reverence and glorification! Prayers and peace be upon him, his companions and descendants, the best company and family, and all those who have followed them with good character, every morning and evening!" He had started to draw a crowd; I could hear him, but could hardly see him for the people who had started to gather around. "And now, to the point! I urge you, brethren in Islam and my brethren, to obey the All-Knowing Lord! Fill the days and nights with your devoutness, in hopes that the Lord will give you a high standing among the faithful and a beautiful afterlife!" He paused. "Trustworthy men, more than one, have been quoted as saying that if you can touch the tip of your nose with your tongue, you shall not go to Hell." Whereupon everyone around him stuck out their tongues and tried to touch their noses. The saddest thing is that, taken unawares, I too stuck out my tongue and tried it. Then I saw him pushing through their ranks with great strides, wrapping his abaya about himself. "That said," he concluded like an imam, "only God is all-knowing. I say this asking God's forgiveness for myself and you! And in conclusion, praise be to God, the Lord of both worlds!"

He extricated himself from the crowd, which began to disperse, and swaggered up to me triumphantly. "How true are al-Buhturi's verses: 'My job it is to write poems in this land, / But not to make the cattle understand.' Look around you." He did so and let out a lowing sound: "Moo!"

I burst out into uncontrollable mirth, laughing until there were tears in my eyes. What wild, reckless man could have done this but Hassan?

### The City of the Rams

I had not seen Hassan at morning prayers, so I searched for him at the Qur'an-teaching school, the *kuttab*, in the forenoon. The school had a large wooden gate facing south, and a spacious dome built out of the same terracotta that formed the khan. I had never sat in a circle at a *kuttab* when I was a child. Grandfather had instructed me since before I could walk; he not only instructed me in the sciences, but in the secrets of life, including the love of this city: the sound of the pupils reciting "By the sun and its brightness, and the moon that followeth . . ." lacked the beauty of skilled recitation and the sobriety in the presence of the Holy Qur'an, but was more like young rams leaping about. My curiosity led me to the classroom door: I wanted to see playful Hassan with the serious mien of a scholar. When he saw me, his face split into a broad grin and he called me over teasingly. "Where do you think you're going, you Lucifer's horn, you? Come on in and I'll teach you how to recite the Sura of al-Shams as it should be done!"

"Lucifer was one of the best of the angels," I said, "and it is he who molded the history of humankind. As for you," I jibed, "you will drag behind on Judgment Day, a mere instructor of boys! Known for their feeble minds and flighty natures, no one believes your like's testimony in a court of law, and it is common knowledge that you resorted to this profession to escape fighting in jihad!"

The boys, divining the lighthearted atmosphere between us, began to fool about and throw pebbles at each other, some of them hitting us; I quickly withdrew. Hassan brandished a cane at them, shouting, the tip of the stick catching a sallow-faced boy sitting in front, as a lesson to his fellows. In the mosque, the guards had picked out the weak boy, on the pretext that he was sitting with the older men, to make an example of him to the others. This city requires a scapegoat to bear the burden of others' transgressions.

I arrived at the mosque early; it was not yet time for the afternoon prayers, after which my sheikh commenced his discussion circle. I went in, seeking the wooden box in which we locked all the writing implements. It was still locked; the key usually hung around Sheikh Muhammad al-Tamimi's neck. He would open it after the dawn prayers, bring out his copy of the Qur'an, and start his recitation with a sweet, melodious voice until his students had all arrived and were sitting around him.

"Sheikh Muhammad ibn Ahmad al-Tamimi has been stabbed in the hand."

I whirled around to face the voice. It was the mosque attendant, the one who had called the police in the fight. He was wearing the same odd pointed cap and the same idiotic expression. With a ghoulish delight tinged with gloating, he was telling some of the students who had clustered around in search of their sheikh and their discussion circle. Glimpsing me out of the corner of his eye, he raised his voice as he told of the incident. "At dawn today, on his way to the mosque, that's when it happened. They don't know who did it. Some say it was heretics who were disturbed by the argument about God being seated on his throne; some say it was the Ayyarin gangs seeking to rob him, and that they stabbed him when he resisted them and he stopped it with his hand."

Amid their cries of "How?" and "When?" and their outraged, wide-eyed stares, I rushed over to him. "Where is he now?" I asked.

"At home," said the attendant. "He didn't come this morning."

The sheikh of the neighboring discussion circle approached. He was short and rotund, veritably rolling toward us, half hidden by his students clustered around him. "I do not think it was the strange young men who come to his circle to cause trouble," he volunteered. The students around him retreated slightly to make space for him when he spoke, so we could all see him. He added, adjusting his black turban, "I do not think that it was because of the altercation last week between Sheikh al-Tamimi and the merchant-born men with their soft and smooth hands. Their only use for knives is to trim their beards and cut their food. They have no stomach for blood; they pass their time listening to music, drinking, playing dice, and amusing themselves. They couldn't hurt a fly." He turned to a young man by his side, whose head was bowed and who was clearly in awe of him. "Jawad! Wasn't it one of those young men whose father called us in to breathe hope into him and recite the Holy Qur'an over him? He had stopped eating and drinking and given in to wailing and weeping when a Turkish boy he owned died, one whom he adored."

Jawad nodded. "It was."

"Yes! Do you see?" The sheikh pointed a finger at him. "Those boys are softhearted and pampered. Their pleasures are closed ledgers, and they walk the city with them concealed in their sleeves. Dalliances and banquets and drinking, that is what they are good at. Go and seek out the one who stabbed your sheikh, for it is not one of these."

There were murmurs among the students. A voice whispered, "Might it be the Persian blacksmith?"

Had Sheikh al-Tamimi really been stabbed? Was it a consequence of the argument that had devolved into a fight, only a few days ago in the great hall of the mosque, between the Persian blacksmith Abu Abbas, who owned a smithy in the khan, and Sheikh Muhammad, when they had argued over the "hand of God"? Sheikh al-Tamimi's students turned to me, rage on their young faces that were just starting to sprout mustaches and beards. They all looked at me with shouts of "The Persian blacksmith is your neighbor, Mazid!"

"Did you see him at dawn this morning?"

I felt myself pale as they stared at me. When I glanced at the door to the mosque and saw some of the Rajilat al-Hanabila coming in, I divined that the matter would only expand. I slipped away to the escape door beneath the minaret and managed to stagger to the home of my sheikh.

*

Sheikh Muhammad al-Tamimi was in his bedroom and was not receiving visitors. People stood and sat in rows in the entryway, the hallway, and the parlor. Some spread out lengths of fabric and lay on the ground outside his house. But when he learned that I was outside, he sent for me to be brought into his private sanctum.

I came inside, head bowed, apprehensive, looking down at my feet with each step. I found him lying on a cotton mattress, bareheaded and looking weak. Around him, his little children jumped and played. This might be the explanation for the stench of urine emanating from his bed. His face was pinched and pale. By his side sat a woman wrapped in a garment that concealed her wholly. All I could see was a pair of kohl-adorned eyes and a pair of carefully painted hands, pleading with him to drink the beet juice in a cup she was holding. Her voice was reedy and thin. "You lost a lot of blood this morning! You have to make it up with this juice." The way his eyes were fixed hungrily on her made me think this was the young wife whose nights he enjoyed and after which he was so cheerful in the morning. She seemed to know it: she was flirtatious in her glances and her speech as she stroked his white beard. His left hand was elevated above his head, wrapped in rags damp with blood.

When he saw me, he immediately started to speak. "There were three of them, all masked. They ambushed me in the darkness. I could not see their faces."

Before I could reply, we heard a hubbub at the door. An older boy, one of Sheikh Muhammad's sons who had taken it upon himself to receive his visitors and oversee their seating arrangements, called, "It is Elishua, the physician, sent by Her Royal Majesty Sultana Sharifa, the consort of our Sultan al-Qadir bi-Allah, God grant him long life, to visit Father!"

A moment later, a thin, old, white-skinned man burst in. His back was bent and his nose crooked, and he was dressed

100

in rich, clean clothing. Behind him trailed a dark-skinned boy carrying a wooden box with a padlock. Elishua went straight to the sheikh's bed without greeting me, as though he were above greeting the common folk. He approached the sheikh without greeting him either, instead saying straight out: "What is the matter with you, Sheikh, lying so feeble abed?" He went on: "Her Royal Majesty the Sultana has bestowed upon you a slave girl and an endowment!"

Displeased, the young wife muttered, "Why not examine him before handing out gifts?"

He ignored her. Taking the sheikh's hand and looking at it, still with a supercilious look almost of disgust, he said, "He must be transported to the *bimaristan*. We fear that his wound may suppurate, as he is feverish. I will precede you." Pausing, he said, "Bimaristan al-Adudi is on the west side of the city. Are you familiar with it?"

I nodded. Without further ado, he went on, already on his way out. "I will await you there."

One of Sheikh Muhammad's sons then suggested we leave by the back door to avoid the press of his students at the front gate. I expanded on his suggestion and said that he should leave with his face covered to avoid recognition. His wife then suggested he leave by climbing over the rooftop of one of his neighbors, but in the end, we settled on the back door.

His son hurried to the market and rented a wooden donkey cart, upon which we placed his bed, and piled bags of barley around it to hide his reclining body from view. Then we took him to the *bimaristan*.

Two three-story buildings on the western side of Baghdad built out of the same red brick as the Wall of Baghdad, one for men and the other for women, linked by a lower passageway on the southern side: this was the *bimaristan*. The sultana's physician, Elishua, was waiting for us at the outer door. Our sheikh gathered up what was left of his strength and walked into the hospital, refusing to be carried. Elishua set down his name in a gigantic ledger upon a short stone pillar erected just inside the entryway, in the corner of a spacious circular atrium from which corridors branched off. Then he said, crooking a finger, "Follow me."

Supporting the sheikh, we hurried to a room at the end of one of the passageways that branched off from the atrium, which they said was the head doctor's consulting room. Our sheikh was ushered in, while we were asked to wait outside in the hallway.

He remained inside for some time; then he came out accompanied by two powerfully built foreign boys. I had never seen anyone like them. They were clean-shaven with shaved heads, their blue-black eyes glinting like the eyes of wolves. They wore white, and on their heads was the Christians' cap. The sheikh was placed on something like a bier, and they went away with him, refusing adamantly to let any of us accompany him. They asked us to return in the evening to see how he was doing. Meanwhile, our supine sheikh was looking at us, terrified, as though being taken to his own burial.

We returned to his house. His sons waited for his students and disciples to disperse, after which we returned in the evening. We found that they had given him a hot bath and clean clothes issued by the hospital, and placed him in a private room with a soft bed and a coverlet of white damask. The sheet was white, and soft as silk. The bleeding in his palm had stopped, and he was loudly and greedily devouring a whole chicken swimming in a great bowl.

We had barely kissed his head and gathered around him, reassuring ourselves of his well-being, when a small man came into the room. Slight of build, bald and bareheaded, his eyes were barely visible through the wrinkles that surrounded them. A great throng of Arab, foreign, and Surianese doctors surrounded him, calling him "the chief physician." Despite his short stature, he had a dominating and awe-inspiring presence. Even Elishua, the sultana's physician, took two steps back and bowed his head in his presence, the perpetually supercilious expression for once gone from his face.

The chief physician took to examining the sheikh's wrist, laying an ear against his chest. Then he gave Elishua instructions in a foreign tongue I could not comprehend. For our waiting faces, he barely spared the ghost of a smile.

A few moments after they left, Elishua returned to us, this time with a broad smile. "He can rise from his bed now!" he said. He went on to tell us that the sheikh could leave the hospital tomorrow, quite cured.

I was not, in truth, overjoyed at this news, for I had glimpsed, on entering the *bimaristan*, on the right of the corridor, a great library illuminated by colorful glass lanterns. Adjoining it there was a grand hall with wooden seats among the shelves; I had had high hopes of creeping into it as long as my sheikh remained here, perusing its contents and reading the titles, if only briefly.

"If my sheikh is leaving in the morning," I thought, "there is nothing for it but to be with the books in the library all night." I then informed his sons that I would keep vigil at the sheikh's bedside all night, and that they could take the donkey cart and return the next day.

After the evening prayers, when sleep began to play around my sheikh's eyelids, the sound of music and sweet, melancholy song began to fill the corridors, emanating from I knew not where. It was as though the stars of that evening had slipped through the fingers of the musicians and were moving around the rooms. My soul plunged into the sorrow of being alone and so far from home, alongside the questions battling in my mind like fierce lions, and tears burst from my eyes, so hot and untamed that I could not stifle them or hold them back. I pretended to be looking out of the window into the garden to conceal my flowing tears from my sheikh, like a motherless child.

There was a knock on the door. One of the foreign boys with the blue-black eyes came in. He seemed fatigued, his earlier vitality having left him. Despite this, he was exceedingly courteous. In halting Arabic, he said, "Your sheikh will leave tomorrow. Would he like to spend some time in the Convalescence Hall, delighting his ears with music, and spending the time in fruitful perusal, to speed the healing of his wounds?"

My heart leapt with joy and I dried my tears on my sleeve. Before I could respond, my sheikh burst out angrily, "After the Lord has healed me, you would have me spend my evening listening to the Devil's own instruments? May you never prosper!"

The foreigner did not, I thought, quite take his meaning; but he did recognize that he was angry. He gave him water in a glass, with a few drops of lavender and sweet basil to help him sleep more deeply.

No sooner did the first wave of my sheikh's snores rattle the ceiling than I was in the arms of the library.

The corridors were heavy white marble, upon which I trod carefully for fear of slipping. The walls smelled of the same healing potion the sheikh had drunk; the music was like a hand massaging my heart and soothing it, and it kept playing until nearly the middle of the night.

Most of the books in the library were Surianese and Turkish. However, I managed to find some Hippocrates and Galen of Pergamon in translation. A shelf of manuscripts also caught my eye for the odd hand they were written in, resembling gilded inscriptions on Chinese paper, padded with silken linings and covered in the well-tanned vellum that never fades. On the face of the shelf was inscribed "The Books of Mani."

They piqued my curiosity. I recalled having read, in the khan's library, a book by the Mutazilite founder Wasil ibn Ataa called *A Thousand Responses to Manichaeism*. I gravitated toward them, entranced by their calligraphy and illustrations. They appeared to be about their Lord Mani. I had seen the Rajilat al-Hanabila burn a picture of Mani. They had snatched it from a young water carrier making the rounds of the houses with a cart upon which was affixed the picture of this man with wide eyes and a friendly face. Most of the books were decorated with delicate drawings and miniatures: rivers, gardens, knights on horseback, and women with long hair sitting on squares of fabric on the grass, shaded by trees with fruit that hung low, surrounded by flowing rivers. Was this their Paradise? How I wished to know! There was a great deal of mysterious writing, surrounded by golden ornamented curlicues.

"Do you like them?"

I jumped, turning around. A man with a young face and bulging eyes was standing there. He wore an expensive silk turban and the sleeves of his abaya were rolled up as though he'd just returned from performing his ablutions. I answered, "Very much."

He smiled. "I saw you admiring them a little while ago. Your eyes were practically falling out into the pages."

I was flustered. He had clearly been watching me for some time. "Are you a patient here?" he asked.

"Accompanying one," I answered haltingly, afraid these blessings would be ripped away from me and I would be cast out of this utopia.

"What you see around you," he said, "is a charitable endowment from my Lord Adud al-Dawla al-Bouhi, may he rest in peace and find a home in Paradise. He set aside countless endowments for this *bimaristan*, to support the salaries of the physicians and staff and treat the patients. He appointed a director of the endowment to manage the moneys and properties it comprises."

I did not know the meaning of "director of the endowment." I thought it was like the man I had met in Basra. I asked him, "Does the director of the endowment supervise the running of the *bimaristan*?"

He raised his eyebrows superciliously at my show of ignorance. "The position of director of religious endowments is a great ministerial position in the diwan of the state. The most competent are selected, and they must have ability and integrity. Only men approved by the caliph are appointed. Everything you see is paid for by the revenue of the endowment."

## The Persian Blacksmith and the Throne of God

Abu Abbas al-Farsi, who was Persian as indicated by his last name, kept a stall in the outer wall of the khan. When I passed it, I was all but struck in the face by the heat from the forge, and the clang of hammer and anvil. I hurried by, barely returning his bellow of a greeting like that of a billy goat. At the time, I had no inkling why he awaited my passage and was so assiduous in greeting me. I was told that he was a slave of al-Hashimi's, who paid his master two dirhams a day. I thought perhaps he greeted me so respectfully because I was always coming and going from the library, and spent long hours there, or perhaps because I was his next-door neighbor—which I did not really credit, for his other neighbors in the khan received no such attention. For that reason, I did not speak much with him, and if he did speak to me, I mumbled back in monosyllables. The tradesmen in the neighboring stalls gossiped about him: he was, they said, a famous bachelor, who had never married because of his love for boys.

He waited for me to pass and stopped me to ask about some grammar issue that perplexed his foreign tongue, saying, for example, "Who are the 'Companions of the Right Hand' mentioned in verse eight of Sura of al-Waqia?" or asking perhaps about the declension of words that ended with -*an*. And when I explained, he raised his hands aloft and bleated like a billy goat, "Good job, Arab of the desert!"

I found his enthusiasm and warm welcome hard to explain. If I lingered but a moment outside his stall, he would rush to pour me a glass of rosewater syrup from a small jar. One time he even made me a gift of a valuable dagger with a handle of banded onyx and an ornamental silver scabbard. I hesitated to take it: I wanted to tell him that I disliked sharp objects, but feared that this would indicate feebleness and effeminacy. I took it from him and turned it over in my hands playfully, then pulled it out of its scabbard, waved it in his face, and said, "This weapon is a saber against all who would injure a neighbor!"

He ignored what I had said, and responded, "You say that in the language of the original folk of Tamim, who hail from deep in the desert! You have never mingled with foreigners or heard strange tongues! The grammar of desert Arabs is instinct but ours is learned!" He added, perhaps to build me up and wear down my reserve toward him, the quotation: "'Incur but the wrath of the clan of Tamim: / You'll find the whole world is against you, it seems.'"

"I am from the clan of Bani Hanifa, not of Tamim," I answered him coldly, "although we are neighbors."

He did not pay much heed to fine distinctions between tribes. "But you are both linked by the native Arabic of the desert."

The next day, he lay in wait for me by another entrance, asking, "What is your custom in pronouncing verse six of the Sura of al-Ala: '*We shall make thee read, so that thou shalt not forget*'?" I repeated it to him the way I had heard it from my sheikh in the mosque, or as I had learned it from Grandfather, not how it was pronounced in al-Yamama. I usually responded to his questions with quotes from al-Asmai, the grammarian of the Basra school, or what came to mind from the discussion circles of the mosque. He would fill with joy and his chest would puff up with pride, nodding in delight at what he thought to be my instinctual grasp of Arabic grammar, making me feel like a divinely inspired prophet spouting miraculous sayings, and possessed of rare gifts with which the other students of Baghdad had not been blessed. But all this did not stop me from keeping the onyx-handled dagger close at hand.

While I spoke, Abu Abbas looked intently into my face. His eyes licked glutinously at my features, lingering lustfully on my lips, as though he wished to drink the words I pronounced in the manner of the clans at the heart of Najd. It increased my distaste for him, and I avoided him so much that, if time permitted, I would leave the khan by a rear exit well away from his stall, leading onto circuitous back roads that passed by palm groves and broken-down walls of estates whose stones moaned and screeched in the wind. They said this was a graveyard for civilizations past, and in part of the wall, there was a wooden gate where a black donkey with a great head was always standing. Sometimes I heard it braying in my room in the khan. "It's a demon manifested in that form," Hassan liked to say, "protecting the people inside the estate from sorcerers and bandits and robbers." I always trembled; but still I found myself obliged to use that road on occasion.

The back roads had not benefited from the great repairs implemented by Adud al-Dawla al-Bouhi in Baghdad. No sooner was I a hundred arm spans from the rear of the khan than I ran into a field of cacti and spiny plants at the end of the road, along with a number of abandoned houses and destroyed aqueducts. Before I turned the corner, there was a barracks for some Daylamite guards watching over the source that provides water to the aqueducts of Baghdad. They wore tattered clothes and were rough-faced and ill-mannered, with long scraggly mustaches. They pestered anyone who passed by with questions, hoping to get a bribe or a gratuity, covering up the abjectness of their begging with a fierce and brusque demeanor that helped save face. When I turned onto the road back to the Chicken Canal, paved with red brick, it was as though I had entered another city, with smooth, paved roads, streetlights on either side, and rows of trees.

The folk of Baghdad never ceased thanking Caliph al-Bouhi for repairing the irregularities in the flow of the river, erecting dams on the canals, and having them cleared of the pigeon feathers and weeds that had clogged them. He also built footbridges above them, had the roads paved and lit with lamps, and repaired some cracks in the walls of the Circular City—in short, he had returned to Baghdad some of its ancient stature and glory.

In recent weeks, when Abu Abbas the smith began to sense my increasing disdain for him, he began to seek out other ways of speaking with me. If I passed by his stall, he popped out suddenly, begging me to stay awhile. Sometimes he would do this and rush briefly into the depths of his stall, while I stood there cursing Shammaa of the House of Wael for giving me the heart of a bird that trembles at every predator that threatens to pluck the blush from its cheeks, and resentful of this accursed infidel lying in wait for me. Before I could think too much, he always hurried back, carefully cradling a leather-bound book in his hands like a newborn babe.

The first time this happened, I was shocked. "This means," I thought, "that he is aware of my passion for books!"

He placed the book into my hands, looking longingly into my face. "Read this," he said. "I know how studious you are, always in the library. I swear, I see nothing behind this bright brow but the signs of brilliance and intelligence deserving of being polished"—he indicated the book—"by these treasures!" He went on: "You know, Yahya ibn Khalid al-Barmaki said, 'What is the worst thing? For an industrious man to content himself with a mean existence.' I perceive that the paper market is corrupt. There are no books for sale now but empty sophistry, collections of quotations from the ancients, and the two good things."

I frowned. "What are the two good things?"

He chuckled. "Food and sex."

Taken aback, I plucked the book hurriedly from his hand and glanced at its title. *Poetics* by Aristotle. I was astonished:

this was a valuable book! How had it come to be in the black-smith's sooty stall? Not only that—it was the translation by Yahya ibn Uday. I tucked it into my sleeve so as not to pique the curiosity of passersby and the owners of the neighboring stalls, who I had started to feel were watching our interaction with a cynical understanding, as though witnessing a business deal. I rushed off to the discussion circle, feeling at the book in my sleeve, looking forward to the moment when I would return to my room and immerse myself in studying it, reading it, enjoying myself, by turns surprised and astonished. Still, I could find no connection between this blacksmith, with his huge, dirty hands, and the contents of this book.

It was a Friday. On that day, there was no discussion circle for Sheikh al-Tamimi: he left after Friday prayers to see to the affairs of his house. However, that day there were two students from Hamadan waiting for him to grant them a degree in Qur'an recitation before their caravan left that evening for that fair Persian city. Sheikh Muhammad al-Tamimi was obliged, after Friday prayers, to sit at his customary pillar of the mosque to examine them. No sooner did his students and disciples see him than they ran to him happily and sat around him, forming three semicircles, although he was ill-humored and bad-tempered that day, with a frown on his face. He did not take out the writing implements for me to use, only asking me to listen to the students with him and go over their memorization with a copy of the Qur'an in my hands, in case he missed something.

One of the young men had an obviously foreign accent, and if I were in Sheikh al-Tamimi's position I would not have granted him the degree. But I had scarcely lifted my head from the Qur'an in disapproval of the student's accent when I glimpsed one of the strange young men, the most argumentative and querulous of them, striding fast toward the circle of my sheikh, bearing in his smooth hands one of the wooden stools used in the mosque as a bookrest for the Qur'an. The strange boy was so beardless and bright-faced as to appear effeminate. He wore no turban, and his hair flowed down to his shoulders. He had come alone that day, without his friends with whom he usually prayed. He drew near Sheikh al-Tamimi's circle, offering the stool with a friendly smile. "Sheikh al-Tamimi, why don't you sit on this, so as to be more comfortable?"

He was affecting a lisp. I was immediately suspicious. Was he making fun of the sheikh, or just trying to be humorous? I had found that the good humor of some of the boys of Baghdad included affecting a lisp for some reason. My sheikh waved a dismissive hand, frowning. "I sit on the ground beneath which the Prophet Muhammad, son of Abdullah, was buried!"

The mincing, lisping young man whispered with intent: "Then why would you give the Lord Himself a chair, upon which He is established? The Qur'an says, in verse two hundred fifty-five of the Sura of al-Baqara, '*His Throne doth extend over the heavens and the earth.*'"

My sheikh surged up and looked about him, then stared at the young man with his eyebrows raised almost into his hair. The young man went on, speaking fluently now, with no trace of a lisp. "The verb 'to establish' gives Him, the Almighty, a form, that is to say, hands and feet."

Sheikh al-Tamimi realized that the young man merely sought argumentation and contention. He shrugged, muttering a proverb: "The clouds don't move when dogs bark." He met the boy's eye. "When learned men speak of matters of the origins of concepts, they do so on a certain basis of knowledge. As for you, who play at it and listen to inanities, you push your way in and seek to argue with scholars and theologians."

That day, Abu Abbas the blacksmith had finished the Friday prayers and gone off to the mosques' discussion circles as was his habit every week: it was the one day he closed his stall and went out in search of what he was accustomed to calling "circles of argument or mirth." If he heard something that bestirred levity in his breast, he sent up heartfelt prayers for the sheikh of the circle; and if he found argument, he cursed him roundly.

I will impute good intentions to—and ascribe to coincidence—the arrival of Abu Abbas the blacksmith at our discussion circle at that precise moment, but be that as it may, the moment of his arrival ensured that every word and scrap and syllable of the argument between my sheikh and the young man regarding the stool reached his listening ears as clear as day. His eyes, red and teary from the smoke of the forge, darted from one of us to the other. Then he burst out, yelling like a bleating billy goat, "Have you no shame, followers of Ibn Hanbal? You would make of God a human figure with organs, He whom no eye can encompass? The Lord is above your base descriptions!"

His bellowing made every head turn toward us. My sheikh was not taking it lying down. "Well, well, and now the Persian infidels are braying!"

"You idolaters," the Persian cried, "giving physical form to the Lord!"

"Idolaters!" yelled someone else in the congregation. Soon the argument turned to shoving, and then a physical altercation broke out, with the Persian blacksmith and some of his supporters in the mosque on one side, and my sheikh's students and adherents on the other.

The fracas only ended with the arrival, as usual, of the captain of the guard, looking around from astride his horse, which he had ridden straight into the mosque. "Have you not had enough?" he said. "Have you not heard of what I did to the Shiites who weep for al-Husayn, and those who weep for Abdullah ibn Zubayr beneath the gates of Basra? Do you not know what becomes of the fomenters of *fitna*? I chained them up by the neck, and the guards walked them seven times around the walls of the Circular City, while people pelted them with rocks and date pits." Then, all at once, he commanded his guards to unleash their whips on the crowd in the mosque, making them all rush outside under his gloating eyes. He left after his horse had scattered its dung over the carpets of the mosque. But the story did not end there.

The Shiites the captain had referred to, who had been chained up and struck with rocks and the captain's whips and forced to wade through horse dung, had had more to say. Baghdad had woken up the day after that incident to find that someone had scrawled on the fishmongers' stores and the stalls that sold fried food: "Prophet Muhammad and Imam Ali are the best of all men; to agree is to be thankful; to disagree is to be an infidel!"

A great outcry followed: the Rajilat al-Hanabila had resumed roaming the streets of Baghdad, foaming at the mouth, brandishing even thicker sticks, despite the threats of the chief of police that he would have them beheaded and hang their heads upon the walls of the Circular City. They paid him no heed, saying that preaching virtue and admonishing vice was a holy duty that was absent and must be restored after the spread of corruption "on land and sea."

The chief of police commanded the stall owners to erase what had been written, but this was only a short truce. This was around the time when my sheikh, Muhammad al-Tamimi, was stabbed; that aroused their ire afresh and their resentment against the Shiites. Back they went to walk the streets, shouting "*Allahu akbar!*" and threatening everyone. It was then I realized that a great evil was about to befall us.

## The Science of Arithmetic
One of the books Abu Abbas gave me was Abu al-Wafaa Busjani's *A Book on What Is Necessary from the Science of Arithmetic for Scribes and Businessmen.* I was overjoyed to receive it and it piqued my interest, not only because it was something outside

the scope of what I customarily read, but because it would aid me in keeping the accounts of the stalls of the khan, a task I performed in lieu of payment for my accommodation.

In truth, the book was the best assistant I could have hoped for. On the first day of the Hajj, just before Eid, Mr. Gecko Hashimi, the director of Ibn Hashim's endowment, told me to do the accounts for the stalls and get them in order before the month of Muharram started the new Islamic year. He always sent me the accounts, which I stuffed under the couch in my room so as not to be confused with the papers I wrote down for Sheikh al-Tamimi, and then completely forgot. Struck with sudden fear that the accounts had been lost or eaten by mice, I took the stairs four at a time. As luck would have it, they were still where I had left them, carefully rolled up and organized, tied with a ribbon of crimson silk that I did not remember having bought. Was that the work of the ghosts of room seven? I did not know, but they must be good fairies.

I then hurried to market, although most of the stalls were closed because of the holy day of the pilgrimage on Mount Arafat and in preparation for the Bayram Eid. I tried to get what I required from some stalls on the outskirts of the paper market that were still displaying their wares; I did not buy the cheap Barmakid paper produced by the factory in Baghdad, but squares of thin luxury paper from Samarqand, which cost a dirham a page. I purchased quality ink made in China, which never fades when applied to paper, not the poor ink made of black vitriol or cedar, which had ruined a great deal of knowledge in the khan's library and here in the paper market.

When I returned to my room, I set out my tools and commenced my labor. I decided to make the cover in *thuluth* calligraphy, with which the scribes of Baghdad were so taken these days. It is known as *thuluth*, or "third," because it is written with a third of the width of the reed pen, making the letters interlace beautifully. Using different colors, I added all the diacritics needed for correct pronunciation. As was customary, I began the document with a *bismillah*, then divided it up: a section for the stalls on the eastern face, with the name of each leaseholder and their industry. These commanded a higher price than the other stalls because they faced the river, and were attended by most of those who were walking on the riverbank or taking boats for pleasure. Other stalls, which paid quarterly, I named "annual stalls." I left the papers in the back of the sheaf for those who paid quarterly. What was more, I left a small space at the end of the document for zakat—one-quarter of one-tenth of the stall according to rent—to make it easier for it to be paid to the needy.

I was hesitant to take this last step, for it was possible that zakat could be taken from other sources of the income, or it might appear I had placed it there out of a desire to be given part of it—there was a fatwa at that time in Baghdad that zakat could be paid to students of learning as wandering travelers. But in the end, I made my decision and set it down. When I had finished, I went downstairs to the binder's at the library of the khan to have it bound. They held out several types and colors for me to choose from: I chose a piece of turquoise leather from the city of Faljan, well tanned and soft to the touch. I asked them to bind it with strong wool thread, all one strand.

I handed over the finished work to Mr. Gecko. To the work, I had added the inscription "To my lord Abu al-Hassan al-Hashimi, may the Lord grace him with honor and long life and all manner of blessings." Mr. Gecko turned it over in his hands, his eyebrows raised in admiration. "I was not told that a desert Arab was capable of such skill and craftsmanship," he said. I swallowed the insult in silence.

I fell into an exhausted slumber the night of Eid. I woke up to Jamra knocking on the door dragging a huge pot behind her, handing out great hunks of meat to the people living there. "Happy Eid!" she said cheerfully. The boy, Maysara, followed her, small baskets on his shoulders filled with dried apricots and nuts.

I took my basket of apricots and nuts with great joy, and said to Jamra, "You may have this leg of lamb. May the Lord always give you His bounty. I have no means of cooking or grilling it. Would you take it home for your children and bring me some to taste tomorrow?"

She showed no joy, nor did she thank me: smiles lost their way on their path to her face. "We'll see," she said. Then she left, Maysara trailing behind her, wearing clean clothes and sandals with shining leather straps. I sat by the walls of my room, nibbling at the dried fruit and nuts, missing al-Yamama. It had been a year since I left.

The new year had come and gone, and the first month, Muharram, was already done, when one morning I heard a light, polite knock at my door. When I opened it, I found a foreign boy with shining blue eyes, smartly dressed and appearing to be well bred. He presented me with a small sack of dirhams. "My master Abu al-Hassan al-Hashimi is very pleased with your work on the stalls he owns, and invites you tonight to his house in Rusafa."

## The Best of Times

My prayers were answered! It was as if the mythical bird al-Anqaa had alighted on the ceiling of my room. I was afraid and hesitant to go: what would I encounter there? I had heard a great deal in the discussion circles about what went on behind the walls of those palaces—the debauchery and dissolution. But Hassan the Egyptian said loudly, unable to conceal the envy in his tone, "You desert brute! Hesitating over an invitation to the famous salon of Dar al-Nadwa? It is the Mecca of Baghdad's intellectuals. It was given that name after Dar al-Nadwa of the Quraysh, where all the learned men congregated in the time of the Prophet. All the Hashimite nobles gather there, Sunni descendants of Abbas and Shiite descendants of Ali ibn Abu Talib as well."

"And are there many of the latter in Baghdad?" I asked.

He tilted his head, thinking. "It is said that there are four thousand of them, and they are given a stipend from the state."

"Hassan!" I cried out. "How do you know all this information and these figures about the Prophet's descendants? Sometimes you make me suspicious."

He blinked and swallowed. "Are you, too, going to accuse me of being a spy for the Shiite Fatimids in Baghdad? Heaven forgive you all!" He went on, changing the subject, "But in Dar al-Nadwa, they soar on the wings of poetry, literature, song, and melody, rising above all petty matters! Al-Hashimi holds his salon with the new moon of every month; he was probably delayed this month because of the festival of Ashoura." He smiled. "In Dar al-Nadwa, they converse, listen to music, share their knowledge, recite poetry, and are bombarded with food and drink. One time, Minister Abu Khalaf himself attended, and the head of the descendants of Abu Talib as well. Abu Hayan al-Tawhidi, the eminent man of learning, used to attend, and it is said that so did Badie al-Zaman al-Hamazani, who wrote the famous *Maqamat*." He bowed his head as if to prevent me from reading his face. In low tones I could barely make out, he said, "Go. Don't you dare decline. It may be the most important thing that will ever happen to you in this city, the thing you will remember when you leave Baghdad."

Had Hassan seen the future in that moment?

I made to leave him, but he caught the hem of my robe. "What of your appearance and dress? You must wear clothing suited to a gathering of gentlefolk. You will find them strutting about in dyed linen, perfumed with nutmeg and saffron, while you will appear in this abaya of yours like a wild moose just done butting!" He went on: "Beware of wearing red. It's the color of the servants who will receive you in the caliph's palace. It

117

is frowned upon for wits to wear heavy Nabatean abayas, but you are far from being a wit! You are but a desert Arab who seeks to be witty."

Hassan rushed off to his students: children in the morning, foreigners in the evening. Heaven help you, Hassan! How have they not driven you mad yet? It was unsurprising that some clerics had ruled the witness of a schoolteacher inadmissible.

But his words still echoed through my head: "Dress finely. Your desert garb is unsuited to the couches and carpets you will be seated on. Don't you dare go in your usual abaya! You shall be like a wild moose. Commit to memory everything you hear and see: I shall question you about it all tomorrow."

What was I to do? Should I wear my old clothes and cover up their faded, threadbare fabric with a strong, embroidered abaya that would eat up all my dirhams, or borrow a garment for one night that would make me proud at Dar al-Nadwa?

Who would lend me one? People who owned rich clothing usually did not lend it to others. At a loss, I went out in the noonday sun to the Karkh marketplace. I asked some of the fabric sellers, who made fun of me, saying, "Nakedness covers nothing!" Another said, "It is essence that counts, not appearance," in a mocking, derisive tone. Still others chose to advise and counsel me. "A garment in which no sin was committed," they preached, "never falls apart."

Finally, at the farthest end of the marketplace, I found a merchant from Maan, displaying some rough abayas lined with soft wool and sleeves embroidered with cords resembling the heads of hoopoes. I bought one, telling myself, "Though you wear white lambswool or silk, in the end you are an Arab of the desert." I dragged my feet back to the khan, feeling somewhat like a camel who has been entered into a horse race.

Abu Abbas the blacksmith saw me coming. Seeing I was downcast, he made to recite the names of books he thought might entertain me. I interrupted him, thinking, "Let's see what this ingratiating infidel has to offer." Aloud, I said, "Abu Abbas, do you know of anyone in Karkh who might lend me a rich garment to fulfill the invitation of a nobleman?"

He tilted his great head, thinking. "Nobody lends clothing in Baghdad," he said, chuckling. "As they say, the naked woman's garb still wears out." But then he muttered, "I'll see what I can do."

The call for the noon prayers was already sounding, so I hurried to the mosque of Karkh. It was not far from the river, built of red brick, its minaret slightly tilted, looking as though it had been built in a hurry. I rushed in, fearing to miss the prayer, then stood transfixed at the inner door, seeing something I had never seen before. A group of blind men were standing in a row, waving their canes, asking everyone who came in, "Are you a follower of Imam al-Shafei?" If he said "Yes," they set his back afire with their canes. Those who came in mocked them, calling them "blind of sight and soul." They pushed the blind men hard, making them fall on their faces. But they leaned on their canes and pulled themselves up again. They remained standing in a line, waving their canes, until we finished praying. I felt sorry for them. Who had filled the breasts of these poor deluded men against the followers of Imam al-Shafei? Were they followers of al-Birbihari? Who was it who kept filling men's breasts with resentment, reducing them to mere rams butting at others?

I left the mosque and hurried to the circle of my sheikh, and started writing. "In the name of God, prayers and peace be upon the Prophet . . ." After the afternoon prayers, I excused myself and ran off without waiting for his permission. This did not keep him from calling after me, "If you don't bring me an excuse tomorrow, I will punish you!"

When I arrived at the gate of the khan that led to our upper chambers, I was waylaid by the dumb boy, the blacksmith's apprentice, carrying a large, wrapped package of fabric, which he indicated to me with a sly smile on his face. He put it in my hands and hurried off.

I took it from him warily, glancing around me, and carried it up to my room. When I unwrapped it with care, I found in it a pair of trousers and a shirt of fine linen, an ivory-colored silk garment, and a caftan of fine green silk embroidered with gold crescents, in addition to a long piece of green silk the color of the caftan, which I guessed must be for the turban. I was stunned at the caftan's beauty. It was wide and a little loose on my thin build, but this might be the fashion among the wealthy men of Baghdad: the young hecklers at the mosque also wore silken caftans that hung loose about their shoulders and draped wide about their bodies, dragging proudly behind them. Did it belong to Abu Abbas? But it had no scent of him: he smelled like a goat that lives among iron ore and firewood. Before I could start to wonder what he would want in return for these clothes, and before I could be overpowered by the spirit of Shammaa of the House of Wael, I hurried to the bathhouse in the marketplace before it closed.

## Dar al-Nadwa

The commander of the armies had forbidden the Shiites from wailing and mourning for al-Husayn the day of Ashoura that year; he had also forbidden the Sunnis at Bab al-Basra and Bab al-Sha'ir from lamenting Musaab ibn Zubayr eight days later. Both parties obeyed, but resentment and rage still simmered in men's breasts.

In the steam, beneath the walls dripping with water and secrets, and the sound of water being poured over bodies, clothing is removed, and wariness and formality are likewise cast off. The heart unburdens itself of its cares and resentment. "How can we not wail over the grandson of the Prophet?" I heard one man saying. "Al-Husayn is foremost among the young men of Paradise. Curse those who murdered the apple of the Prophet's eye! How dare they forbid us from mourning?"

The words reached my ears from afar, as though emanating from a deep well. The veil of hot steam, the shadows of the walls, and the scent of the perfumed lather half drugged me. I had divested myself of my garments and left them in an outer passageway, a towel around my waist. I sat on a stone platform encircling a fountain topped with a great stained glass dome, while a bathhouse attendant approached me, muscular of build, big of belly, and foreign of tongue. He instructed me to lie down by the fountain.

The steam released the memory of dust from my skin. Hot water pouring, a loofah dripping with lather scrubbed cruelly over my back and shoulders, lifting layers off me. The lethargy and the cloud of steam allayed my doubts; here I was, free of the specter of Shammaa of the House of Wael, the loofah leaving me peeled and clean, the voice of the angry man who wanted to mourn still reaching me from afar, as the bath attendant undid my braids and lathered my hair.

The bath attendant handed me over to another boy, who started to comb my hair, pouring jasmine oil onto it. With a *miswak* that he dipped in crushed salt and charcoal, he cleaned my gums and teeth, then clipped my nails and pushed back my cuticles with a twig dipped in vinegar and rose-scented fat.

I, Mazid al-Hanafi of Najd, emerged from the steam of the bathhouse as pure as the day I was born, clean and free of sin and impurity.

When a playful little moon appeared on the horizon, the scent of the river rose, green and tempting. I didn't have to ask around to find the location of Abu al-Hassan al-Hashimi's house: its wall, of gleaming pink stone, can be seen across the river by most of the inhabitants of eastern Karkh. All I had to do was to cross the bridge over the river from Karkh to Rusafa. But, to be sure, I asked the lamplighter at the wall of the Circular City where the house of Hashimi was: he pointed without hesitation at the pink wall and muttered, "Everyone knows it. It's next to the endowment lands of the Bimaristan al-Adudi at Rusafa."

On the bridge of Rusafa, my eyes did not search for the doe-eyed ladies of pleasure; my heart was beating fearfully, in awe of the gathering I was headed for. What would come to pass? What faces would I see that night? Would they seat me with the nobodies in the back row, "next to where they put their slippers," as they say—nearest the door?

When I drew near the wall, I found that, up close, its color was not pink; that might have been caused by the reflection of the afternoon light on its great stones, or the flickering of the odd glass-covered brass lamps, the like of which I had never seen in Baghdad. I swallowed and whispered my name to the guard at the door. He kept me there for a few moments, then handed me over to a boy who came running from within and requested politely that I follow him. He had a shyly glowing lantern in his hand. The sound of the waterwheels was feminine and soft, like the alabaster of the path we trod.

There were vast gardens in which peacocks strutted proudly about; my companion was obliged to pause several times and wait for me as I stopped and stared, astonished. This was before we reached a wooden door with great hinges, ornamented with brass, flanked by two marble pillars, each as high as five men, with carvings of vines wrapped around them.

The door opened onto a passage entirely carpeted with rugs from Samarqand and lit with ornamented wall lanterns, the ones they call *karmaniya* in Karkh. I followed the boy, looking about like a lamb following its mother. Finally, there reached my ears an imposing but melodious voice saying, "I'm not praising anyone, Lord preserve you and defeat your enemies. That said, the Mutazilites are men of justice and good monotheists. There are many good scientists and men of letters among them who remain loyal to taqiya rather than face the dungeons that lie in wait for them. It is said that our comrade, Abu Hayan al-Tawhidi, is one of their imams."

My innards churned as though I were about to face an army when I stepped into the gathering.

I had caught fleeting glimpses of Abu al-Hassan al-Hashimi on one or two of his visits to the khan, surrounded by his friends and retinue. I had been afraid, as I entered, that I might not recognize him, so full of trepidation was I, and so full the gathering of men, but I found him the moment I entered. As for him, he watched me keenly as I entered, while continuing his conversation: "I regret that al-Tawhidi, the great imam, the fount of learning, has been obliged to quit Baghdad for Shiraz, unable to stomach the heckling and contentiousness of those with closed hearts."

His eyes followed me as I stepped into his gathering, a welcoming smile on his face. I knew not whether to go to him and greet him, or to seat myself at a distance until he should finish his conversation. But I merely stood speechless in the center of the hall, the sound of the fountain loud in my ears. Immediately he handed the book he had been holding to his companion and stood, coming toward me all smiles. "Welcome, Mazid al-Hanafi, maker of books, master of the elegant pen!" He turned to his companions. "Anyone who enters a strange place is perforce perplexed. Let us therefore begin by greeting him."

He seated me not far from him, which piqued the attendees' curiosity as to who I was; perhaps my borrowed finery increased it. All the while, he kept repeating, "Welcome, a thousand welcomes, al-Hanafi."

I was trembling and confused; I jammed myself into the couch, wishing the curious eyes would disperse and return to what al-Hashimi was reading out of his book.

The room was circular, its walls adorned with gesso and its ceiling inlaid with gold leaf, surrounded by an arcade supported by marble columns with colored garlands; in its center was a fountain sparkling with blue water, with rose petals in its basin. Before the guests were brass dishes with feet about two hand-spans high, in the shape of birds facing one another: upon them were set out peaches, pears, and grapes, and next to them was a glass dish for the pits. I had not been there long when a group of young men came in wearing garments of red silk, turbans on their heads with a feather on the front, bearing trays with glasses of *sekanjabin*, palm wine, *jallab*, and buttermilk.

The boy who had brought me the invitation was among them; when he glimpsed me he smiled, bowing his head in a polite and refined manner. He disappeared and returned quickly, then bowed to me and presented me with a garland of jasmine, which he hung about my neck. It was then that I real-ized everyone there was wearing a similar garland, perfuming the entire place with the scent of jasmine.

I began to discreetly watch al-Hashimi as he spoke: he was squat, but he sat on the couches and silken cushions with his head high like those of noble birth. His face shone with a handsomeness whose source I could not identify: it might have been his broad brow, or where his eyebrows met above a nose that split his face like a sword. He had taken his turban off in a gesture of informality, placing it next to him, and his neatly combed black hair fell to his shoulders. From the first moment, I intuited that the conversation rolled from one guest to another like the round gem on the top of a scepter: he let no one monopolize the conversation for too long, and gave everyone a chance to speak. This disturbed my innards anew: I would certainly be called upon to speak.

This instinct proved true when he said, "And how are you, Mazid?"

I responded, sitting up straight and raising my head, "Well, and in good health, praise the Lord."

"And how is the clan of Bani Ukhaydar, descendants of the Prophet? Do they rule justly in al-Yamama?"

I was filled with suspicion. He knew more about me than I thought. "There is no better ruler nor yet a better court. Prayers and peace be on the Prophet and the good descendants of his house."

He inclined his head, pleased at my words. "Mazid al-Hanafi!" he said. "They say that you are in the company of the books in the library day and night. Tell us what the books have whispered in your ear."

Suddenly I heard a rough voice from close by al-Hashimi. He said mockingly, "And what can the folk of al-Yamama have to say? There is no worse liar than Musaylima al-Hanafi. Have you not heard our imam al-Tawhidi saying, in his book *al-Basa'ir wa al-Dhakha'ir*, that a man returning from al-Yamama was asked, 'What was the best thing you saw there?' and he replied, 'The exit.'"

The assembly roared with laughter. My face reddened and I stammered; this was too much for someone green like me, here for the first time.

My face was so red that Abu al-Hassan al-Hashimi noticed, and attempted to mend matters, saying, "Speak well if nothing else, Abu al-Darayn! This young man may well have knowledge up his sleeve that will put your laziness and dissolution to shame. Have you not heard the words of al-Fadhl ibn Yahya when he divided people into four classes: kings who deserve obedience and respect; ministers distinguished by insight and good counsel; noblemen lifted up by money and power; and well-mannered men of the middle class, trying to reach the station of the aforementioned? All others are but flotsam and jetsam, caring about naught but their food and sleep." He turned to me. "And what will you set out on our table today?"

I divined that Abu al-Hassan had dragged the business about the classes of people into the conversation to grant me an opportunity to calm my trepidation and catch my breath. I soon gathered the scattered threads of my thought and thought I might recite the poem of Ali ibn al-Jahim upon

Rusafa Bridge; but it had been cheapened now, on the tongues of storytellers and sung out of tune by singers at bars. Even the common people repeated it. I looked for something to contain the assembly and bind the demons waiting for me: I had no wish to direct the conversation to the books of heresy in the library in which I buried my head. Finally, I decided to recite a poem my grandfather and I had sung, by the greatest poet to come from al-Yamama, al-Asha.

I looked up at the ceiling: above me, my grandfather's window opened, bringing in the smell of date-palm pollen and the hoofbeats of the evening stars, the bleating of the herds returning from grazing, and the clangor of the gates of the Citadel of Bani Ukhaydar. . . . My breast filled with all of these before I recited:

> Take your leave of Hurayra; watch the receding caravan!
> Can you bear to say goodbye to her, you loving man?
> Her hair is long, her smile is bright, and oh, she walks
>     so slow,
> As barefoot in a mud puddle, so leisurely she goes.
> Not lingering nor hurrying, she walks to the girl next door,
> Like a passing cloud she moves, floating over the floor;
> Her ornaments and finery all rustle when she goes,
> As the desert wind sighs through the evening primrose.

Because every eye was fixed on me in shock, I dispelled my nervousness by imagining the faces to be the sheep returning from grazing, except for Abu al-Hassan al-Hashimi, whom I imagined as my grandfather. Then I recited the rest of the epic poem.

The hush that fell over the assembly was like that which fell over every creature in al-Yamama when my grandfather and I sang that poem; the bees building their honeycombs in the trees paused to listen. I sought out the rest of the verses in my head until my throat felt tight and my chest was fit to burst. I could not go on: I had not known that homesickness is a jackal lying in wait that, once released, buries its fangs in you. I was overcome with embarrassment and shame: I feared that the veil of my melancholy would cast a shadow over the lightness of the company.

Abu al-Hassan said loudly, saving the moment, "Bless you, al-Hanafi! I swear, your recitation has been music to our ears, even though our hearts have no strength this night for the longing call of the desert! Let us avoid the paths of poetry, for they are traps lying in wait for the unwary heart."

But Abu al-Darayn said, "Mazid has recited the verse of his tribe's poet. The desert Arabs are tribal and proud of their own folk, and that will never change."

I fell silent, not knowing why he singled me out. Was it because I was new and only passing through, and so he allowed himself to appear waggish at my expense? Or perhaps he had divined my reluctance to make a retort. His unamusing taunts only redoubled. I watched him from my seat after I had calmed myself.

Abu al-Darayn was an older man who sought to look younger: his beard and mustache were dyed with henna, and his silken abaya had fallen about his shoulders in a show of simplicity. His eyes were as piercing as those of a bird of prey, catching every scrap and tittle that took place in the gathering, and never took his attention off those seated around him, not to mention his assiduousness in gaining Abu al-Hassan's approval, agreeing with everything he said and nodding admiringly when he spoke. He was definitely a sycophant who would not hesitate to lord it over those beneath him and abase himself to those above him. This type of man is careful to seek out gatherings and salons, rush to them to flatter the master of the house, recite the poems they have memorized, convey to the lord and master the news of the marketplaces and mosques, fill their stomachs, receive some gifts, and go.

When the meal was served, he was seated near me. I was shy to eat, and the closest dish to me was the *haris*, or wheat porridge; I contented myself with reaching for this dish exclusively. Noticing, he said, "Why do you only eat *haris*, although it is the food of low-born riffraff?"

I could tell that this monkey had seized upon me to make me the laughingstock of the assembly, probably because I was new to the gathering, or because I was young or visibly withdrawn. But a man sitting next to him, divining his intent, said, "And what is served in your house every day, Abu al-Darayn, if not porridge and bones?"

Abu al-Darayn obviously cared nothing for these words: his seat at the table clearly filled him with joy and contentment. He launched into a mimicry of folk from every region, imagining each as they would sit at the table, as though he had brought them all into the room with us: now he mimicked a desert Arab, now one from Najd, now a Nabatean, a Sindhi, an African, a Turk. "This is how a Nabatean eats," he said. All the personages he mimicked were in a state of ravenous hunger, providing a convenient excuse for him to stuff his mouth with handful after handful of food, crumbs scattering about him. The louder the laughter of those around him, the more greedy and unpleasant he became. He was the last to leave the table, and he did not leave until he had filled every cranny of his swollen belly.

When we concluded our meal, some boys came in, each bearing a bowl and two urns. I washed my hands with water and a paste scented with orange blossoms before the boy washed the traces away with the rosewater in the urn in his left hand. We dried our hands with kerchiefs of Egyptian silk from Dibaq.

## Zahira

We returned to our gathering. "I shall never forget as long as I live," one of them said, "the death of one who was the light of this assembly, and the flower of its company. His speech made the mind fertile, and comforted the heart, and dissipated all care: Badie al-Zaman al-Hamazani, may he ever have a cool resting place! His life was cut short; he was snatched from us."

Abu al-Darayn leapt to catch at the thread of the tale. "Is it true what people say and the common folk bruit about, that Badie al-Zaman swooned, making his family think he was dead? They buried him quickly, they say, but he lived on in his tomb, and they heard him screaming: they dug up the grave, but found him truly dead, fallen over on his beard from the horrors of the grave."

Al-Hashimi cut him off. "Here Abu al-Darayn would not rest until he dug a grave where we sit," he said. Then he added, "Let us not give ourselves over to poetry entirely nor to talk entirely nor to song entirely. We must seize the day. Sing, talk, recite poetry, and let us seize life with both hands."

He glanced to the right, gesturing with his hand. Silken curtains that had been covering the southern gallery of the room were raised. From behind them emerged a line of slave girls so extraordinarily beautiful it was as though they were born of the rain. Their garments were red with a hint of blue, embroidered at the hem, and they had the fine, fresh features of the women of the Sindh. They bowed before us in a pleasant greeting, then sat in a half circle among some couches and pillows set out for them. The lute player and the flutist sat before them; behind them sat others holding a tanbur, a tambour, and brass castanets. They spent a long time preparing their instruments, adjusting the strings, and tapping them with slender fingers. Their eyes were on Abu al-Hassan al-Hashimi, waiting for his command to start. "Let us hear some music," he said, "No, allow me to repeat that. Let us have some music to welcome our new guest Mazid al-Hanafi from Najd."

I blushed and looked down. I would have preferred to do without this greeting: it might turn those present against me, and bring a more intense scrutiny upon me, one I could do without. Abu al-Darayn, of course, seized this opportunity to get at me. " Ladies!" he chortled. "Be gentle with al-Hanafi! We don't want him to end up like Bashar ibn Burd, who spouted heresy when he was drunk on wine and song. He turned to a man next to him and said, 'I swear, Abu Abdullah, this is better than the Sura of al-Hashr'—that's what he said." He turned to me. "Such hospitality merits that you kiss al-Hashimi's hand, young man. Up with you, go and kiss it!"

I could not help scowling. I had never kissed the hand of anyone but my grandfather. I rose and hurried to al-Hashimi, who tried to catch me and motion to me to sit down, but I had already reached him, so I kissed his brow. Just then, the women I had dubbed the Daughters of the Rain burst into song:

Look back on Najd; my eyes do seek it,
Even though it is in vain;
Its soil is perfumed with ambergris,
Musk, and agarwood in rain.

Then they fell silent. Apparently these verses were all they knew in praise of Najd. The assembly went back to laughing at some unfunny story told by Abu al-Darayn about a judge by the name of Ibn Siyar, who had an immense turban and a long beard. He was, the story said, approached by two women, one accusing the other. "'What say you to her accusation?' he asked the second woman," Abu al-Darayn recounted. "'I am so affrighted that I cannot speak,' said she, 'by the sight of a beard an arm span long and a face an arm span long. I am so awestruck I am dumbstruck.'"

I could not tell whether his tale was meant to entertain or to make him the center of attention, and I knew not whether to laugh at his unamusing tale; I settled upon a quiet chuckle amid the gathering's uproarious laughter.

Suddenly the gathering fell silent as the musicians began to sing a poem by Abu Nawas:

You are the full moon of the house,
The musk that perfumes the halls;
The fleeting scent of the dog rose,
The flowers on the trees so tall;
With heels like ivory, you are
Like a tanbur breaking hearts all;
You are the throne of Solomon,
Full of wisdom both great and small;
You are the Holy Kaaba with
Its pilgrims, curtains, and its wall;
For love of you I am adrift:
In Paradise, or Hell to fall?

Everyone applauded, having swayed along to the music. After this, I heard murmurs and saw everyone looking about. "Where is Zahira?" I heard them say. "These verses always announce her arrival."

Suddenly there she was, tripping and swaying by the fountain. I fell silent, stunned at the thought that this much beauty could have been among us without my perceiving it. Back home in al-Yamama, we sang of the beauty of the women of the House of Wael and their long braids: what to say, then, of the hair of this wild mare, rippling about her like curtains of night? She began to sway. She slipped two silver daggers from her belt and moved them in slow arcs, their light reflecting off her figure and face.

In the beauty of women, there is tempting beauty, and companionable beauty, and miniature beauty like the melodies of the musicians; but Zahira's beauty was painful, like the way the moon spills its light over the river, or the way honey spreads over butter.

I could not take my eyes off her, as though she were one of the women of Paradise who neither menstruate nor suffer from mucus. Her beauty was incapable of being moderate; did the very air change color when she passed?

She shook her breasts: the waterfalls of her hair spilled over her face. Her stomach was bare, a ribbed belt around her waist. Her pantaloons were of transparent silk that showed off the roundness of her thighs and the splendor of her legs. Over her navel was a pearl, upon which every eye that devoured her was affixed.

I was lost in bliss. I kept stealing furtive glances at Abu al-Hassan. He maintained his composure and dignity, unchanged: he did not so much as blink, drinking glass after glass. I had no idea what was in them, but he never over-stepped the bounds of chivalry, to say nothing of drunken indiscretion. He contemplated her with admiration that was innocent of any lust; when the gathering concluded, he stood tall and steady as his guests took their leave of him, his eyes only a little fatigued, I knew not whether from the cups of whatever he had drunk, or from sleepiness.

Delight, the reed-scented river air, and the companion-ship of the stars: was it a woman like her who tempted Harut and Marut, making them, who had been angels of heaven, fall damned to the bottom of a well?

I caught a glimpse of Zahira leaving. She climbed into a sedan chair mounted on a camel, covered with two layers of shining curtains that fell to cover the body of the animal. At the gate of the mansion, a sullen older man accompanied her, and two Ethiopian boys loaded the musicians' instruments and bags onto mules. Next to her, the sullen man trotted on a sprightly mule, upbraiding the musicians over matters that remained a mystery to me. He was sharp-voiced, his foreign words blazing with ire. I knew not whether he was her com-panion or her father, but she alone appeared unimpressed by him and spared him not so much as a glance. When she danced, she shook her rear seductively in a manner that a girl would not in the presence of her father.

If it had occurred to me in that moment to uproot every date palm in al-Yamama and plant them all along the paths of

Abu al-Hassan's palace in thanks and gratitude, I would not have hesitated. I took his hands and bent over them, thanking him. Suddenly he tightened his grip on one of my hands. Leaning closer, he whispered, "Come to the house tomorrow after the sunset prayer. I require you for something."

His whispered words, despite their pleasant delivery and innocent nature, struck my delight in the face, scattering me far and wide. What did al-Hashimi want of me? I was overcome with unease. Had I made some error in the accounts of the stalls of the khan? Or did he want me to be a bookkeeper at his home? But he hardly stayed in Baghdad—he was only there between wintertime and the season of trimming the date palms; then he was gone again.

The next morning I woke early. Despite this, I performed the dawn prayer in my room, lingering a little, recalling the events of the day before, and the Zahira of Harut and Marut. She and I breathed the same air, the air of Baghdad. She was displaying her wares, all the glory and beauty she possessed, in the capital of the world, and she wished to captivate me and keep me there.

I told Hassan some of what had taken place, in order to stop his mouth and put an end to his incessant questions. I kept a great deal to myself, secretly drowning in its delight. A great many of our inner joys will fade when exposed to the air and to others' questioning. When I mentioned that Zahira had danced, his eyes widened. "Was she there?"

It disturbed me that others knew her: I had thought to keep her exclusively within my breast, mine and mine alone. But Hassan said, "Baghdad is completely taken with Zahira. Some call her 'the Blossom.' And here you are, buried in books and discussion circles, knowing nothing." He sighed. With some melancholy, he went on, "In the desert, when a caravan passes by a palm grove and the palm fronds sing, people know there is a bride in the caravan. And now, when the palm fronds in Baghdad sing, people know the sedan chair of Zahira, the Blossom, has passed that way."

What a disappointment! It was painful to learn that I was not the only man captivated by her; the dreams of everyone in Baghdad clung to her. But Hassan added, "They know not who her master is. She came from the east with all of those who accompany her. Some say she's a Persian; some say she's from Sindh. They say she was a slave girl owned by a Bouhi prince, who fell so deeply in love with her that he never left her bed or her side, paying no heed to his family and friends. Disturbed by this single-mindedness, he instructed one of his men to take her to the sea and drown her. The man, having fallen in love with her, took pity upon her, and escaped with her to Baghdad: they say it is the older fellow who is always in her company."

Was Hassan telling the truth, or was it another one of the tall tales that he told to drive home that he knew everything while I was a green bumpkin? "Do you remember the feast of Ashmuni?" he asked me. "When we had that fish? She was the one singing in the great marquee. But she was wearing a veil to protect the people from her beauty. In any case, everyone who has seen her says she is one of those nymphs who never live long, but die in the flower of youth."

"Truly?" I asked. But deep inside me, an evil impulse was overjoyed that Zahira would die young, for I did not wish to leave Baghdad if it meant leaving behind this nymph. I did not know then that my overweening love for her had plunged its hand into the Book of Fate and written therein.

"Heaven protect her," Hassan said. "She refused to join the caliph's harem, on the pretext that she is the wife of that old man who goes about with her, and will not be shut into a house of slave girls where only her admirers can see her. Some people come to Baghdad only to delight their eyes with the sight of her; but she is retiring, which only makes her more attractive to them. The commander of the armies of Baghdad no longer extends his protection to her, now that she has refused to spend the night in his company." He added, "They say that even the slave mistress at the palace, who is an adherent of Sappho and loves women, sent her a doll of wax on an ornamented base, which is a Persian custom they call 'the bride.' If she should accept, the beloved places a necklace around the doll's neck, and rewards the go-between who brought her the doll with a new chador; but if she refuses, the doll is returned with a black veil over her head. But Zahira did not respond, leaving the door ajar without closing it. There are many who would do her harm: the commander of the armies has but to leave for Rayy or Mosul on business for the Rajilat al-Hanabila to rampage through the marketplace, smashing musical instruments, emptying jars of wine, and beating and attacking slave girls and slave boys. Also, the Ayyarin gangs have become more savage in recent times, and will commit robberies in broad daylight. All this is sufficient to keep her distant and remote."

"What about you?" I teased. "How do you manage your affairs with the Rajilat al-Hanabila and the Ayyarin when you come home at midnight, or if they catch you staggering through the streets smelling of wine and the perfume of the women at Ishaq al-Wasati's tavern?"

Hassan left. I remained in my room: I had no wish to leave it. There were three new pomegranates lined up on my windowsill, and a buzzing around the window of a small creature—I knew not whether it was bird or insect, but it had green wings and flitted back and forth, describing circles around the window as the sun rose higher.

I curled up in my bed like a fetus, my clothing wrapped around me, with no desire to move out of my ecstasy, knowing that Jamra, with her face like dried river mud, would knock at my door now wanting to clean the room.

What would al-Hashimi tell me tonight? I rose lethargically, did my ablutions, and prayed. I replaced the borrowed garments I had worn, wrapped it all back up, and went to the stall of Abu Abbas.

Before I reached the bottom of the stairs, I heard a hubbub in the street: running footsteps, voices yelling and shouting "*Allahu akbar!*" and the stall owners whispering, "It is the procession of the caliph, al-Qadir bi-Allah, Heaven protect him!"

It was a great procession, coming from Rusafa over the bridges, among the stalls, heading for the gateway to the Circular City. I stood stunned, watching a sight more majestic and awe-inspiring than anything I had yet seen in Baghdad.

Six horsemen preceded the procession on magnificent horses, with saddles fashioned of shiny colored leather, bearing shields of silver. Their turbans were of black damask, set with a great white feather that appeared to be from a male ostrich. Three of them were to the right and three to the left of the procession. There were two lines of men on foot, led by men with black flags upon which was written in white, "Muhammad is God's Prophet," which is the emblem of the Abbasids. The horn players were blowing so hard I fancied their cheeks would burst. There were three rows behind the caliph, weapons and shields clanging so loudly that they could be heard above all the clamor.

The stall owners stood outside their stalls to cheer and greet the procession and call blessings down on the caliph. "Heaven preserve Caliph al-Qadir bi-Allah, steward of the Prophet!"

The caliph was riding a giant black horse with a great chest and massive legs, which appeared to be a Byzantine mount; next to him scurried a guard bearing a black parasol shot through with gold thread. I could barely see his face for the crowd and the sun's glare; I merely caught a fleeting glimpse of him, the Prophet's garment, the *burda* handed down from sultan to sultan, around his shoulders. His ring and scepter glinted in the sun; his henna-dyed beard was thick and his nose sharp.

When he drew near to the gate of the Circular City, the crier preceding the procession called, "His Majesty, Servant of the Holy Line, the Caliph of the Prophet and the Imam of the Faithful, al-Qadir bi-Allah, has been disturbed in his rest by what he has heard of *fitna* and the spread of discord and hypocrisy among his subjects, and the introduction of seditious talk in the mosques and marketplaces. He commands everyone to remain on the straight and narrow, and the right path of religion as laid out by the Prophet Muhammad. He calls upon all to abandon the practices of the Mutazilites, and the Rafida, and speeches that are counter to Islam. He will prepare a document to that effect and publish it soon before witnesses. All those who have arguments shall sign it, and anyone who shall go against this shall receive swift punishment, to serve as an example for his fellows, the Mutazilites and the Rafida and the Ishmaelites and the Qarmatians and the Jahmis and those who would embody God. They shall be crucified and imprisoned and exiled and cursed from the pulpit. This decree is binding; if you do not accept it, on your own head be it." Then the procession turned and headed back to the Circular City.

The stall keepers and passersby burst out with one voice: "We hear and obey, Heaven preserve the caliph, may God grant the Prophet's steward long life," and so on. Despite my awe at the impressive scene, I could not but be irritated by the cunning and hypocrisy of the stall owners. They spent their days complaining of the high prices, the scarcity of goods, and the injustice of the submissive ruler, when they knew full well that the solutions to all these matters lay in the hands of the commander of the Bouhi army. No sooner had the procession disappeared through the gates of the Circular City than they went back to whispering mockingly about the reason he had come out to meet the people; it was rare for him to go abroad in his procession, for normally he went out incognito, disguised as one of the common people. No doubt there was something serious afoot: there must be, as the saying goes, coals burning underneath the ashes.

They went back to whispering: "So submissive is he that the sultan's preachers do not obey him; he named his son 'the Conqueror,' but the preacher, al-Sabi, refused the name, saying, 'There is no conqueror but the Lord,' and the sultan obeyed."

There were two disgusting men from the clan of Khathaam, known for their sharp tongues and wiliness, who owned a stable of donkeys, which they rented out at the gates of Karkh. If a Shiite tried to rent a donkey from them, they took turns praising Imam Ali, so that he would pay them generously; if a Nasibi came by, they praised Abu Bakr, so that they would not sacrifice the coin of this man or that. In the city, we mockingly called them Nakir and Nekir, after the two angels who keep accounts on each shoulder—and sometimes Ass and Jackass.

Despite this, it was they who fanned the flames of foment in Karkh; it was said that it was they who had set the caliph al-Qadir over his people. They were the loudest to yell, "Heaven protect the caliph!" and ran after the procession until it disappeared. They staggered back, cheeks puffed out, bawling noisily, "There is a copy of the list of sects and groups forbidden to speak hanging on the wall of our stable for anyone who wants to read it! If you want a copy, come with your scribe." I could not tell whether they meant some subtle jibe by hanging the list of sects on the door of a barn, or whether they were serious.

When I came to the blacksmith's door, he was deep in the bowels of his shop. He did not come out to watch the procession pass, careless of the chaos caused by its passage. His face held subtle mockery. He smiled when I arrived at his store, broader than the smile he had worn to see the caliph's procession. "Did you see the procession?" I asked, making conversation.

"O follower of Abu Hanifa!" he snapped. "The document from the caliph al-Qadir is coming! Mouths have been stopped! Heads shall roll! The jails shall fill up! Not so fast!

Your head might be next if he learns that you have fallen in love with the books of heresy!"

He put his head near mine and whispered into my ear: "Al-Qadir himself was chosen by the Bouhis; he was on the run in the time of Caliph al-Tai; he came to Baghdad and was well received by Bahaa al-Dawla, who appointed him caliph, but now he has turned tyrant."

I had no wish to engage in conversation: the market-place of Karkh appeared congested, and after the fights at the mosque, everyone was on edge, watching and listening. I held out to him the suit he had sent to me yesterday. "Thank you," I said.

"Please," he said, "keep it, and remember me."

He insisted, flatly refusing to take it. I put the bundle down on a pile of firewood in the corner of his stall. "I am not myself in this garment," I explained. "I lose Mazid of Najd. I want to remain a poor student who looks up at the sky and down at the earth in search of answers."

He smiled slyly. "Has Dar al-Nadwa given you some of the answers you seek?"

I stared so deeply into his eyes that I could make out the red veins in the whites. Avoiding a direct answer, I said, "Gatherings are private, Persian."

He clapped his big soot-stained hands. "I was born and bred in Baghdad! My father came with the armies of Ali, son of Khosrow, who named himself Adud al-Dawla al-Bouhi. When he settled in Baghdad and it became the capital of the Caliphate, it became the capital of the Bouhi Dynasty as well. The minarets and pulpits said prayers for Ali Khosrow in addition to the Abbasid caliph. Since that time, my family has lived here. Despite all this, you all still call me foreigner?"

I felt he was about to become garrulous, and withdrew quietly, confused and preoccupied with what Abu al-Hassan al-Hashimi would do after the sunset prayer at his house.

# The Pomegranates of Rusafa

Evening fell. Jamra caught sight of me when I was ready to go out to Abu al-Hassan. "Where to, fair-faced Arab of the desert?" she asked.

"Rusafa," I replied curtly.

"The people of Baghdad say the best pomegranates come from Rusafa. Are you going to pluck pomegranates there?"

"What is it about this woman, who only thinks of pomegranates?" I thought. "And her imps, placing pomegranates on my windowsill every night!"

"What kind of pomegranates are you going to pluck? Are they the pomegranates of someone's breasts, or . . . ?" And she burst out into a debauched laugh.

I pushed past her, eyes on the floor. "Jamra," I said, blushing fiercely, "you must have been raised in a brothel!"

The minarets of Karkh called for the sunset prayer. Loud flocks of birds flew past in the sky over the river: thin beaks and long legs. Were these the cranes of the river? They did not coo like doves or pigeons, but made a sound like a moan of pain.

In the evenings, on the shores and on the bridges of Rusafa, I usually heard the croaking of frogs, but that evening the sounds of birds surrounded the place. I stared up at them, speechless, then replied, "And a very good evening to you too, birds! Are you singing with joy at the path I am taking, or crying out in mourning?"

I neared the mansion of al-Hashimi and, as I had last time, took to contemplating the color of the wall. Was it really as pink as it appeared from the opposite bank?

The carpets of the previous day had been taken off the pathways. I followed the boy, who turned into a different doorway from the one I had entered yesterday. A rear door led us onto a passageway, and then a wooden door on the right that opened onto a small room with high windows. It was jammed with shelves of books and manuscripts, and beneath the shelves were couches with silk cushions. In the center sat Abu al-Hassan al-Hashimi, who had lost none of his imposing stature or vigor.

My heart beat hard. Was this his library, the one that Hassan the Egyptian had told me about? The room was perfumed with Indian sandalwood; it looked like the cell of some devout monk. Despite its small size, it was richly furnished with carpets of Persian silk, embroidered with river scenes crowded with sailboats.

Abu al-Hassan stood to greet me. I rushed toward him deferentially, so that he would not have to come all the way to me. He wore a robe of white silk, in which his body moved with dignity and poise. I know not why, but I sensed he was less welcoming today than he had been the day before. In vain, he tried to conceal the slight frown on his brow with a polite smile, evidence that something was troubling him.

I took his hand in both of mine, bowing slightly. "In my haste to arrive in time for our appointment, I did not have the chance to pray," I said. "I should like to do so in your company."

He gestured carelessly to a corner of the room. "You may pray here," he said. "For, as the Prophet says, 'I have made a pure mosque of the earth entire.' I've already prayed," he added. Then, pointing to his chest, he said, "I have prayed here. I prayed to God within these ribs of mine."

I asked no more, nor spoke, having learned from the mosques of Baghdad that silence is a treasure. When I finished my prayers, I approached him. He had me sit on his right side, a book in his hand. "Yesterday wine, and today momentous things. Dar al-Nadwa is held with each new moon. I do not hold the gathering for poetry recitations, entertainment, and the clinking of glasses, but there is no avoiding these salons to keep up the appearance of wealth. You must show power to the eager, give relief to the afflicted, offer help to the weak, grant charity to mendicants, bequeath gifts to poets, bestow largesse upon writers, and provide shelter to guests, or else glory and power will be taken away from you."

A boy came in, placing two glasses of pomegranate juice on a small low table. I was reminded of that she-devil Jamra with her pomegranates. Hashimi finished: "There is my book for all to read." He remained silent awhile. A tired smile still on his face, he said, "Every book lover has three books: the first is the tempting book that leads you into the temptation of its lines. The second is the turning point—the book that moves you from one point to another in this life of ours. And the last is the book you write or copy, to return the favor to men of letters."

I looked at him, feeling that what he said had the tone of an introduction to what came next. But he merely looked at me. "Have you found your own book?" he asked.

His mysterious manner disquieted me. What was he getting at? However, I answered quickly enough, as I wished to appear bright and quick-witted and deserving in his eyes. "My favorite books are the *Life of the Prophet* by Ibn Hisham and *The Classes of Poets* by al-Jamihi. I read them in al-Yamama. The turning point was the great collection of books I found in your library at the khan: the books of al-Kindi and the House of Wisdom translations of the Greek wise men—"

"It is said," he interrupted, "that you pour out the light of your eyes for hours upon hours among books."

I was flustered. Were they spying on me? Reading is a private and intimate activity. I did not want anyone to come between me and my books. I folded myself into the pages of a book as into my mother's arms. What did these people want from me?

"And the final book?" he said with gentle curiosity.

I fell silent. "I haven't written or copied it yet."

"You will," he said.

He picked up a book, which I noticed was covered in the same leather as the books in the khan. He leafed through the

pages with his long, spindly fingers. It was entitled *al-Mughni*.
"Have you read this book by Abd al-Jabbar ibn Ahmad?" he
asked. I shook my head. "You must read it," he said, "and
think well on the concepts and what it says. There is a copy in
the library of the khan." He added, "People no longer respect
books and don't long to read them; they merely lie in wait to
attack each other, bandying about accusations like 'Mutazilite' and 'heretic.' And the spears and arrows with which the
Shiites fight the Sunni Hanbalites well, those strike everyone."

He leaned back. "In the khan's library, I have brought
together the best books and the most valuable manuscripts. I
have filled it with good translations, some dating back to the
House of Wisdom. The last addition to it is a collection of rare
and valuable books that were part of al-Sahib Ibn Abbad's
library in the city of Rayy, which had started to arrive in
Baghdad and were distributed secretly. There are also works
by a young physician who has become famous in the court of
the Samanid Empire in Bukhara, Avicenna by name." He fell
silent awhile, then almost moaned, "All this treasure, possibly
destroyed by the spark of *fitna!*"

I said, encouragingly, "It is *fitna* indeed. Even the caliph,
God preserve him, rode around the marketplaces today, asking
everyone to abandon sedition and stay away from argument
and debate."

The light of mockery flashed in the depths of his eyes.
"Does the caliph want anything else?" He looked down. "It is
he who opened the door to the *fitna* that is now rolling forth
like the waves of the sea. It is *fitna* that keeps him situated
between the two scales, now pulling this one near, now pushing that one away. He will raise up the Prophet's descendants
until they grow wings and claws, whereupon he clips them."
He took a breath. "Then he turns to the Hanbalites of Sheikh
al-Birbihari and lets them send their Rajilat al-Hanabila
out into the marketplaces with their repulsive preaching
and harsh ways. The *fitna* in the marketplace remains in the

marketplace—away from his throne. He does not know that, as the proverb says, 'Most incidents start with a glance; great fires from small sparks grow perchance.'"

He fell silent for a while, measuring my reaction. It appeared that he saw something in my face, for he said, seeking to calm me, "When Greek philosophy comes together with Arab religious law, that will indeed herald perfection."

I said—phrasing it as a question so as not to appear pretentious—"But sir, Greek philosophy is fleeting human wisdom; how can we compare it to eternal divine wisdom?"

He said impatiently, "And this is what makes me even more sure that religion is for the common folk, while philosophy is for the few." He paused before saying, "We were visited by a blind poet from Maarat al-Numan, whose heart had a vision for all that. His name was Abu al-Alaa al-Maari. When he saw some people in Baghdad awaiting the return of al-Hallaj, standing in the river before the place where he was crucified, and others weeping and wailing over al-Husayn, awaiting the return of those who were absent, he indited the lines:

> These sects are means for the leaders
> To seize power, free from fears.
> People want pleasure, not the poetry
> Of Shammaa and Khansaa with their tears.

"I swear," he said, "the farseeing blind man spoke truth!" He went on, warming to his subject, but his speech and lack of formality made me tremble. Why was he showing this face to me? "And what is coming is perhaps worse and more bitter. Baghdad is no longer a place where one can abide; I hear that you were thinking of leaving. I, too, intend to leave. I see hands bearing torches of *fitna*, of which some spark must touch the khan's library. Any accusation that one of the books within it contains heresy means that it may be burned to ash." He took a breath. "I must spirit it away little by little, and distribute it among safe countries: the paths between different lands are now burning coals."

At this point, two boys came in once more, another pile of books in their arms, which they laid down in front of him. He patted them with one hand as one might pat a thoroughbred horse. "You spend a great deal of time leafing through books of philosophy; you borrow others from the stall of Abu Abbas the blacksmith."

I felt the blood drain from my face. Did he know Abu Abbas? Was the man a spy? Was it he who had recommended me? Was it the very man who had given me the silken suit? All these questions surged through my head; I hoped they did not show on my face. I did not stop him to press for details: I was eager to know what he would say after this introduction.

"What you heard today in the marketplace," he said, "is not the first time death threats have been made against the levelheaded, sober, monotheist Mutazilites, leaving the way clear for charlatan sheikhs and preachers in Baghdad threatening the science of the Mutazilites. Even grammarians and linguists now poke their nose into these affairs: Abd al-Qahir al-Girgani claims philosophy is heresy, and places those who study it on the list of those who follow their own judgment and are apostates from Islam." He sighed. "When the scales of the mind are not available to weigh words, the tongues of fire will definitely touch books that scientists have spent the better part of their lives recording, and poured out the light of their eyes in writing and translating. They were safe and sound under the wing of Caliph Mamoun in the House of Wisdom. The ulema know nothing of the precision of the words of these books," he went on, "nor the noble meanings they convey. If one is not a thinker and endowed with free will, one is not responsible for one's actions, which would make it unjust to divinely reward or punish one for those actions."

I nodded, astonished by his intellect, his lucid phrasing, and the depth of his knowledge. "How can they burn books of philosophy, just like that, when Sheikh al-Kindi always said, 'Philosophy is the science of the first truth, which is the reason behind all other truth'?" I asked.

When I said these words, his face broke into a smile for the first time that evening. "You are now quoting the Just Monotheists, the Mutazilites! This is the nature of free spirits, flying high in the kingdom of knowledge, like a line of great cranes that never becomes extinct! Bless you and bless your path. I know that the sharp eyes of the blacksmith are never wrong. He chooses our men with care."

"Our men?" A tremor went through me. What men had I just become one of? I did not ask him. I let him speak, pouring out his heart without hesitation or suspicion as I merely nodded my head calmly. I recalled that my sheikh, Muhammad al-Tamimi, had spent an entire month telling us about the things that spoiled one's ablutions and how to divine the direction of the qibla, while Abu al-Hassan al-Hashimi unfurled his prayer mat between the parentheses of his ribs, and I was obliged to accept them both as they showed themselves to me.

I bowed my head. "My sheikh warned me against the books of philosophers, because their authors are not Muslims and so it would not be a sin to kill them—and this is exactly what made me creep out in the evenings after his discussion circle to the paper markets or to the khan's library, to seek out the books my sheikh had cursed!"

Al-Hashimi burst into helpless laughter. "This is why I called you to be one of my trustworthy secret keepers, for the mind is the measure of what is right and wrong, by comparing what is acceptable and unacceptable, and permission and prohibition."

My eyes must have widened: what he said was not so far from what Aristotle had said! I opened my mouth to say something, but he threw me a quick glance and went on. "I am leaving Baghdad soon. I know not when I shall return. I have married a Surianese woman who lives in the Levant, on the borders of the Byzantine lands, and I have a daughter by her. Perhaps I shall live out my life on a peaceful estate of mine there. I do not wish to liquidate my business and my properties as I don't want to arouse suspicions about my absence; however, I have devoted most of them to religious endowments to benefit the students of knowledge coming to Baghdad. My other estates, and this house of mine, will be taken care of by my cousins.

"As for the books, I shall give some to the paper market, although I know that their fate may well be the flames. Others I shall keep in the library at the khan for the edification of bright students. They may be taken as damning evidence against me, but perhaps they will light up someone's mind. The libraries of the mosques are closed to us, the caliph's sword hanging over our heads." He paused. "But I have poured molten gold and distilled wisdom and the cream of the ages into crates of valuable books that I plan to distribute among different countries, on the wings of cranes: you, and a group of selected sober and just folk like yourself.

"These crates are like pomegranates: each one bears many books, like pearls. I shall give you your share: make sure to place them in a place worthy of them. It is the secret that turns base metal into precious metal. They shall remain for future generations of bright minds, to light the deep darkness of this nation." He added: "There will be a crate waiting for you at the eastern gate when you leave."

He rose, taking his leave, indicating that our meeting was at an end. Placing a hand on my shoulder with tender trust, he said, "Mazid, where did Aristotle place virtue?"

Fearing he would back away, I responded straight away: "Between two vices."

"You did well," he said. "He placed it between two statues, and this is what we seek to do: to wash Islamic religious law clean and purify it with philosophy, now that it has been defiled by ignorance. When you plan to leave, pass by the door of Asad al-Furati. He lives east of Baghdad. Everyone knows his house. His father is one of Baghdad's most eminent merchants. Ask to see him, and greet him with the words 'A status between two statuses,' and he will complete the bequest I have given you."

I left, wondering: "The bequest he has given me? Here are the pomegranates of Rusafa, come from the windowsill into my hand."

## The Monkey's Sorrows

I went out of the khan early next day to meet Abu al-Hassan, the face of the river misty in the morning, a flock of cranes wheeling about it. I walked around the rear of the khan on the path of the abandoned estates. I had no wish to meet the blacksmith so early with my doubts and fears; I needed to arrange the mosaic tiles of my mind in a manner that would allow me to burn my bridges and go into this new land bare of everything but my mind. A fetter had been placed around my wrist, though I did not know where the chain led. I wished to be alone with my thoughts.

But what was happening here? The rear path was nearly empty. The black donkey with the big head was not there; but no sooner did I reach the Chicken Canal, from which I went around to eastern Karkh, than I heard tambours, horns, and singing, splitting the calm of the morning with rude effrontery. I saw a handsome Indian in clean clothes spreading an expensive carpet out by the mosque. He had a monkey with him and got him to shake hands with the passersby, walk around with a *miswak* in his mouth, lift the prayer beads in his hand, run them through his fingers, and weep. This was exactly what I needed: to watch this monkey, taking me far away from the suppositions and presumptions that had stolen my sleep last night. I followed the monkey and his keeper as they went around every mosque in Baghdad until the afternoon prayers.

After the faithful had quit the mosque following the prayers, the monkey was dressed in a special costume like that of a prince. His owner scented him with expensive per-fume. He put on him shoes embroidered with gold thread and placed him on a mule. When he was done, three Indians arrived, one of them leading the monkey's mule, the second carrying his shoes, and a third carrying a parasol with which he protected the monkey from the sun. Then they walked through the streets, the people chasing after them to shake the monkey's hand.

At the end of the day, exhausted by walking around everywhere, we stopped at the door to a mosque for the sunset prayer. One of the Indians rose, telling the story of the mon-key. "Listen, one and all! Whoever has been cured of an illness must be grateful to the Lord for His boundless gifts. Know that in his youth, there was none better than this monkey, nor more obedient to the Lord God. But a devout man is always sorely tested, as they say: his stepmother cursed him into the form of a monkey after he caught her fornicating with a slave of hers. She struck him down from his noble mien to this form."

When the Indian reached this point in his speech, the monkey pulled a kerchief from his pocket, put it over his face, and took to sobbing bitterly. The men's hearts melted: their imam himself started by going to the monkey's kerchief and putting two dirhams therein. He was followed by the rest of the men who had been praying in the mosque.

The Indians invited me to supper with them that night. They had bought grilled meat, bread, stew, and sweetmeats, and I became more certain that Baghdad was but a great market where everything could be bought and sold, even the monkey's sorrows.

## "And We Made the Iron Supple unto Him"
The Persian blacksmith stopped supplying me with books. He was waiting to see the effect of my visit to Abu al-Hassan al-Hashimi—I still saw him bursting into the mosque some Fridays, looking in every way like someone lost, hands dirty,

clothes soot-stained from the forge. He did not respect the discussion circles enough to wash himself and don a turban and a garment appropriate for the revered status of the mosque, instead coming in barefoot to sit at a far corner of the circle, listening. Sometimes he would ask a question that showed he was avidly following the lesson. Whenever asked his name and profession, he would always answer with verse ten of the Sura of Saba: "And we made the iron supple unto him," indicating that David, a prophet in his own right, had been a blacksmith.

I still had two of the books he had passed to me: one was by al-Kindi and the other Aristotle's *Metaphysics*. They remained in my possession for a long time; I did not return them because, in truth, I could not let go of them. He ceaselessly reminded me of them when I passed by his stall: "Have you read al-Kindi's book? If you're done with it, I have another by him refuting the claims of those who say they can make gold and silver."

That subject was not exciting to me, so I would hang back and say, "I've read it all. But of all the sayings I took to heart, the most significant was al-Kindi's 'Be not ashamed of loving what is right and acquiring it, even if it cometh from faraway lands. There is nothing as deserving of demanding your rights than what is right.'"

When he heard that this quote, his perpetually red eyes glinted with pride. "That is what is right," he said. "Not the tradition of quoting the ancients! The books I give you are for thinking and learning about the kingdom of heaven."

I said, teasing, "Atheists started in heaven. The first deviation was when Lucifer disobeyed God, after all, and the reason was that he used his head and logic without accepting what he was told."

I had heard this from the odd young men at the mosque, and I said it to Abu Abbas to provoke him. He pulled more books out of his store, which seemed like a depthless dark cave, but definitely protected a gate to a secret garden of which nothing could be heard over the sound of his workers' hammers and anvils.

The morning of that day, the attendees at Sheikh al-Tamimi's discussion circle numbered a few over ten thousand; his students were obliged to make use of human amplifiers who stood close to my sheikh and placed their hands around their mouths like a horn, to convey his words to the listeners like an echo.

How I wished to leave them for the neighboring circle, where they were arguing about whether or not it was sinful to quote a debauched poet like Abu Nawas, or a modern poet like Abu Tammam. The sheikh of the circle saw this as a blot on the sanctity of the mosque and a reduction of the status of the ulema, but one of his students offered as evidence the great Imam Shafei, who listened to the poetry of Abu Nawas, although he kept it at a distance from his notes and books. How I wished I could cast my papers aside and go listen to them. But I was tied to my papers and inkwells like a sheepdog guarding a flock.

## The Head of the Beast

There was nothing special about the day I decided to return the books by al-Kindi and Aristotle to Abu Abbas the blacksmith, except that the morning was thick with a cloud of dust as yellow as turmeric: I planned to negotiate and buy Aristotle's book from him, as I could no longer part with it.

He was praying in the corner of his stall, prostrating himself long and devoutly. I remained out of the way until he had finished, whereupon he came to me hurriedly, smiling, as was his habit. I said cheerfully, "Here is al-Kindi. The Arab returns it to you, foreigner! And it is the foreigner"—I motioned to Aristotle's book—"that I wish to buy from you."

"Would you buy me also?" he asked lewdly. "You could be my master, and I your slave who must do whatever you say."

He never ceased conveying his debauched messages to me. I no longer paid it any mind, having realized they were but empty words. I went on, presenting him with a book I had bought from the paper market recently: "I found at Abu Yusuf Abu Durri's at the paper market: a book by Galen of Pergamon, translated by Hanin ibn Ishaq, and he claims that it is the original copy from the House of Wisdom. Examine it; I doubt it is. The writing in it is soft, and the paper looks like new Barmakid paper. Also, the colored embellishments in the corners of the pages indicate its newness."

He took it from me, pushed his great head into it, and scrutinized its lines, muttering. "Many books have been copied," he said, "and these copies may be an exact facsimile of the original. They are good books."

"But," I responded, "how can Abu Durri sell it as the House of Wisdom copy? The way it is written and organized does not resemble the copy of Aristotle at the khan's library, which I think came from the hands of the translator Bukhti-shu himself."

Abu Abbas was rubbing the pages between his fingers and sniffing them. He could tell the age of a book by the smell of its pages. I watched his great thick fingers stained with coal dust, saying to myself, "Do these two hands, which have lifted hundreds of hammers, still retain the delicacy needed to examine paper?"

As we were deep in conversation and looking at the books together, I suddenly felt a darkness fall over Abu Abbas's stall. The light seemed to have been blocked. I glanced up at the entrance to the stall to find two great figures in the doorway, with heavy wool abayas and long braids, leaning on thick sticks resembling shepherd's crooks. A great terror came over me, taking me over so the air turned to stone in my lungs. What had brought the Rajilat al-Hanabila here? I whispered to myself, "You are dead, Mazid, for in your hands you hold the book of Galen of Pergamon!"

Before I could look at their faces, one of them roared, "Are they the books of heretics and atheists in your hands? You would put out the light of the Almighty? What evil!"

The voice turned me to stone. Images poured into my mind unbidden: the Sura of al-Rahman; "*the sun and the moon are made punctual*"; the braying of camels; the sand dunes of the al-Dahna Desert. I turned with difficulty; my neck was frozen. It was no other than Musallama and Sakhr of Tamim, their beards longer and their shoulders broader, their prominent cheekbones rounded out with flesh. Their eyes had abandoned the look of the wily hunters about to attack their prey, and replaced it with the airs of arrogant religious clerics. Their faces showed nothing but rage and resentment, so much so that I could not even smile to see them. I went to the entrance of the stall, looking fully at them. Had they joined the Rajilat al-Hanabila? But Musallama cut my ponderings short. He approached me, flinging his arms open for an embrace. "Mazid! Mazid al-Hanafi! You old bookworm, where have you been!" He whispered in my ear, "What are you doing in the company of this accursed Rafidi foreigner, may God punish him as he deserves?"

At that moment Abu Abbas bellowed, "Some people have no shame!" He rushed into the bowels of the shop, coming back with a great hammer he used to forge the edges of shields, and brandished it in their faces. "I swear, if you two don't get out of my shop," he roared, "I'll bash your faces in with this hammer, and if you don't understand me, well, too bad for you!"

"How dare you, infidel who lies with men!" Sakhr yelled back. "I swear we will crush you! You Rafida, you fire worshippers, you who dare speak of faith!"

At these words, Abu Abbas's face split into a snarl the likes of which I had never seen. The veins in his neck pulsed violently. "*The desert Arabs say: 'We believe,'*" he quoted from the Sura of al-Hujurat. "*Say unto them: Ye believe not, but rather say 'We submit,'*" *for the faith hath not yet entered into your hearts.'* Damn you! You are accursed until the Judgment Day! You embody the Almighty, you give Him hands and feet! The Lord is above what you describe! You pretend that your ugly, charmless faces are made in the image of the face of the Lord of Both Worlds and that your obnoxious forms are made in His likeness? You speak of hands and fingers, and feet with golden soles? And thick hair, and ascending to the sky, and descending to the earth? The Lord is above what you unjust ingrates say, far above it."

By now, the owners of the neighboring stalls had arrived, crowding into the space between Sakhr and Abu Abbas after they had almost come to blows. My bones were quivering: all I could do was push them violently out of the stall, saying, "Let us go now!" and quoting the Qur'anic verse that says, *"Those who control their wrath and are forgiving!"* having first stuffed Galen of Pergamon's book up my sleeve. I had no desire to walk with them: my speaking with them and their whispers in my ear stunned every one of my neighbors in the marketplace of Karkh; it would ruin everything I had built by being meek and reluctant to draw attention to myself. They would now think me a spy planted among them. Therefore, I gestured goodbye to Abu Abbas, still standing in his smithy like a demon of rage, hammer raised. In a halting, shaky voice, I recited to them,

> Ignore the barbs of the ignorant man,
> For all he sayeth doth lie in him.
> It never harmed the great Euphrates
> That dogs dived therein to swim.

Please," I said, "let us go upstairs to my room in the khan." I had no idea what to do with them in this crowded marketplace where all eyes were on us.

I took them up to my room, and then wished that I had not. There they told me of their intention to "cleanse the whitest city of the world from the impurities of idolatry and polytheism, and shed blood until it be so." The first one they would slaughter, they said, was "that filthy blacksmith who stabbed our sheikh, Muhammad al-Tamimi."

Terrified by what they said, I burst out, "But how do you know that it was Abu Abbas who stabbed our sheikh?"

"Where have you been, Mazid?" Musallama thumped the floor of my room with his stick. "We have heard that you keep company with the sheikh, and take notes from him and for him. Did you not hear of the altercation between the blacksmith and Sheikh Muhammad? Those who witnessed the incident said that he left the mosque foaming at the mouth and muttering threats. And then it was only a few days until the sheikh was stabbed. You left our sheikh alone, God forgive you! As the proverb says, 'Those who are too heavy for their friends become too light for their enemies.'"

Feigning stupidity, I said, "Why do you not raise the matter of Abu Abbas with the wali or the commander of the armies?"

"The chief of police is an infidel like him," Musallama said derisively, "and he will definitely take his side. It is we who will set up the scales of what is right: the Bouhis themselves have presumed to divinity, giving themselves such names as 'Prince of the World,' 'Lord of All Princes,' and, for their ministers, titles that belong only to God: 'The Perfectly Capable,' and 'The Only Authority.' May they taste humiliation in this world and the next."

I did not bend to the storm of their rage, which seemed too fierce for my diminutive room at the khan. "But the sheikh has many enemies," I said. "A few weeks ago, for example, we were besieged by a group of privileged young merchants, who exchanged sharp words with my sheikh and his followers."

"We know them!" Musallama shouted. "Seraj al-Din al-Furati and his band of heretics who pass around the books of atheists. They live in the lap of luxury; they could not so much as shoo a fly away from their well-washed faces. I doubt it was they who stabbed the sheikh. Still, we are not unaware of their heresies; their heads must roll, and soon." He snarled. "The sick shall find their cure with us."

"Those effeminate fops!" Sakhr roared, waving his stick. I knew that he did not speak unless it was time for action, leaving most of the talk to Musallama. "They are nothing but a band of heretics! How I wish to smash in their clean-shaven faces with a stick such as this!" He snorted, brandishing the stick. "But we must avenge our sheikh upon the person of that filthy fire worshipper first."

Musallama took up the thread. "Those fops are like asps, like an incurable disease. Their poison is slow-acting; their evil has touched the Prophet's descendants. Abu al-Hassan al-Hashimi holds audiences with them, and goes to the paper stalls that sell their books, and brings them together in his home in Rusafa in the center of vast estates and lush gardens." He shook his head. "And instead of thanking God for His great blessings and abundant gifts, he has made a library in his house, which they say is filled with the books of atheists and heretics, to say nothing of the ones he brings in from Byzantium smuggled among the carpets and inks he claims to have purchased from Persia."

Sakhr added in a high voice, letting some of his idiocy slip out: "We reported him to Sharif al-Radi, head of the House of the Descendants of Ali, but he excused himself from the whole affair, saying he had no authority over him, and merely prayed for the Lord to guide him. But in any case," Sakhr continued, "the eye of God never sleeps. God has punished him with a small animal that nibbles away at the plants of his orchard day and night, and no tree or shrub escapes unscathed, no matter how they wipe it down with tar or set it alight." He smirked. "Here he is, seeking a buyer for his estate and about to leave for the Levant, where, it is said, he is married to a Surianese woman who bore him a daughter who will grow up beneath the domes of churches, Christian crosses, and infidel creeds."

I could not quite keep my composure when he mentioned al-Hashimi, his pink mansion, and the date palms heavy with the perfume of the river, thinking of the carpets woven with bounding gazelles and Zahira poured out of a honeypot. I feared that these thoughts would show on my face, letting them know that I, too, frequented that paradise.

They were filled with rage. Their abayas smelled so powerfully of sour milk that I found it hard to breathe in the confines of the little room. I thanked God that I had hidden Aristotle's book in a box in the corner of the room, or mine would have ended up on the list of the heads that would roll. I now understood why al-Hashimi insisted on leaving; for whence had these two obtained the story in minute detail if not through spies sent out by them?

"That fire worshipper," Sakhr hissed, "has been planted here to draw people away from their religion and cast doubt upon their creed. Do you not see that his stall is unique among the tailors, cloth merchants, and sellers of nuts, located among the stores and not at the craftsmen's market? It is planted there incongruously for a reason. Have you not seen that his dumb apprentice is a fire-worshipping Sabian? He closes the stall at night and commits debauchery with his apprentice, whereupon they spend the night in worshipping the fire."

My soul trembled at the depravity in his words, which he spoke in the refined language of the tribes of al-Yamama. "How do you know?" I burst out. "Have you seen them? Have you pried open their hearts?"

"Pay that no mind," Musallama responded, catching Sakhr's idiocy, "and let us speak of what concerns our sheikh. The blacksmith wormed his way into the discussion circle of our sheikh and questioned him and started the *fitna* that would have killed our sheikh if the Lord had not protected him with soldiers who descended from the sky and shielded him from the daggers aimed at him."

Because I had been there, I realized that news becomes distorted in the telling, and the more people tell a story, the more falsehood enters into it, and the more twisted it becomes with each retelling. And now, here was this pair of jackals in my room, waving swords and spears. What was I to do? "Musallama!" I snapped. "You are raising your sword and placing the sacrificial animal on the altar: what is your excuse for severing heads and committing murder, which God has prohibited?"

Eyes blazing and hawk-like nose flaring, he said, "Do you really need more than this? I swear, I fear for you, lest their books and their writings have corrupted you and made you turn away from the Holy Book and the Prophet's Tradition. I swear that I will not rest in my bed until that Rafida is resting in his grave, and I have rid our world and our religion of him!"

I tried everything to calm his ire: I asked him the secret of the abaya he wore, of a style normally only worn by ministry clerks. He said, "Our cousin, may God reward him, registered our names on the list of ministry clerks, so that we now receive monthly salaries and wear the garb of the ministry." He stood abruptly, and Sakhr did likewise. At the door, he turned. "You must come and pray with us at our mosque near Bab al-Sha'ir." He gave me a reproachful smile. "I swear that I see the marks of the softness and lassitude of the city in you. You must join us for the dawn prayers and regain Mazid the wolf that we know."

Without another word, they left.

I lay down on my back, terrifying images filling my mind. What if they knew I was unconvinced of the image of God in human form? I was a firm believer in "he who describes the Lord limits him," and that God was greater than any image in which He could be embodied. My beliefs would not please them. They had been pleasant with me because it was our first encounter, but they would not be so forgiving a second time.

Their visit left me confounded. I was now certain of two things: first, since they knew where I lived, they would never leave me in peace; second, they had prepared the sacrificial altar and the sword for the head of the Persian blacksmith. I must leave Baghdad with all speed; I must also hurry to Abu Abbas and warn him. That was what any honorable man would do, out of respect for neighborliness, not to mention breaking bread and sharing books. But I was not an honorable man. There were other thoughts in my head. What if Abu Abbas lost his temper and went on a rampage—not unexpected, given his fiery temperament—and went to confront them with a group of his friends? That would make me the instigator of a flame of *fitna* in Baghdad that would never die down. What if I slipped away in secret to tell the captain of the guard? I would, at the very least, be dragged into an unending interrogation. What if I went to Abu Hassan al-Hashimi for guidance? But I did not wish to appear like a fearful, ignorant yokel to him after he had chosen me and entrusted me with the secrets of the Just Monotheists. He would definitely doubt my competence; the matter would arouse suspicion, and he would withdraw the valuable crate of books from me, my life's dream. I prayed to God to help solve the conundrum, reciting the poem:

There may be an affliction that tightens around you,
Of which but the Lord holds the key.
Like a noose it did tighten, and then it released—
When I thought I should never be free.

I fell asleep to the sound of muttering and shouting: I knew not whether they were coming from my own head or from the Pomegranate Window. I was accustomed to sleeping on catastrophes and waking to find them gone: I was sure this calamity would dissipate with the night and its nightmares. This time, though, it failed to evaporate.

*

Baghdad woke to a light drizzle pattering against the bitter orange trees that filled the khan's back garden. But it was not only the rain to which Baghdad awoke: there was also the news that the blacksmith had been murdered.

There was a heavy knocking on my door. I had missed the dawn prayer at the mosque that morning and had prayed in my room, preparing to collect my things for departure. I opened the door fearfully. Hassan was standing there, pale and panting. "They found Abu Abbas the blacksmith in his stall with his throat slit!" He gasped for breath, visibly searching for words. "Something dark is on the horizon. *Fitna* is coming. I fear you will be the first target. You are the recordkeeper of Sheikh al-Tamimi, and I your friend: they have seen us together often. We must flee and escape Baghdad."

I caught at his hand. "Calm yourself." It was difficult for me to take in the rush of his words.

"Mazid," he said, still wide-eyed, "you *must* take this seriously. We may be killed and our money confiscated as part of the *khums*. I have seen many Shiites here washing their hands after shaking hands with me because I am, according to them, one of the Nawasib. It is preferable not to spend the night in our beds here. During the *fitna* that broke out in Karkh before, when they burned the copy of the Qur'an belonging to Abdullah ibn Masoud, who they say wrote it down as it was revealed to the Prophet, a great many people were declared apostates and fit for execution, and a good deal of blood was shed. It was a copy the Shiites had kept for years, and they say it is completely different from the standard Sunni Qur'an commissioned by the third caliph after the Prophet in its meanings and the order of the suras. The Fatiha and the suras of al-Falaq and al-Nas are completely missing from it." He dragged in a breath. "Sheikh Isfaraini commanded that it be burnt because of that discrepancy. After the burning, the Shiites revolted, flooding the streets beating their breasts and

160

cheeks, and some of the more weak-minded among them went to the house of the judge, meaning to set it alight and murder him, but the captain of the guard caught them and beat them back. News of it reached the caliph, who was incensed and sent his men to defend the Sunnis, and thus many of the Shiites' own homes were burnt to the ground. Their blood, you see, has still not dried and the slightest thing will set off *fitna*. What do you think will be their response when they wake to find one of their number with his throat slit in his own shop?" He took my arm. "Our presence here is dangerous. We shall be rats trampled underfoot."

But he lingered awhile before he left. A veil of tears covered his eyes. "Yesterday, a stray dog killed my cat, Morgana," he said. "Everything in the universe is telling me to leave."

## A Full Moon, Waning

His imposing presence and powerful build had not protected him from being found in the morning in his stall with his throat slit; in fact, he had been completely decapitated. They found his dumb apprentice crouching, trembling, in the farthest corner of the shop, describing with shaking hands two men who had entered the shop in the dead of night and cut off his head.

A great horror crushed my chest: I recalled the head of the animal tossed carelessly beneath the garden wall in Basra, flies buzzing around it in the morning mist. Would the stall owners gossip much about how I had frequented his stall? Would they tell the chief of police that I had taken Rajilat al-Hanabila to my room in the khan? Would my neck be the first to be placed on the altar of revenge?

There was no time to waste. My hands were steeped in blood, up to the wrist. I'd wait a few days so as not to arouse suspicion, and then I would quietly leave. These days must be spent far away from Karkh, for I knew not whence the knife would come. I must start now by looking for a camel and a caravan to take me away. The few dirhams I possessed might not be enough for the good caravans capable of carrying a heavy crate of books; but no matter, for I could distribute the books among several cloth or leather bags.

Hassan the Egyptian had resolved to go to India and teach the boys in a *kuttab* there: this incident only sped up his decision, and he also went to contract with a boat that would convey him to Basra, thence to set sail for India. But, for all his worry and disquiet, he was still his playful self: that night, he secretly brought in a small jar of wine. His eyes glistened with tears. His gentle soul made parting difficult. "Hassan," I said, wishing to see what he would say, "are you grieved at parting with me? I am nothing but an odd desert fellow, silent and bookish."

He leapt up from where he had been sitting, as though he had remembered an important matter, and waved a warning finger in my face. "Have you concluded your affairs in preparation to leave Baghdad? Never think that your comrade al-Hashimi will save you, for none of us will escape the wrath of the caliph, and no one has power over the caliph." He shook his head sorrowfully. "Most of his anger is directed at Egyptians. He sees us as nothing but spies for our Fatimid caliph. Once he called in the followers of Ali ibn Abu Talib who were descendants of the Prophet, and made them sign a document casting doubt on the ancestry and creed of the caliphs of Egypt, stating that they were not descendants of Muhammad at all, but of a man named Disan ibn Said al-Kharmi; that they were infidel Manichaeans and fire-worshippers, and that they were sinners who did not punish what the Lord had forbidden, and who made free with women's virtue and spilled blood and cursed the Prophets, and a great deal more beside. It is said that a great many men signed it, including Sharif Murtada and his brother Sharif al-Radi and a number of eminent members of the clan of Ali, and the judge Abu Muhammad al-Akfani, and Abu al-Hassan al-Hashimi."

As usual, I forgot in my disquiet to ask Hassan where he had obtained such full information if he were not, in fact, a spy for the Fatimids. I remained silent.

Hassan never abandoned his know-it-all role. "If you want to buy your camel for a caravan," he said, "go at the end of the day as the market is drawing to a close, and everyone wishes to be rid of their wares at low prices."

I ignored his advice, asking instead, "Is there a book market in Egypt?"

"There is always a book market in Egypt," he said. "It has never ceased, and never will. Most importantly, we have a jewel buried in the mud of the land of Caliph al-Hakim bi-Amr Allah: Ibn al-Haytham!" He smiled. "They say he invited him to Egypt from Iraq after hearing that he could control the Nile waters and build a dam to hold back the annual flooding, but he failed. The caliph gave him a job in the Egyptian ministry, although he desired it not. And because the ruler is as changeable as the wind and spills blood for no reason, Ibn al-Haytham sought a ruse to escape his punishment. He found nothing for it but to feign madness. He did so, and the news spread to the caliph. The caliph set a guardian over him and seized his moneys, assigning him a servant and leaving him in his home not far from the mosque of Ahmad ibn Tulun."

I bowed my head, thinking. Euclid's *The Elements* on geometry and Ptolemy's *Almagest* on astronomy would be the best gift for Ibn al-Haytham in his distress.

The next day dawned. It pained me that I was obliged to take the rear gate from the khan, not this time to avoid meeting Abu Abbas, who had watched me so avidly in life, but to evade the eyes that would doubtless stare at me after his death.

I would not go to Abu al-Hassan to say goodbye; I had no wish to arouse more suspicion. I went only to my sheikh and said goodbye. I did not tell him that I was leaving for good, only that I was going away for a few days to visit a relative of my mother's who owned a farm in Wasit. He cared nothing for my words: he was incensed that day, as there had been a quarrel the day before in the mosque between two students in his circle, and the Daylamite guards had entered the mosque again and sullied it with their horses' dung. He was busy cursing them and calling them the root of all evil.

I spent little time in my room. No more pomegranates appeared on my windowsill.

At dawn, in two days' time, I must hand back the key and leave. I would give Jamra a big present: when asked where I had been the night the blacksmith was murdered, she told them I had not quit my room all night. Only one thing was left: Seraj al-Din al-Furati and the crate of books.

## Voyage of the Cranes

I headed for Bab al-Sha'ir, examining the houses and streets and looking at every wall and gate, in search of al-Furati. But when I reached the house, I froze.

It was opulent and lavish: no sooner did you reach the outer wall than you recognized that those inside had never known hunger or thirst. It was ringed with palm trees and Christ's thorn jujubes, whose branches leaned on the solid rock of the wall, flocks of doves nesting within. There was a spring for whoever wished to drink, as a charity, flowing from the wall into a stone basin over twelve arm spans across, from which passersby, animals, and birds all drank. There was a towering wooden gate decorated with brass rings beneath an arch with mosaics and vines executed in gesso. This was one of four gates surrounding the mansion of al-Furati.

The magnificence of the place stopped me in my tracks. I could not advance, but stood staring at a large group of guards at the gate. I could hear the clatter of their shields as they came and went before the great doors. I slowed my step, and concealed myself around a corner, watching them closely, until they walked away from the gate, only four of them remaining. Only then did I come forward slowly to ask after Seraj al-Din al-Furati.

How would I walk out of here with a chest without arousing suspicion? Did they provide visitors with wings with which to transport crates full of books?

The guards scrutinized me suspiciously when I approached. I asked after Seraj al-Din al-Furati. A bright-eyed young man appeared, light of step and dark of skin, and asked me to follow him down a long corridor opening onto a sitting room with blue silk couches, glowing in the light spilling in from the arched windows. The boy bowed, indicating I should enter. "My master Seraj al-Din is on his way to us."

It was not long—mere moments—before I heard the sound of footsteps in the corridor. But when their owner stood at the door, the blood froze in my veins. It was none other than one of the odd young men of luxury who came to the circle of my sheikh al-Tamimi, heckling and arguing, bags under his wide eyes from late nights, soft hands like a slave girl's, and glossy hair that spilled onto his shoulders. He slowed, pausing at the door for a while, an unreadable smile on his face. He stepped forward, muttering, "Welcome, I'm sure."

I overlooked his lukewarm greeting. "My lord al-Hashimi sent me." I paused, then whispered, "He says there is a chest . . ." I fell silent.

Somewhat reproachfully, he said, "You are al-Tamimi's scribe, are you not?"

In low tones, like one excusing some transgression, I explained, "He selected me for my good hand and the speed at which I followed his speech."

His glance was mocking. "You mean following his ramblings, sophistry, and errors. In any case, where is the key to the chest?"

Only a few times has my intellect come to my rescue despite my panic: this was one such occasion. Slowly, looking him deep in the eye, I said, "It is in a status between two statuses."

He raised his eyebrows and looked at me. Then he gestured to me to sit down, saying, "Rest awhile: take a seat. I have been told that you impressed everyone with your recitation at Dar al-Nadwa last month." Still he scrutinized me, gathering his velvet caftan about himself. Then he sat with the air of a lion in his own den, although I had last seen him buffeted by screams, crowds, and those running from the whips of the guards.

He did not cease his close inspection of me, but now it was as though he was submitting to a great will that he could not disobey. "Subh!" he called, and a foreign boy, with a red nose and red hair, came running. "You and Layl," he said, "bring the third crate of books."

Layl was the dark-skinned boy who had brought me inside. Al-Furati turned to me, smiling and showing even, shiny teeth. "You see?" he said. "I named them Subh and Layl—Morning and Night. I divided the day between them, for we are a just, monotheist people."

I raised my eyes to him with a conspiratorial smile, indicating that I was a Mutazilite like himself. "Justice," I said, "is one of our five pillars." Meanwhile, I was thinking about the "third crate" and the two who had come before me: had they taken the rare and valuable books and left me the dross?

My host pulled me from my musings. "They say your sheikh is battling a fever, and sick at home," he said, "and no longer spreads his ramblings at the mosque."

"He was," I responded calmly. "His wound was infected, and he was feverish: but he recovered after the sultana had him treated at the Bimaristan al-Adudi."

He nodded. "What a wonderful location chosen by the fever! Perhaps it will burn straight through his bones and purify

166

him. 'A wound healed over pus and pestilence / Shows naught but the physician's negligence.' The disease in your sheikh is not in his wound, but also in his mind." He paused a moment. "And after all this, he is treated at the Bimaristan al-Adudi." He shook his head with regret, running his soft fingers through his beard. Then he burst out, "They are always like that. They have all the luck. When the cleric al-Isfaraini issued his fatwa that Abdullah ibn Masoud's copy of the Qur'an be burned, the Shiites revolted and almost set al-Isfaraini himself on fire. The caliph repressed them and had their houses burned down to pacify the cleric. So how do you think the clerics repaid the caliph al-Qadir for ingratiating himself to them?"

I tilted my head questioningly. He went on, "With disobedience and disrespect! When he desired to dismiss al-Isfaraini from his position, to balance the scales between the Rafidis and the Nawasib, al-Isfaraini wrote to him with barefaced insolence: "I know that you cannot dismiss me from my position because it is God who has appointed me to it, but with a word from me to Khorasan, I can have you dismissed from your position as caliph." He bowed his head and said with venom, "That is the way of all clerics: if a sultan panders to them too much, they seek to share their power. Even the head of Ali ibn Abu Taleb's descendants, al-Murtada, did not dare go against them. I hear he plans to leave Baghdad after what he said about *sirfah*, which caused the preachers to stir up the rabble and the common people against him."

His lack of formality and his openness encouraged me to interrupt him curiously. "What is *sirfah*?"

He shook his head in exasperation. "Al-Murtada followed the Mutazilites in affirming the miraculous nature of the Qur'an. The Mutazilites believe that any person could have written the Qur'an or similar, but that God deterred them from it. That is *sirfah*—determent. Baghdad shook at these words of his, and but for their respect, or what was left of it, due to the descendants of Ali ibn Abu Taleb's lineage, the senile old man al-Isfaraini would have issued a fatwa that he be killed."

"I have never heard of this in the two years I have spent in Baghdad," I said.

"Voyager," he said, "never regret what you have not seen in Baghdad, for there may be great evil within: the lash of the caliph's proclamation is now a threat hanging over all our heads. Now it remains for us to preserve the wisdom of the world and the cream of the ages, and keep it away from the charlatan preachers and the sophistry of would-be theologians and the sycophants of the powerful." He took a breath. "We, the Voyaging Cranes, the Just Monotheists, must distribute these books among libraries and houses of learning, and place them in the hands of brilliant and insightful thinkers and those who have chosen the intellect and rationality as a beacon to bring good and defend against evil."

Subh and Layl returned, bearing with difficulty between them a great wooden chest studded with brass nails. It was engraved with rounded patterns polished with shiny wax, locked with a padlock with a circle of leather around it. My heart fluttered. Here were the pomegranates of Rusafa, stuffed with pearls! I wanted to leap up from my seat and peruse its contents.

"Hold on!" Al-Furati put a hand on my shoulder. "We have not yet concluded our business." Seeming to sense my urgency, he said, "Patience. Voyagers do not race against time. They are careful, reserved. They turn matters over this way and that before coming to a decision."

He gestured with two fingers to dismiss the boys. Then he looked at me. "Abu Abbas the blacksmith, may he rest in peace, attempted to give you to understand some things, but you did not listen. Al-Hashimi has given you some of the landmarks, but not the map. The Voyagers are descendants of ancient human wisdom, which believes in God, in justice and monotheism, in preaching virtue and dissuading from vice and injustice. We have made the intellect our imam, and any matter our minds cannot accept, we reject and do without.

"We are the keepers of the legacy of the House of Wisdom, which was a pearl in the crown of rationality. Now it is being overtaken by preachers, schoolteachers, and idiots, and has lost its wisdom; nothing remains but chains of quotations from the ancients that put paid to rational thinking. We have decided on preserving this legacy, not only in our breasts, but by conveying it far and wide via the Voyage of the Cranes, to every city and every land."

He fell silent and looked down at his feet. Suddenly he sat up. "I do not wish to go on for too long. These books are the repositories and keepers of knowledge. They are lanterns that will light up a dark *fitna* on the horizon. They are seeds planted in fertile hearts that understand them and take them seriously." He looked from me to the chest. "Do not concern yourself with their price, but rather with where you will plant them."

He dropped his head back to lean on a cushion behind him, letting out a sigh that came from the depths of his soul. I felt that he had exhausted himself. He closed his eyes for a moment before sitting up straight again and recollecting himself. "Yesterday, I witnessed an auction for the book explaining auditory science by Alexander al-Aphrudisi of Damascus. It sold for one hundred and twenty gold dinars. There is nothing wrong with making money from them, but do not let money be your master. In every land you find yourself, you will take the torch and pass it on. You will hear and be heard. You will listen and enlighten. You will be a learner and a teacher at once.

"Look for your own secret garden. It might be hiding in the shadows, or in the depths of the seas, or within a person's breast. Look deep, use your vision, and it shall be revealed to you. Seek out the flocks of Cranes and watch them quietly and patiently; they shall surely alight on your fingers."

*

He insisted that I stay and share his meal. He passed the time setting out items of advice and wrapping me in instructions. He left no detail unmentioned. "When you arrive in a city, go to its Great Mosque. Observe its clerics and its libraries. That is where the Voyagers fly. Be secretive: what goes beyond two people is public. Beware of spying eyes, for they may ruin you. Do not stay too long in one place, especially if you should become well-known there and you find heads turning to you and the envious multiplying. . . ."

In the end, I tried to retreat; I felt overstuffed with his advice, which made me seem like some naive bumpkin. As I was drawing my caftan about me and adjusting my turban to make my exit, he asked me to stay back a moment, and disappeared into his house. He returned quickly, bearing in his sleeve a brass folder meant for keeping papers, with mysterious words engraved on it. He held it out to me, then put his hands behind his back, as if announcing that he was finished with his task, and with me. He said, as if imparting some great news, "This is a copy of the road map. Read it as though it were written expressly for you. The Lord creates at every moment, depending on circumstances, the word, and the manner in which it is read and spoken."

His words enveloped me. I felt that the earth was moving beneath me, so I leaned on the wall. Seraj al-Din went on: "When you arrive at the status between two statuses, you should have, like a disciple, some signs and symbols, that you may seek out what is too high or concealed from your stairway. Some of these instructions will seem mysterious to you. Others you will have already left behind in your journey. Some will appear too general and not applicable to you; but their interpretation will become clear in the places and situations through which you pass. There is no eternal, changeless interpretation: interpretation is formed through situation, as I have told you. If you do this, the commandments I shall give you will tell you how far you have ascended on the staircase of the Way of the Voyagers."

I fell silent. I had no idea what to say, so I shook his hand warmly and said, "Thank you."

"Where are you headed after Baghdad?" he asked.

I said, "Jerusalem."

He smiled. "That city has not lost its questioning spirit. You will find there a noble imam from the clan of Qays, named Amr al-Qaysi. Tell him that his cousins greet him and say to him, "Is morning not nigh?""

## The Mirrors of the Djinn

I am Mazid al-Hanafi. I have left al-Yamama behind for what glory I can pluck from the streets of Baghdad. What shall I do with myself? To what ruin am I headed?

The books of the House of Wisdom captivated me: they transformed me into a voyager spreading good tidings and bad, yet I was nothing but a fleeing, terrified man with blood on my hands.

Voyager? Was that a title, a description, or a rank? I dared not ask.

I had agreed to meet the Daylamite perfume dealer at the eastern gate of Baghdad. I would pass by this house tomorrow with my she-camel, Shubra, to take the chest of books, garlanded with the mists of dawn.

I still had the book of al-Kindi. I had not returned it to Abu Abbas the blacksmith. How death turns every tyrant into a saint! It had completely erased any resentment I felt against that book-loving blacksmith. He made metal melt, but the world had been hard to him: he had made locks, but not keys. Knowledge for him was an antidote and an excursion of hope, that he might inhale a breath of fresh light in the darkness and smoke of his stall. Life had not been kind to him: he had not had a chance even for a final wish, a knife lying in wait around a corner to cut off his head, casting him aside by the fire and molten metal of the forge.

I must spend the night away from Karkh, as though I were feeling it already disappear and fade away. I had not returned since I had left there that morning. I prepared a bed beneath the wall of a garden not far from the caravan, and slept there so as to comfort myself with the travelers' voices, but not so close as to be confused or distracted by what they were saying.

After afternoon prayers the next day, the travelers began to arrive in succession. I busied myself with arranging my things on the back of my camel, and feeding her, and stealing glances at the people coming to join the caravan. There were not many: most were merchants, and some were Christian pilgrims headed for Jerusalem, with four guards bristling with weapons staring curiously at everyone from their spot underneath a pair of nearby date palms.

I was eager for evening to come so that I might read the commandments. I had no wish to be seen reading them.

The evenings in Baghdad were still cold, and fell fast. They brought with them melancholy yearnings and dark fancies. I curled up in my abaya and lit a small fire, nibbling at some wheat cakes, of which I had purchased a great quantity to eat on the journey. When everyone began to disperse around me, dissolving into the darkness, and only their shadows remained, I glanced about me fearfully. Then I carefully pulled out the brass folder and started to work on its locks. I was nervous: my hands were trembling as though I were about to release a djinn from its depths. Instead, the scent of perfume overwhelmed me. Was the wind bringing me the perfume of the wares on camelback? Or was it the ghost of the perfumes worn by Seraj al-Din al-Furati?

When I opened the package, a faint light glowed. I raised it to my eyes and stared at it again. The words were as though written on water, their letters rippling as though floating. I was afraid.

What was this? A fairy mirror? It shone in the misty night. Was it made of mercury? I closed it, fearful.

Shubra was ruminating placidly, watching me indifferently through her long lashes. I opened the folder again. Its letters lit up in the darkness once more. I had no need to light my small lantern to read them; they were written in *diwani* calligraphy, and started with the Qur'an verse, "Therefore of the bounty of thy Lord be thy discourse." It went on:

When He of the absolute Will, He whom the mountains have sung of His power and might, He who with His great authority makes the planets move, He to whom every creature prays in the night and the morning, desired to guide His faithful to the right path, and shelter them beneath His great throne, and wake them from the somnolence of luxury, and lead them to the path of truth and verity, He blessed them with the Two Ways, giving them free will instead of predestination. He bestowed upon them enough of the light of rationality and proof to lead them to Paradise; glory to the One who is bound by neither space nor time. Now that the Voyagers are besieged by trials and tribulations, and folk resent them in many nations; now that everyone is lying in wait for them with tooth and claw, and voices are raised against them among those who would extinguish the light of God with their maw, we find it prudent to set down the contents of our minds on paper, that it might be passed around among disciples, and spoken of among knowledgeable Voyagers, that they might remain as lights on a path besieged by seditious plots like fragments of the night.

As to you, Voyager: we have written down these commandments for you. Read them with the eyes of your circumstances before those of your head, that they may be as a lantern and a companion to you.

*

First Commandment
Do not hesitate if you find you have chosen the long and circuitous path: do not look back.

Second Commandment
If you seek knowledge, knock on the door of your own self. Consult your heart, but before taking its advice, show it to your mind for approval or disapproval. Knowledge is a gate with two doors: one of the heart and one of the mind.

From afar, the braying and snorting of camels came to me as the men tied them with ropes and prepared their food and water: I was like a man transported. Had I consulted my heart?

Third Commandment
The world is light and it is fire: drink from the cups of the sunlight of knowledge without being burned by its flames. Your greatest aspiration here is to be saved.

Fourth Commandment
Erect no dam, raise no veil between yourself and the truth. If it cometh in the shape of a person who claims to possess the truth in its entirety, remove him far from your path, for this is nothing but his own truth. If it cometh in the form of certainty, purify it with the water of questioning and doubt; if it cometh in the form of a mountain, climb it to seek what lies behind that mountain. Do not submit your mind to any creature who seeks to direct or lead you on the pretext that they alone have claim to certainty: in so doing, you become like the donkey who gives its reins to a thief to steal it.

### Fifth Commandment
Monotheism is an unattainable goal: each one finds it through his mind according to his ability.

### Sixth Commandment
Beware! Never become the enemy of the wise sciences, never be tribal or feudal or bias yourself toward one creed or knowledge: he who hateth any of the sciences remaineth ignorant of it.

### Seventh Commandment
Burn all these commandments, that they may not become a parallel religion to entrap you in bars of their own. Life is greater than instructions and commandments. Life is ever-changing and nothing remaineth the same. Time flows on and takes all. Everything leaves its place; nothing remains forever.

The desire for learning is the mother of all virtues. Burn these commandments and start anew.

I did not sleep that night. I remained suspended between the beating of the wind and the pulsing of the commandments made of rippling water, to pour into my mind whenever my soul thirsted.

The first commandment: I had taken the longer path, away from sleepy al-Yamama, safe in the embrace of its date palms, placing the North Star before me and heading for Baghdad, full of rage and *fitna*. The second: had I consulted my heart and asked my mind? That was what had snatched me from the presence of al-Tamimi and to the paper market and the library of the khan, and placed me on the path of the Voyagers. The stock in trade of al-Tamimi was nothing but a long string of quotations from the ancients.

I could hear the sounds of the camels and the rustle of the wind. It was my last night in Baghdad—the city where I had spent two years, baptizing myself in its river, washing myself clean in its libraries, cradled in its clouds. It had stripped Mazid of al-Yamama away from me, making me a blank page upon whose ribs Fate now inscribed its seven commandments.

The last thing I left behind in Baghdad was an anonymous message I wrote with my left hand, that my handwriting would not be recognized.

> In the name of the God who never sleeps, nor ignores the rights of His servants, and prayers and peace upon the prophets:
> Justice is a universal law. It was placed in the hands of rulers and responsible figures. If it is implemented by those with twisted horizons and the common folk, sedition runs rampant and chaos is the order of the day. Blood shall flow. Blood has already flowed—the blood of Abu Abbas, the Persian blacksmith, who was killed by Musallama and Sakhr of Tamim. They are members of the Hanabila; they enacted their own judgment within his stall. This is the truth, as God is my witness.

I placed the note in one of the cracks in the outer wall of the khan, where it could be seen. No doubt it would soon pique the curiosity of some passerby. I knew not what would come of it—if justice would establish itself in Baghdad now that blood had been spilt, houses burned down, and mosques filled with fighting.

Baghdad was no longer a place to abide.

# 3

# The Pillars of Bosra

WE STAYED A FEW DAYS in the town of Bosra, in the Levant. It was a city carved out of solid rock: domes, brackets, and pillars of ancient stone, roosting on the fringe of the desert like the she-camel of the prophet Salih, and the cool air that passed through its pillars bore the murmurs of fear and disquiet. Its stores were occupied with trading and bartering between the caravans of the Arabs of the Peninsula and the Levantines: woolen garments, buttermilk, and carpets, while the caravans bought grains, pulses, receptacles, fabrics, and perfumes. I heard them haggling with a trader from our caravan over two bottles of heavy perfume distilled from Byzantine roses.

There were only a few bookstores in Bosra. The curious, welcoming eyes of the booksellers tempted me to divest myself of some of the books in my possession and barter for some of theirs. However, their marketplace was sleepy and lacked customers: most of what I found there was in Surianese, of which I only spoke a few words. I also feared to show them my books lest they languish long on their shelves, for everyone in this city had turned away from books, busy mourning the fall of Aleppo into the hands of the Byzantines, and the Muslims' inability to defend it. They feared that the hand of Byzantium would extend to Bosra in the Levant, the presence of the Fatimid wali in Damascus notwithstanding. But what could a small force there do against the crashing waves of the Byzantine army?

Most of those who passed by the city went to see the Byzantine ruins on its outskirts, including a great circular structure with dozens of concentric tiers of stone seats within, carved out of rock. Between the seats had sprouted plants and thornbushes. Opposite the seats was a raised stone dais, surrounded by pillars. The people of Bosra called this place "the Byzantine playhouse." I found no Byzantines there, only flocks of sheep, grazing on the wildflowers and gamboling about its seats. I sensed a great dignity in the place: there was something awe-inspiring about these great tiers and the high boxes surrounding them on the edges. Some of the pillars were topped with carvings of fearful or shouting faces, as though they were wailing or warning of some danger. Upon some of the seats, strange letters had been carved, or perhaps numbers. I found some builders coming to fill mule-drawn carts with stones from the playhouse looking at me oddly as I stood on the lower tiers of the raised dais and yelled, "O dwelling place!" and listened to the echo of my voice as it rang off the curved walls and the graduated seats. The walls captured my voice, magnifying it as though a thousand throats called out with me.

"Do not disturb the demons of the Byzantines," a voice told me. "They may follow you and destroy you."

I whirled around, startled. The Daylamite caravan owner was there, together with some of the guards of the caravan. I had formed a stronger bond with him, and he had warmed to me when he heard some of my song and poetry recitation, and he kept asking me to raise my voice in song to help his camels along in return for two bottles of valuable perfume he selected from his stock. Because I could not tell the difference between poor and good perfume, I left the choice up to him. To tell the truth, in this, he was an honest man: when Shammaa of the House of Wael used to be visited by the grooming women from Khadrama to sell their perfumes, she insisted that it be aged, thick, and dark; the bottles that the Daylamite gave to me were so.

# 4

## The City of Prophets
## Ramadan 2, AH 402; March 28, AD 1012

AFTER THREE DAYS' WALK FROM Bosra to the west, there appeared close by us a great mountain with peaks and valleys, set in a tangle of shrubs and bushes, dotted about with minarets and church spires. "Praise the Lord!" called the caravan leader. "It is the Mount of Olives and the City of Prophets." We were almost at Jerusalem, on the second day of Ramadan.

The Muslims called out *"Allahu akbar!"* while the Christians wept and sang melancholy hymns. The camels slowed as the road sloped uphill to the gates of Jerusalem. I dismounted from Shubra, who was close to collapse from fatigue, and we headed for the gate known as the Damascus Gate, on the northern side of the walls of Jerusalem. A great many caravans were clustered there, the camels of travelers and pilgrims seated all about; the bleating of sheep mixed with the braying of donkeys, and everyone racing to drink from a well surrounded by rectangular rock pools, filled up from the well for those arriving.

It was the end of the day, and I was exhausted and thirsty, waiting for the sun to set so I could break my fast: I delayed entering the City of Prophets until the morning. I needed a safe place for the box of books, and the place around me was teeming with travelers.

When dawn came, I let Shubra go to graze in the grassy, green environs: the hills around us were covered in dark red flowers with a powerful scent like that of the earth after rain. Beasts of burden were not permitted to enter by the Damascus Gate; therefore, I left my crate with the guard of the caravan, entreating him to care for it in exchange for a bountiful sum. His naive, imbecilic face reassured me that he would not lust after a pile of books.

I went into Jerusalem with a group of merchants. The air of the city bore the sounds of beating wings. Were they the wings of birds, or were the angels familiar with the city?

The crowding at the gate was intense. When we entered through the doorway, we found a broad, paved road running from north to south, which seemed to divide the old city into two halves. On both sides of the main road were towering buildings constructed of white rock, with stained glass windows.

The style of the buildings did not resemble the ones I had seen in Baghdad: some were still occupied, while some were abandoned, their doors and windows fallen off and grass growing beneath their walls. They called them the Umayyad palaces. I would have liked to stand there for a long time, staring at a kingdom that was now in ruins, but I was obliged to quicken my step to keep up with the group of merchants who appeared familiar with the city and knew the way. I gave my ears over to what they spoke of and pointed at; they thus gave me the keys normally denied a gawking visitor looking around the squares and talking to the silent walls.

The path sloped uphill, leading to spacious, carefully paved squares, located southeast of the city wall. Next to one of the mosque walls, a marble tablet was inscribed: "This Mosque Was Renovated in the Time of Caliph Ibn Abd al-Malik."

The merchants said, "We have arrived at the Aqsa Mosque! Greetings to you, first of the two destinations for pilgrims!"

On a small elevation was an octagonal mosque topped with a gilded dome, to which we mounted on broad steps.

They said it was the Dome of the Rock, and there they parted ways. Some went to the Qibli Mosque to pray, some to the Marwani Mosque, and some went straight into the Aqsa Mosque, at whose door I stood awestruck, listening to the beating of wings in the air. It was from here that the Prophet, the best of all men, rose on his journey to Heaven.

Inside it was dim, and I could barely make out the rock in its center. It was like a great table, chest-high, as long as it was broad. I stood transfixed, staring at it, listening to one of the merchants of the caravan calling out, *"Allahu akbar!* This stone descended from Paradise and remained suspended in the air and has never rested on the ground. When it falls, that will be the sign of Judgment Day. It is blessed, brought from Heaven with the Black Rock at the Kaaba, and we shall be reborn and judged around it on Judgment Day."

Another was pointing out the irregularities and protrusions on its surface. "Look! Here is the footprint of the Prophet. Next to the footprint, here is another place where his turban fell when his magical mount, Buraq, began to carry him up on his journey through the heavens."

I stared at the smooth rock, feeling its slippery surface. I could not find the footprint or the location of the turban, but took to contemplating it. When it fell from Heaven, had it witnessed the mysterious longings and passions in Adam's breast as he walked around that exalted garden, isolated and lonely, before his wife sprang up out of him? Had Eve stood upon it one day, her feet anointed with the musk of Paradise, the loveliest of all the women God had created? Had this rock heard the conversation between the Lord God and the rebellious Lucifer before he was cast out of the Divine Kingdom?

I was overcome by the loneliness of Adam, our father. My feet were weighted with the ponderous awe of the place and the hunger and thirst of fasting. The group of merchants milled about with quick, impatient movements. Out of their pockets they produced long chains of prayer beads that hung almost to the floor, their faces turned to the ceiling, contemplating it. Meanwhile, I wondered what suras the Prophet Muhammad had recited to the other prophets as he led them in prayer in this place?

I walked slowly through the markets and alleyways: the paved pathways and stone walls were not unlike the city of Bosra, but these were wider and the air was purer. In the squares and culs-de-sac were orange trees bearing early blossoms, for it was still chilly around us. The folk of Jerusalem were mostly Arab and Surianese, though there were others whose provenance I could not make out; at any rate, they did not resemble the folk of Baghdad. Their faces were ruddy, their features finer and more delicate, and their movements more graceful and smoother. No one paid any attention to me. The city was packed with pilgrims, and it appeared that they were accustomed to seeing strangers here; or perhaps it was my mean and poor appearance after a month on the back of Shubra that made their eyes look through me. Even the store owners did not cry their wares when I passed; they turned away from me carelessly. "I must do something about my appearance," I thought.

I went to a barber and asked him to cut off my two long braids. It was no easy decision: I felt shorn, as though I were cutting off Shammaa's braids. My mother always took care of my hair, perfumed it with nutmeg, and braided it with powdered cloves. All the people of al-Yamama wear their hair in braids. In Baghdad, I wore them rolled up under my turban to avoid mockery. After the barber cut them off, I took my braids, dug a hole in a corner of the city, and buried them in the same place as the graves of the prophets, muttering wryly, "Perhaps my braids will help me on Judgment Day; they say that those buried in Jerusalem will never be damned."

I had my beard and mustache trimmed, relieving them of the repulsive unkempt look they had acquired, keeping only enough for a manly appearance without looking like a wild man or a Bedouin. From the roofed-in marketplace, I bought a new shirt and pantaloons, and went into a bathhouse in the market whose steam seemed to penetrate to the bottom of my lungs. It was built upon a spring that gushed hot water without ceasing.

When I finished, I put on a few drops of the Byzantine rose perfume that the owner of the caravan had given me: thus I was ready to meet Amr al-Qaysi as a well-groomed bookseller from Baghdad, not an unkempt desert Arab who had leapt out from behind some sand dune and landed in Jerusalem. After I emerged from the bathhouse and donned my new clothes, my movements suddenly became more graceful and my voice lower. My steps grew slower and smoother, and when I sat, I did so with some fastidiousness, so as to avoid the places that might tear or stain my new clothes.

I went to the Great Mosque of Umar for the afternoon prayers, in search of the discussion circle of Amr al-Qaysi. I approached the attendant, or perhaps it was the muezzin—I could not tell, for he wore a bright white turban and a green caftan. I greeted him carefully and asked, "Are you from this city?"

He answered me readily, courteously, with no trace of wariness, "From the moment I opened my eyes. We trace our ancestry to the Arabian tribe of Kalb, which came and settled in the Levant, its origins being from the Peninsula." He added, familiarly and a little proudly, "We are the uncles of Yazid ibn Muawiya, on the mother's side. His mother is Maysoon, daughter of Bahdal, from the clan of Kalb."

The minarets of Jerusalem pray the Shiite prayer for the Prophet's descendants, while this muezzin prides himself on being related to the enemy of Ali ibn Abu Taleb, Yazid ibn Muawiya. I sensed that his world was limited to the confines of this mosque. At that time, I was not yet accustomed to the nature of the Levantines, who were open and friendly with foreigners and expansive with strangers. I had learned from my stay in Baghdad that a stranger had strict limits, beyond which one was expected to hold one's tongue, for you never knew what you might say that would result in a dagger being brandished in your face.

He adjusted his turban, then raised his white eyebrows and said as though just remembering, "Where are you from?"

I said shortly, "I am a Hanafite Sunni from al-Yamama." I paused to see the effect of the name on his expression. Would he recite the black list that they always teased me with: kin to Musaylima, horn of the Devil, and so on?

But his face showed no indication of having ever heard of it. He only said, "Oh, you have journeyed a long way. Are you a student or a merchant?"

"Both," I responded.

His simple demeanor and clear responses allowed me to look my fill at the beautiful colored ornamentation in the colonnade and its pillars and arches. He kept talking, not realizing my distraction. After some hesitation, I asked, "Do you know Amr al-Qaysi? I was told that he holds his discussion circle here."

His smile made three deep vertical lines in his cheeks. "Why, whom should we know but Sheikh Amr al-Qaysi, God bless him? He is our sheikh and speaker and the preserver of our knowledge, a good man and devout, full of inexhaustible wisdom." I had clearly sparked his interest with my question about the sheikh: he appeared to have a great deal to say. "Tell me about the way you took, and the caravan you went with."

"I am a bookseller," I said shortly. "They told me that Jerusalem is thirsty for books."

He puffed up with the air of one with pretensions to knowledge. "Who does not love books? Show us what you have, Arab of the desert. Are there any true God-fearing men who are not men of knowledge? We Jerusalem folk are fond of learning, and students always come to us: they all say, in praise of the city, 'I would fain be a straw in one of the mud bricks of Jerusalem.'"

His expansiveness did not sit well with my wary and cautious nature. Quietly, I said, "God willing, I shall bring some of them here." I added hurriedly, "But where can I find Amr al-Qaysi?"

He pointed at the gravelly floor where he stood. "Here," he said. I stared at him, astonished. He went on, "He has held a discussion circle here after the afternoon prayers daily since he arrived in Jerusalem." Before I could ask, he went on: "But I could not tell you where he lives, as he prefers not to receive visitors in his house."

I guessed deep within me that he had said this so as to watch my meeting with Amr al-Qaysi and find out what I sought. He added, "Everything in the pot comes out with the ladle. Just wait until the afternoon prayers."

I found his expression to be in poor taste.

When I concluded my prayers, I looked about me in search of the muezzin to point out Amr al-Qaysi's discussion circle to me. However, I did not require much assistance, as it was the only circle with four large circles of students around a sheikh, who I guessed was he.

I approached the circle hesitantly. I found a place by a marble pillar so that I could watch him without being observed; but the sheikh still glimpsed me as I stepped in carefully.

Beams of colored sunlight spilled in through the stained glass windows of the mosque to form a pool of light on the gravel floor, making it look clear and glistening like the bottom of a brook. I scrutinized the features of Amr al-Qaysi, or, as his students called him reverently, "Our sheikh al-Qaysi." His face was long and sharp-boned like the faces of the folk of al-Yamama. He was light-skinned, and his features still had the look of youth about them. His beard was coal black; he had wide shining eyes of a deep black, curled lashes, and amid all this, a big nose overpowering all his other features.

When he invoked the name of God and called down blessings on the Prophet to begin his lesson, a sense of security filled me at the sound of his voice. Was it his confidence, poise, and clarity of diction? He was like those men who appear all of a sudden to repair what is broken and settle matters, whose word is his bond, whose speech comes without hesitation; one of those who make the rules, and leave it to others to argue the details.

He was speaking about the names and attributes of God, a subject it was forbidden to even touch upon in Baghdad. "'*There is nothing whatever like unto Him*,' says the Qur'an: that is to say, God transcends names and descriptions, for He is above earthly imperfections."

It is not in my nature nor part of my instinctive reticence to address strangers, but I know not what, at that moment, moved me to say, "This is what the Mutazilites say, our sheikh!" I was mortified the moment I blurted it out: I appeared like an idiot student who draws attention to himself by his mischief.

He sat quietly for a while. Everyone in the circle was silent, every head turned toward me. Staring at me, al-Qaysi said, "You mean the Just Monotheists, who hold that God does not create evil or cause it to occur; for if He did, and then punished us for it, it would be unjust, and the Lord our God is a just God."

I saw clearly that Amr al-Qaysi had no qualms about announcing he was a Mutazilite in front of witnesses. Maybe he was far from Baghdad with its quarrels and insults and accusations of heresy and swords poised to strike and spill blood, or maybe these dark clouds had not yet arrived in Jerusalem.

Seeking to pass a covert message to him in my reply, thus paving my way to him and what I had come for, I said, "Yes, our sheikh. The circles of Baghdad and the gatherings of Basra have taught me that. They are the Just Monotheists and their five pillars are as follows: justice; monotheism; promises of reward and warnings of punishment; a status between two statuses; and finally, to preach virtue and admonish vice. They are devout and God-fearing folk, despite the doubts raised around them."

All heads turned toward me once more. Unheeding, I went on, "But until now, I have not understood the meaning of the phrase 'a status between two statuses.'" I said it slowly, enunciating carefully and clearly like one engraving the words deeply into rock.

Amr al-Qaysi fell silent. He looked so hard at me that I began to quail. I could barely swallow. Then he half closed his eyes, as though in ecstasy, and looked at me through his long eyelashes while the students in the circle looked from one of us to the other, awaiting what would become of this contentious interloper of a student come to snatch away the water their sheikh was pouring into their cups.

The muezzin was sitting close by Amr al-Qaysi, facing the students as though indicating that he occupied a position higher than them. Suddenly he let out a great yell that split the silence: "Ah, Hanafite! Welcome to the circle of our sheikh, who lights up the minarets of Jerusalem with his presence!"

Without looking at him, al-Qaysi held up a hand to silence him. "Hush." The muezzin snapped his mouth shut and went back to what he had been doing: scratching behind his ears, staring at everyone's faces, watching anyone who came in, and looking around the mosque with thick, sleepy eyelids and a bored expression, uncaring of what went on in the circle.

Al-Qaysi looked down for a long moment. Then he said, "A status between two statuses. Well. Abd al-Jabbar ibn Ahmad says that the origin of the phrase is to be used for something that falls between two others, each of which attracts what resembles it: that is the meaning in plain language. As for the idiom, it is the knowledge that a sinner has a name between two names, and a judgment between two judgments: he is not called an infidel, nor a believer, but is called a sinner; and if a believer dies while insisting on sinning, he is not punished, but rather referred to the Lord God. If He punishes him, that is His justice; if He forgives him, that is His mercy, of which no mind or religious law can disapprove. That said," he concluded in the customary manner, "only God is all-knowing."

As he said this, he looked from one attendee to the other; when he came to me, he planted his eyes on my face as though he wanted to find out what lay behind my silence. I was astonished by his immediate response to my interruption, for in Baghdad the students of a circle do not interrupt their sheikh, instead waiting until the end of the lesson for questions and discussion, at which time the sheikh would offer only unintelligible answers and mutterings. I had not yet heard a sheikh say "only God is all-knowing." But al-Qaysi had expanded and explained and clarified, which emboldened me to give him more of my doubts and worries: "What has he done to be eternally damned?"

"Because he has free will," al-Qaysi said. "*Did not God say that He 'hath shown him the Two Ways,*' in verse ten of the Sura of al-Balad? He knows the sin, and yet commits it: knowledge is the cornerstone of judgment and responsibility."

The time for the sunset prayer approached and everyone left Amr al-Qaysi's circle to eat and drink for iftar, but he stood there staring at me, and I divined that it was time to approach him. I approached haltingly; I wished to begin by reassuring him. "Our venerable sheikh," I said, "bless your knowledge, which dissipates the darkness around our hearts. But," I asked, "is morning not nigh?"

He said only, "You are right. Come with me to my house for iftar."

We walked with slow steps on a paved road parallel to the covered market. Weakened by hunger and thirst, we passed through the city. Amr al-Qaysi remained silent, his prayer beads running through his fingers. I walked alongside, not breaking the reverence of his silence. I contented myself with looking at the façades of the houses, surrounded by pots of flowers and climbing plants, and listening to the sounds of the folk of Jerusalem preparing their iftar. The air still hummed with whispers and murmurs like prayers or hymns. From time to time, the smell of burning wood would strike us in the face. Sometimes we passed through streets crowded with Christian pilgrims, their possessions piled high upon their backs, their eyes staring and thirsty, some ringing bells they held in their hands and singing hymns. I was torn between staring at them and following the steps of Sheikh al-Qaysi. Perhaps noticing my astonishment and perplexity, he motioned with his head at a group of Christian pilgrims and said, "Palm Sunday is nigh. It is the seventh Sunday of the last and greatest fast before Easter Sunday. The week it starts with is called Holy Week, which it is claimed is the anniversary of Christ's entry into Jerusalem, and we call it the Sunday of the Palms and sometimes of the Olives, because the folk of Jerusalem received him like a conqueror with palms and decorated olive branches. The palm fronds and decorations are reused in most of the churches to celebrate this day."

Suddenly he slowed his pace. He was walking more comfortably and less stiffly the farther we went from the mosque, not appearing as severe as he had in the center of his students and disciples. "How is Baghdad?" he asked in his melodious voice.

I responded immediately: "I left it in an unhappy condition. Prices were rising and calamity reigned."

He held up a hand. "My boy, I am not asking you about the marketplaces. Tell me how the Voyagers are, the Just Monotheists."

Oh Lord! I only knew al-Hashimi and Seraj al-Furati, and perhaps Abu Abbas the blacksmith. I knew that he had asked this question to test me, that he might trust me. How should I answer? Trying to avoid answering the question as much as possible, carefully so as not to arouse his suspicion,

I said, "They are well. Or shall we say, they are in a status between two statuses."

He burst out laughing and patted me on the shoulder. "You cannot be in a status between two statuses unless you are a sinner! Heaven forbid they be sinners!" He went on, "How is al-Hashimi? Has he settled in Baghdad, or is he still running about planting God's green earth?"

I responded more confidently, "I left him planning his departure and preparing for it. I doubt that Baghdad is a suitable place for him to remain."

"Baghdad is angry," he muttered as if to himself. "There are coals burning under the ashes. The Bouhi soldiers are unhappy with the caliph. The people are unhappy with the soldiers. When tensions are high, there can be no prosperity, and everyone will remain afraid of what tomorrow may bring."

"You are correct," I said. "I have seen many hungry and homeless folk there, and the Ayyarin gangs prosper and proliferate under the eyes and ears of the guard."

He laughed bitterly. "The Ayyarin. The alleyways of Baghdad spoke the names of their leaders with terror: Aswad al-Zubad, Abu al-Arda, and Abu al-Nawabih." I guessed then that he was well acquainted with Baghdad. I did not wish to press him with questions: he appeared preoccupied, and weakened with fasting. He added, looking down, but with a great deal of eagerness and curiosity, "Are al-Qadir's men still persecuting those they call Mutazilites and heretics?"

"I could not see anything clearly," I said. "All I could see was that the police and guards were trying to prevent fights breaking out in mosques and discussion circles, to avoid bloodshed between the Sunnis and the Shiites. *Fitna* is still afoot after Sheikh al-Isfaraini burned the Shiite copy of the Qur'an that they say belonged to Abdullah ibn Masoud."

"That is an old *fitna*!" he said. "I mean, has the caliph announced his document that he set out to cut short those he calls 'the contentious and argumentative folk'?"

Before I could tell him what I knew of this matter and what I had seen at the sultan's procession in the marketplace of Karkh, two young passersby who appeared to be his students stopped us and kissed his head.

The road soon turned to the right, bringing us to a garden with a low wall of large and sturdy stones, the gathering dusk darkening the trees, twittering birds thick on the branches. The evening breezes were spreading the smell of fresh-cut foliage. A gate opened onto a garden path leading to a two-story house with a great green wooden door with two leaves; most doors I had seen in Jerusalem had only one.

It appeared that the birds had betrayed our arrival: before we arrived at the door, it opened with much noise and creaking. A slight boy in a clean blue caftan looked at me warily out of narrow blue eyes beneath a protruding forehead. He ran to Amr al-Qaysi, saying, "Welcome home, Master." He took his master's turban and caftan and hung them on the nearby stand.

"Tell the family to lay the table for iftar, Abdullah," said al-Qaysi, "and prepare a place for our guest to sleep tonight."

His hospitality took me unawares. Grateful, I turned to him and said, "Heaven reward you, but I shall not be a burden. I must return to my camel and my crate of books, for they are still outside the city walls. All I wish for is a safe place for my books—" I caught myself. "I mean the books in my possession, until I find a room in a boardinghouse for my stay in Jerusalem."

"Fear not," he said. "It is difficult to find a boardinghouse or a room at this time, for Jerusalem is overrun with pilgrims, but be glad. Tomorrow I shall find a place for you and your books, and you shall sell them carefully, at your leisure."

With a deep sigh, he walked farther into the house. I followed him. "Although you are young," he said, "a father's love for his children has not yet robbed you of your sleep. Choose for your books the best buyers and owners that you can, as though you were choosing a husband for your daughter, and be as careful of them as you would be careful where you sow your seed."

My eyebrows rose at the odd comparison, but he merely went on: "Mazid. You are a Voyager now. A Just Monotheist only accepts money that is pure and without taint, rising above the greed and insistence of merchants, who lie in wait like vultures awaiting a carcass. Voyagers are falcons perched on the highest peaks, rising above the seeds scattered about for the common folk and the riffraff." He smiled as we mounted two steps into a spacious, high-ceilinged reception room ringed with couches and pillows, faced entirely in bookshelves. "This is especially true as you are a bachelor, and have not suffered the hunger of another's stomach."

I looked at him, finding his words strange. "I mean," he explained, "you do not have offspring to feed."

His serving boy, Abdullah, came in just then, bearing a tray laden with various types of food, which he laid down between us before going to fetch a low table placed behind the door. The boy spread this with a clean cotton cloth, then placed the tray atop it, saying, "Eat, good sirs."

The banquet was prepared with love. I had not a moment's doubt that the one who had laid out the slices of lime, poured the soup, put out the dried fruit dipped in honey and butter, and set the spoons in a row was sending a letter of love to Amr al-Qaysi. This was certainly a wife who had awaited him the length of the day. How wonderful to come home to a house with a woman who has been all day awaiting your coming, where the very walls sing to celebrate your return. Her refreshing breath pours over your pillow every night, your feet touching soft, warm feet in your bed.

The minarets of Jerusalem rang out with the sunset prayers, as though the same cup of the river Kawthar in Paradise had been poured over them all at once. Amr al-Qaysi stole glances at me, in an attempt to divine what had distracted me for these few moments. "Come," he said, "let us eat. Tomorrow will come soon." He added, "Remember what I have told you. Be diligent and only sell the books to those who will hold them in their deserved esteem. You will have no trouble finding buyers in Jerusalem, especially as it is the season of Christian pilgrimage, and their priests and monks are eager for books and pay the highest prices for them."

There came to us the incessant noise of children from within the house. A small boy with a blond shock of hair and two missing front teeth poked his face around the door, then ran in and buried his face in the folds of Amr al-Qaysi's robe. He held him and inhaled the child's scent. "This is Qays, the apple of my eye, and the first of five children borne to me by Nour Dana, my Circassian slave girl, now the mother of my children." With a broad smile, he said, "I have followed the Prophet's saying and not married a cousin, as many do. There are none weaker than the children born of relatives, none stronger and better than the children of those who bear you no relation. The Arabs say 'Cousins are more patient,' but women not related to you bear better fruit."

He paused awhile, sipping a sweet drink smelling of flowers. He bowed his head. As though telling me a secret that was trying for him to tell, he said, "Nour Dana is a younger sister of Tamani, the mother of Caliph al-Qadir. But I have never tried to exploit my marriage to worm my way into the caliph's court. The day I signed the Mutazilites' petition, I could have spared my pen and myself; the caliph holds his late mother Tamani in high esteem and makes much of her memory. But being a Mutazilite is a charge I deny not, and an honor of which I am unworthy; and I shall not betray the Covenant of the Voyagers."

Qays tugged at his father's robe, and his father pushed him away and dismissed him from the room. "All that is desired is chosen," he said, "but not all that is chosen is desired, like beating a bright boy or drinking bitter medicine."

My hunger was sated, my thirst quenched, and the feebleness of my limbs from fasting reinvigorated. It was clear to me that al-Qaysi was a brilliant Voyager; his speech was articulate, steeped in wise sayings, proverbs, and valuable observations. It was rare to find a man with such wisdom so intertwined with his heart, mind, and tongue.

When we had performed the sunset prayers, I resolved on emptying my pockets of the last pieces of news I had that might interest my host. I said to him, "Baghdad is still abuzz with the news of Caliph al-Qadir bi-Allah bringing together the wise men, the clerics, and the eminent men of the sects of the Mushabbihah, the Shiites, and the Mutazilites. He held a banquet for them at his palace and brought out the sword and the leather beheading sheet. He laid out the banqueting tables in his court; then he prepared a document commanding them to relinquish and recant all their beliefs—and the sword and beheading sheet were the reward for whoever should refuse."

To my shock, al-Qaysi's face crumpled suddenly as though in pain or disgust. He choked out, weak and grieved, "That night, the beheading sheet was crimson leather, edged with wool. The executioner was masked. A smell of rot and decay came off him: I knew not whether it was the leather or his body that gave it off. It disgusted me so that I could not eat of the banquet." He was breathless, a slight tremor deep in his voice. "Perforce, I signed the document of repentance. And that was something I shall not cease repenting all my life." He sighed. "A group of preeminent Voyagers signed with me. Caliph al-Qadir was filled with rage against the Mutazilites that night, for the preachers of the court, to relieve the monotony of their idle existence, had gathered about him and told him, 'The Mutazilites are saying that good Muslims are infidels! They call them sinners and transgressors! They have ruled that good Muslims belong in Hellfire with the distorted logic of their twisted minds,' whereupon he instructed his ministers to start preparing the al-Qadir document for them and those like them. I would ask: Has it been issued to all and sundry, or not yet?"

I responded immediately: "They are passing around passages and lines from it, and are threatening people that it will be issued soon, and speak of it incessantly, but it has not been issued yet."

He contemplated the ceiling, running his hands through the hair at his temples. "I signed that night," he whispered, "having drunk a bowl of milk that the serving boys of the palace were bearing around over our heads, in the stead of the wine we were accustomed to being served in the palace. And I breathed not a word."

The wounds of Baghdad seemed still raw in al-Qaysi's breast: he expanded on his subject like a lion whose claws have been torn out and roars all the more fiercely. Where al-Hashimi had evidenced a nonchalance born of despair and a desire to depart, al-Qaysi's coals still burned bright, unquenched. I could see my fate starting to move in a direction from which I could not free myself.

"That night," he resumed, "when al-Qadir bi-Allah saw my silence and my frown, he concocted a scheme against me. He announced my appointment as the overseer of his stables: this would allow him to keep me under observation, while conveying the impression to me that he had privileged me and admitted me to his inner circle. But he was at bottom humiliating me: for the overseer of the stables, or what they call in Baghdad 'the Hoof and Trotter Club,' is responsible for every animal in the royal stables: horses, stallions, workhorses, mares, mules, donkeys, and camels, as well as overseeing the camel drivers and jockeys and giving them their pay.

"I spent a week in this position. When it concluded, I left the Circular City having resolved to leave; I quit Baghdad under cover of night, and never looked back. A few months later, I was followed by my family and my children. I settled here in Jerusalem under the wing of the Fatimids, where I intend to remain to the end of my days."

He dragged in a deep breath and turned to me with a weak smile. "I must cease. I have spoken too freely. A Voyager must be wary and not babble or chatter." He appeared to be attempting to dispel the melancholy that had overtaken him and filled his eyes, I could see, with tears. "Well, tell us, how many books are in your possession?"

I said haltingly, "I do not know precisely, my sheikh, but they must surely number from forty to sixty books and manuscripts, the preponderance of them from the House of Wisdom."

He nodded admiringly. "You have done well! Have you ventured to bear this quantity of books alone? Why, when I left Baghdad, the people of that city were cursing the Voyagers and the Mutazilites, saying, 'God damn the Mutazilites, for they muddy the waters and rend the tenets of religion!' Did not that quantity of books alert the guards as you left Baghdad, or provoke their curiosity? Did it not surprise the folk of the caravan that brought you here?" He did not wait for an answer. He merely smiled as he clapped me on the shoulder. "Al-Hashimi knows whom to choose, indeed! The sons of the desert are brave of heart!"

I bowed my head, looking at the floor. This was not out of modesty, but from a fear that he might see, deep in my eyes, a cowardly bird that quailed at the sight of blood. However, Fate was clearly pushing me down this path, and I could not escape it.

The birds were now asleep. The garden was quiet. Through the windows, the scent of flowers and rain-dewed leaves wafted in. An ecstasy flowed through my veins, whether from the spiced food I had consumed or from this brilliant man's conversation I knew not. I felt that I was embarking on a hard and troublesome road alongside him, leading up to a falcon's nest.

The room they had prepared for me was a small, elegant guest room by the entrance. We stood at the door, and al-Qaysi said, "You will spend the night here."

Red-faced, searching vainly for words of thanks, I said, "Sir, I know not how—"

He interrupted me, laying a hand on my shoulder with a friendly smile. "Did they pass on the seven commandments to you?"

"Yes, yes!" I said enthusiastically. "Seraj al-Furati passed them to me."

He held up a hand to stop me, looking deep into my soul. "Do not tell me. The commandments are never the same for any two people. You must remember yours. See what answers they bring you." He clapped me on the shoulder. "Good night. I shall wake you for *suhour*."

After the *suhour* meal, we went to the mosque for the dawn prayers. At the gate, I heard the beat of wings approaching. The mosque attendant was putting out the lamps; inside the mosque, a group of men who had been up praying all night were gathered in a dhikr circle praising God, swaying this way and that as they repeated, "Glory to Him who never sleeps and never ends! Glory to the Self-subsisting Sustainer of All, Glory to the Ever-living, Glory to the King, Glory to the Most Holy, Glory to the Lord of the Angels and of Souls, Glory to Him in the highest." As the air vibrated with their voices, I heard again the rustle of wings.

Outside the mosque, on our way home, the roads were subsumed in the deep blue of the Kingdom of Jerusalem. Amr al-Qaysi's voice sounded deep and melodious in the valley of dawn, like a hymn. "I will go now and see to some affairs of mine. In the fullness of the morning, a Christian priest will come to you, and you will go with him and stay in a room prepared for you at his house." Before I could ask him why he had chosen this priest, he said, "Jerusalem is bursting with

Christian pilgrims at this time of year. The Byzantine soldiers protect the passage of the caravans from Byzantium; there is food and water along their paths; and so there are rarely any dangers for those caravans, except for the inclement weather on the Anatolian Mountains. Others come from Macedonia or from Rome. There are huge numbers of caravans, and Jerusalem can barely hold them all."

He went on: "They are claiming that the millennium has turned, and they believe that Christ will appear to the faithful; and, so thinking, great hordes of foreigners have commenced pouring into the Holy Lands from Byzantium. The pilgrims do not wish only to visit; some have resolved to remain in Jerusalem until their death and be buried here."

He fell silent for a while, then resumed. "The burning of the Church of the Resurrection, site of the Holy Sepulcher, by order of the ruler of Egypt, has only increased their conviction that Christ will rise again soon. It is said that they number seven thousand men and women—and some say ten or twelve thousand."

He added in a whisper, "In the midst of all of this, you can sell your wares easily—" He broke off suddenly, as though he had been about to tell me something else, but stopped himself. "Goodbye, then," he said, taking the garden path leading away from his house.

My she-camel, Shubra, paid my arrival no heed; she turned her face away from me as though repulsed by my arrival, which reminded her of fatigue and suffering. She chewed her cud, ruminating nonchalantly. I nobly endured her lukewarm reception of me, undid her reins, and set her free. "Go," I said. "I hereby free you: you are at liberty. You have the right to live the remaining years of your life free from the humiliation of slavery."

A gold dinar summoned those who would help me carry my crate of books to the house of Amr al-Qaysi. "Truly," I muttered to myself, "people gather around those who have gold!"

No sooner was I alone with the box in my room than I rushed to examine the books. They were stacked in tight piles, holding hands and terrified like small, hungry grouse chicks seeking shelter from the beak of an eagle.

## God's Locusts

The house was quiet, the cries and giggles of small children reaching me from afar. I was only interrupted by the serving boy, Abdullah, who poked his big forehead into the room from time to time to ask me if I needed anything, to which I shook my head with a grateful smile. I spent the morning looking through Amr al-Qaysi's library. On a shelf to the back, I found some manuscripts, half worn away: they were pages from Aristotle's *Organon*. I decided to copy it out again and edit it according to the copy I had in my possession, and present it to al-Qaysi.

There were collections by al-Mutanabbi, Abu Nawas, and others, and some works, such as al-Isfahani's *Aghani* and Abu Hayan's work, which I had read in Baghdad but felt an overwhelming desire to reread. A bizarre ecstasy filled my body, the tremor that customarily overcame me in the presence of books. They seemed to me like unopened jars and welling springs: perhaps it was this passion that steered me away from adventures in moneymaking or trade or even dalliances with women, keeping me chaste and careful. My lusts were packed away in a concealed pocket in my mind, coming to me only in my most secret dreams. It was only Zahira who had shaken me to the core and scattered my composure to the winds; the rest I could keep at arm's length, immune to their temptations. Was I chaste and virtuous, or was it merely that I had yet to enter the demons' battlefield?

What book should I give to Amr al-Qaysi? His generosity and hospitality left me tongue-tied. Or should I let him choose? Should I give him a translated work, although these were the most expensive and doubtless the most sought-after by the Christians, or a work by al-Kindi? I had a valuable manuscript by Ibn al-Haytham about music, which I had acquired from Sheikh Zakir in Basra. It would doubtless capture his interest. Finally, I settled on giving him the book of the Brethren of Purity, although they were garrulous and a great deal had been attributed to them that they had not said, and they said a great deal without evidence or proof. Finally, they hold that their imam is rationality, though often they deride the rational mind and mock it. But perhaps Amr al-Qaysi would approve of what they said: "There are rational people who will not accept imitation, but require proof, reasons, and truths." Al-Qaysi would no doubt like this, in addition to the copy of his book of Aristotle.

In any case, I had only looked so far into the top layer of the box of books, and I knew not what lay concealed at the bottom: as I fell deep into the ecstasy of turning pages, I heard Abdullah saying, "Samaan, the priest, is at the door waiting for you."

I adjusted my appearance and hurried to the door to greet him. I found a venerable gentleman standing a few paces away from the entrance, underneath an apple tree in the front garden, hands clasped in front of him, head lowered, in the black garment of a monk with a yellow patch the size of a man's hand on his robe and a wooden cross hung around his neck. I ran to him and greeted him. But for a smattering of white hairs in his beard, his broad-browed face had not lost its freshness. He had delicate features and a ruddy tint to his face.

It became clear to me from the first glance that his eyes were filled with a weighty sorrow, so that one might think he was coming from a graveyard or a funeral. Sorrow shone in his eyes, accompanied by a degradation that was painful to see in such a man. I greeted him and clasped his hand in both of my own. He was looking at me hard and deeply. To cut short the inevitable embarrassment and diffidence that must exist between two strangers, I said, "I shall bring my effects from within and accompany you."

*

I followed him as he walked quietly and smoothly through the city paths. We passed through archways, stone gateways, and paved squares. We took the path leading down from the Damascus Gate and headed north through the fabric market, then the spice market, then the meat market, then the cotton market, and the goldsmiths' district, followed by the carpet weavers' market, until I thought we should reach the end of the world.

Before the priest turned into a side street and began to walk faster with his hands behind his back, we entered a clean, bright street whose folk had arranged pots of flowers and myrtle outside their homes. They gave Samaan the priest a friendly greeting, smiling at him and calling him "Father." The press of Christian pilgrims around us grew thicker, waving palm fronds and chanting sweet, melancholy hymns, sometimes stopping the priest to kiss his hand. I divined his high status among them, which only increased my respect and veneration for him, belying the meek and broken look he had on al-Qaysi's doorstep. This, however, disquieted me: he was a man whom many knew and many sought out, and had numerous visitors, which might draw attention to me and the books in my possession.

The path opened out onto a circular plaza surrounded by houses. In the center were some blossoming orange trees. In a corner of the plaza, Samaan stopped at a door in the front of the building and pulled a key out of his pocket.

With our first steps into the house, a breeze wafted over us bearing the perfume of a fragrant plant with a spicy scent not unlike that of the Mount of Olives. We sat upon wooden seats in a passageway by the door, with cushions of a delicate white fabric with worked edges. We had barely sat down when Samaan tore off his cross and sighed deeply. He stretched his head and neck as though to get the stiffness out of them, then disappeared into the house.

201

I took to looking at my surroundings. A blooming oasis, where everything was dewy and refreshing, as though an aquatic creature lived here, making it cool and moist. I recalled the words of my sheikh, Muhammad al-Tamimi, about Christians: how they were unclean and did not wash their private parts with their left hand, as they should, and did not bathe after lovemaking, as they should. The only good thing about them, he said, was that their women, especially the Byzantines, were fertile, with childbearing hips.

Samaan returned with a brass tray laden with a glass jug and some glasses, his broken demeanor quite gone, as though his soul had been set free upon his arrival in the house and his removal of the heavy cross around his neck. He poured a drink for me with the same sweet smell that filled the house. I asked him what it was, and he said, "Anise."

"Can I keep the glass with me," I said, "and drink it at iftar?"

With a friendly smile, he said, "Of course. I shall have them put it in your room. May the Lord bless both our fasts," he continued, since in this millennium, the seasons of fasting for Muslims and Christians coincided. As he spoke, my attention was caught by his beard: it was squared off carefully and his nails were clean and neatly trimmed. As he spoke, he brushed down his sleeves to ensure they were smart and in order. "Amr al-Qaysi tells me of your valuable collection of books," he said. "I doubt that we will have trouble finding a safe place for them in our house." With an abrupt laugh, he said, "Perhaps we can buy some from you. The pilgrims will definitely take many of them."

"My main concern," I said pleadingly, "is to conceal them in a safe place, away from prying eyes and the curious folk of Jerusalem."

"We pray to the Lord to preserve them," he said in troubled, choked tones. "We managed to rescue some of the books from the library of the Church of the Resurrection before it was burned down, and they were distributed among people's homes. We prefer that they should stay there until we gather enough funds to rebuild it. But for now," he concluded, "it is sufficient to pray."

I know not why, but he seemed wary when speaking of the Church of the Resurrection: he was not forthcoming with details. But I felt that it was the source of the grief at the bottom of his soul, although not the only one. He had a chestful of sorrows.

I excused myself, saying I would return before sundown. "With the sunset prayers," he said politely as he withdrew, "we hope you will share our ascetic, simple table, as simple as that of Christ. We are also fasting. Your room will be ready."

I resolved to go to the market and buy a bag, then go to the box of books and begin to move them into the house gradually; a great chest carried through the streets of Jerusalem would naturally arouse suspicion.

It was clear from Samaan's speech that he was extremely respectful of the books in my possession, and he hinted that he would pay a goodly sum for them. Still, I was full of restlessness and unease. Despite this, I desired to set my affairs in order so as to attend the afternoon discussion circle of Amr al-Qaysi. I had a room in the Christians' Alley for the duration of my stay in Jerusalem, a pleasant heavenly blessing that would keep suspicion away from my books.

When I entered the mosque, al-Qaysi's discussion circle had commenced. His deep voice was ringing out, filling the curves of the stone archways. His tones were careful and measured, only entering your mind with the greatest certainty. I stood waiting in that mysterious status between certainty and doubt, between the Unseen and this world: it seemed that my perplexity would abide forever, in a status between two statuses.

When I approached the circle, I found an argument brewing between al-Qaysi and two young men in his circle, one with a thick red beard and the other young and devoid of facial hair. The latter was frowning and saying, "The Christians are like locusts! Jerusalem is teeming with them! They gnaw on everything! They have raised prices, devoured our stores, filled our streets, scattered their debauched women with their rippling flesh all about, and settled in our city's houses, following the mumbo jumbo of their holy men who tell them it is the year Christ shall appear now that it has been a thousand years since his death. They are waiting for him to rise again!"

"Jerusalem is ours!" said the owner of the red beard. "It is where our Prophet walked and ascended on his journey to Paradise. They are nothing but heretical polytheists. Although the Fatimid caliph, may God grant him long life, destroyed the Church of the Resurrection and burned it down, they still walk around drunk and pray with their crosses, ringing their bells and filling the air with their incense and their wailing!"

Someone spoke from the circle—he was hidden by a pillar so that I could not see him. "Where are you, Muslim clerics? Where is your role, now that Jerusalem is being ravished by Christians? Where is the purification of the whitest seat of religion, now that Aleppo has fallen, and they are approaching like locusts, and those we see around us crowding the streets are naught but spies for their armies? Expect the armies of Byzantium to attack us at any moment!"

This was the ball of fire that they flung into the hands of Amr al-Qaysi. But his voice did not change; his tone was the same. He turned to the youth with the red beard. "Do you say that they entered Jerusalem," he asked, "or that they were already here? This is where our Prophet was born, and their prophet, Jesus. Here he is buried; from here he rose again. They have been here for hundreds of years. There is naught between us but the Pact of Umar, which protects their persons and their moneys and their places of worship. Do you pretend to be holier than the caliph Umar and think yourself better than he?" His tone sharpened. "Beware contention, my boy. Too much argumentation is a sign only of weakness." He added, "There is no absolute right, nor absolute wrong. The Prince of the Faithful, Ali ibn Abu Talib, has said, 'A part of this is taken, and a part of that is taken, and they are thus mingled.'"

The muezzin of the mosque, in his usual spot next to Sheikh al-Qaysi, did not miss his opportunity to interject something or other he felt would please the sheikh, or air some of his scarce knowledge. He added mockingly, "You are playing a game of one-upmanship with the Holy Qur'an itself! Does not God say in verse eighty-two of the Sura of al-Maida, *'Nearest among them in love to the believers wilt thou find those who say, "We are Christians": because among these are men devoted to learning and men who have renounced the world, and they are not arrogant.'* Also, they are bound to us by a treaty and they are dhimmi, and the Prophet has said, 'He who murders a dhimmi shall never see Paradise.'"

Despite the tone of reproach in the muezzin's voice, I was confident that he would have quite a different opinion if Sheikh al-Qaysi contradicted him; it appeared that the awe-inspiring presence of the sheikh had affected the muezzin, for he always agreed with him and seized the smallest chance to praise every word he said.

Amr al-Qaysi motioned to me to approach where he sat. I was flustered: I had no desire to attract attention and arouse curiosity, nor to be roped into the task of the notetaker that had enslaved me in Baghdad and kept me from the joys of contemplation and meditation by listening to the conversations in the circles around me. I wished to be calm and retiring in my stay here, like the wary and fearful cranes by the river walls.

It would appear that all discussion circles are alike: here, in Baghdad, and in Basra. There are brilliant students and common folk and riffraff, all congregating around their sheikh to hear what they want to hear. But let the sheikh say something unfamiliar to them, and they burst into a frenzy; therefore, he must be armed with knowledge and arguments, and prepared to throw the stone of proof at the head of the troublemaker.

It appears that when the student is ready, the teacher comes to him. I was the first one in need of that stone, to silence the whispering doubt inside me about the uncleanness of the houses of Christians, their food and drink, and my unease about the time I was to spend in a Christian home.

Amr al-Qaysi said to me as we were leaving the mosque, "Those young men are ruled by the common law, their anger, and their lusts, more than evidence, proof, and argument. Therefore, they are ruled by predestination rather than free will, and will remain followers as long as their minds are inactive."

I arrived at the priest's house as the sun was seeking a path to descend behind the mountains. When I made to knock at his door, I found it standing ajar. He called to me from within. I went into a courtyard with two olive trees in the center; at the farthest end beneath its wall, a table had been set up next to the mouth of an oven blazing merrily in the wall. By it stood a thin woman baking, trying to force a smile onto her disgruntled face. The table was set with round earthenware plates filled with broad beans, olives, black-eyed peas, garlic steeped in vinegar, olive oil, and hot loaves.

Samaan gestured to the woman: "My sister, Zulaykha."

Zulaykha's cheeks were sunken and her nose hooked. She resembled the women who had been with us on the caravan coming from Baghdad: withered, nothing like the women of Byzantium with the great hips that the sultans chose to bear them boys. But Zulaykha's food looked delicious: and her figure like a dry stick, and her severe temperament, were no doubt what had made this house so fresh and welcoming. By her side crawled an infant that she gave a piece of dough with which to amuse himself. He tired of it and took to crying; she placed some loaves in the oven, picked him up, and held him, gave him her breast for a while, then rushed back to her loaves.

The sun had not yet set. They were waiting for the sunset so that I would be at liberty to eat with them. The silence at the table was uncomfortable, so I told the priest the story—in a disapproving tone—of what had taken place at the mosque. "Pay them no heed," he said jocularly. "If they tasted the wine in our cellars, they would forget their evil in an instant. Have you not heard the verse: 'They asked, "Are you a Muslim?" I said yes, on the outside; / But with my gullet full of wine, a Christian inside.'?"

I was delighted at this playful, even impish, side of the sober Father Samaan. And to think I had been nervous about living in a dark room in the house of a stern priest who, I thought, would make my life miserable.

After the Christian banquet, he led me up to my room, then took his leave, saying he must be up early the next day. The pilgrims were due to carry an olive tree from the Church of St. Lazarus to the ruins of the Church of the Resurrection, which were a long way apart. They would sing hymns and say prayers all the way, carrying the cross, and he must be with them to protect them from any would-be troublemakers who sought to block their path. "If you require anything, you may ask it of Zulaykha, and she will bring it to you. Forgive her for not smiling: she is a grieving widow. She lost her husband in the clashes, which still continue, between the Christians and the Fatimid soldiers. These confrontations have never ceased, not since they tore down the Church of the Resurrection and defiled the grave of the Son of God."

## My Heart, Speak to Me of God

The streets were packed with pilgrims. Most were on foot, a small number on donkey back. Most of them, especially those from Byzantium, wore odd clothes and robes: pantaloons topped with shirts, coats of leather or fur, and wide cotton *gallabiya*s topped with embroidered caftans, all without a turban. The women's heads were covered with thin veils.

The beauty of the Byzantine women stole my breath. Their fine features, their radiant complexions . . . when they were next to me, I wished to dip my fingers into their cheeks, which shone like springs untouched by heat or dust. Each group of them was preceded by a man ringing a bell, whereupon they would sing their hymns behind him, tears of deep grief in their eyes. They waved palm fronds and olive branches; sometimes they suffered a small boy to sit on the trunk of the olive tree, whereupon the rest of the little ones would cry and squall and complain, asking for food and a respite from the long walk.

My room was full of books. My head was filled with the command of Seraj al-Din al-Furati: "Beware of selling them to those without the sensibility to grasp their worth, without the intellect to plunge into their oceans. Do not cast your pearls before swine."

The way was crowded with pilgrims, which forced me to take a serpentine path, brushing shoulders with all, careful to keep the orange plaza behind me and my face north, toward al-Qaysi's house. I began to feel reassured, for in this great press of bodies, footsteps, and noise, none would concern themselves with a desert Arab carrying a bag filled with books. "Hallelujah!" they cried, and chanted Surianese and Arabic hymns in melancholy tones. The current of pilgrims embraced me: they drove me to whisper along with them, as if wrapped in the warmth of a great abaya that enfolded me.

I listened to the man chanting in the front: "Come unto me, all ye that labor and are heavy laden, and I will give you rest. Take my yoke upon you, and learn of me; for I am meek and lowly in heart: and ye shall find rest unto your souls."

With my bag stuffed with books and manuscripts over my shoulder, I suddenly recalled the warning of Amr al-Qaysi:

"Beware! Do not take them to the common market or to the booksellers', for the spies of the Fatimid caliph are everywhere in the marketplace."

The hymns filled the path with a sense of security. Was it a true security, or the shock of being struck in the face like the overpowering silence of a disaster? The air sang with the voices of the pilgrims: "Hallelujah." The Christians of Jerusalem had gone to bed one night and awoken to find their church, the Holy Sepulcher, the tomb of their prophet, burned to ash. I looked at the sky over our heads. Clouds had begun to gather, portending heavy rain. Jerusalem was a city shadowed by clouds of discontent: no sooner did a cloud disperse than the horizon grew thick with another, raining blood and tears onto its streets.

As I was transferring another load of books from al-Qaysi's house, I hardly recognized the house of Samaan but for its bright green windows, so crowded was the plaza outside with a group of pilgrims just arrived. They were babbling in foreign languages, calling to one another, and unloading their belongings and supplies from mule-drawn carts and setting them out before the house of Samaan. I was unsettled: what should I do? Should I advance, or draw back?

Samaan, who was standing at the door with a small but welcoming smile, appeared to catch sight of me. He waved a hand and motioned me closer. "You can go up to your room, Mazid," he said. "These are pilgrims just arrived from Antakya."

I picked my way through their effects with difficulty, without raising my eyes to them. I walked with my head down, listening to them talk and make noise in a language that sounded familiar. It was not the Arabic spoken by Samaan, but it sounded similar: I managed to make out some words. As I followed him through the inner courtyard of the house, Father Samaan said, "My aunt, her husband, her son, and two daughters. You are fortunate in that your room has an outer balcony with stairs leading directly into the street: you can come in and go out without the embarrassment of passing through the house."

I could tell that Father Samaan was implicitly conveying to me the bounds I should keep to when moving around in the house—I could not walk about the house freely. This pleased me, for I too required some liberty, and I did not wish to be embarrassed by having to pass among their womenfolk and their rooms. Besides, Zulaykha's brow was always furrowed against me: whenever she saw me going upstairs, she fixed me with a scrutiny that bore slight disapproval. I would nod to her respectfully, but she never responded.

On my way inside, I caught a fleeting glimpse of them as they attempted to find a comfortable spot for a crippled boy sitting on a chair borne by two men. When I arrived in my room, the noise beneath the house continued for a long while, until I finally leaned over the balcony. I could not see the gate, for it was concealed by the western wall of the house, while the branches of the orange tree all but covered the inner courtyard before me. The scent of the orange blossoms was everywhere, overpowering. It penetrated my soul, and filled me with simultaneous pain and ecstasy. Through the branches, I spied the crippled boy seated on a chair surrounded by pillows. A fair-haired girl was placing a small table before his seat, and as I watched, she lifted his legs and placed them upon it. I could not make out his features from where I stood, but his golden hair was parted in the middle and hung down to his shoulders. He spoke in a loud voice I could hear from above: perhaps it was a recitation of some sort. Zulaykha approached him with a small tray bearing food. "The Son of God," he cried out. "Man does not live by bread alone!"

I know not why he said this, when he was gobbling up the loaves on the tray with gusto. Perhaps he was expressing his joy at arriving at the City of God—or the Son of God. I knew nothing of Christian heresy. I must find out from Samaan their disagreement with the Nestorians over the two natures of Jesus Christ—his humanity and his divinity. I had not grasped the finer points of their disagreement in the books I had studied in the khan. Those who reported them had always made light of the whole affair.

Although the room Samaan had prepared for me was no larger than my room in the Khan al-Hashimi in Karkh, it was clean and bright, like sleeping in the heart of a jasmine blossom. In addition, it opened onto a balcony that formed part of the rooftop of the house: it overlooked the inner courtyard on the east, and to the north of the balcony were stairs leading onto the street. The room was simply furnished, with nothing but a wooden box to hold possessions, a strong, narrow bed with cotton bolsters, and a lantern in a triangular stone-framed alcove. The great advantage of the room was the large window overlooking the balcony and a grapevine. This window must bring the morning in early in all its awe-inspiring glory. If the sun did not wake me, the cooing of the doves would surely accomplish it.

I sat and placed the bag of books in my lap to see what I had brought from the box: I had just grasped at whatever I could reach. There was Hippocrates's *On Regimen in Acute Diseases*; *The Humors* by al-Kindi; al-Farabi's critique of Aristotle's *Metaphysics*; Aristotle's *Ethics*, translated by Hanin ibn Ishaq for the House of Wisdom; *Physics* by the same author; and Yahya ibn Uday's translation of Aristotle's *Poetics*. Finally, there was Ibn al-Muqaffa's translation of *Kalila wa Dimna*. Each of these was a treasure in its own right, and I had no intention of leaving more than this in Jerusalem.

I was glad I had found *Ethics* among these, so that I could start to copy it. Every day I would copy five pages; I would then have it bound and would give it to Sheikh al-Qaysi to replace the tattered copy in his library.

How would I sleep in a room where my only coverlet was a cloud of perfume, and my companions great Arabs and prodigies of Greek wisdom?

Before sundown, I heard a swishing and whispering at the door to my room. Was it birds or cats? I opened the door a crack, and waited awhile before looking out. Two girls, ten arm spans from the door to my room, were hidden in the branches of the orange tree. The sunset light had spilled over their hair, turning it the bright gold of chrysanthemums. They wore bright cotton clothing. One was fair-skinned and a little taller than the other, who was barely out of childhood. Both had delicate fingers that were plucking orange blossoms from the branches of the tree overhanging my room.

When they glimpsed me, they drew back shyly. Then the lighter-skinned one said, "I'm sorry! Did our talking disturb you? We're just trying to pluck some flowers. We'll make sweets with half, and the other half we will carry home. We have a small soap-making workshop there."

From her halting speech and many pauses to remember words, I could tell that she spoke Arabic with difficulty. But the girls were like two radiant streams sparkling in a grove, or like angels from my dreams that had landed on the balcony. I thanked the Lord that I had cut off my braids and trimmed my beard so I didn't frighten these two doves!

I approached them. There was a pile of blossoms in the corner, conveyed there by the evening breeze. I scooped up a double handful and carried them over to the girls: when I drew near, I could see that the fairer-skinned girl's face shone like a loaf of bread on hot coals. With naive softness, she said, "We shall repay you with the jam we make to celebrate the end of our long fast."

It was several days until I tasted the jam. I spent those days going to and fro between the house of Amr al-Qaysi and the house of Father Samaan to move all the books and stack them in their boxes. I placed some of them in the alcove and gazed at them with pride. That was before the light led me to the church of the Christians.

## The Saturday of Light

I woke with the dawn mists to the sound of footsteps rushing hither and yon beneath me in the house, water being poured, furniture being moved, and women calling to one another. I leapt out of bed and hurried outside, looking discreetly through the branches of the orange trees to see what was taking place below. The women had emptied the courtyard of furniture and were pouring water and soapsuds onto it, scrubbing the tiles and the fountain. Then they poured more water and swept it out of the courtyard with brooms of straw; they beat the rugs and draped them over the edge of the fountain and trimmed the plants around the orange tree.

They seemed to catch sight of me, and I retreated quickly to my room. I heard a knock on my door like the beating of wings. The younger of the two girls was holding a hot fresh loaf. There was nothing more beautiful than this loaf, save the smile she wore. The fairer-skinned girl was carrying a plate of the orange blossom honey and a glass with some drink in it. She whispered, still shy and hesitant, "Blessed Resurrection. This is sage, the drink of the Virgin: it clears the blood and the mind." Then she held out the plate. "Your share of the orange blossom honey."

I had no idea what to say in response in order to make her stay as long as possible. Her eyelashes were thick, I saw now, in the light of the morning sun on her cheeks. When I remained silent, staring at her, smiling like an idiot, she went on, saying, "Father Samaan says that we are all going to mass now. If you want anything from the house before we lock the outer door . . ."

I finally came to myself and said, "To which church are you going?"

"The Church of the Resurrection," she said. "It's the Saturday of Light, and the sacred flame will come out of the Holy Sepulcher and light up the world, and the candles in our hands, too."

Meaning to correct her naive beliefs, I said, "You mean you will light candles at the Holy Sepulcher."

"No!" she said. "Each of us will bear an unlit candle, and when we go around the Sepulcher, they will be lit by the light of the Lord!"

I nodded, unable to argue with these two radiant doves. All I said was, "When will the door be locked?"

Putting a hand on the shoulder of the younger girl to go, she responded, "We're only waiting for the men to help us carry Hamilcar's chair to the church." I guessed that Hamilcar was her crippled brother.

I retreated inside and placed her gifts aside for my breakfast. Such joy surged through my blood that I could not stay in the room, so I went out onto the balcony. The morning touched all things and made them unfurl: breezes sighed like the breathing of a great and magnificent woman passing through Jerusalem, carrying the spring in her wake. Doves fluttered, murmurs sounded, the smell of bread filled the air, horses neighed from the nearby fields: it was the Saturday of Light. What light engulfed the place! She said that they saw a flame coming out of the Sepulcher that became light. There was no reason I should not go with them and watch the sacred light illuminate their candles. I resolved to go. I would spend my morning with them and see the mumbo jumbo of the Christians for myself.

Their brother needed men to carry his chair. I would be one of them.

I washed and prepared myself, then hurried down the stairs for fear they would leave without me. Their chants and hallelujahs reached my ears: "This is the day that the Lord has made! Let us rejoice and be glad in it! Your light is the Light of the World! Light of creation entire!"

When I arrived downstairs, they had gathered in the courtyard of the house, wearing brightly colored clothes, with silk sashes around their waists. The women had adorned their hair with flowers and the men had waxed their mustaches and turned the corners up. I barely recognized Zulaykha: she was a changed woman. It was then that I realized makeup could turn a barn owl into a woman.

I hesitated, not knowing what to say, then repeated what the girl had said to me: "Blessed Resurrection."

They smiled in response, looking at each other as though watching a performing monkey. I offered to help them carry Hamilcar's chair: the priest was delighted, and brought a small chair made of wood and ropes and asked me to sit upon it until they completed their preparations. They were unhurried, occupied in discussing a recipe for some remedy for the cripple—a poultice of powdered sage, the Virgin Mary's plant, mixed with the milk of a mother whose infant was about to walk or was taking its first steps. The mother was saying, "After this recipe, the Lord sends the angels of walking. They surround a person to lift them from the baseness of the ground to the dignity of standing erect."

It appeared that they had prepared this recipe, and Zulaykha was walking around them proudly, carrying her infant who had been taking his first steps in the courtyard, while Hamilcar's knees were wrapped in the poultice, covered with green silky fabric. Hamilcar was sitting among them, fresh-faced and radiant, his blue eyes of startling clarity, so transparent that I had at first thought him blind. His face was cheerful, resembling the images of Jesus hung up in their churches. His mother was dry and withered, all beauty gone from her face. He leaned his head and shoulders against her. I gazed at her, astounded that the womb of this ugly creature could have produced the two doves and Hamilcar as well. I thought of Hassan, who always said, "Do not be deluded by the beauty of Byzantine women in the first flush of youth: they age early."

It appeared that everyone had surrounded Hamilcar and was preoccupied with him, except for the father, who had slumped over a nearby chair, complaining of continual weakness and thirst, until Samaan turned to him and said, "You have the symptoms of sugar in the blood."

The father responded, barely able to speak: "I know not. Possibly. My heart beat faster after eating the orange blossom jam."

"All last night he was weak and sleepless," the mother said. "He sweated without cease, and went to urinate constantly. Be with us, Blessed Virgin!"

Father Samaan rose and said, "We shall see." Asking the father to accompany him, he exited through the rear door to the barn behind the house, which supplied the house with milk and eggs and chicken. He was absent for a while. Suddenly we heard the priest calling loudly, "Come and see!"

Unable to contain my curiosity, I rushed with the others to find that the ants had collected around a mound of sand damp with the urine of the ailing father. Proud of the accuracy of his diagnosis, Father Samaan said, "This is the sickness of sugar in the blood. A strict regimen is necessary, that your blood may not consume you."

I never imagined that the pile of sand damp with urine would one day confer upon me a doctor's degree.

Samaan preceded us to the church. Two carriages stopped outside the door, each drawn by two powerful mules, one to convey Hamilcar and the other for the women. They mounted, carrying white candles garlanded with myrtle and ornamented crosses. Zulaykha was smiling, her resentment dissipated: she had brought baskets of bread stuffed with boiled eggs, carrots, and other vegetables, a small jar of olive oil, and some herbs. The two doves wore garlands of flowers on their heads, making them shine and take flight like birds of good omen. When our carts passed each other on the road, the fair-skinned girl would smile and wave at us, filling my heart with childlike joy.

The entrance of the street was decorated with wooden arches adorned with garlands of jasmine and leaves, hung about with colored kerchiefs. Everyone passed beneath them singing hymns: "The Redeemer hath returned . . . He hath risen again." They rang the bells they held in their hands, as the spire that had held the church bells was now burnt to the ground.

Today their Redeemer returned. I recalled the folk of Baghdad, also still waiting for the Mahdi who had gone into the cave to come out . . . everyone was waiting. I knew not if either of these dear departed had resolved to return.

Amr al-Qaysi had told me in secret two days ago to be careful in the Christians' Alley, as they were justifiably resentful, and often lost their composure when they looked at the charred remains of their church. When I arrived, I could not but sympathize. The sight of the ruined church was indeed enough to make anyone lose his wits. The church had no roof, and some of its walls had been destroyed. What had been the floor was covered with charred wood and shattered glass, swept to the sides; some of the mothers had leapt over the stones of one of the demolished walls into the interior of the building, carrying their children on their hips for fear their tiny feet would be cut by the stained glass shards.

Samaan saw me looking at the ruins in dismay and immediately pushed his way through the rows of people to me. "Welcome to the Church of the Lord, Mazid," he said. "I wish you had seen it in a better state, before it burned down." Then he became occupied with trying to clear a space for the chair of the crippled boy, whom I could barely make out among the crowds pouring into the church, its walls, and its soot-stained stones. Through one of the gaps, the Mosque of Umar could be seen.

*

We placed Hamilcar's chair close to one of the priests, a man wearing an imposing robe and a giant headdress that set him apart from the rest of the holy men. He knelt and sang by the entrance of the sepulcher, sobbing and wailing so violently I could barely make out his voice saying, "A single drop of Christ's blood is enough to make me pure; a single touch of Christ's hand is enough to set me free!"

He appeared to be an important personage, surrounded by a group of priests who protected him from the press of people around. He stopped weeping suddenly and sprang to his feet, then strode toward what was left of a dome inside the church with steps leading deep into the earth, which was the sepulcher. This behavior seemed tantamount to announcing that it was time to pray: a great murmur went through those assembled in the church and they all raised their hands, palms open, looking at the sky as though waiting for the light to rain down upon them.

All around the opening of the tomb there were murmurings and hymns: the priest went down into it, and there was a press of bodies like the waves of the sea, raising their candles on high, awaiting a light from a great candle three arm spans tall, which the high priest had taken down into the Sepulcher, and would come out lit with his light. The smell of the tallow candles and some unfamiliar herb . . . I stayed close to Hamilcar, fearing that his chair might be overturned in the crush. His face was shining and his eyes, filled with tears, glanced about him as he clutched his knees tightly. Suddenly he motioned to me to come closer and whispered in my ear, "Now a great light shall come out of the Sepulcher. Only pray. Pray with all your heart."

I was at a loss for words in the rush of that moment, but I found myself murmuring with them:

A great light shall burst forth from the Sepulcher of the
    Lord Jesus;

218

Shine, O Jerusalem, shine with a great light!
Shine with fire, shine with the Lord's flame so bright;
Kyrie eleison.

Suddenly it was as though two flashes of lightning met above our heads in a line whose arc extended from east to west. I trembled and my knees all but gave way. I looked around me, shivering: the candle of the high priest glowed softly as it glided out of the Sepulcher, alight with a burning flame. He raised it up high, pale and bewildered with joy.

The crowd burst into a frenzy, pushing and shoving, all holding out their candles to receive the light, to light their candles with the Lord's holy flame. Samaan had a long candle with him, lavishly decorated and ornamented and wound about with myrtle, which he extended and managed to set alight. He then lit the candles of those with him. As I had no candle, the fair-skinned girl gave me a white one. "Pass your fingers over it," Samaan said to me. "Its flame gives light but does not burn."

I did so and felt no heat: my fingers came back unscathed. I murmured verse sixty-nine of the Sura of al-Anbiya: *"Allah said: O Fire, be coolness and safety upon Abraham."*

Samaan heard me: for the first time, I saw a brightness in his eyes that broke through his sorrow and broken demeanor. He said to me with conviction, "It is not fire, but light."

The two sisters' faces were red and their eyes swollen with tears as they swayed and repeated with the others, "Christ is risen again. . . . Kneel in joy, he is risen again!"

Those with bells rang them loudly as everyone prayed. They prostrated themselves on the church floor carpeted with shards of stained glass. I feared to refrain from following suit lest I appear like the Lucifer in this gathering: I prostrated myself; not knowing what to say, I muttered, "Glory to God in the highest." I repeated it, but God did not respond. I repeated it a second time, but He paid me no heed. Then I whispered resentfully, "If you hear me, O God, forgive me and have mercy upon me, for all I do brings me in the end to You."

As I raised my head, Hamilcar's toes were moving before my eyes: his legs were trembling all over. For a moment I did not realize what was happening, preoccupied as I was with calling for God. But that morning, I recalled, his legs had lain as still as sacks of sand. "Christ is risen!" the girls cried out. Hamilcar's mother was shaking in a paroxysm of weeping, her tears mixing with her mucus, and she poured water perfumed with orange blossoms over his legs, saying, "This is water from Siloam, where the blind man saw again, and where Mary washed his clothes as an infant!"

His feet shook harder. Suddenly I saw his hand grasp at the hem of my garment. "Help me," he said. "Christ is risen."

I put my hands under his arms. I lifted him up. He stood. His mother and sisters were gasping with sobs. "Hamilcar walks!" they cried. "Hamilcar walks! May the spirit of the Lord bless him! Christ rose again and healed him!"

All the while, Hamilcar was clutching me with a pained smile. He was hunched over, not walking straight, but he was taking steps. He took about six steps away from the chair, clutching at my robe. I tried to return him to the chair, but he begged, "Let us go to the Light of the World! Let us walk to the sepulcher!"

What have you done to yourself, Mazid? What has planted you here among their crosses and bells? But Hamilcar was walking, and he whispered into my ear, "Jesus bless you, Arab of the desert."

For a while, I saw the church rise from the ashes, solid stone again thanks to their prayers and hymns. The stones rose up all around the pillars, light spilling forth and the marble shining. Doves fluttered over it. It was then I knew it had not been destroyed: it stood tall in their souls.

I glanced down at Hamilcar. His face was so near mine that I could see the depths of his irises, no longer blue but green. He said slowly, like a man transported and raving, "Do you know the secret of those doves flying up there?" I shook my head. He said calmly, "It is the Holy Ghost. It is with us now."

In my room that night, I felt that beings of light were gathered around my bed. This talk of flame and of light, who had whispered it in my ear before? Without hesitation, I went to the folder bearing the commandments and took out the papers. The third commandment unfurled:

Third Commandment
The world is light, and it is flame: drink from the cups of
the sunlight of knowledge without being burned by its
fire. Your greatest aspiration here is to be saved.

Knowledge is light, while certainty is a fatal flame of delusion. It traps the spirit in its folds until its edges disintegrate. O God, bless me with the ever-renewing flood of your light and glory!

The crowds slowly dispersed from the streets of Jerusalem as the pilgrims commenced their return journeys. Hamilcar did not walk with the same vigor he had shown on the Saturday of Light, but he could now stand and leave his chair to walk a few paces, holding on to the walls. I had managed to sell some of the books in my possession: a priest from Antakya had purchased al-Kindi and Hippocrates. He had come to visit Hamilcar's family to congratulate them on the miracle of Christ that had touched their son. Samaan whispered in his ear that I had some books, so he waited until I returned from the circle of Amr al-Qaysi. I found them awaiting my arrival, Samaan anxiously wringing his hands and the priest from Antakya sitting in the courtyard, in his hand a long rosary of yellow beads that he was running through his fingers. His hair hung to his shoulders, pure white like cotton. Zulaykha had brought out what seemed like the entire contents of her kitchen to welcome him.

He did not ask me to show him the remainder of the books, as is customers' wont: he merely placed the books carefully in his sleeve, paying me handsomely for them. Before he departed, he told us there would be a meteor shower tonight after sunset, which they said were the angels sent by the Lord to prepare the earth for Christ's return.

Hamilcar and his sisters were eager to see them. I invited them to come up that evening to the balcony adjoining my room to watch the angels dressed as meteors.

There was a low stone seat along the wall embraced by the branches of the orange tree: the sisters furnished it with a carpet and pillows to form a comfortable seat for Hamilcar, propping up his feet on a rattan chair. Then they ran downstairs to get some bread and the cakes they baked for Easter to eat on the roof at sunset. As they came and went, I quelled the desire that had stayed with me, to dip my fingers into the spring of their rosy cheeks.

Hamilcar was excited, his face no longer pale. He said loudly, "Your face shall ever remind me of my steps by the Holy Sepulcher, and the happiness I felt when the blood rushed through the veins of my feet!"

I seized the opportunity of his sisters' absence to ask, "Would it please you that I recite some of our Qur'an over you to bolster your recovery?"

His eyes shone. "I entreat you! Do so before my sisters return and betray it to my mother!"

I recited the Fatiha, al-Falaq, and al-Nas, and breathed, "*When I sicken, it is He who cures me,*" and recited verse 255 of the Sura of al-Baqara, known as the Verse of the Throne. I raised my hands to the sky and whispered, as my grandfather used to when I had a fever or trouble breathing, "*God, do away with illness, Lord of All. Heal, for you are the Healer.*"

At that moment, the meteors began shooting down powerfully in mighty showers, so bright that they lit up the darkness of the eastern horizon. The rest of the family ran up to the balcony to watch with us.

After the Night of the Meteors, Hamilcar and his sisters, the two doves, often came up to my balcony. The older girl was named Elissar and the younger Hanna.

In front of the orange tree, Hamilcar told me the secret of his unusual name. "My father dreamed," he said, "that I would be a great general like Hamilcar Barca the Carthaginian, but as ill luck would have it, I became a cripple."

His sisters were accustomed to these sorrowful moments from him, so they hurried to praise his intelligence and beauty, and rub his legs, and tell me of impressive things he had done when he was a little boy, such as committing to memory everything he heard. "Why, he spoke fluent Arabic at six!" one sister said, giving me to understand that this was before the fever that had crippled him. The girls were convinced that part of their duty in life was to make Hamilcar happy.

Elissar leapt up. "He reads! He is wise! He reads in Surianese and Arabic, and all in Antakya bring him their letters to read for them." She entreated, "Will you permit me to bring him a book from your room, that you may hear him?"

Without waiting for an answer, she bounded out of her seat and disappeared into my room. She found only the books arranged in the alcove, as I had locked the others securely in the crate. She returned with *al-Muqabasat*, a copy I had acquired for a paltry sum from an indifferent merchant who had placed it under his water jar. Hamilcar took the book and reverently turned it this way and that in his hands, while his sister lifted the lantern by his head. He began to read Malik ibn al-Rayb's poem in sweet, haunting tones:

If only I might pass a night in Najd!
To my camel I lament with all my might;
If only the caravan had not left Najd;
If only Najd could walk with us by night.

He read fluently and well, despite lacking the lilt of the Arabic verse meter of *al-raml*. His melodious voice and the light of the lamp spilling onto his face made him seem like a priest speaking a prophecy. Hamilcar, the miracle of Christ, with his great soul unfurled over the world. We spent several nights going over what Hamilcar read and studying it together: I could see a depth of awareness in him and a rare talent, one I had never before seen in any student.

It did not require a great deal of thinking on my part to resolve to pass the torch of the Voyagers to him, and let him take the book to Antakya. Although I was busy with discussions and conversations and revising books and preaching to Hamilcar that he might be a secret crane in Antakya, there was another who had me in his sights and for whom I was the subject of his preaching.

After the event at the church, Samaan came up to me more frequently, perhaps on the pretext of bringing food, perhaps to ensure that the door was locked from the inside. Each time, he brought me small porcelain icons of Christ and Mary, then thanked God for Hamilcar's recovery, and told me how he had seen the face of the Lord shining in mine when we were in the church, and how the Kingdom of the Lord had opened its doors to admit me. He repeated, "When one forgets the Lord, the Devil takes his place, for the human soul is a house, and if it be not inhabited by the Lord, the Devil shall make his home there."

I sat with him and listened without attempting to silence him. I enjoyed the soulful, slightly idiotic gaze he fixed on me and wanted it to continue: I wanted to let him enjoy the pride of being a missionary in return for his friendly and thoughtful hospitality. I had no desire to tell him that this talk was soporific, that there was a great deal of what he said in my own religion, and that I was still examining it in my own head. How, then, should I make the leap and become a Christian when I had not yet settled matters in the faith into which I had been born?

Still, he was relentless in his invitations to the Kingdom of Christ, so much so that he sometimes knocked on my door in the middle of the night, asking me to wake and look at the face of Christ in the moon.

I decided at that juncture to be somewhat unpleasant, that he might stop. "I am unconvinced by the doctrine of atonement: how can one bear the sins of all? In our religion"—and here I quoted verse thirty-eight of the Sura of al-Najm—"*no laden one shall bear another's load.*'"

But it appeared that my question only kindled an unquenchable passion in him to tell me repeatedly that the Son of God is as meek and mild as a lamb: he told me that Christ did not ask for even bread or water when they were withheld from him. "The Son of God will save us, along with God's mercy and His vast kingdom that embraces all."

Two days later, Samaan sat with us—Hamilcar, his two sisters, and I—on the balcony, although it was his custom at that time of day to accompany Istafan, the monk, to pray at the ashes of the church.

Istafan had been one of the monks of the Church of the Resurrection before it was destroyed. He could now be seen by its ashes, perpetually kneeling. His face was sunken and pale, lost always in prayer, while some old women who passed by combed his unruly hair and gave him food to eat and rubbed his chapped feet with olive oil and perfume. He told the story of the night of the fire to all who passed: curious pilgrims, itinerant vendors, the stray cats, and the birds of the sky. He repeated it in every detail and word for word, and concluded, "And so the Fatimid caliph al-Hakim bi-Amr Allah commanded that the Church of the Resurrection be torn down and the Holy Sepulcher sabotaged. It was leveled to the ground, and this was on the second day of the imprisonment of the Coptic pope Zacharias. His uncle Armia, the Orthodox patriarch of Jerusalem, was also summoned, and the Fatimid caliph had him beheaded." And between the gasps and wide-eyed glances, he would mention that it took fifty-four buckets, which he had carried on his own from Siloam, to extinguish the blaze.

With every sunset, Samaan would go to the monk Istafan and kneel by his side before the ruins and ashes, and they would pray together: "The lion cub is imprisoned, who can sleep? Can any believer in Christ close their eyes thinking of the humiliations heaped upon Christ, bringing Him to stand like a criminal before criminals when He is the embodiment of compassion, ruling that He should die when He is life and the giver of life to humankind? His followers escaped that the proverb might be true: 'Strike but at the shepherd and the sheep shall scatter.'"

Many pilgrims and the denizens of Christians' Alley would join them in prayer: "Strike but at the shepherd and the sheep shall scatter!" Their voices reverberated through the streets.

But this was one of the rare nights when Samaan abandoned this practice, leaving Istafan the monk in favor of bringing me into the Lord's flock. How I wished to whisper to him of my bitter struggle with my demons and the heresies of philosophers and the sacrilege of al-Farabi, that he might cease this suicide mission! In an attempt to acquaint him with the abyss of my demons—for then perhaps he would be silent and only pray for me—I asked him, "What is the secret of the conflict between the Christians at the Council of Chalcedon on the nature of Christ?"

He blinked hard and stuttered. I went on: "Some say the Lord will rule over humanity on the Judgment Day in his human form, because He appeared in human form before creation, and some reject this."

Samaan looked at me silently, brow furrowed. He seemed to sense that it was time to retreat and regroup. However, nothing would dissuade him from his attempts to convert me, despite the way I stared at him, trying to infuse a measure of idiocy, and my heretical questions about the nature of Christ, which roused his ire. He ceased his ascents to my room for a number of days; perhaps he was absorbed in aiding the many pilgrims leaving Jerusalem.

We met every evening. Elissar and Hanna would prepare Hamilcar's seat, while I brought my collection of books, and we would start to read them. The girls would sit with us for a while, listening silently without remark; soon tiring, they would slip like breezes into my room and impose order on my scattered things. They arranged my pens in rows, washed my clothes, filled my jug with flower-scented water, and set out some cakes for me. Then they left, filled with gratitude for the joy that shone on the face of their brother in my company.

The scent of orange blossoms never left the folds of their clothing. The scent made me melancholy and filled me with yearning, and I imagined them sleeping by my side every night.

Christ had awoken, and the world with him: the bells of spring chimed and the cats yowled their mating calls and the demons stirred in the depths of our minds. I wanted to tell Samaan, "The demon inside me is now whispering with desire for Elissar and Hanna together; the demon wants them together. I am captivated by their beauty and naiveté, their mouths half open with all the lustfulness of a bunch of grapes."

I preferred not to tell Amr al-Qaysi of Samaan's proselytizing forays, and his attempts to bring me into the fold; I could see that they shared a profound friendship and a great deal of mutual respect and affinity. I did not wish to ruin it, being merely a passing guest who would soon be gone.

However, in the end, when Samaan began to ask me to come with them to mass on Sunday instead of going to Amr al-Qaysi's discussion circle, I hinted to al-Qaysi about this. With a sly smile, I said, "It appears I am an uncommonly welcome guest in Samaan's household."

Al-Qaysi was undisturbed, merely nodding. "What else did you expect from a man of God? This indicates that you are now dear to him: he hopes to make you one of his flock, fearing for you and wishing to grant you this gift." He tilted his head. "Do you and Hamilcar not spend long hours in discussion? Are you not attempting to bring him nearer you, and grooming him to become one of the Voyagers' cranes in Antakya? Just so, Samaan wants you in the flock of the Lord's sheep." He smiled. "Fear not. Be glad. Whatever is set before you, subject it to the judgment of your mind. If your mind accepts it, then take it; else, reject it. A Voyager has no truck with the faith of sheep. While with them, pluck the best fruits only from the orchard; discard the rest."

He fell silent. Then he put a hand over his mouth as though remembering something. "In any event, we Mutazilites, men of science and monotheism, have a great argument with the Christians. The first to challenge the Qur'an, to say that it is created and not eternal, was John of Damascus, called Saint John by the Christians, who presented the argument to the Muslims of the Levant: 'Do you say in your holy book that Jesus is the Word of God to Mary and part of His spirit?' And when the Muslims responded in the affirmative, John of Damascus said, 'And you say that the Qur'an is the Word of God, not created but eternal, on the Preserved Tablet?' And when they said, 'Yes,' he then said, 'Then Jesus is a God eternal, not created.'"

Al-Qaysi raised his long-lashed eyes and blinked several times. "You see, Mazid? It is a marketplace for answers. Each displays his own wares. Cleave to that which your mind tells you: it is that which will tell you what is good and what is evil, and you can then make your choice." He nodded. "This earth has been trodden by a great many prophets. Each of these leaves behind people, Paradise, and Hellfire, in addition to a disciple who weeps over his grave."

He rose, performed his ablutions, and led us in the evening prayers.

Customarily, before the Ramadan dhikr circles, a number of preachers come to recite the stories of eminent men's lives, of conquests, and of tales from the lives of the prophets. They exchange seats until the prayer of *qiyam*, of those who sit up all night to worship. But what piqued my curiosity and left me astonished and openmouthed were their tales of the history of Jerusalem. Whence had they come by all this information? Or had apocrypha crept in? They sat cross-legged, closed their eyes, and, their faces filled with a kind of delight, recited reverently: "This is the House of Prophets, the Place of the Righteous, the Home of the Abdal, and the destination of the virtuous. It is the first of the two Meccas, as we call the holy pilgrimage sites; it is the site of the Resurrection and of the Prophet Muhammad's ascension to Heaven; it is the Holy Land; it is where the virtuous soldiers of the Lord never sleep; it bears the glorious caves and the noble mountains; here Abraham came and was buried; here Job lived and kept his well; here were David's altar and his gate; here were Solomon's miracles and his cities; here Ishaq and his mother are buried; here Christ was born and raised; here were Saul's village and his river; here David slew Goliath; here Jeremiah was imprisoned; here were Uriah's mosque and his home; here were Muhammad's home and his gate; the Rock of Moses; the hill of Jesus; the altar of Zacharias; the battlefield of Yahya; the tombs of prophets; the villages of Job; the home of Jacob."

He paused for breath, looking around to see the effect of his words on the assembled faces, then resumed: "The Aqsa Mosque. The Mount of Zeta, also known as the Mount of Olives. The city of Acre. The tomb of the *Siddiq* Abraham; the tomb of Moses; where Ibrahim lies; the city of Ashkelon; the Springs of Siloam; the dwelling place of Luqman; the Valley of Canaan; the cities of Lot; the place of divine gardens, the mosques of Umar, and the endowment of Uthman; the location of the two God-fearing men who came out to Moses, and the meeting where the two adversaries met; the dividing line between torment and forgiveness; the location of Baysan; and a portal placed on Earth by the Almighty."

And so the preacher continued until he felt the listeners had tired of his speech, at which time he would tear off his turban and make the rounds of the attendees that they might place whatever sum they wished into it. I would sit there openmouthed, perpetually stunned. Once I whispered to Amr al-Qaysi, "Is all this information true?"

"If it is, he's a wonder." He laughed. "The words of preachers and biographers are filled with *Israiliyat.*" I nodded, knowing that this meant false information from a foreign source, not necessarily Israelite.

From that day on, whenever I passed through the streets of Jerusalem, I looked about me in search of the ruins of the things the preachers had described: I found naught but a grieving city, its air now bearing the scent of orange blossoms, now the smell of burning.

I was unhappy, even grieved, to learn that Hamilcar and his sisters were returning to Antakya. They were preparing to leave in a matter of days. This meant that I too must go. It was time to dismantle the tent of friendly company and talk and the wisdom of the ancients that had been set in motion by the shower of meteors and the wings of angels upon the balcony overlooking the courtyard, which I had once thought would last forever.

Hamilcar no longer needed to be helped up and down the stairs, for he had a stick upon which he leaned, and ascended, albeit slowly, catching his breath at each step. But he arrived in the end, and hurried to my room, looking around in its corners for a manuscript or book that I might have forgotten to pack away in the chest. That evening they prepared a light supper for us: loaves sprinkled with thyme and olive oil. Elissar brushed each of these with a spoonful of buttermilk before pouring olive oil over it and handing them to each of us.

I was accustomed to concealing my grief behind a veil of mystery and silence. But that night, it was as though I wished to stand and mourn over ruins like the ancient Arab poets, and the words escaped me perforce. "I am overcome with sorrow at your departure," I confessed.

They responded with sighs and sadness equaling or passing what I felt—words of regret and tear-filled eyes. We dried each other's tears with promises to meet the following year. And so we filled the breaches of parting with wishes that we knew would not come true.

Suddenly, after a moment of silence in which our food stuck in our throats, Hanna whispered, in her girlish voice like the cooing of a dove, "There is something I wish to ask you, but I fear it may disturb you."

I wondered what she wanted. Had Samaan told her something of my heretical ramblings? Or had she sensed something of my thoughts about her? I nodded. "What is it?"

"Do you desert Arabs really eat lizards?" she blurted.

Her sister kicked her under the table; Hamilcar burst out laughing and roared with mirth for a long time. I looked at her face, bright red with embarrassment, and thought, "What an enchanting girl! Her beauty is ruinous! Did she see the remnants of a lizard's tail on my mouth, I who spent many nights longing to pluck the grapes from her lips?"

I laughed along with them and said proudly, "I am Mazid, Mazid of Najd, al-Hanafi, from al-Yamama. My land has flowing springs and blossoming date palms. My homeland is like a stunning beauty covered in a burka, who is savage and wild to strangers, but once she trusts you, takes off her veil and shines. Her springs burst forth with meteors and honey—honey that has been stored in her hidden places since the time of Tasm, Jadis, and all the extinct tribes that are no more."

They left the balcony, going downstairs, the sound of their laughter and chatter lingering. Hamilcar's transparent eyes, filled with wonder; Elissar's and Hanna's hands that made everything they passed over shine; their delicious, satisfying meal steeped in the perfume of the fields of wheat. I resolved to leave Jerusalem, having left a scrap of myself here, on this balcony. I had stuffed my pockets with knowledge and pages turned to ash; I had poured into my heart that mysterious thing that keeps you on the banks of the river of speech, unable to scoop any of it into the pots of language.

With care, I had passed three books to some pilgrims who I had sensed would keep them well, on the shelves of respect and veneration in their homes or at the book market. I had also finished copying out Aristotle's *Ethics*. I must prepare to depart, I could not remain standing and staring at ruins, listening to the reed flute of sorrow until the last breath. I should gather my things and flee. I would give the requisite respect to grief; I would not begrudge it. I would feel its pain, and be a good host. But afterward, I would wash myself of its dark discouragement, and would carefully take down the lesson it bore me. I would close the ledger and go. The grief of Jerusalem still settled in my breast and held sway over me. It had its own sly methods, slipping in whenever evening came and Canopus shone again, or when the doves cooed by my window.

But I must go. If water does not flow, it stagnates. I would go. It was no lie when I said that my heart longed to see Egypt.

*

I could not sleep that night. I left my bed and climbed down the outer stair to the street, feeling my way by the light of a sleepy slip of a moon and the far-apart torches on the winding stone walls of the alleyways. I would tell al-Qaysi that I was going to Egypt, and he would certainly tell me the name of the Voyager I should visit there.

I had chosen Hamilcar to be the repository of the Voyagers' torch. He had a brilliant intelligence and a spirit eager for knowledge, and was a voracious reader. In the libraries of Antakya, he could found an active cell of Voyagers. I would copy the seven commandments and pass them on to him. I knew not how they would appear to him: most importantly, Samaan must not see them, for fear he think I were proselytizing to him.

The street was quiet but for the sounds of the insects of the night and the crowing of confused cockerels thinking it already dawn. I arrived at a spring pouring out of a wall, forming a clear pool in a basin. I plunged my hands into it, scooping out a double handful, and drank and drank. I washed my face, feeling my worries fall away with the drops of water. Then, fearful of losing my way in the dark, twisting alleyways, I decided to turn back. But suddenly I heard the sound of footsteps approaching.

I trembled. What had brought me out now, so close to dawn? Then I saw the shadow of someone approaching from the end of the street. It was either a night watchman, who would be suspicious of one walking alone at this hour, or a robber or member of the Ayyarin, who would steal my garments and leave me naked. I froze and stuck close to the wall, not making a sound, hoping he would not see me. But to my astonishment, when the owner of the footsteps approached, I could make out a woman with her hair loose. Oh God, was this the ogress of children's stories?

When she drew level with me, I made out that she was wearing a fur garment and a head covering of sheep's wool. She was

233

muttering, "How narrow the way if You are not one's guide; how terrible the loneliness if You are not one's companion."

She would have left me behind and walked on had I not whispered, "What keeps us from God, then?"

She turned her face to the sky and responded without looking at me, "The love of the world. There are those whom God has given of his love to drink; these are so consumed with passion for Him that they love none other."

"And what is the path to Him, sister?"

Then she turned to me. Despite the dark, I could see tears in her slightly protuberant eyes: her glance was sharp, plunging deep into my chest and taking my breath away. Then she said, "Some carry understanding to those who understand better than they. Your answer you shall find always in your heart."

As though handing her some of the stones that weighed heavily on my heart, I said, "But what of the whisperings and mutterings of the Devil?"

I could hear her saying as she walked on and left me standing there, "Sometimes the soul feels tightness and darkness; sometimes it feels free and light. Follow your own light, young man, follow your own light."

Afterward, I ran to my room with the fourth commandment reverberating in my head.

Fourth Commandment

Erect no dam, raise no veil between yourself and the truth. If it cometh in the shape of a person who claims to possess the truth in its entirety, remove him far from your path, for this is nothing but his own truth. If it cometh in the form of certainty, purify it with the water of questioning and doubt; if it cometh in the form of a mountain, climb it to seek what lies behind that mountain. Do not hand over your mind to any creature who seeks to direct or lead you on the pretext that they alone have claim to certainty: in so doing, you become like the donkey who gives its reins to a thief to steal it.

I remained staring at the wall, unable to think clearly, until morning came.

The next morning, Samaan was standing at the bottom of the stairs, still smoothing down the hems of his sleeves with his clean, neat fingernails. He told me that a group of Coptic priests would be visiting him within two days, and that he wished to show them some of the books I had acquired. With a sad, wry smile, he said, "They say that the Egyptian caliph has established a great library comprising many varied texts in the sciences and arts, and appointed skilled copyists to replicate them; they would like to select some of your valuable books to sell to the library. They will pay great prices for them."

I fell silent. I could feel that Egypt awaited me: it was I who would pass the books on to the library.

I could not sell all my books here, for I must pass the seeds of the Voyagers to many cities, and I must keep some books in my possession for Egypt, and, if I were blessed enough, the libraries of Cordoba, where the learned folk would no doubt receive them eagerly. "I have only a few books left, mostly books of poetry and quotations from the ancients, which I doubt will interest the priests as much as the House of Wisdom translations in the sciences, but in any case I will see what remains."

I paused awhile. I wished to ask him about the woman I had encountered the previous night, but feared he would ask me why I had left the house before dawn, so I was silent, looking around at the white gypsum walls of the houses, embracing windows adorned with flowers, and listening to the bleating of sheep and lambs in the fields and meadows around the city walls.

I bought a handful of green almonds from an itinerant vendor and nibbled at them eagerly despite their acidic tang.

Jerusalem had no running water or canals like Baghdad: its water came from wells. But it had the best fruit of any city. The folk around me walked slowly, secure now that the bustle of pilgrims had abated from the streets. How had things fallen apart so drastically for me that none of the stories I was told answered my questions? The flood of facts had burst forth, destroying the architecture of my mind. I had not one room left in which to take shelter. How had al-Qaysi's structure remained standing and stable, with light in his face and peace in his heart and tact in his conduct, while I was being pecked at by the birds?

I had settled upon giving Amr al-Qaysi *Kalila wa Dimna* instead of *Ikhwan al-Safa*. Not only was it bound splendidly and intact, it was entertaining and exciting and good for both adults and children. As for *Ikhwan al-Safa*, the copy I had not only appeared to be by Ikhwan al-Safa, but it had many additions and errors introduced in copying, and included sections on astronomy, alchemy, magic, and talismans, sciences I needed to read about and explore their mysteries. One is greedy at heart, after all.

I had completed Aristotle's *Ethics*. I would take it to the paper market to have it bound, knowing for a certainty that al-Qaysi had read it before. But a Voyager must have a book by Aristotle in his collection, and a scale that allows a mind to weigh pros and cons.

I was distracted as I walked: my feet led me to Istafan the monk, still kneeling in the ruins of the church and praying: "O Lord Jesus! You who said, 'Come to me, all you weary, who are heavy laden, and I will give you rest,' I am coming to you. I place all the burdens of my life at your feet, for I believe you will carry them for me, today and every day, as you once carried the cross."

Istafan's face was tanned and leathery and cracked by long exposure to the sun in his long prayer. Around his neck was a large wooden cross, as big as the one hanging around the neck of Samaan. I pitied him. The cord of the cross had rubbed the back of his neck raw. I tried to move the cross to relieve the pressure, and it left a perfume on the tips of my fingers. "Is this sandalwood?" I asked.

He did not look at me, merely murmuring, "Perhaps."

I left him, asking myself the secret of this refreshing, wonderful smell around Istafan. Was it the perfumed oils with which the old women anointed his hair, hands, and feet? But they too said that this smell was from the sacred dust stirred up by the beating of angel wings and the soles of the feet of the prophets who walked around this saint.

When the afternoon prayer call sounded, I went to the Mosque of Umar to pray with Amr al-Qaysi, bend my knee at his discussion circle, and drink my fill of his wellspring: perhaps it might quench the fire of the questions burning within me. Perhaps I would tell him of my desire to leave for Egypt.

I arrived at the mosque as Amr al-Qaysi was shaking the ablution water off his hands. We prayed together. His discussion circle was not held immediately: some Catholics and their great priests were paying a visit to the mosque, and had obtained the wali's permission to enter the mosque that they might contemplate its construction and architecture from within. I was joyful, for I should be in al-Qaysi's presence and obtain a private audience with him until such time as the Catholics' tour of the mosque was concluded. I gained knowledge and learning every time I found myself in his presence; I still stammered before him and became an overawed student searching his brain for some observation to make his teacher think him bright. But instead, I found myself telling him what occurred on the Saturday of Light: how I had gone there to assist the crippled boy on his journey to the Church of the Resurrection, and seen with my own two eyes the flame that shone out from the sepulcher to light the candles. Disapprovingly, he responded, "That is what led to the destruction of the Church of the Resurrection and the site of the Holy Sepulcher: someone told the Fatimid caliph, al-Hakim bi-Amr Allah, of the flame that comes out of the sepulcher. His opinion was that this filled their minds with idolatry and their hearts with doubt, and drove them to light lanterns at the altar and resort to ruses to bring the light to them, such as dipping them in elder oil, which is flammable when mixed with oil of lily, and burns with an intense and dazzling flame."

My eyes widened in wonder. "But the Christians have been doing this for dozens of years, nay, hundreds! How could he embark upon such a course?"

Shaking his head, he whispered, "He is an unstable leader, of unsound mind, and disturbed. Ever since he ascended the throne, he has been seeking an opportunity to harm them, although his mother is a Christian, and he was raised by his maternal uncle. That may be the reason, we know not." He sighed. "The wali of Jerusalem showed me a letter he received from the caliph saying: 'Undertake the castration of the Christian priests in Jerusalem.' The city fell into an uproar, stunned and disturbed at the cruelty of such a command. When they remonstrated with him, he said that he had said, 'Undertake a census of the Christian priests in Jerusalem,' and that flies had muddied the ink to change it to 'castration,' or so he claimed!"

He took a deep breath. "He has perpetrated bizarre deeds upon the people of Egypt. He has made it a crime to sell dates, and had a great quantity of them collected, which he burned. He prohibited the sale of grapes, and destroyed the date harvest that the Christians might not turn it into wine. He has gone so far as to compel Christians to wear a cross about their necks weighing a pound and a quarter by the Damascene scale, like the cross you see on the neck of Samaan. He also compels the Jews to wear a piece of wood around their necks weighing fully as much as the cross, in a reference to the head of the calf they had worshipped, and to wear black turbans only. Christians and Jews must wear the cross and the piece of wood even in the bath. It is said that in his Cairo, he created special bathhouses for them that they might not mingle with Muslims. Therefore, when news reached him of the flame that emerges from the sepulcher, and the customs of the Christians every year, singing hymns and waving palm fronds and olive branches, he wrote to the wali of Jerusalem commanding him to demolish the Church of the Resurrection."

He gestured with his head to the men going about the church: "Imagine that you have come from far away to perform a pilgrimage, only to find that the Holy Kaaba had been demolished. Not only that: you are prohibited from circumambulating it as usual. You would be bound to feel that the world has been shaken to its foundations. That unbalanced boy on the throne of Egypt has done to their church what the infidel Abraha dared not do to the Holy Kaaba. And as though that were not enough, he commanded in the same year that the churches of Egypt be demolished into the bargain." He lowered his voice and looked about for fear of being heard by one of the Catholics walking nearby, contemplating the walls and ceilings, impressed, their embroidered silken robes making them appear like proud cockerels. "They have a base title for the Church of the Resurrection: they call it the Church of the Refuse to further demean and degrade it!" He shook his head. "This despite the fact that you will never find a prouder people than those of Jerusalem. You will not see a drunkard here; the traders do not cheat in their measure; there are no houses of ill repute, in secret or in public, but it has a rash and reckless ruler. It is said that he hated his Christian teacher, who humiliated him as a child, so that when he grew up and wished to take vengeance, he visited the teacher and mocked him, saying, 'The lizard has become a dragon.' Then he had him killed."

After hearing this news of Egypt, I thought better of telling my sheikh al-Qaysi of my desire to go there. Perhaps I would tell him the following day.

Not long after, the Catholics quit the mosque. Al-Qaysi accompanied them to the gate out of respect and shook their hands warmly. Then he returned to us to hold his circle.

Some of the Christians had lingered, obtaining al-Qaysi's permission to listen to him. They clustered around his discussion circle next to his students and disciples, rubbing shoulders with them. He called out, "Thanks be to God, and prayers and peace upon the Prophet. Prayers and peace upon the One who hath made the good and righteous man, Jesus, peace be upon him, and empowered him to hold prayer. Our Qur'an calls peace and prayers upon Jesus, upon the day of his birth, the day of his death, and the day he is resurrected to live again." He quoted hurriedly from the Sura of al-Ghashiya, when he perceived that heads had begun to turn this way and that in curiosity: "'*Remind them, for thou art but a remembrance; Thou art not at all a warder over them.*' The Just Monotheists follow the path of rationality. Rationality is their imam." His eyelids drooped for a moment, his long lashes casting a shadow over his cheeks, as was his wont when struck by inspiration. A faint smile of ecstasy played about his mouth. "When we just folk seek to speak of language, we find that it is formed by rules and practice. It is a pure creation of humanity; it developed together with history, and in accordance with the changes in time and place. Our wise man, Abu Ishaq al-Kindi, says that there is nothing more important to a student of Right than Right itself. Islam is a structure, built upon the five pillars. What lies within this structure is yours: you have the free will to build and establish your life with what choices you will."

"If I had said this aloud in a mosque in Baghdad," I thought to myself, "I would fear that the mosque would be brought crashing down around my ears! But," I mused, "it appears that the City of the Prophets is more tolerant of a little heresy."

On my way home, I entered the covered market adjoining the western side of the Mosque of Umar. They said that it was the gate the Prophet Muhammad had entered by on his journey up to Paradise. It was packed with close-set stalls, the floor paved with great, ancient flagstones, smooth with curved edges, and before each stall stood the vendor crying his wares. The seller of rosaries waved two of them, crafted of perfumed wood; the spice trader sang the praises of a powder that would return an old man to his youth; the seller of caftans called out that he had robes just arrived from Byzantium. Everyone was crying his wares, each roaring loudly so as to drown out his neighbor. It was a battle of voices all around me. But they knew full well when to cease their shouting so as not to escalate into a physical altercation; long neighborliness had created tacit boundaries between them, which they respected. Each of them displayed his wares, and the market was for everyone: just as a prophet appears at the head of every nation, allowing whoever wishes to believe or disbelieve the freedom to do so. Why was it not so outside the marketplace? In Jerusalem, in Iraq, and in al-Yamama, rivers of blood flowed between the adherents of every prophet; and in the Agate Cities, steeped in blood and screaming, the poem was recited that al-Qaysi was ever repeating to me:

> Jerusalem's folk, with all their might,
> Quarrel 'tween Muhammad and Christ.
> Some ring the church bells day and night;
> Some cry to prayer as to a fight;
> Fain would I know, for 'tis a blight,
> Just who is wrong and who is right!

At that moment, I was fiercely resentful of al-Qaysi: he had thrown me into my own perplexity, and escaped unscathed himself.

## Zulaykha's Spring

In my final days in Jerusalem, Zulaykha's treatment of me changed. She was more pleasant and less forbidding. This pleased me. I had a fondness for her, and a deep respect that made me seek her favor, hoping that her resentment of Muslims, whom I embodied, would fade. I had had no hand in her husband's murder.

She smiled at me, her yellow eyes glowing like a cat's. I had always wished to voice my admiration of her housekeeping and how well the house was managed: this grim figure, with her hooked nose and sunken cheeks, had spread the perfume of flowers about the place like a garment adorning her home. Her children played about her, fresh-faced, clean, and well-dressed. She pushed some logs and wood scraps into the oven, and in a twinkling set the table with food and delicious bread. She scattered sprigs of mint and thyme over the dishes, dividing the food among those who lived there, and prepared glasses of anise or sage. She brought water from a basin beneath a spring that flowed from the wall of the house, and poured it equally among small pots on the balcony and in the rooms after mixing it with drops of orange blossom water.

Her skill at cooking was the talk of the neighbor women: on that day when the Egyptian priests had visited us, she made for them a small roast pig, adorning it with fragrant herbs and orange slices. They cleaned their plates so thoroughly that there was not even a scrap left to give to the hungry men of the church!

## Before Departure, after *Posterior Analytics*

Ishaq ibn Hunayn's translation of Aristotle's *Posterior Analytics* was the book I had decided to bring to meet the Egyptians who had congregated in Samaan's house before I showed them my collection. My keen interest in meeting them lay not only in the sale of my books; the main source was my desire to accompany their caravan to Egypt and learn about their country from them.

There were four men. They sat in a row in the sitting room, imbuing it with a heavy masculine scent mingled with the smell of their sweat and the sandalwood I customarily smelled in churches. Three of them had taken off the crosses about their necks and placed them in their laps. The fourth, who seemed to be their master, sat among them, leaning back in his seat, while they sat politely on the edges of their chairs and looked at him to show respect and obedience. When he spoke, they all fell silent; at a movement from his hand, they rushed to fulfill whatever command he had given.

The leader was slight of stature, with an incongruously loud, hoarse voice. Perhaps its imposing nature lent strength to his feeble physical presence, swimming in his loose ecclesiastical garment. But a look at his glittering eyes made you recognize that within the folds of the black garment lurked a wily fox, skilled at making his way through the twists and turns of life to achieve his ends. His piercing gaze scrutinized me, making me fall silent at first.

To break the stillness, Samaan extended his hand to the book I held. "This is Mazid," he said, "a bookseller from Baghdad. He says that he has a goodly collection of the translations of the House of Wisdom." Then he rose from his seat and presented the book to the wily fox with a slight bow.

I had not missed the implicit ridicule in Samaan's tone as he introduced me. It was as though he were saying, "Well, and something may come of the desert Arabs yet: wonders will never cease!"

He called the small priest "Father Basilius." Without bothering to look at me, Basilius responded as he turned the book over in his hands: "The market is filled with books copied from Aristotle, especially his *Ethics*, and Plato's book on politics. Not every book is trustworthy. It might be filled with apocrypha from copying: scraps and lines from here and there, unrelated to the original book. I previously bought from

243

a charlatan bookseller a collection of Pythagoras, Empedocles, and Themistius, or Euphrades as he is sometimes called."

I took umbrage at his belittling tone and the weighty names he dropped as though to intimidate me. How was I to gauge his veracity? I rose with alacrity and plucked the book from his hands, returning to my seat. "In matters of buying and selling, if the buyer has no desire for the goods, he is under no obligation to acquire them."

He stared at me, slack-jawed. It appeared he had thought that his old man's bargaining tactics, which rely on denigrating the wares being sold, would garner him the best offer. "Where are you from, young man?" he asked.

His tone reminded me of Hassan the Egyptian. They sounded extremely alike, as though they had lived together in the same house. His *r* and *l* sounds mingled in the same manner. Hassan's presence, suddenly there between us, softened the harsh moment, at least to me. "I am Mazid," I responded, "Mazid al-Hanafi, from al-Yamama. I was educated in Najd, and I have a degree from some imams of Baghdad in grammar, the Prophet's tradition, and Qur'an recitation. I frequent the discussion circles of Amr al-Qaysi, the sheikh of the Mosque of Umar."

"My ear is never wrong!" he boomed, his voice still filled with arrogance and disdain. "You buy and sell books of philosophy, when your sheikhs say that philosophy is heresy, and brand those who choose it as a profession as apostates from Islam? What have you to do with books of philosophy?"

The provocative question caught me by surprise. I could find nothing to say. Naturally, I could not use philosophy to argue with him: he was a cleric, and the Church has always burned books of philosophy. I could not respond to him in kind and say, "And what have *you* to do with them?" The three men around him were staring at me with narrowed eyes, awaiting their master's command to know what to make of me. But I shall not deny that I was pained.

I contented myself with saying, "None rejects philosophy but a narrow-minded fool, be he a Muslim or a Christian priest." I added, "The Just Monotheists have a long and profound connection with philosophers." I took a deep breath, holding Aristotle's book tightly in my hands. "Al-Kindi, the Arab philosopher and sage, says we must elevate that which rationality elevates and denigrate what it denigrates. The philosophers did not only stay with the Arabs in the House of Wisdom in Baghdad; they visited our caliphs in their dreams. Have you not heard of the dream of Caliph Mamoun?" Without waiting for his answer, I went on: "Aristotle often visited Mamoun in dreams. In one of these, Mamoun asked him, 'What is beauty?' He responded, 'What the mind finds beautiful.' Mamoun asked him, 'And then what?' Aristotle said, 'The best of religious law.' Mamoun pressed him, 'And then what?' Aristotle answered with finality, 'There is no more "then," unto infinity.'"

"Then," the wily old fox snorted, "we had best wait for a visit in our dreams from Master Aristotle!"

I was gathering the sharp barbs of some conclusive retort from all about my head, when suddenly glasses of honey-sweetened sage tea were being handed out by Elissar. Still uneasy, I was obliged to look down; however, I caught the fleeting wink she gave me. That was odd: what did she want?

"But that is a time long past," said Basilius. "Now, books of philosophy are burned or thrown into the river in Baghdad. Use your eyes: but for the Christians' tolerance, you would not be in the house of a Christian priest in Jerusalem, nor indeed I in the house of Samaan. The priest of the Church of the Resurrection should be appointed by the Metropolitan Bishop of Alexandria, but in Jerusalem they seized the Metropolitan position. The Lord says, 'From Egypt I called my son.'"

He seemed to have directed his attack at Samaan. I turned to the latter: he was swallowing and blinking hard. Just then, Hamilcar appeared in the doorway, leaning on his cane with his left hand and on his sister Elissar's shoulder with his right. I understood then the secret of Elissar's wink. I ran to assist him and prepared a seat for him. Elissar whispered, helping me pile pillows behind his back, "When I heard the conversation, I wanted Hamilcar to be here: he will no doubt enjoy it."

I returned to my seat. I must not fall silent or appear retiring before my student, the Voyager-to-be: he must be impressed by his teacher. Craning my neck as though we were standing at the gate of philosophy itself, I said loudly, "Philosophy is wisdom: our prophet, Muhammad, has said, 'Wisdom is the ultimate goal of any believer.' The theological sciences in Islam are naught but an attempt to reconcile rationality with inherited sayings. Texts, as you know, may have many interpretations. Our sage Abu Ishaq says, 'Nothing is dearer to the seeker of truth than truth.'"

"What is this wisdom of which you speak, young man," Basilius retorted, "when the heads of Copts are being mounted on the Fatimids' gates?"

Sensing that the conversation might devolve into an argument and a fruitless exchange of accusations, I turned to Samaan in hopes that his cool temperament might calm the heat of the moment and asked, "Why do you think the Egyptian caliph ordered the destruction of the Resurrection, although Caliph Umar never touched a single stone of the church when the Muslims took Jerusalem, instead writing the Pact of Umar that makes much of the dhimmi and all they hold sacred?"

Basilius interjected, voice rising and eyes reddened. "The caliph commanded that the church be leveled! He called the patriarch Armia, the patriarch of the Eastern Orthodox Church, to Egypt—his own uncle!—and had him beheaded with a sword."

One of the priests with him looked at the floor and shook his head. "We still do not know where he is buried."

Why did they all repeat the same story? Was it the truth, or had they heard it from the monk Istafan? I feared to fall victim to the grief of a pilgrim whose Mecca has been destroyed with a breast full of hatred, especially seeing Samaan's face darken and his lower lip tremble slightly. Evasively, seeking safer ground, I said, "Philosophy is a just scale by which right may be measured. Bless the soul of Ishaq ibn Hunayn the Surianese, who translated Aristotle. Aristotle says that virtue lies between two vices: courage lies between impetuosity and cowardice, and generosity lies between miserliness and extravagance. This golden mean has reached Islamic jurisprudence, even the jurisprudence of the monotheist Mutazilites: they built for the sinner a new world between Heaven and Hell, named 'a status between two statuses.'"

My display put paid to my disgruntlement, and it seemed to have calmed the room somewhat. Basilius fell silent and one of the priests next to him said in a ringing voice, as though preaching a sermon, with tears in his eyes—from anger or eye trouble I knew not: "The Lord waited not to punish the sinners of that time! The wrath of God descended upon churches because of them! They were dismissed from the churches because they had become like the current walis who persecute holy men, finding excuses to collect money on any pretext, trading in the churches of God, and selling indulgences for money, handing over the Church to whoever paid them an additional dinar; men unfit to serve or work for the Church: this was why the Lord set upon them the lizard that grew into a dragon, and leveled their churches."

Basilius looked at him sharply, as if to say that this was not the time nor place to insult the mourning Christians, and that this kind of talk should be between themselves, not in the presence of this Arab would-be logician and Samaan, who had disobeyed the Church of Alexandria. "O Jesus," he said in a dry voice and with a stiff tongue, "we were lost sheep and are returned to the shepherd of our souls." Then he said to me, "Show us what books you have, Arab, that we may see if there is anything worth spending the money of the Church on."

From my first step into Basilius's company, I had disliked his manner. He had the air of a lizard that had not turned into a dragon, but remained a lizard. He felt like a vacant vessel: there was no one in our gathering he had not attacked. His knowledge was like rain that falls on desert sand, bringing forth no fruit or flower, merely soaked up by the passageways of his empty soul. I contented myself with waving *Posterior Analytics* at him, resolving to demand such a hefty sum that he would be unable to pay it. Suddenly, for the first time since he entered, Hamilcar spoke, as though he were speaking a prophecy. "Your Eminence Father Basilius," he said, "I have spent long nights reading Aristotle, and I doubt that I have understood but a fraction of it. But in my understanding, it makes the attainment of truth or wisdom contingent upon following proofs and extrapolating what is unseen from what we can perceive. As I read it, he uses a greater and lesser premise, and via these, he arrives at a result that proves the truth of what he says."

All heads turned to him like the heads of the family of Mary saying, "How can we talk to one who is a child in the cradle?"

Unperturbed, Hamilcar continued: "I shall take an example from our conversation. The greater premise: the Lord lost patience with the actions of his flock in that time. The lesser premise: the keepers of churches sinned. The result: God unleashed his anger upon all churches due to their actions."

A deep silence fell over those assembled. Then I glimpsed Father Basilius swallow in preparation to speak. I feared that he might say something to break down Hamilcar's as yet unsteady steps into philosophy; I feared he might steal away the joy of a month of miracles, philosophy, first steps, and the conversations beneath the orange tree that had brought Hamilcar to his recovery. I burst into speech, I know not how. "O God!" I slapped my forehead as though I had forgotten something. "Forgive me, Hamilcar! I completely forgot that you have already bought *Analytics*!" I turned to him, my face radiating sincerity. "Forgive me for putting it up for sale! O Eminence Father Basilius, forgive me! The book is Hamilcar's! I doubt that I own any more books by Aristotle."

I was overwhelmed with relief, as if a great weight had been lifted off me. I had no wish to further embarrass Father Samaan; I also had no wish for the people of Jerusalem to bruit it around that the desert Arab had in his room manuscripts worth their weight in gold. I took the book and returned it to Hamilcar. His face had lit up and his eyes were shining. He wriggled his toes in delight.

I was aware that Hamilcar was not in the least crippled—had never been a cripple. When he leaned on me in the Church of the Resurrection, in the press of bodies and the frenzy of emotion, he had walked like a normal man. I had no sense that I was holding him up at all: in that moment, his feet barely touched the ground when he was walking straight and steady. However, I know not the reason he had chosen to live as a cripple. Was it rebellion against his father, who had wanted him to become a general? Did his father bring him little lambs to slaughter, then slap his face if he refused to kowtow? Was it a rejection of his father's fate, forever stooping? Did he wish to lift his face and stare at the higher kingdom of the Lord, sending his sisters every Sunday morning to the church library to return to him with a goodly collection of books without rebuke for being absent from the fields? This is the nature of Voyaging Cranes: they are born with wings that it is nigh impossible to muddy.

I handed him the book: his handsome face was shining and his neatly combed hair gleamed on his shoulders. Deep within me, I knew that I had only placed the book in the best location possible, in the possession of this boy who had willingly cut off his own legs, sprouting great wings in their place, formed from the pages of books. This was how I would remain faithful to the tenets of the Voyagers. I had planted this book in a sunny field, rather than in a dark and moldy storehouse of books within Basilius's house of worship.

Once the rich feast was over and Basilius's belly was full of roast pork, he forgot about everything, including his desire to acquire books. He even told me, scraps of bread and fat still clinging to his beard, how to find a caravan of pilgrims due to go shortly to Egypt.

Hamilcar was among those standing and waving to me as I left for Egypt. I had sold some books to the priests returning to Damascus and Byzantium, and Hamilcar's father had introduced me to a deacon who worked for the patriarch of the church in Konya, who had bought from me three books with gold dinars.

I passed one of the dinars to Zulaykha: she was truly a sprig of sage that overflowed with refreshing bounty from morning to night. As I was preparing myself for travel, she presented me with two jars of water and a bag she had filled with dried meat, hard cheese, jars of olive oil, and wheat cakes. My room and my balcony, where the stars came out, were hidden behind the branches of the flowering orange tree.

I wrote out the seven commandments and passed them on to Hamilcar. His path toward the Voyage of the Cranes was smooth and verdant: it had never passed beneath the Document of al-Qadir, or the blades of swords; he never had to know that the head of the Persian blacksmith had rolled onto the floor in his store like the head of a camel.

I performed the dawn prayer with Amr al-Qaysi, who recited verses one and two of the Sura of al-Najm: *"By the star when it setteth; Your comrade erreth not, nor is deceived."* We could barely make out the columns of the mosque in the morning mist. He stood tall and imposing, as befitted a Voyager, wearing a black silk abaya and turban. He laid a hand on my shoulder. "Mazid," he said, "of all God's gifts, he is least generous with certainty. Hold to the vocation of the Voyager like a burning coal, as they once told the early Muslims to grasp their faith in their hands though it burned them, and leave it not."

I could say nothing; the words stuck in my throat for sorrow. "Al-Jahiz has divided up every country," he said by way of comfort, "and says that they are ten: industry in Basra, rhetoric in Kufa, kindness in Baghdad, treachery in Shahr-e Rey, envy in Herat, coldness in Nishapur, miserliness in Merv, chivalry in Balkh, and trade in Egypt. Pray to the Lord to bless your business, Voyager, as you go to Egypt." He departed, leaving me behind him, repeating, "Go with God, al-Hanafi, go with God."

I made my way to the caravan stop, rebuking myself. How feeble I had seemed, fighting my tears in front of Amr al-Qaysi like a child leaving its mother! Jerusalem held the cloisters of prophets and the fluttering of angels and the beating of the saints' feet in its streets.

The caravan was headed southward. Warm breezes surrounded us; bells were ringing out from some mysterious, faraway place, filled with a sweet, sad melancholy.

## Come to Egypt

I left Jerusalem in the company of the Coptic pilgrims' caravan. I left Jerusalem in pain and bleeding: my songs and recitations were not needed, for they were going home, ringing bells and singing a melancholy song: "Glory to God in the highest, and on earth peace, good will toward men."

Although I was bereft at quitting my companions in Jerusalem—a grief that would remain in my chest like a wound—when I embraced the journey, I was alert and watchful, entranced by a new beginning. I seemed to plunge into a spring that washed away all that clung to me: fatigue, disappointment, and the tedium of custom. At the fabric market in Jerusalem, I had managed to acquire a length of fabric, the edges embroidered with scarlet thread in the form of tiny crosses that came together to form the shape of posies of flowers. It appeared to have been a tablecloth or an altar cover. I had bought it and made of it a cover for my box of books, to protect it from both dust and prying eyes.

The caravan was so long that I could not see its end. Its camels were energetic, with massive feet. We came out of Jerusalem, or Bayt al-Maqdis as it is known, as the stars were still whispering to each other in the sky. When I had left Baghdad, it had been torn apart by swords and harsh words, filled with sinners and poets and the hungry: a ruby steeped in blood and the struggle for dominance. Today, as I left Jerusalem, angry bees were buzzing around al-Aqsa. There were unquenched coals beneath the Church of the Resurrection, rage on resentful faces against the Lord's locusts who had defiled the churches and courtyards of Jerusalem, and more resentment within the hearts of the pilgrims who had climbed the cold mountains and crossed the ice-capped hills and freezing valleys only to find the Holy Sepulcher had been leveled.

Jerusalem was beginning to recede behind us, a red halo surrounding it. Was it the line of dawn breaking? Or was it the suffering of a city within whose walls there had been enmity and fighting since the beginning of creation?

The returning pilgrims' caravan took the route known as "The Path of Ancestors and Kings" back to Egypt. It passes through the central mountains of Palestine, and they say it is the path taken by all the prophets. I was overcome by this thought, and by my camel's side I heard the echo of their footsteps in their simple leather shoes and sensed their breasts burdened with a dream of delivering humanity from sin and damnation. Moses of the bulrushes, striking the earth for the first time, causing twelve springs to burst forth, and striking it a second, causing the Red Sea to part. Bright Joseph, whose face lit up the pit, yet cast no light into the dark faces of his brothers. Jesus and Mary, followed by the stars and the kings. Who else? How great this path was! Peace be upon them all.

We moved on in slow stages: first we came to Bethlehem, where the pilgrims stopped for some days to pray in its churches and visit its shrines. Then on to Galilee, where we spent two more days. The caravan then went on in fits and starts, not picking up a steady pace until we arrived at Rafah.

The sale of books had given me some dinars around my waist, but I must remember always that I was a Voyager, my primary task to place the books where they belonged, not to trade in them. This time, I had managed to buy a strong camel: I had not let the trader choose for me and take advantage of my naiveté and ignorance, as when I had bought Shubra, my old camel, whom I had set free to live out the remaining years of her life grazing around Jerusalem. I had bought a saddle with many straps from a pilgrim arrived from Byzantium, upon which I could set all my things, including the box. It was sturdy, of strong leather, adorned with silver scrolls—all this in addition to a young, well-behaved mule that carried the rest of my things.

When we arrived in Arish, the entire population seemed to have come out of their mud-brick houses to stand in a line with their baskets, waving to the pilgrims, offering them carpets, baskets, and early crops of dates. I noted that many of the pilgrims bought the dates, hiding them beneath their things and in hidden pockets upon their camels, to bring back as gifts from the Holy Land. I knew not the secret of their eagerness, until they told me that they could not display the dates before the guards and spies now that the caliph of Egypt had commanded that all the crops of dates and grapes be burnt that year: they were now sold in secret at astronomical prices.

For all this, I felt a desire for some dates. I am from al-Yamama, after all, and the first thing in my stomach, even before my mother's milk, had been a date from the palms of al-Yamama that my grandfather had let me suckle on. My mouth watered for a date between my teeth. I stopped by a thin date vendor, a frown on his dark face. His wife stood by him, face covered by a burka. She had beautiful hands painted with henna. He was displaying his wares some distance away from the line of date vendors: he also sold the dense dried yogurt known as *jamid*, animal fat, and small baskets woven of palm fronds. I bought some of his con-cealed supply of dates, and *jamid*. The taste of the latter in my mouth filled me with longing. Ignoring his disgruntled face, I asked, "How does the Arabian Peninsula?"

"Well," he said indifferently. He was looking at me dispar-agingly, thinking I was a Christian pilgrim. I attempted some pleasantries, but he coldly rebuffed me. As the proverb says, "Moving mountains is easier than bringing hearts together!" Our wars with the Byzantines had left no room for affection.

As we were on the outskirts of Egypt, one of the priests, who had ridden on his donkey all the while, said, "We shall tread the path of the Holy Family! I would not have endured riding this slow animal were it not to imitate the Holy Family."

I heard one of the pilgrims by my side mutter to him, "And are you riding a donkey to emulate Jesus and his mother when they fled to Egypt, or because the caliph of Egypt has forbidden Christians from riding on horseback?"

He trotted away from us at that, still astride his she-don-key, muttering, "The Lord Jesus was riding on the back of a speedy cloud: he came to Egypt, and its graven idols trembled with the light of his face, and Egypt's heart melted therein."

## Cairo of the Caliph al-Muizz
## 18 Dhu al-Hijjah AH 402; July 11, AD 1012

Not only had Amr al-Qaysi confided in me the name of one of the Voyagers of Egypt, but he had written out a document for me to facilitate my passage and the sale of my books in the climate of that country, filled with suspicion and teeming with spies.

We continued our path southward, the breezes becoming warmer but not losing their freshness. We arrived at a small town on a hill among green fields and palm trees, called Tal al-Zagazig. There were simple mud-brick houses, their fronts shaded with palm fronds, surrounded by fruit orchards and fields of barley. There was a crowded market whose folk were delighted to see us and examined our wares with curiosity, seeking all that was fit for sale. On the outskirts of these were abandoned graveyards and the idols of extinct peoples.

Most of the pilgrims had separated, and the long caravan had split up into smaller ones, the travelers getting rid of what raisins and dates were still in their possession before arriving in the caliph's Cairo. Four pilgrims who had been walking alongside me all the while cautioned me against openly selling the dates and raisins I had bought: the buyer might be a spy for the chief of police or the ruler. I was, they said, to be subtle about it. "How?" I asked. "I do not mean to sell them. I only mean to eat them." I thought of feeding the dates and raisins to my camel, or giving them to the first hungry man I came across, but before I could announce my intentions, one of the four pilgrims, whose camel had a large nose ring and whose woolen saddle was decorated with brass rings of the same type, and who seemed to be the master of the group, offered to buy them from me for a paltry sum, claiming that he knew where to sell them without arousing suspicion.

"That is even less than what I paid for them," I said.

"As you wish," he said, shrugging, and left. At that point I realized that the story of the police spies and the caliph had all been part of a complex setup: eager eyes keeping track of what I had bought in secret. In the end, I submitted to their wishes to rid myself of my burden: I kept only two containers of raisins and one of dates, pretending to be the innocent Joseph who had believed his brothers' lies. Why not? It was not unlike the idiot's smile I feigned when I preferred to distance myself from some disagreement.

The four men, whom I dubbed "Joseph's brothers," paid me four Fatimid dirhams, with the inscription "Ali is God's steward" on one face and the name of al-Hakim bi-Amr Allah, the Fatimid caliph, on the other. It was the first time I had held one of these in my hand: in Palestine and Bosra, the Abbasid dinar and dirham still inspired confidence in the marketplace. But who knew with Joseph's brothers? The dirhams might be forgeries, and might prove to be made of dates if I put them in my mouth.

We walked on through great farmlands traversed by canals with tree branches and feathers and dead rodents floating in them, the smell of plants and animal dung clogging the air. The size of the tree trunks nourished by Nile silt astounded me: if five men attempted to hold hands around them with their arms fully extended, their hands would not touch. There were boys playing in their branches, and energetic peasant women walking beneath them in colorful clothing that clung to their curves, with swaying steps and flirtatious smiles. They bore earthenware jugs of water on their heads like an adornment that only enhanced their beauty.

Finally, the town of Ain Shams came into view as the sun was setting. I asked after a place where I could rest, pass the night, and feed my mounts. A farmer volunteered the name of a boardinghouse a little way outside the city called the Travelers' House, and before I could ask him for assistance, he took the reins of my camel and walked me there.

My crate made my movements heavy and my travel hard; I feared that it might be lost and I also feared prying eyes. I always needed to keep it beneath a safe roof. My journey to the boardinghouse did not inspire confidence or security, but only pride in myself and disgust for the mean clothing and cracked bare feet of the man leading my mount. "Lord," I prayed, "let not vanity find its way into my nature."

Outside the boardinghouse was an old woman selling bread and stuffing sugarcane and tree branches beneath a hot iron plate, baking large loaves that she then steeped in fat and sugarcane syrup. I bought a delicious hot loaf from her. "Don't you want two more for tomorrow?" she asked. "After a full night in the fat and sugar, they are even more delicious."

I bought the extra loaves, but ate them before I fell asleep: they were, no doubt, the reason for the wild dreams that came to me with the murmuring of the river in my veins as the Egyptian women brought water from it in their round pots.

We continued our journey at dawn from Ain Shams to the walls of Cairo. There were houses and civilization everywhere around us; only a limited number of the original caravan remained, between seven and ten men. At noon, we saw the wall of Cairo of the caliph: towering, sturdy, well guarded, more impressive than the wall of the Circular City in Baghdad, as though the djinn and the spirits had erected it. Around the wall, it was crowded with people and caravans, and vendors crying their wares sold exotic fragrant fruits. I left my camel and mule and my belongings with the caravan guard without yet paying him the fee he had stipulated when we were in Jerusalem. He had begun to make the rounds of the travelers, seeking his fee. When he arrived at me, I placed the reins of my camel in his hand, saying, "I shall go to pray at the al-Azhar Mosque. I shall not be long, and then I shall return to give you your money."

At the gate, the Fatimid guards stopped me—those whose power and savagery had been the talk of the caravan. They were brought in, I had been told, from the desert mountains, so that they had the endurance of a camel, and its cruelty. Dark-skinned, they wore heavy white turbans and held long spears in their right hands. They spoke broken Arabic. One of them looked closely at me. "I am a student," I said to him, "coming to al-Azhar."

"From where do you come?" he asked.

"I come from the Arabian Peninsula. Al-Yamama, from the clan of Bani Ukhaydar, the pure descendants of the Prophet."

I had my doubts that he had understood all I said. He spoke in Berber with a group of guards at the gate, and I heard them repeating, "Student." They soon opened the gate for me, although their faces did not soften.

Despite the scowling guards, after I'd taken a few steps inside, Cairo appeared to shine with the proud glow of a new city. There were wonderfully ornamented buildings, most three stories tall, with carved wooden windows. There were plazas with pots of flowers and fountains, and paved aqueducts filled with water running beneath the walls of the houses. On the walls were brass lanterns set with colored glass. By every mosque was a place for ablutions and a charity fountain from which pigeons and doves drank.

All the roads of Cairo curved to eventually lead out onto a long street they called al-Muizz Street. On both sides of it were collections of shops and stalls, and it was clamorous with the voices of itinerant vendors. I walked down this street, looking at the shop windows, my stranger's face attracting no one's attention. It appeared that they were accustomed to strangers in this city, especially students attending al-Azhar.

At the end of al-Muizz Street, to my right, were one-story buildings set close together that opened onto a pale courtyard in their center: this appeared to be a barracks, for I could see groups of soldiers standing in the square on parade. In the sun, their helmets, swords, and shields gleamed. Their flags were white with a gold crescent, and within every crescent a lion executed in red silk. I could hear their yells and the tramp of energetic, unyielding, grim marching. I trembled. These, then, were the ones who were fighting with the Abbasids for power.

But the awe-inspiring nature of the soldiers was swiftly forgotten when I stood at the steps of al-Azhar, at the end of al-Muizz Street. High minarets called to me, towering over heavy domes set with mosaics. I entered the mosque from the eastern side, immediately finding myself in an inner courtyard with a roof inlaid with gold. From this courtyard five colonnades branched out, supported by marble columns topped with intertwined, colorful garlands, beneath which the discussion circles were held. Perhaps this was the courtyard angled toward Mecca that was known throughout all the lands, whose fame had reached Baghdad. I spent a long while staring at the decorations above me, overcome by a moment's fancy that they were birds whispering to one another.

I faced the east and prayed two prostrations. As I was concluding my prayer, I looked around once again at the ornamentation of the structure and the ceiling. Suddenly I felt a presence next to me, staring at me deeply without blinking. I startled and quickly finished praying.

I trembled when I laid eyes on my neighbor, not only because he had surprised me, but because of his odd appearance and his round, startled eyes. Although his unkempt hair was white, his face was still young. In his eyes was the odd glitter of madness. He wore a loose, ragged garment, but it smelled of luxurious rooms in a well-kept home, and not the rottenness of someone who slept in alleyways. He motioned with his hand to the garlands adorning the ceiling of the mosque, whereupon I looked up at them again. In a deep voice he interrogated me: "Gardens and paradises with nobody in them. Where are their inhabitants?"

His question startled me. I shook my head. "I do not know."

In a voice that seemed not to come from him, he said, "These are the scenes of empty paradises that burn with longing for those who shall live there." Then he leapt up from my side and walked away. He appeared to walk with difficulty: he had a wooden cane with a silver head in the shape of a lion. My eyes followed him as he walked through the arches and pillars of the mosque and disappeared into the light like a spirit.

I had to return to the city wall now, where the camels were. The books were there, and I needed to find a safe place for them, for now I was like a jackal hunting with her pups on her back. I was in need of a house in some discreet and far-flung location. While matters had proceeded smoothly in Jerusalem, with the great crowds of pilgrims awaiting the resurrection of their Christ at the turn of the millennium, it was a different matter in Egypt, for I could see fear and caution on everyone's faces and in the way they moved. Some spoke in low, choked tones. The vendors shouted heedlessly, but if a soldier passed, their voices stopped in their throats and they bowed their heads and only whispered in the ears of the passersby.

I could rent a house as a visiting merchant: I would not go to the Voyager whose name Amr al-Qaysi had given me until I settled down. I had been told in Jerusalem that the rulers and princes here had religious endowments to support the students of al-Azhar, and to grant them room and board. If they found no room there, they took them in to spend their nights in rooms set aside for students in the gardens of their mansions. But that was the last thing I desired here—me and my box of controversial books! A fellow student might betray me there, and my head would soon roll beneath one of the many gates of Cairo.

I resumed my search for shelter, not knowing that my shelter was also searching for me. After my exit from the mosque, I took to walking through the maze of streets around it, crowded with houses and stalls and the large collections of stores, called *wikalas*, with great wooden doors. It seemed to me that the best people to ask after a house to rent would be the itinerant vendors and the water carriers, for they were walking the streets all day, gathering news. Next to the northern gate of the mosque, I found a vendor selling prickly pears. He stood at a wooden cart piled high with them, hoarsely crying out as though it had been his habit all his life.

I stopped at his cart. With his rough hands, he deftly plucked up the prickly pears, peeled them, and then presented them to his customers, still calling out. My foreign accent piqued his curiosity, and he burst out in a chatty tone, "I thought you were from the Levant! Some of the best and brightest students come from Damascus."

I cut off his babbling. "What is the best and closest place where I can rent a room?"

"The students are many," he said. "Why not go to the housing for the students of al-Azhar?"

Instead of answering directly, I said evasively, "I am a man who stays up all night reading the Qur'an and saying prayers; I would disturb my companion or roommate."

He remained unconvinced: I did not look much like an ascetic. Nevertheless, he jerked his thumb at a path to my right. It was an alley slightly elevated from those around the courtyard of the mosque I stood in. "You might find what you want with them."

"Whose house is it?" I said, looking in the direction he'd indicated.

"The owner is a good and devout man, a descendant of the Prophet. He has a large retinue of servants who, I think, will take care of matters. His treasurer is a man named Yunis. You can rent a room in that house."

As I had been chattering with him, he had peeled a number of prickly pears for me, and when I told him that this was too many and that I only wanted two, he was incensed. He turned to a comrade of his, close by, selling green pulses of some sort, and began to insult him with great depravity. I understood that some of these insults were meant for me, as I had not bought all he had peeled. With difficulty, I refrained from answering, and left without thanking him.

The long time he had spent in the company of prickly pears had made him spiky as well.

I went into the alley indicated by the prickly vendor with wary steps. In Jerusalem I had slept in the heart of a jasmine blossom. I hoped that Cairo would be so kind to me. What if the house were narrow and dismal? In fact, its outer appearance was as harsh as the prickly fellow who had pointed it out, but once I stepped over the threshold, I found some details that encouraged me to rent it. By the entrance there was a little room that seemed to have been used to store wood by its previous inhabitants, as its walls were covered in shelves of gesso, and the door had a sturdy lock—a perfect place for me to store my books and bring in some of my would-be buyers without attracting attention. The upper room was sunny and fresh, adjoining a wide roof that overlooked the roof of the house next door, separated only by a low wall.

The boy they sent in with me to open the doors was thin and energetic, leaping up the stairs three at a time. He wore a cap with a bobble on the end: it looked new and he seemed rather proud of it, as he never ceased tilting his head this way and that to make it move and shake. Still, he remembered to tell me all about the walls that had been freshly whitewashed and a spring where I could wash myself without needing to go to the public baths. He apologized for the narrowness of the staircase.

The upper room was furnished with a carpet and a straw mattress, a cotton coverlet and worn pillow atop it. It had a small window with a pot on the sill, full of water, cool and damp. I took it up and drank several gulps, moistening my throat and reviving my spirit: I could feel it enter every corner of me. I knew then that the waters of the Nile taste like nothing else.

I rented the house, which appeared to be a section of a larger dwelling, taking up the entire end of the alley. Perhaps it had been a room for a servant or groom. However, the boy told me that it had been set aside for the teachers of the boys of the house, and had recently been put up for rent with the influx of students to al-Azhar.

It was time to bring my chest of books. I exited by the southern gate and went around the wall to where the caravan was. On the horizon, I could see clusters of close-set buildings, almost on top of one another. They were quite close by. Their windows were narrow, and they were built of red brick. Some of them had many stories—up to eight—so that I thought they were minarets at first glance. I went southward to look at them and stared up at them from nearby, stunned. I only learned that it was the old city of Fustat when I drew near. This was the city originally built by Amr ibn al-Aas: its streets were narrow, crowded with passersby and vendors, refuse and broken pottery. Its doors were low and battered, and thick weeds grew beneath its walls. From time to time, beasts of burden stopped and ate a mouthful. Was it because I was coming here from Cairo that I perceived it as so ugly and repulsive, the faces of the people there so disgruntled and lacking in joy? They had none of that smiling nature of the Egyptians in their fields and farms embraced by the Nile.

I was fatigued and sleepy, and could not stay long. I turned and went back to the walls of Cairo to bring my things from the caravan owner. I feared that my long absence might have incensed him, but quite the reverse: he had made use of my absence to find a place for my camel and mule at a camel trader's at the entrance of Fustat, who pledged to take the camel and mule out to pasture and care for them in return for two dirhams per week, on condition that if the camel became pregnant—for it was a female—he would keep the calf.

I scoffed inwardly at the bargain, for a camel remains with child nigh on a year, and I would only remain in Egypt for a matter of weeks. There was an odd look in the people's eyes here, and they never stopped looking around them.

It did not occur to me then that Egypt would embrace me for two years, during which time I would see wonders that would add years to my life, and white hairs to my head.

A porter approached me with a she-mule pulling a rickety wooden cart, and offered his assistance in moving the pile of boxes and crates at my feet. He wore a monk's habit with a patch on it, and had a large cross hanging from his neck. His cross was unlike the one worn by Samaan, or even Istafan, and some of the pilgrims: it was closer to two tree branches he had lashed together with cord into a crude cruciform on his chest. He offered to convey my things to my preferred destination. "I am going to Cairo," I said, looking at his mule with the air of one doubtful that she could carry my things.

In the sprightly, fluid tone of the Egyptians, he said, "Fear not! I will call a comrade of mine and we will divide up your effects!"

"No!" I motioned to him, afraid to attract attention by appearing so rich that I required two carts to carry all my things. "I entreat you. I have no desire to parade into the alley where I am staying like a bride carrying a trousseau."

Fearing to lose a customer who had not haggled with him over price, he said, "Fear not; I shall take you first, then return to bring the remainder of your things. Do not pay me until you have all your things with you."

"What are the few dirhams I owe him," I thought to myself, "in comparison to the great chest of books, if he were to take it and run?" I was exhausted and in no mood for more negotiation, especially now that we were surrounded by a great crowd of porters waiting for our deal to fall through so as to snatch up a customer.

I looked into the face of the porter, trying to gauge his honesty. He was sad and serious-faced, dark-skinned, with a straight nose and thick lips. His features sat together trustingly, with that air of nobility possessed by devout men who have managed to tame their desires and look upon the world from the high window of decency, purity, and the type of dignity that is too proud to ask for alms.

He loaded my crate and some of my other things onto his cart and we set off, moving parallel to the city wall. He drove along paths where Fustat and Cairo appeared to intermingle, while on the horizon, a group of buildings appeared beneath a great mountain he said was called al-Qatai. I had started my conversation with him with a little lie to pique his avarice: "I am an Arab trader who travels often between Egypt and the Arabian Peninsula," I said, "and if you do your job well, I shall ever be your loyal customer." But he made no response to my lie, only walked on in dignified silence. It appeared that my attempt at ingratiation had failed and my lie had not made him avaricious, but rather the reverse: it had made him draw back out of fragile pride.

I wished he were more pleasant and informal with me, so that I might draw him out on what still remained mysterious to me in the affairs of Egypt, and inquire about the sword that clearly hung over their heads and made people's faces so wary and fearful, especially in Fustat.

When we entered by the southern gate, he turned to me coolly. "Where to?"

His question took me by surprise: I knew not the name of the quarter, nor the alley, where I had rented my house. "Al-Azhar Mosque," I said.

"Which gate?"

"The northern gate of the mosque," I said, and added in an attempt at levity, "The one with the prickly prickly pear vendor."

We went through the streets of the caliph's Cairo, the Coptic porter and I and the box of books, which I had decided to start with, leaving the remainder of my effects with a companion of his whose trustworthiness he vouched for. They spoke among themselves in a strange tongue that was certainly not the Berber spoken by the guards at the door. I could almost make out the meanings of some of the words, but they slipped through my fingers: I was so overcome with curiosity that I asked them, "What language are you speaking?"

"Egyptian," they said. "Coptic is Egypt's original language." I was silent: it is unbefitting of a stranger to scrabble at closed closets.

I was overcome with relief when the minarets of al-Azhar appeared before us and I could make out the location of my home. I motioned to the entrance of the alleyway. When he approached it, the Coptic porter shouted, "Ah! It is the Madman's Alley!"

I whirled to him. "Yes," he said, "that is the name they give it." His face was still sad, glancing about him with a reserve that spoke of his unwillingness to enter into conversation. When we arrived at the gate, I found the boy, Mabrouk—for that was his name—waiting for us, eyes alight with pride at his achievements and expecting his reward, for I had asked him to clean the house from top to bottom of the dust of abandonment and scatter water about, and also to bring me some food.

Together, we brought in the heavy box of books, and the porter whispered to me, "Well, I shall go to bring the rest of your things before night falls; the daylight has eyes, as they say."

Evening came without my realizing it, so engrossed was I in emptying the box of books and removing the dust that clung to them and setting the books upon the gesso shelves. The minarets called us to the sunset prayers with sweet melancholy, the sound pouring down over the ear like water after thirst. It stirred my longings, and I missed my grandfather's room, always filled with treats brought from unknown places. But where was the porter? He had not yet appeared, and the paths of Cairo were dark now and the guards were due to close the gates. Had he decided to steal my things? But there was nothing within them worth the gamble. My most valuable possessions were my books, and here they were, upon shelves in the shadow of the minaret of al-Azhar. My money hung about my waist; the rest was but the scattered effects of a traveler.

How stupid I was! The Christian had tricked me and taken advantage of my ignorance. The Devil had whispered in his ear, "He is nothing but a naive Arab." I had trusted him, and he had thrown that trust away. But I should pay that no mind, after all: it was but some garments and carpets and bottles of perfume, an astrolabe, and a compass that always pointed to the North Star, the last two of which I had exchanged with a trader from Byzantium for a book by Galen of Pergamon. But the original manuscripts of the House of Wisdom were safe on the shelves before me.

There were also some utensils I required in my travels and where I settled: a gourd for water, two plates, two bottles, the raisins and the dates, and some bags of dried sage, chamomile, and thyme given to me by Zulaykha; their scent made me think of Elissar and Hanna. I should sleep this night, then search for him tomorrow; the daylight has eyes, as they say, and I was all but dropping with fatigue. I had not slept between four walls for close on a month.

With the break of dawn, I washed myself and prayed. Then I rushed out of the city walls by the north gate, where the porters congregated, looking around me all the way in hopes of catching a glimpse of him in some alley or other. I caught sight of his companions walking in groups with their shaved heads, leading their mules or donkeys, and wearing the heavy wooden cross, but he was not among them. I feared to ask after him so as not to arouse curiosity and make tongues wag; instead, I preferred to go to the exact spot where I had met him yesterday.

The place was even more packed than the previous day: a caravan had just arrived from Andalusia. Camels, horses, mules, men on horseback and on foot, masters and slaves, all poured in. My things had disappeared from the place where I had left them, and the porter with them. I began to look from one face to another, trying to make out the Coptic porter among those who had gathered about us, awaiting the travelers from the Andalusian caravan; but in vain. I could not find him. I remained there, tired and hungry, until after the afternoon prayers.

Warily, a porter approached me. "Are you looking for Zacharias?"

"The porter with the wooden cart is named Zacharias?" I replied eagerly.

"Yes." He nodded. "I saw him yesterday moving your things."

I grasped his hand, saying pleadingly, "Yes."

Even more warily, looking right and left, he said, "The police took him away last night, him and his mule."

"And my things?" I cried.

"They are on his cart," he whispered.

Stunned, I breathed, "Why did they take him away? Is he a thief?"

"No!" The man shook his head violently. "It is a long story: in brief, the cross about his neck does not conform to the regulations set out by the ruler concerning shape and weight."

"Whatever is happening in Egypt?" I thought. "The *weight* of the cross?" Out loud, I said to my interlocutor, "Where is your police headquarters?"

"Most probably in Cairo," he whispered. "The guards have a place where they gather, by the entryway of the northern gate. Go to them and ask after him: you might find word of him there." Then he hurried off, as the porters were dividing up the Andalusian caravan's things among them.

I went to the place he had pointed out. I found a section beneath the gate roofed with palm fronds, enclosed with low mud walls, strewn with gravel and a few poor mats. Inside, gathered around a dish of dried figs, were the guards.

I approached them and they took to scrutinizing me. They were dark-skinned and long-limbed, like the men I had seen yesterday. I greeted them; they responded only with murmurings and more staring. But I plucked up my courage and said, "I have lost my things, which were with the porter Zacharias."

They appeared indifferent. In an accent that was clearly foreign, they asked, "Where are you from?"

"I come from Baghdad," I said.

"And what do you want here?"

"I am a student at al-Azhar. But when I came here I rented a cart . . ." and I told them the story all over again.

They spoke among themselves in a foreign tongue of which I understood nothing. But one said to me, "What does the porter look like?"

"I know not how to describe him," I said, "only that he is dark of skin, tall and thin, and his name is Zacharias."

"Ah!" he said through a mouthful of figs, and nodded. "We arrested him. He is now in the police headquarters behind the mosque in the caliph's Cairo." He added hurriedly, seeming to want to get rid of me—after all, I had spoiled the enjoyment of their figs—"Go to him there."

I was overcome with the desire to rain down invective. "Shame on you!" I would say, perhaps, and "You threaten the very folk you are pledged to protect!" But the foreigner's tongue is short and his hands are tied, as they say; so back I went to Cairo, doubting that I should regain what I had lost.

After losing my way in the streets several times, and needing to ask the prickly pear vendor for directions twice, I arrived at the police headquarters. I did not recognize it as such at first: it blended into the soldiers' barracks facing al-Azhar, a great, spacious structure with a high, solid wooden door, ringed by a low mud wall around a neglected garden at the end of which the house stood. The inner door stood open, flanked by two red-faced *saqaliba*. I tried to speak with them, but their mouths were stopped by their foreignness: they could not make out what I wanted, save for some motions and gestures that gave me to understand that their chief was absent, and that I should come back the next day. Well, why not? I had come this far.

I walked around the building on my way home. Behind it was a barn where some horses and other beasts of burden were gathered, and there I saw Zacharias's mule, head lowered, the flies collected about her ears, but without the cart or my things. I decided to come back the next day: the daylight has eyes. I passed a bakery thronged with people and bought hot, puffy loaves of bread, not thin like those of Jerusalem, but thick, with black seeds sprinkled over the top.

The doves cooed, opening the gates of evening. A guard with a torch was lighting the lamps of the streets leading away from al-Azhar, while everyone's feet headed for the mosque. When I was nearly at the house, I saw a light shining from beneath the door. I was immediately disquieted. But the key to the storehouse was in my pocket. I hoped my books were safe!

The light turned out to be a simple lantern held aloft by Yunis, the manager of the house. "Welcome to our new guest," he said. "I hope you are comfortable. I am here to reassure myself of your well-being. Has the boy Mabrouk prepared the place and done his duty toward you?"

Yunis had round eyes that darted about slyly, although the remainder of his features resembled a child's. I did not think he was a servant: he might be a steward. He was smartly dressed, and the silk belt about his ample paunch was carefully tied. I understood from his tone that he was here to receive the rent in advance, as I had agreed with him yesterday. "Do come in and share my supper," I said, as politeness dictates. He demurred, but I insisted: a stranger must pave his path with friends.

I spread out a mat I had found rolled up behind the balcony door at the top of the stairs, and we sat sharing bread and honey and careful conversation. The atmosphere between us was more friendly: Yunis excused himself for some time, then returned with a special oil from the main house that would light the lamps of the house without leaving soot stains, along with more rugs, couches, and pillows. "These are for if you would like to furnish your balcony to receive guests," he said.

The space he called the balcony was outside the small room with steps up to it, leading onto the roof of the main house. "This place," said Yunis, "was the quarters of a private teacher my master brought in for his sons. When they grew older and began to go to the discussion circles of al-Azhar, it remained abandoned or used for storage. We revived it and began to rent it to the students and sheikhs of al-Azhar: and it fell to you."

His air as he said the last words gave me to understand that I should pay now. "How much do you require?" I asked. "I will only rent it for two months, as I know not how long I will sojourn in Cairo."

With a false smile, he said, "Sir, we only rent by the year, or six months at the least, no less. Payment is to be made in advance."

I had no choice; out of my meager purse he took three gold dinars as six months' rent. Although I found the sum exorbitant, the advantages of this house would not be easily found again: being part of a great house gave me a secure cover and dissuaded prying eyes, and I had no wish to arouse suspicions about myself with more traveling about Cairo in search of a new home.

He took from his sleeve a sheaf of papers. "What is in the head must be set down on paper." He quoted verse 282 of the Sura of al-Baqara, "*O ye who believe! When ye contract a debt for a fixed term, record it in writing,*" and then started writing, while I consoled myself that I had a great many books that I could sell and make up my losses. I was so tired and sleepy that I could not haggle with him, and I gave him the three gold dinars, my head seeking my pillow.

Suddenly we heard a noise in the road close by the gates, and the sound of muttering and cries, and a man loudly reciting the Qur'an. When we rushed to the gates to see what the matter was, we saw a shadow staggering through the dark, waving a flaming torch. By the light of his torch, I could see it was the madman who had told me the day before at the mosque about the paradises awaiting their denizens. But that was not all. Yunis ran toward him, lantern swinging, then took the madman's hand and kissed it. He took the torch from him, saying, "Come, Master. Let us go home."

My jaw dropped. So this was his master? The passersby were walking past them uncaring, merely greeting them, some stopping to kiss the hand of the madman before going on their way; some clucked their tongues and shook their heads, muttering the proverb "When the world is kind to a man, it gives him the attributes of others; when it is cruel, it robs him of his own."

Yunis headed back into the house, leading his master by the hand. They went to the great wooden gate that formed the end of the alley. This madman was Yunis's master? The man he was speaking of, and in his name, concerning renting houses and teaching sons? Was this the madman the alley was named for? I was not certain, but that day I had learned far more than enough for the curiosity of a stranger on his first day.

## The Woman of the Eggplants

The cries of the river birds and the breezes that reached me in my upstairs room; the small well beneath the house; a safe place for my books: all of these made of this house a little oasis. Despite its modest size, its stairs led to a space that opened docilely onto the sky, where I would spend many nights watching the stars.

I had a great desire to visit a bathhouse, for it appeared I would have a long day. A good breakfast; a bath, lather, and steam—these might return my vitality to me and the vigor to demand what was rightfully mine. The alley was quiet with morning breezes and the footsteps of serious-looking students hurrying to the circles of learning, as they call them in al-Azhar. I was burning with desire to attend the circles of the sheikhs of al-Azhar and hear their words tempered with the waters of the Nile. I am Mazid al-Hanafi of Najd, on the banks of the Nile, performing the traditional rain prayer that it may quench my deep-seated thirst, born of the desert I belong to.

Only a few sheikhs had captivated me after Grandfather's passing, among them al-Hashimi and Amr al-Qaysi. Both Voyagers: was I predestined to become one of them, to admire them and be captivated by their deductions and interpretations? I could have been in the mosque of Baghdad even now, at the right hand of my sheikh al-Tamimi, taking down what he said with reverence and veneration, if my head had not been turned by the booksellers' wares, if varying opinions and leanings had not snatched me away, if I had not been bitten by the lust for knowledge. My sheikh Muhammad al-Tamimi had possessed no knowledge to outstrip my grandfather's. He had exhausted himself with the arguments of the circles and the accusations of embodying God. He had chosen the path of Iraq to reach God. Each of us performs the task he is created for; my place was not there at his side.

On my way through the market to the bathhouse, I passed many porters, Copts leading their donkeys, or water carriers conveying water to the various houses. Around each of their necks hung a heavy wooden cross approaching that worn by Samaan and the Christians of Jerusalem.

When I came out of the bath, restored and reinvigorated, I decided not to ask Yunis to accompany me to the police headquarters. I had no wish to arouse his suspicions, and decided instead to solve my problems myself, only asking for help if I ran into some obstacle.

As luck would have it, this time I was told at the gates that the chief of police had arrived and was inside; he had not gone out on his morning rounds yet. Then the two guards pointed out a gate at the far end of the garden leading to a long, dark colonnade. I had walked only a few paces through it when I froze. I had heard wailing that was more like an animal howl: it was a woman, screaming and begging for something, I knew not what. I thought of fleeing, but kept pushing myself forward.

The colonnade led me to a wide, sun-drenched passage-way with a roof open to the sky, the right side supported by columns surrounding a great chair like a throne. Upon this, a large-headed policeman sat erect, surrounded by pillows of crimson silk, wearing a turquoise-studded brass helmet that seemed jammed onto his big head. His complexion was dark. Upon closer scrutiny, he looked like the bull that stands at the gates of Hell. His men stood around him, their heads lowered. His awe-inspiring impression, though, faded a little when you approached him and found that he was barefoot, that there was no small amount of vacuity and stupidity in his face, and that, furthermore, he did not understand what was said to him the first time, but needed it repeated over and over.

My new clothes that I had bought to replace those I had lost, in addition to the hot bath, appeared to bolster my appearance as a man of high standing, making him leap to his feet in welcome. "Have a seat," he said, "while I finish with the whore," as he called her. The woman continued her wailing, clutching at one of the columns of the colonnade and beating her head against it until her forehead bled, blood dripping down over her face. Her veil fell away, and the things she had been carrying in a bag in her right hand were scattered about.

"I swear by God, three times," she cried, "I never walked in the marketplace! The seller is a low man and chooses the worst eggplants to give me! I went downstairs to select them myself when your men arrested me on the charge of speaking with men!" She tore one of the bracelets from her hand and rushed to the seat of the chief of police, falling at his feet and crying out, "My children have been alone in the house since the morning! My husband is a tanner! He will tan my hide and wipe the stable floor with me if he finds out!"

She was shrieking and crying and beating her face with her hands. The chief of police looked from the bracelet she had left on his boots to the one still on her wrist and said, "The crier has called it in the marketplace dozens of times: any woman walking in the market will be imprisoned and punished. But you women are like Potiphar's wife: you would tempt any man to sin, and are impelled by your natural inclination to seduction."

She cried out again and beat her head against the column, more blood oozing out. Suddenly, I knew not why—perhaps her screaming had disturbed him, or perhaps as part of a tacit agreement among everyone that the chief of police always softened before a woman's wailing—he reached out with a rattan cane and took up the bracelet with it. He turned it this way and that in his hands, then quickly stung her thick buttocks a few times with the cane as she writhed at his feet. "Return her to her home," he said. "As for the vendor who sold to her, take his wares for yourselves today as a punishment for him."

Before I could fully overcome my shock, he turned to me with his great head and flaring nostrils like a bull's. "What's your story?"

I did not know how I found the halting words and breath to tell him the story of the porter and my things.

"Ah!" he interrupted me with a voice that resounded from the depths of his great belly. "So you are the man who came here the other day. We would have returned your goods to you, if we had not found magic and sorcery in them, and plants with a bizarre smell." Before I could open my mouth to explain, he said, "Yesterday we arrested the Coptic porter cheating on weight: he disobeyed the sultan's orders and removed the cross weighing a pound and a quarter, which bears the hallmark of a workshop that makes them for the Copts, assuring us of their proper weight, and donned a light one of tree branches in its place. He must be punished. You will not get your goods back until you tell us the secrets of these tools and plants."

What was I to do? How should I deal with this man whose tongue was a whip and whose hand was a scourge? Should I tell him that these tools were the pinnacle of human invention from the House of Wisdom, and the compass and the astrolabe for the stars and planets? I guessed at that moment that I must lay something at his feet to liberate my things, but feared to misjudge matters or underpay him. I found it prudent to draw back until I had asked someone how to deal with this matter.

Meanwhile, two men embroiled in an altercation had come in behind me. The first said the other had split his head open, while the second was yelling and swearing that he had not; indeed, he claimed, the first man was the one who sold dates in secret outside the door to the mosque. The chief of police's nostrils flared anew. "Come closer!" he cried, and the colonnade was in chaos once more. While the policemen reprimanded the adversaries, shouting at them to be quiet, I saw my chance and slipped away without being noticed.

I stopped at the gate, in search of a guard who spoke good Arabic to ask him how Zacharias the Copt was faring. I finally found Zacharias in the stable room behind the neglected garden of the police headquarters, shaven, with wounds and raw places on his scalp. He gave me a somewhat foolish smile. "Zacharias is well," he volunteered. "His people have taken up a collection for him and he shall be set free. God has liberated him. The chief of police is kindhearted and forgiving, unlike many chiefs of police. Some of those who have arrived from Damascus say that his counterpart in Damascus ordered a Moroccan man be paraded around on a donkey and publicly humiliated, then had him beheaded." When he saw the shock and horror on my face at his words, he added smugly, "That is the reward of those who love the Sunni caliphs Abu Bakr and Umar."

I recalled the document Amr al-Qaysi had prepared for me, addressed to an Egyptian Voyager called Rashid ibn Ali, who lived in the city of al-Qatai below the Muqattam Mountain. I had thought to land on his house like a voyaging falcon, flying high and above all want, but circumstances had dictated that I come to him bearing a sack of troubles.

Coming and going between Cairo and Fustat remained tricky, always arousing suspicion and questions. My third day in Egypt dawned and I still had not visited their great river and greeted it; I had not gazed my fill at the boats sailing upon it and the flocks of birds flying above it, but instead had wasted my time parleying with policemen.

The skies of Egypt were filled with birds migrating from the north. Was this their season? I was no hunter, for I had slipped on the first line of a book and couldn't get out. The reeds clogged the riverbanks, thicker than those in Basra. Golden, shining reeds tangled, taller than a man, interlaced like the bars of a cell; but as they swayed they revealed a winding path along which I picked my way carefully.

Suddenly, in the middle of this swamp, there appeared a cluster of houses fashioned of cane and reeds—clearly huts constructed for fishermen. They were spreading their nets wide, washing their clothing and hanging it out on the reeds to dry, and cooking their food on the banks of the river. As I passed, they stared at me in a friendly manner and entreated me to share three grilled fish from their table. I thanked them and retreated hastily: I am a man of the desert, and fish is pungent and repugnant to my nostrils. Although Hassan the Egyptian in Baghdad had often tried to make me learn to like it, he had never succeeded. I had eaten rabbit and dried meat, yet I could not stomach fish. Did not Jurayr al-Tamimi of Najd say of pure

Arab women: "They live not with Christians, desert-bred; / They never ate of pure fish yet."

The fishermen had set out their baskets and their catch the length of the riverbank. The fish in the baskets stared at me from the bottom of the well of death with round eyes like the eyes of my pet Shaqran; when I slit his throat, his eyes had stopped pleading and only stared at me.

The sun's heat was blistering, shining over the river with the ripples of calm, sweet waves. The slight mist of high noon turned the river into a shattered mirror whose every shard told a story. I wished then that I could know where Moses's mother had set the papyrus basket afloat bearing her infant, and the location of the great clumps of sedge where the basket had run aground. The Qur'an says in verse seven of the Sura of al-Qasas that Moses's mother was inspired to place him in the basket and was told, "*We shall restore him to thee, and We shall make him one of Our messengers.*" But who had told her that? Was it God who had spoken to her directly? That would make her a prophetess. Had He sent an angel to her? Had he breathed it into her soul?

Who lets himself question will ever fall prey to suspicion and remain in eternal doubt. There was a fertile and delicious thing between the reeds the length of the riverbank: the soul of everything that grows awakens what lies slumbering within one's veins. How tempting is Egypt, the repository of history and the mermaids' playground.

I felt hungry. I turned and headed for the Muqattam Mountain and al-Qatai. I would go to the market and eat before commencing my search for Rashid ibn Ali. Egypt was now divided into three cities: Fustat built by Amr ibn al-Aas, Cairo built by al-Muizz, and between these, al-Qatai built by Ahmad ibn Tulun and embraced by the Muqattam Mountain. Each leader, drunk on victory and domination, builds a new city in his own image. Ibn Tulun had come to Egypt as a wali before deciding to secede as a princedom. These were the flags of the victorious and the rule of armies: Egypt had tempted conquerors throughout history. From the north, over and over, a victorious conqueror would come and claim it as his own.

## Al-Qatai

I waited until the noonday heat had cooled, then walked through the streets seeking Rashid ibn Ali. Finally, one passerby asked, "You mean the carpet dealer?" as though he found it strange that I was asking directions of one who was himself a landmark.

A carpet dealer! Was the Voyager hiding behind carpets, then, and camouflaging himself in their patterns? I had thought the Voyagers were only crafters of sentences and sciences.

A great many neighborhoods in al-Qatai were all but abandoned, but the neighborhoods beneath the Muqattam Mountain were still populous, comprising a tanners' market and a spear makers' market. Al-Qatai and Cairo were much like two wives: the former older, abandoned, and neglected, those in power turning away from it and toward the caliph's Cairo, fresh and charming in her youth. The houses of Cairo were built of sparkling stone, with spacious balconies and steps leading up to them at a distance from the public street. There were gardens separating them, and they were more spacious, and the marketplace was at a distance from al-Azhar Mosque and School out of respect and veneration for the latter's status. But in al-Qatai, there were still the remnants of some of its ancient glory in some of its neighborhoods, especially those next to the Ibn Tulun Mosque. The mosque itself still preserved some of its luster: in the center of its courtyard was a dome held up by ten marble pillars. Beneath it was a fountain overflowing with sweet, cool water.

I felt my way forward, asking and guessing, delving deeper and deeper into al-Qatai in a westerly direction, heading for the Muqattam Mountain, until I reached the outskirts of a market selling leather goods and carpets. On the corner where two streets intersected was a grand store selling carpets, the size of three of its neighbors put together. Inside were vast rolls of carpets and fabrics, both silk and wool. Some of the carpets were rolled up in rows in corners and against the walls, while some valuable silken pieces were hung up prominently. The air was full of the smell of wool.

I stood at the door. The shop was crowded with elegant men who had a supercilious air. They seemed familiar to me. Their clothing was clean and their features well-washed; their perfumes were overpowering, and they spoke with quick, leaping phrases, unlike the speech of the Egyptians. Before I could step inside, I recalled where I had seen them before: they were members of the caravan that had arrived from Andalusia and settled by the walls of Cairo the day before. They clustered about their master, following him with respect: because he was fat, with a great paunch, the shop attendant had brought him a chair upon which to catch his breath, and was now displaying his carpets in the man's hands and at his feet. The shop boys spread out the carpets, and he fingered them dubiously and turned them over to examine them. "Ah," he would say, "this is Samarqand wool," or "Chinese silk," then gesture to another of the carpets hung up. "Bring me that Persian rug hanging there." Those around him seemed disinclined to offer any opinion that differed from what their master said. The group of men around him: were they his guards? They wore ribbed belts and silk turbans with shining jewels on the front. They smelled of perfume, and their eyes glittered. They say that their eyes are not afflicted by weakness or blindness because they are always looking at green pastures. Bless you, Andalusia! When shall I lay down my wandering staff on your shores?

Eventually, one of the carpet trader's men noticed my presence as I stood at the door, stunned by what I saw. He hurried toward me from the other end of the store. "What can I do for you?"

I cut him off. "I'm here to see Rashid ibn Ali," I whispered.

He fell silent at first: he had been engaged in divining my nature and class so as to seek out the best manner to sell me a carpet, but I had cut him off, breaking his train of thought. I was definitely a foreigner, not an Egyptian: my clothing did not indicate that I was a poor man seeking work, but it was nowhere near the extravagant beauty of the Andalusians.

Just then, a white-haired, bearded man came over, clearly making an effort to appear friendly while attempting to retain his dignity and maintain a respectful distance between himself and his many shop attendants. It appeared that it was his custom to intervene when some matter arose that was beyond the shop attendants' abilities. I repeated my request to see Rashid ibn Ali. His eyes did not widen in surprise, but he did say politely, "The man you seek is not here now. Whom shall we tell him asked, when he returns?"

I slumped. With some hesitation, I said, "Mazid al-Hanafi. Kindly tell him I want carpets for my house, which lies in a status between two statuses." And I left.

Ah, this phrase that opened all doors for me; it had not let me down yet among the Voyagers. When I returned the following morning, the shop attendant received me eagerly. "Where did you disappear to, man?" he asked. "Our master Rashid ibn Ali has been waiting for you since yesterday."

The man with the white beard ushered me into a room at the rear of the shop. I thought I would meet Rashid there, but it was an entryway to a great red room. All the furnishings were red. The ceiling was ornamented with gilded miniatures and there were wooden closets along the walls carved with curlicues and intricately formed branches, the height of two men and perhaps five arm spans across. The table was piled high with books and ledgers.

In the center of the room sat a man engrossed in a book. He only looked up when we were five paces away, and even then he could barely tear his eyes from the page. He planted his eyes on my face. A silence ensued which I felt must have been long; he had uttered nothing but mumbled to return my greeting. At first he appeared distracted and absent: I could tell that he was still lost in the book he held in his hands. He stared at my face as though emerging from underwater and seeing the world for the first time. He was swarthy and had coarse features, but there was a quiet manliness in his look and an air of nobility in his demeanor—that of a man whose essence is held up on pillars of wisdom.

He motioned to the shop attendant to go, and I remained there, observing him. His face was not that of a merchant, with their greedy, grasping mien concealed behind a pretense of decency to draw you in. He was not wearing his turban, only a striped caftan over which was an abaya of the well-made, expensive silk that, in Baghdad, was brought in from villages in the mountains of Surian. On my way there, I had vacillated: should I give him the document al-Qaysi had handed me or content myself with the "between two statuses" I had conveyed to him the day before? He cut my thinking short by handing me a book by al-Kindi that had been in his hand and commanded, without inviting me to take a seat, "Read the last two lines."

I took it from him and murmured, "Philosophy is unattainable if one does not know mathematics. Mathematics is unattainable without the science of logical deduction."

When I finished, he said, "What is your opinion of this?"

I was shocked by this sudden test, and knew not what to do. Inspiration struck, however, as it had been wont to do of late. I recalled what Amr al-Qaysi had discussed in his circle, and recited, "With the advancement of humankind and the wars that require justice in dividing up the spoils and equal numbers in the ranks of an army, they used the sexagesimal system: sixty signs as the base, before the Ancient Egyptians developed the decimal system currently in use."

I looked into his face, hoping my response was sufficient. But I was struck with fear to see a thread of mockery lifting his lower lip. "Also," I said, catching myself, "al-Kindi employed mathematics in creating the Arab musical scale, as mathematical truths are immutable and precede all their counterparts in the world of the senses. The mathematical method requires rational proofs."

"Good," he said carelessly. Then he gestured to a book on a shelf, covered in red leather. "Bring that book, and let us see what Abd al-Jabbar ibn Ahmad has to say about this." I rushed to the spot he had indicated, asking him the name of the book. "It is on the second shelf. It's called *The Classes of Mutazilites.*"

I handed it to him and it fell open to a specific page, as though the book was opened to it habitually, and he read in a deep, hoarse voice: "There are three types of evidence: the evidence of the mind, because it weighs pros and cons, and because it knows that the Holy Book, the Prophet's tradition, and any matter upon which the four imams agree are all sources."

My heart beat faster. I could no longer hear what this venerable man was saying: I recalled that, one day, my sheikh al-Tamimi had cursed Abd al-Jabbar and called him an infidel, and said it was a sin to stand behind him in prayer, and if the latter had not been living in Rayy, under the protection of its ruler, al-Sahib ibn Abbad, he would have called for his death.

When Rashid ibn Ali saw that I had fallen silent and become distracted, he surprised me with the question: "And how are the Voyagers?"

"The Voyagers of Baghdad," I said, "repeat this verse by a blind poet with a great insight, who visited the city. His name is Abu al-Alaa al-Maari. He says: 'Young man possessed of intellect, if you be sound of mind, / Know that each mind a prophet is, and follow on behind.'"

It was as though this verse had rained down flowers upon the face of Rashid ibn Ali: the sun rose in his face and his garden blossomed. "We Just Monotheists," he said, "have no guiding light but our intellect. Bless you!"

He cleared a space for me to sit by him and asked me my background and where I was from. My reserve fell away, and I took to chattering in comfort and security. "My name is Mazid al-Hanafi . . . al-Yamama, Basra, Baghdad, Jerusalem . . ." and so on. Mazid, the voyager through the Agate Cities and the uncharted lands of knowledge, who knows more keenly every day how much he does not know.

He asked me how Amr al-Qaysi was and about his affairs. He did not ask about al-Hashimi or Seraj al-Din al-Furati. I guessed that most probably, in the secret laws of the Voyagers, no disciple knew more than one person in his voyages, to break the chain and keep their story from spreading. In Egypt there were many Voyagers, but Amr only knew Rashid ibn Ali. Or perhaps, for some reason only he knew, he thought that Rashid had the water that would quench the thirst of my parched soul. That seemed to be why a disciple arriving in a country only knew the sheikh he was going to, and the one he had come from.

My sheikh in Egypt, whom I had come to, seated me close to him and resumed his perusal of his book. He raised his head. "Where are you lodging?" He went on, "Beware of renting a lodging in the alleys where the police are quartered: you will be placing yourself under suspicion and many eyes will spy on you. When Jawhar al-Saqilli, who built Cairo, finished building the Eastern Castle and the mosque, he divided his soldiers among twenty alleys, and named each alley by the name of the tribe that settled there: there is Zuweila Alley next to Zuweila Gate, Barqiya Alley, the Byzantine Alley, Kutama Alley, and so on. Now, as you see, Cairo has become a military encampment. Al-Qatai and

Cairo are practically interconnected. If you go out of the Zuweila Gate you immediately find the Ibn Tulun Mosque. Therefore, choose for yourself a room or boardinghouse next to the mosque, one devoted to students."

I told him the tale of my arrival and the rental of my house, deferring the story of my confiscated articles. Now I understood the confident unpleasantness of the soldiers I passed by at the exits of the alleys as I came and went: I was nothing but an interloper in what was effectively a military barracks. "Have you started to attend the discussion circles of al-Azhar?" he asked.

"I am following them," I replied, "so as to find someone worthy of bending my knees to sit in his circle and place myself in his hands."

"Do not expect to find Voyagers only as theologians and clerics in these circles," he said. "They are everywhere. Their light moves in their hands, and I was careful to surprise you with a question about al-Kindi and the intellect so as to put you on my path and see where you would tread. I placed you upon my scales to see which of the balances would descend."

The ease with which I had joined the path of this imposing, suspicious giant of an Egyptian emboldened me to say, "Since I am upon your path, I wish you might permit me to avail myself of the paradise of your library when I desire."

I said it and immediately fell silent, afraid I had over-reached. But he laid his hand on my shoulder in a friendly manner. "It is yours."

At this juncture, I informed him of the book collection in my possession, and asked as to the ideal method of distributing them. "I will be straight with you," he said. "In these dark days that Egypt is experiencing, you will not find a thriving book market. However, books are still like gold: their price multiplies with age and provenance, and they will not remain without buyers."

I felt I must leave, since after saying this, he had returned to his book. Head bowed, I said, "There is one last thing."

He raised his eyebrows curiously. Only then did I take note of his large, slightly protuberant eyes.

"What is the best way to get my things back from the chief of police?" I asked.

He blinked. I told him the story of Zacharias and his cart. He shook his head sorrowfully. "Come by tomorrow for the midday meal, and I will have obtained the answer in relation to your possessions." He went back to reading. "Close the door behind you, and call Yakout in to me."

I exited with alacrity and no little joy, my path paved with rubies. In a short interview, I had been given the right to visit an astonishing library and gained a promise of my things being returned to me!

I went out into the shop, looking at the shop attendants, searching for Yakout, who was, as I had expected, the polite white-haired gentleman. I told him that his master wanted him, then added a question before I left. "I would like to take a tour of al-Qatai," I said, "and perhaps go a little way up the Muqattam Mountain. Is there any danger in it?"

His eyes gleamed. "No. But be careful, and do not investigate too thoroughly or linger in abandoned places, where thieves hide. Also, the caliph's guards, informants, and spies are all about the place to organize a safe passage for him." He lowered his voice and said with wry derision, "In recent times, our caliph, who has set himself up as the Imam Who Can Do No Wrong, has taken to leaving the palace at night on his donkey and going to read the stars and interpret their signs on the summit of Muqattam. And because he refuses the company of any of his guards, the captain of the guard, who is responsible for his safety, is obliged to scatter his soldiers about the path in the guise of informants or itinerant vendors."

*

It was not an easy thing to forget Rashid ibn Ali once you were out of his company. The way he raised his eyes from his books and fixed them on his interlocutor; the way he paused between sentences to choose his words; in a word, his presence impressed itself upon me as the other Voyagers' had. The coarse features of his face; his neck, thick and veined like a tree trunk; his curly hair shining with perfumed oil, shot through with white; and the library he proudly displayed . . . what manner of books lay in it? I must not be too hasty in seeking answers nor tear them open too roughly. Answers lie dormant like butterflies in their chrysalises: when they are complete, they flutter free to perch on your finger.

My heart trembled as I walked, knowing that this was the path taken by the caliph every night on his way out of his palace. I glimpsed around me ruined mansions and abandoned houses, whose inhabitants had left them empty to be taken over by some shepherds and their handfuls of sheep, and a few water carriers: these sat, smiling and friendly, outside houses with the windows taken out, the doors broken in. I was certain that if I entered the house of any of these men, they would share their supper with me.

On my way back to Cairo, I walked along the Water Car-riers' Alley, so as not to become lost in the many streets. The water carriers of Cairo had their own streets, through which the camels and mules, gourds and containers of water on their back, came and went from the Nile. They were always squab-bling with the passersby, either because the water in their gourds had splashed on someone's clothing or because they insisted on being paid in advance: half a daniq, which is one-sixth of a dirham, for every floor ascended in someone's house.

I must return to my home now. I had asked Mabrouk to purchase for me some mugwort and sweet basil and plant it in pots around the circumference of the upper balcony and throughout the house, for the mosquitoes had given me great distress the previous night, especially with our proximity to the river. My "blood was sweet," as Shammaa had told me when the mosquitoes bit my face as a child.

Shammaa of the House of Wael! Her memory was like a needle pricking at my heart. I thought of her headscarf with its yellow flowers: she always bought a new one from the pilgrims returning from Mecca. In the evening, when she slept, she removed it and washed it, then undid her long braids and let her hair hang loose over her back. The next morning, when it dried, she would wrap it up and place dried lavender in it, so her hair would smell of lavender all day. I would not remember her too vividly, for my heart ached.

The scent of mugwort and basil was powerful at the entrance to my house. Although it was tempting to remain beneath these shelves reading the books, I must not give in to this desire. I must join the discussion circles of al-Azhar. If I lingered here reading only, it would no doubt give rise to suspicion.

It was not the sound of the evening prayers that brought me out of my house, but the sound of screaming, almost yowling. I could not find its source until I approached the door and it sounded again. "The Lord is everywhere! He speaketh all tongues! He manifests in every person!"

The voice was coming from the main house at the end of Madman's Alley. I recalled then that my search for Rashid ibn Ali and what remained of my things and the porter had kept me from asking about the madman and his relation to Yunis. I opened the door and looked around, seeking the source of the sound. Despite the dusk starting to descend on the alley, Yunis was attempting to pat the madman's shoulder in a calming manner as he led him into the house, lifting his hand and kissing it from time to time. From behind the gate of the house, women's hands protruded, some bearing glasses of a drink they were trying to hand Yunis to give the madman, some catching at his sleeve to pull him inside. The madman himself had his eyes fixed on the sky and cried out, "The Lord is everywhere! He speaketh all tongues! He manifests in every person! Glory be to Him who has no equal, nor companion on His throne!"

I retreated into the interior warily, sensing Yunis's embarrassment: he surely had no wish for me to see, as I had, this man pushing him, kicking him, and throwing his turban to the ground. But a strange tremor went through me, making me leap up suddenly. I felt that I was being watched in secret.

I closed the door of my house, overcome with loneliness. Egypt does not go to bed early. There are voices everywhere. I felt that every voice had its own secret, quite unlike its fellow. That same night, the sound of some string instrument being plucked descended upon my rooftop, ruinous to the soul on account of its great beauty. The music was enthralling and sweet, as though the musician had plucked the melancholy and longing of every migrating bird over Egypt that year and poured it over the strings.

I woke on Friday morning with the melodies still in my head. Foreigners always tread lightly, walking by the roadside and leaving the center of the road to others, and they do not beat about the bush in conversation; they make way for others; they are never expansive in their conversation; and they are careful to avoid confrontations, be it with a vendor or a chief of police.

I passed by al-Azhar for Friday prayers before going to Rashid ibn Ali. Before I went inside, my attention was caught by an opulent carriage pulled by an extraordinarily dapper mule, its saddle adorned with silver; a group of mosque attendants had gathered around it, in their center a black-skinned beardless man, well dressed, with a magnificent turban. He turned his nose up at those passing by. His appearance suggested that he was a palace eunuch. I heard him speaking to someone in a commanding, impetuous tone: "Bring the stamp from the imam to indicate you have received the mosque's supplies from the palace!"

An attendant rushed inside, while others took to enumerating the various supplies sent from al-Azhar in loud, pompous voices. "Four mats from Abdan; four plaited mats; Indian oud; musk, one month's supply; wax and wicks for lanterns and coal for burning incense; four ropes; six buckets; ten baskets; two hundred brooms; earthenware water jars and their stands; fuel oil; a silver chandelier; twenty-seven silver lanterns. . . ." He repeated them as though going over supplies, but it soon became clear to me that he was taking advantage of the crowds coming in for the Friday prayers to show off and boast of the supplies sent by the palace to al-Azhar.

The sermon that Friday was on Islam's benefit to every nation, the justice of the Almighty, and returning power to the Prophet's descendants—namely, those who ruled Egypt.

After prayers, the discussion circles were held. Although I was hurrying to the house of Rashid ibn Ali, I could not keep myself from a circle I passed; I heard the sheikh saying, "Why is a verb formed from a noun without the element of time?" The students around him were either African or foreign. I guessed that this lesson was a review session before the students began their examinations to earn their degrees. I recalled with pride, in the mosque in Baghdad, how my sheikh, al-Tamimi, had always chosen me to go over lessons for the foreign students from Persia and Sindh. That pride drove me to yell from where I stood in the outermost circle: "Because time is always present. A verb is meant to indicate a meaning: since verbs are finite but time is always present, nouns are what we must take verbs from."

Every head turned to me, while the sheikh of the circle stared at me in silent surprise. I suddenly feared that what I had said might be a Mutazilite belief that had stuck in my head, but the sheikh smiled. "Well said, young man. What is your name?"

As my grandfather always says, "A man is judged by what he says, not what he wears." My words about the sources of verbs had opened the gates to me: I walked out of the mosque with information about most of the sheikhs' discussion circles, the times they were held, the place where I should set down my name tomorrow, and the identity of the treasurer of the mosque who bestowed the palace's monthly stipend upon the students.

Al-Qatai was teeming with people that day: some itinerant vendors had even laid out pumpkins, Armenian cucumbers, and garlic among the ruins. I had barely arrived at the carpet store when I found it closed and shuttered. I was overcome with disappointment. What had happened? Should I go back, or seek some other door?

I did not have to search for the door, for it sought me out. One of the boys who worked in the carpet store, whom I had seen inside yesterday, waved to me from across the street, telling me to follow him. We walked down a paved street. On both sides, houses had sprung up with high walls and wooden windows that protruded like boxes. At the end of the street, we went through a passage that led into the same red room where I had met Rashid ibn Ali the day before; we had entered by the large south gate.

Rashid was at the head of his gathering, surrounded by his guests, looking quite different from the day before. He was in full finery—a caftan and a silk turban—and tall, bright-faced young men were sitting on either side of him, although they appeared bored and lackluster, looking about the guests' faces. As soon as one of the young men spotted me at the door, he leapt up to welcome me with a warm smile on his face. "Is this why a verb is formed from a noun?" he asked.

His energetic welcome tied my tongue. He led me to greet Rashid ibn Ali, saying, "I am Ataa, son of Rashid, and I heard you today at the circle in the mosque. I am in the habit of frequenting discussion circles." With a chuckle, he whispered in my ear as we walked to his father, "But many of the circles in the mosque go beyond charlatanism to sheer quackery."

I liked the light of fun and mischief in his eye, and hoped to speak more with him. As soon as I greeted Rashid ibn Ali and sat close by him, I heard him commanding one of his boys: "Bring Mazid's things." The boy rushed off and, after a short absence, arrived with the rest of my bags and boxes, dust and all, that the chief of police had confiscated on his shoulders.

I was embarrassed by my humble belongings making an appearance in this opulent company, with the towering ceilings, the gilded ornamentations, and the couches that embraced you like a mother. I feared he might open them up in front of everyone, revealing my herbs and old sandals with goatskin straps, which I still kept with me from my time in al-Yamama. "Please," I said to the boy, "put them somewhere close by, and I will take them when I leave."

"We liberated your things!" Rashid ibn Ali called from where he sat at the head of the table. "We also interceded for the Coptic mule driver. He promised to hang a cross around his neck of the required weight, but he had no money to buy it. We paid for his cross and his fee in one."

I tried to ask him for more details, but was interrupted by a group of boys coming in with trays bearing glasses of a sweet drink with a wonderful scent. The boy who gave me a glass saw my confusion and hesitancy, and said, "This is made from dried apricot. In Egypt, we call it *qamar al-din*."

At that time, the assembly was abuzz with the story of an Azharite sheikh who had been found with a copy of the *Muwatta Imam Malik*, the earliest written collection of the Prophet Muhammad's sayings, compiled by Imam Malik. The Shiite rulers had had him whipped and paraded around on a mule for fear that the School of Imam Malik might spread among the Egyptians. Rashid ibn Ali looked at me meaningfully, as if to say, "See?" Then he introduced me to his assembly: "Mazid al-Hanafi, a student from al-Yamama." He immediately gestured to the young men on either side: "My sons, Ataa, Abd al-Jabbar, Ibrahim, and Idris—in honor of the prophet Idris, who was the first to write and settle in Egypt."

The glances of mischievous youth and the natural pride of nobility were in his sons' eyes. Their bright garments and silk turbans suggested they were young men who had never yet suffered; the greatest challenge they had faced was shooting down a wild goose with their arrows. Did they swagger along the Nile, followed by girls staring and women sighing? I, too, sighed deeply. Is this envy, Mazid? Have you lost the pride you felt in the al-Azhar discussion circle a little while ago?

I drove these thoughts from my head and took to observing Rashid ibn Ali, surrounded by his sons, of whom he appeared as proud as a peacock fanning his tail this way and that. My father had not been proud of me. He thought that my long sojourn at my grandfather's side, my face buried in a book, had made me soft. He made me suffer under the lash of hard tasks, cutting up dry palm fronds and turning waterwheels and carrying water. When my grandfather stopped him, telling him I had an extraordinary talent for reading and writing, he would lose his mind, sending me away to the camels' grazing ground for a week at a time. I would return with my feet full of cactus spines; Shammaa would anoint the soles of my feet with flaxseed oil to draw them out, quarreling with my father all the while.

My father wanted his sons to be a collection of fighters on horseback: strong, powerful men. But when he grew old and sick, and his sons were scattered about every land and valley, he would find none to tend his weakness but some of his women and his daughters: they alone would sit by his head when he died, and mourn and bury him, wailing at his grave.

The sons of Rashid ibn Ali had bright faces, pleasant demeanors, and features that had never known privation or hunger. He appeared to have forced them to attend this gathering to bolster his own pride. He went on by way of introduction: "I named Ataa after Sheikh Wasil ibn Ataa, one of the heads of the Just Monotheists, who left Imam Hassan of Basra and let his intellect be his imam. In the second and third—Ibrahim and Abd al-Jabbar—I brought together both names of the Judge of the Mutazilites, bless his intellect and rationality."

It appeared that Egypt would not brandish its knives in the faces of Mutazilites as yet—or was it just that Rashid ibn Ali trusted his assembly? Most of the men there appeared to be merchants, distracted by moneymaking from science and contemplation; they were discussing the affairs of the market as they enjoyed their *qamar al-din*.

Soon, however, Rashid ibn Ali turned to his son Idris, as though continuing a conversation they had started before my arrival. His eyes fixed a little above his son's face with a half smile, he said, "My question is, was the Holy Qur'an created in the time of the Prophet and concordant with the events that happened then?" Idris lowered his head in silent confusion. His father added, "Or is it as the folk of Basra say, that it was created with Life itself, and preserved in the Tablet?"

Idris appeared to like the latter answer, as it seemed to give more dignity to the Qur'an's eternal status. He responded quickly, as though afraid that someone else would beat him to it, "It is eternal, in the Preserved Tablet!"

His father smiled triumphantly, as though he had won some contest and was now leading the conversation in the direction he pleased. "Well, if that is the case, what of verse one of the Sura of al-Masad, which says, '*Perish the hands of Abu Lahab! Perish he!*' Is Abu Lahab's infidel nature born of the moment, or old as eternity?"

He looked at the faces around him, victory in his protuberant eyes. But everyone around him was silent. "Abu Lahab cannot have been created an infidel," he explained.

"The evidence being that the Prophet Muhammad, peace be upon him, called upon him to believe, and was insistent in his preaching. There was a possibility that he could have become a Muslim, like the uncles of the Prophet, Hamza and al-Abbas. But he did not. And the Qur'an descended with the verse that described these events. Therefore, the Qur'an is created and not eternal. The Divine Meanings lie not in the letter of the words, but in what they engender in ourselves and the ideas they inspire in the mind." He paused, gauging the effect of his words on the faces of those around him. He shook his head, "This is the reverse of what the Hanbalites say, that one must judge by the general intent of the text, not by the specific occasion." He immediately turned to me. "What do you say to this, Mazid?"

I had already divined that he had embarked upon this topic that I might empty my mind's pockets in his gathering, and also to get the merchants to quit their discussion of the wheat caravans on their way to Hijaz. I racked my brain in an attempt to recall a few lines from the discussion circles of Baghdad on this subject. I sought something impressive, awe-inspiring, even if I did not understand some portion of it; something by means of which I could outstrip these young men born in the lap of luxury and make them feel inferior in the presence of my vast knowledge. I said, "God has described His own book as created, for he says in verse two of the Sura of al-Anbiya: *'Cometh unto them a new message from their Lord.' There is nothing eternal in this world but God.*"

I saw Ataa's eyes sparkle, not with jealousy but with warmth. Even his breast was pure and free of envy, radiant as his face. The assembly whispered and chattered about the Preserved Tablet and the preservation of the Qur'an. Rashid ibn Ali pressed his thick lips together, clearly afraid that the chatter would devolve into an uproar, and pushed the boat of the conversation far from the Preserved Tablet. He turned to me. "Have you seen the giraffe and the elephant of al-Ikhshid?"

I gaped. What was he speaking of? His sons laughed. "The giraffe and elephant of al-Ikhshid have an interesting story that everyone who visits Egypt must know. Al-Ikhshid looked at his minister Kaffur one day, the day they brought in a giraffe and an elephant from the land of the Negroes. All the servants and slaves tilted their heads to look, but Kaffur's eyes never left al-Ikhshid, for fear that he might call on him only to find him distracted. Al-Ikhshid and Kaffur long gone, the elephant and the giraffe remained, handed down to generations of the stable boys of al-Ikhshid, who cared for them on a farm not far from Fustat, and people began to go there to see the animals and wonder at them. They were cloistered away from people, so that you could not see them without paying a dirham. When the giraffe died, they sent for another from the land of the Negroes, and brought back two; a space was cleared for them next to where the rams and cocks fight, and the people go to see them every week."

I feared that this talk of the giraffe and the elephant meant that he was making light of me, and that I was still viewed as a naive disciple in the caravan of the Just Monotheists, although deep down I resolved to seek out the giraffe and the elephant.

Suddenly Rashid ibn Ali rose and gestured to us. "Lunch is served; step this way." We rose behind him, surrounded by his sons: I could see that the races had mingled, manifested in Rashid's dark skin, compared to his fair-skinned offspring.

Atta approached me and whispered, "I'll see you tomorrow in al-Azhar after the noon prayers."

Suddenly Rashid ibn Ali stopped and looked at us, as though remembering something. "What affirms that the Qur'an is created," he said, "is that the Divine Meanings lie not in the words, but in what they engender in ourselves and the ideas they inspire in the mind. Therefore, each of us creates and understands them according to where he is on the journey of his own mind."

My heart beat so fast that I tripped over the edge of the carpet. I would have fallen on my face if it hadn't been for Atta, who grabbed me and asked, "Are you all right?"

Rashid ibn Ali had raised me to the fifth commandment on my ascent:

Fifth Commandment
Monotheism is an unattainable goal: each one finds it through his mind according to his ability.

Had he meant to say it, or was it the machination of Fate to build steps leading each disciple to a higher place in his ascent?

On my way home, Rashid ibn Ali asked one of the grooms to accompany me. I placed my things on the horse's back and we walked alongside the animal until we were through the gates of the walled city. We made our way to the narrow alley where my house lay: he stopped there and swiftly carried my things inside on his shoulders. As I did not have any dirhams to give him, out of gratitude, I took loaves with black seed from the bread basket and presented them to him. In retrospect, this was probably ill-considered of me, given the lavish banquet served to us in the house of Rashid ibn Ali: mutton, duck, spiced soup . . . But he responded with a polite slap in the face, saying, "Thank you. It will make a good meal for the horse."

Embarrassed, I blamed myself, as I was still dealing with the world through the memory of hunger and thirst.

I undid my packages. My things appeared untouched: nothing was missing, even the compass and the astrolabe, although the chief of police had showed a keen interest in them and turned them in his hands, and I doubt anyone could have blamed him for taking them. But the power and influence of Rashid ibn Ali appeared to have ended the matter.

I spent the rest of my day at home, filled with contentment and a sense of security, thanks to my ascent in the journey of the Voyagers and a full stomach. I spent the evening with Hippocrates, translated by Hunayn ibn Ishaq. He mentions in his preface that, according to Galen of Pergamon, "Hippocrates compares the human being to a small concentration of the big world, because to care for the human body is to care for the world."

I performed the dawn prayers at al-Azhar. The gifts of the palace had begun to appear about the mosque: the place for prayer was perfumed, and the lanterns had imbued the air about me with a pleasant purplish hue. I spent the morning and early afternoon there, moving from circle to circle, observing the teachers who might grant me a degree. Ataa accompanied me—or perhaps I accompanied him, although he was three years younger. Ataa was still at the stage of playing and having fun, swaggering around with his spear-straight figure and elegant clothing. The world had not spilled its dark liquid on him. He did not care to attend all the circles and told anecdotes about the sheikhs. If their talk bored or disgruntled him, he rose and found another. Despite this, he was my guide through the colonnades and gates of the mosque: he crept with me to a row of windows in the northern cellar of the mosque, saying with a sly laugh, "If we listen closely, we can hear the girls' discussion circles from here. If we set up a ladder, we might catch a glimpse of them."

We did not stay long there, for fear of being spotted by a guard, and went to the library instead. Finally, he led me to a row of discreet columns in a far corner of the mosque where one could lie down to snatch a nap. In one of the discussion circles, I maintain that I saw the madman, with his wild hair, the silver lion on his stick, rushing down the corridors: I guessed he had managed to escape that day from Yunis and from the hands that dragged him inside.

That day, I had been looking forward to an intimate evening with a book I had borrowed from the al-Azhar Library, the book compiled by al-Sharif al-Radi of the sayings of Ali ibn Abu Talib and named *Nahj al-Balagha*. Here was a book worthy of solitude and contemplation.

That was what I thought, but then my evening took a turn for the bizarre.

I had just finished the sunset prayers and was heading for the gate of the mosque, when I found the madman standing before me. I jumped and trembled to hear his voice. "Deeds never end," he said. "They last; they stay. The wounds in the heart bleed, taking your soul and your heart's light with them."

His voice and appearance froze the blood in my veins. He had followed me without my sensing it. This was all I needed—a madman following me! I stopped, wondering if I should humor him and lead him back home, but at that moment Yunis arrived in a rush. He bent over the man's hand and kissed it, grasping his stick. As though speaking to a small child, he commanded, "Come, master, to the house."

Suddenly the madman became a respectable master: he raised his chin and asked Yunis in a calm tone accustomed to giving orders, "Have you prepared Lamis to come to my room tonight?"

Yunis hesitated, flustered. The madman screamed in a voice coming from the depths of his soul, "Have you dressed Lamis in her finery to come to my room tonight? Or is the she-devil still pinching her hands and fingers with pins heated on the coals of my heart?"

By the time the screaming started, Yunis had already been careful to lead us into Madman's Alley, away from the passersby. The madman turned to me and whined, "Lamis's hands were like white jasmine. They were tiny. Shining. But they were disfigured with heated needles, until she grew angry with us and left."

"Lamis is waiting for us now," Yunis said, embarrassed.

The madman's eyes bulged. "Silence, filthy slave! You are nothing but the cur of your she-devil mistress!"

With these revelations and mysteries, I saw Yunis's face freeze. I started to withdraw and head for my own dwelling. "Please stay," Yunis whispered. "Help me walk him to the house. Master appears especially agitated tonight. I fear he may run off to the top of Muqattam, or into the desert."

I walked with him. The whole way, the madman complained to Yunis and insulted him. But I had not the courage to ask what had occurred. It was the first time I had approached the great gate in which the Madman's Alley ends: sturdy and wooden, it was studded with nails and decorated with brass crescents and stars, with a great padlock the size of a camel's head. It was a nobleman's house and no mistake. You could tell from the spacious halls with their high ceilings and columns, couches and furnishings, the fire in the brazier, and the cloud of Indian incense over all. "Stay," Yunis entreated, "and recite some Qur'an for him. You are an Azharite: your recitation will bless the house."

The madman was calm and pliant in my company. Yunis ran to get more mastic and Indian incense for the censer, muttering, "Life has taught me that it holds many lessons."

"The Qur'an heals people!" I heard a suffering female voice cry. I raised my head, and saw a woman waddling toward us like a dignified goose, rustling in her flowing garment of silk that she drew along behind her. She had a diaphanous, silken face veil the color of wheat. Every time she moved, her bracelets and finery jingled and whispered. "In the name of the One who heals all . . ."

When she reached us, I heard the madman mutter, "You are what ails me, she-devil!" She retreated to a corner by the door leading into the house, covered her face with her veil, and started weeping.

Mabrouk and another boy brought a low table and placed it between me and the madman. They set out a meal upon it under Yunis's instructions. At the same time, I had the powerful sensation that there were eyes watching me from some hidden corner. The goose woman waddled away from us, wiping away her tears and overseeing our hospitality. When she removed her veil, wet with her tears, I looked at the floor politely so as not to stare. "Witchcraft," she lamented, "and what it does to people! May that day never come again, the day that Berber girl came to our house!"

The madman surged up. "Silence, she-devil!" he roared, spittle flying from his mouth. She fell silent immediately, tilting her head to the side. Yunis leapt in to smooth matters out, pouring a drink into a cup and offering it to me.

It appeared to me that the woman was still clinging to her fading youth. There was still something of it left, however: a pair of beautiful eyes surrounded by thick kohl, and a complexion like honey. Her worry and disquiet could not hide an attractive hoarseness in her voice, which matched the wringing of her beringed and bejeweled hands as she spoke. She ran her hands over the parting of her thick black hair, which hung in a braid down her back. Her beauty still tugged at the edges of her face and collected around her enticing mouth. She was afflicted: she sighed deeply and called down God's help, beating her hand against her thick thigh, soft as a feather pillow. Her eyes never left the madman. The food was set out on the table, but no one touched it. Although I was hungry, I was embarrassed to start when no one else was eating. My feeling of being watched only grew stronger.

At that moment, I felt it was absurd to keep up the pretense of the stranger, the neighbor who had been dragged into this tale by chance, especially as it seemed that there was a sense that I would save them—that everyone in the room was helplessly looking to me for some nonexistent protection. "Would you recite some verses of the Suras of Yasin or al-Rahman to bring him peace?" the woman entreated.

I wished I could tell her, "Your presence has only agitated him; please leave," but that would have overstepped my position. I could not leave without giving them some sort of assistance, even if it involved feigning knowledge. I recalled Galen of Pergamon's explanations and his addenda to Hippocrates: it was just what they needed in this congested room. I lowered my head and took to recalling the words I had read. "There are two causes for illness: remote causes, caused by the atmosphere and the climate or the foods eaten by the patient, and proximate causes, caused by the imbalance or predominance of one of the four humors of which the body is composed."

After I had said my piece, they all craned their necks toward me, as though I were waving a lantern for a caravan lost long ago in the desert. Perhaps I enjoyed the attention; or rather, was reassured by the deep reaction that had spilled over into this large, comfortable reception hall. I continued: "Therefore, diseases must be cured by means and methods that lead to the maturing of humors and extracting them from the body." I breathed in deeply: seeing them still stunned, staring at me, I continued: "When the humors are well mixed in manner and measure, the body remains in good health. We are now in fall, which does to the body as it does to the leaves of the trees: the air makes a man lonely and melancholic, and affects the liver and the gallbladder." I turned to Yunis. "Make sure he does not sleep directly under the sky and the stars." Then I asked, "Is there a bathhouse you can take him to?"

His eyebrows raised in surprise, he said, "Sir, my lord is a nobleman and cannot visit the baths of the common folk. We have his own private bath in the house, for which we have brought in a special aqueduct from the Nile."

In a tone so calm and confident that I half imagined Galen of Pergamon would chuckle to hear it, I said, "After he has bathed and his humors are in balance—air, water, fire, and earth—in the bath, we shall give him raisin water to drink."

The woman was shocked and cried out, "But there are no raisins on the market!"

I did not answer her and turned to Yunis, getting ready to leave the house, "Do not forget what I asked of you. When he is done with his bath, pour water with sweet basil over his feet: the vapors of evil leave through the feet, and his humors will then be in balance, and he will sleep deeply. I shall come to see him after evening prayers."

I left with the sound of the muezzin calling for the evening prayers, great waves breaking on the shores of the Nile, as though it were calling for an absent lover. The sound echoed through the passages and colonnades, erasing the fatigue of the day.

I went to my house and took the raisins and sage out of my bag. I prepared the raisin water in a small jar. Then I prayed at the mosque, returned home, and read some Galen. Did madmen have humors of black bile? Galen quotes Hippocrates in saying that they are melancholic, with dark hair, and their bloodstream sluggish, especially in the fall. He did not think that bloodletting was the best cure for them, but rather expelling impurities from the stomach.

I took the raisin water and the sage—it is said that they are laxatives—and hurried to the home of the madman. He had calmed down after the bath, and his face was tired and drowsy. His unkempt hair had been smoothed down with perfumed oil, and he wore a white cotton garment with an olive-colored wool caftan over it. I handed him the jar: Yunis rushed to pour some of it into a glass for him. The smell of sage was so powerful that I felt Zulaykha might step through the door at any minute.

The sense of being watched this time returned to me insistently, before I raised my head to see a girl at the door staring at me with a smile on her face. She shone so brightly, as if made of pure gold, that I was speechless. Her skin was like gold dust; her eyes were glittering amber. She was walking toward us slowly, her mischievous eyes fixed on me. She paid no attention to Yunis, as though he were not there. When she reached us, she approached the madman and whispered, "Master," then ran her henna-dyed fingers through his hair.

His head had been bowed: now he raised it, put his arms around her waist, seated her in his lap, and buried his face in her neck. He kissed her lips chastely, as if she were a cat that one might pet in passing. She responded, pliant, as if it were an action repeated dozens of times a day. She kept watching me intently, as though planning something.

To conceal my embarrassment at this turn of events, I announced, "It appears that our master is well now. I wish him a peaceful night. If I am able, I will come by tomorrow and bring him another draft."

On my way home, I was filled with an alchemist's joy. The madman had calmed down. But who was this girl of gold? Was she one of his slave girls? Her eyes stayed with me. When I arrived at my house, I resolved to go out and buy some of the herbs mentioned by Galen, marjoram and cumin, which he said were intestinal cleansers.

A doctor takes on some aspects of a god: he encounters people on the battlefield of hope and prayer. After disease has sapped their strength and removed their fangs, they eagerly await the path back to life, guided by a superhuman doctor who will pour life down their throats once more.

Should I become a physician by profession? It would abbreviate years of my suffering in life, and spare me having to introduce myself to the Egyptians I met now as a merchant, now as a vendor, now as a student. A doctor is allowed access to the most closely guarded houses, all doors are opened to him, and all veils are lifted from him; he sits at the head of the table and the choicest morsels are presented to him. I took up another handful of raisins, put them in a cup, and set it aside.

Grapes are mentioned eleven times in the Qur'an: I would take the drink tomorrow to the madman of the black humor, to see what would become of his case.

Between sleeping and waking, I heard the strings of the lute. They were still sad, suffused with longing and the song of migrating birds.

I went to see the madman the next day after sundown. I knocked at the door and the boy, Mabrouk, opened it, welcoming me warmly: he appeared to feel that now there was something that brought us together, over and above my being a mere visitor to their master.

He let me into the reception hall. The goose woman, or "mother of the children," as they called her, was at his head, smoothing his wavy hair and anointing it with sandalwood and jasmine oil, as he lay on his back, hands behind his head, staring at the ceiling as though avoiding her gaze.

When he heard my voice, his face split into a great grin. He sat up and said, "Welcome to the one God has granted wisdom and given the answers! Al-Jahiz was right to say that wisdom descended from the sky to three of the denizens of the earth: the Greeks in the head, the Chinese in the hands, and the Arabs in their tongue! I had such a deep sleep last night as I have not enjoyed in ages."

I was astonished: he appeared well-balanced and dignified. I gave him more of the raisin drink and said, "This is your dose tonight."

The mother of the children was pleased at his joy and said, "If only you would live next to us for always, Mazid! He has been so much better since yesterday. If you were a slave, we would have bought you from your master, and if you had been a master, we would have asked you to stay."

Her words disturbed me. She would buy me? It appeared that my face showed something of what I felt, for the madman snapped, "As the proverb says, they fall on their tongues because of their tongues. You have ever been foolish, and speak foolishly." Then he quoted the verse: "You have no horses nor money to give; / At least speak no ill as long as you live."

Why so much hatred between them when they still lived together? What had she done to him that he held so much resentment for her?

To lighten the embarrassment that filled the room, I said, "Be sure to drink the raisin water tonight. The Prophet, prayers and peace be upon him, was fond of raisins, and said that they were good for the nerves, lighten affliction, quench rage, sharpen the taste buds, remove phlegm, and improve the color. Imam Ali says that one who eats twenty-one red grapes a day will never fall ill. Not to mention the poem that says,

> The grape is the king and sultan of all the fruits;
> Its moisture and sweetness render all things moot.
> Each other fruit has something of which to boast;
> But no book could grapes' virtues adequately host.

It appeared that my words were his cure, not the raisin water. He raised the glass and drained it, and then chewed on the raisins. When he finished, he lifted his head to Yunis and asked him to take down everything I had said.

Yunis disappeared for a moment, then rushed back, bearing a pen, inkwell, and papers, and asked me politely to write down what I had said to his master about grapes, for he had not followed it accurately. I wrote it down carefully, feeling the amber eyes on my face again like burning coals.

Tomorrow would be the second Friday I had spent in Egypt. Rashid ibn Ali sent me an invitation via his son Ataa to lunch after Friday prayers. His youth was no impediment to the deepening of our friendship: Ataa said to me playfully, quoting Abu Nawas, "You desert Arabs are nothing in the eyes of the Lord!"

"The Egyptians worshipped their kings," I shot back. "According to the Qur'an, Pharaoh said, 'I am your Lord, Most High.'"

Ataa's vigor made one think he was preparing for a great vocation. He was quick-witted and a voracious reader, but not enslaved and controlled by books like I was: he made surprise forays into them, devouring them and reading an entire book in a day and a night. Afterward, he might cease reading for close to a month and absorb himself in hunting or sitting with the guests at his father's gatherings or cantering about on his horse in al-Qatai, knowing that many eyes were watching him and many women wanted him.

I felt secure in his presence: he was my eye on Egypt, and he kept my path open to Rashid ibn Ali. I told Ataa of the madman's vacillation between absent rambling and keen observation. "It is not strange," said Ataa. "I have seen him do worse. Many say that he is feigning madness, because the caliph would have forced him to take on the job of a judge, which he loathed. He says in his private meetings that theologians will be resurrected with the prophets, while the judges will be resurrected with the sultan's men!"

I had not attempted to sell any books until now. I was still fearful of prying eyes. Amr al-Qaysi had said, "Voyagers' books are their mind, their ancestry, their seed, so be careful where you deposit them." Rashid ibn Ali told me, "There is nothing wrong with demanding a high price for them: that will keep them out of the hands of the common people, and place them with noblemen and the highborn. He who wants them will give anything for them. Beware of selling them to pay for your own needs; find a profession that will protect you from want and asking for charity."

Although I now received a stipend from al-Azhar, riches are, as they say, company in a strange land; and the proverb says: "He who asks for alms shall never live with dignity." I must find a profession to support myself, and to guarantee my daily bread. I had hired the boy, Mabrouk, to take care of my home in exchange for a small sum every month.

That day when I went out for Friday prayers, I found a great marquee erected before the gates of al-Azhar, with boys and slaves crying loudly, "General Zaffar al-Islam, His Majesty the Caliph's general, was blessed with a boy last night, whom he named Husayn! Pray to him for long life!"

The faithful were crowded in the marquee, with tables set out with bowls of the sweet pastry *zalabiya*, glasses of rosewater, and dishes of fish. It is the custom in Egypt to spread out a shade or sail at the time of the sermon, which the preacher started that day by saying, "Prayers and peace upon the Prophet, and Imam Ali, and the Prophet's daughter Fatima the Pure Worshipper, and Hassan and Husayn, the Prophet's grandsons, whom God has raised above all sin, and purified; and pray for the pure imams, the fathers of the prince of the faithful, our caliph, al-Hakim bi-Amr Allah."

Would the list of the Prophet's descendants be crowded with more names year after year? If so, the imam would be reciting their names from one Friday to the next. It was the custom of the Fatimids when they went to war to take the coffins of their ancestors with them. How foolish they were.

Then I realized that my thoughts were transgressive: I asked God for forgiveness and protection from the Devil. O Lord! Ever since I became involved with the Voyagers, I have only to set foot outside the mosque to question all I have heard and everything around me, breaking it down into little pieces crowding into my mind—and now my doubts and fears were following me into the mosque itself. God help me!

I found Rashid ibn Ali's gathering, as usual, packed with the eminent men and great merchants of Cairo, the sound of discussion and heated back-and-forth within the hall louder than my first visit. The caliph had issued an edict that an inscription be placed on every mosque cursing the Prophet Muhammad's caliphs Abu Bakr, Umar, and Uthman, as well as the Prophet's wife Aisha, and Talkha, al-Zubayr, Muawiya, and Amr ibn al-Aas—in other words, every Sunni descendant of the Prophet's lineage. A toothless sheikh sitting by Rashid ibn Ali said, "We used to curse the Nawasib from the pulpit only after the Friday prayers. But for this to be inscribed on the walls of mosques! It is a great sin, and will be accompanied by lethal *fitna*. The people of Egypt are new to the Shiite sect."

Another toothless man by his side said, "Are we to curse the two of them when Abu Bakr was with Muhammad in the cave, side by side, as they were fleeing the infidels? Are we to curse Aisha, Mother of the Faithful, when the Prophet died in her lap?"

One of the sheikhs of the discussion circles, whom I always observed beneath the pillars of al-Azhar, said, "We know not what lies in wait for us after this, nor where these boats shall take us. The Christian king of Ethiopia now collects *jizya* taxes from the Muslims there, as we do from the Christians here. And the greatest blow is that the burning of the Church of the Resurrection has driven the monarchs of Europe to sound the trumpet for a holy war." He went on: "The king of the Bulgars and the king of Byzantium have joined forces in defense of the Christian holy shrines, chiefly the church that we now call the Church of the Refuse, although it holds the Holy Sepulcher where Christ is buried and rose again."

I shrank in the presence of this overpowering resentment and unconcealed ire. Was this assembly safe from spies? Our host made no reply, merely shaking his head as he listened attentively. I was somewhat reassured that he would not notice my presence in the crowd, but it appeared that he had, for in a moment of silence he asked me, "What is your opinion, Mazid of Najd?"

"You and your 'Mazid,'" I thought resentfully, "as though there were none but me in this hall." I knew not how many spies were hanging on my every word, and there was still a great deal of my life that I wished to live: I had no desire to be stabbed on my way home, or have my head roll off the summit of Muqattam. But I must say something worthy of this learned gathering, not reflecting cowardice and apathy. I must earn the trust my interlocutor had placed in me by asking me out of all the others. "Metaphor and metonymy," I thought, "were created for moments like this. I shall speak in a manner that may be interpreted in any fashion, and thus not fall into error." Aloud I said, "Prayers and peace be upon our Prophet Muhammad, and his noble and good descendants. Humanity was created to people this earth and carry out the great ends of religious law, we must not insult one another and so scatter our efforts to the wind, whomever the Lord fills with unbelief cannot be brought to the right path, whomever He fills with belief cannot be brought to the path of perdition; human instinct is monotheism and justice. In conclusion, thanks be to God, the Lord of both worlds."

I glimpsed a small smile on Rashid ibn Ali's face, making light of what I had said. He invited us to finish our conversation over a meal: the conversation subsided and became more pleasant, filled with joking, laughter, and good cheer, especially as the dishes on the low tables were filled with goat meat, chicken breast with vinegar and eggplant, chicken boiled in pomegranate sauce, grilled goose with lime, wheat cakes with sugar, and sweet, delicate, puffy *khushkanan* pastries stuffed with almonds. The toothless old man said, "Faced with such a banquet, Ali and Muawiya would become brothers and give up insults and fighting—they would only fill their plates and their stomachs!"

After our meal, the gathering of Rashid ibn Ali usually dispersed, whereupon Ataa and I would go on a walk on the banks of the Nile or around Fustat, sometimes taking a boat to the island in the center of the Nile, returning with the sunset prayers.

That night, the lute played again, crying and bereft, as though the brides of the Nile—virgins whom legend has it are sacrificed to the river to make it flood—were all sitting in a row, mourning their stolen youth swallowed up by the river, reducing them to wandering spirits fluttering over it.

I no longer saw a great deal of the madman at the mosque; when he needed me, he now called for me. One day, I found Mabrouk waiting for me at the stairs to my house. "My master wishes to see you."

I accompanied Mabrouk to him, filled with apprehension. In his house, I always saw something that left me speechless for a week. This time did not disappoint. He was sitting with his golden slave girl in his embrace. She had papers in her hands, and an inkwell and pen close by. I bowed my head and took a step back at the sight of her, but he called me forward. Then he said, "Mazid, I would like you to give your seal of approval to these words we have copied from yours, and make sure that they are accurate. Read what you have written, Kahramana."

Kahramana? So her name meant *amber*. Before I could pursue these musings further, she raised a sheet of paper with writing on it and read in a sweet voice with a crack in its depths: "The Prophet, prayers and peace be upon him, was fond of grapes, and said that they are good for the nerves, and lighten affliction, and quench rage . . ." and so on, reading in a playful voice with a hint of flirtation in it what I had said about grapes that night.

Sometimes she would break off her speech and look at me, licking her lips lustfully, whereupon her master would nudge her and say, "Read on."

"But," I remonstrated in surprise, "the words are not mine; I copied them from some—"

The noble madman interrupted me: he seemed at the height of wisdom. "Be that as it may. But all we need to hear about the benefits of grapes, prohibited by the tyrant, are set down therein."

I was stunned to find that they had prepared dozens of copies about the benefits of grapes, carefully rolled up till they were no thicker than your ring finger, tied up with woolen thread, and carefully stacked on the low table.

I returned home with the certain knowledge that this noble house was drawing me in, day after day, and calling me to its deep waters; I knew not that this very night I should drown.

After evening prayers, I was accustomed to go out onto the balcony that formed part of the roof, eavesdropping on the conversations between the stars and the caliph's Cairo, and waiting for the sound of the lute that would pierce my evenings like a meteor of joy. I listened for the river birds that refused to nest and remained circling on high, crying mysteriously. I was accustomed to devoting this time to reciting some of the poems I had memorized for fear of losing them to the slippage of memory. I started with one by Umar ibn Abu Rabia:

> The eldest sister asked,
> "Know you the boy over the dune?"
> Said the middle, "It is Umar."
> Said the youngest girl, who loved me,
> "We know him: who can hide the moon?"

The upper room and its balcony were separated from the rest of the roof by a low mud wall, upon which Mabrouk had set out the pots of sweet basil. This wall separated me from the rest of the madman's house.

In the night, things begin to move beneath the cloak of darkness, creeping out of their holes. Cats meow, crickets chirp, leaves rustle on the trees, spirits come out of hiding. Suddenly a gigantic cat crashed onto the roof. The sound was coming from the low wall between my roof and the noble madman's. I froze, trembling. At last I stood, looking at a dark shape padding quickly toward me. I feared it was one of the demons afflicting the madman's mind, but when it was ten arm spans from me, two amber eyes shone in the darkness. She whispered, "Did I startle you?"

She drew near. Her breath smelled of cloves. "How goes your evening, Arab of the desert?"

I took two steps back. Before I could stop her or rebuff her, she let her abaya fall. There was nothing underneath but her body, the light from the slip of a moon spilling over it, turning it the color of apricots. Here was someone who had made up her mind.

We wrapped ourselves in her abaya. When she saw how disturbed I was, she held me and said, "Let us start by drinking from the spring before we go for a swim." I knew not what she meant to signify. But she seemed to sense my greenness and inexperience, so she guided my hand beneath the darkness, and together we went to the river.

I feared the thing that burst from me then, the thing that set me all aflame. She was laughing, perhaps at my unschooled enthusiasm and passion, or at my greedy mouth that bit her and drank the nectar from her folds.

Suddenly she opened her palm to reveal a red silk kerchief. "Put it in," she said, "for I still fear the punishment of the Lord for sullying or mingling bloodlines." I know not where I put it in, or if I put it in at all! She was leading me seductively, and I was drinking of her like a stallion after a thousand days' thirsty journey.

I could not say when she left. I was like one drugged. But I thought I heard her rustling by my side at dawn.

\*

Her presence had been a flood that subsumed me, a wave that drowned me. When the light dawned, I took to wandering the alleyways of Cairo: through the gates I went to the river, perhaps to gather the threads of my mind that were scattered through the air. I remained distracted until the sun was sinking, the late-afternoon sun spilling jars of gold into the river. There were many fishermen, people taking the air, and some boys crowding and splashing in the water, swimming and trying to catch fish with small, tattered nets, while the fishermen reproached them for frightening away the fish.

Though the ruler had made a law prohibiting outings by the riverbank, he had not been able to keep the Egyptians away: the Nile remained their father and their lifeline, without which they would shrivel and drop off the tree. All they did, when they heard the police passing, was hide among the tall reeds by the river, or behind the large mimosas whose branches trailed into the Nile. Flocks of cranes landed on the water and swam around fearlessly, accustomed to the gentle nature of the Egyptians.

"*And flesh of fowls that they desire,*" says the Sura of al-Waqia: if I, from the Arabian Peninsula, ate the flesh of cranes, would it benefit my body? According to Hippocrates, the sick are healed by the drugs of their own land: I hoped that the raisins I had bought from Arish would be a good cure for the madman.

It was as though I had confessed my worries to the universe. A group of boys approached me, passing a piece of paper among themselves and tossing it about wildly. One of them came up to me and said, "Do you read, sir?"

I nodded. He held out the paper to me. To my surprise, it was none other than one of those written out by Kahramana yesterday about the benefits of grapes. I paled. Who had brought this paper here? What was I to do with it? The boys had seen my confusion and perplexity, which only caused them to come closer. In a panic, I told them, "Beware. It is a wicked spell from the time of the Prophet Moses. Anyone who recites it turns into a river hog."

They drew back, frightened. "There are many of them all over the city!" they cried.

I tore it up immediately and threw the pieces into the river. Full of ire, I rushed to the madman's house, seeking answers. Was it true what the boys had said, that the papers about grapes were everywhere? I glimpsed one on a window-sill, another at the threshold of a mosque, and a third with the prickly pear vendor. The benefits of grapes filled the skies of the caliph's city, in defiance of the orders of her ruler, who had outlawed them. I plucked up two and secreted them in my sleeve, then rushed to the Madman's Alley.

What was happening here? The caliph had issued an edict banning grapes, and the papers extolling the benefits of the fruits of the vine were fluttering in every alley. All that remained was for it to appear on the walls of the police headquarters. What kind of challenge was the madman undertaking?

When I arrived at his door, I knocked. Quickly, as though he were expecting me, an albino boy opened the door. He was white down to his eyelashes, with red eyes like a rab-bit's. I drew back slightly, frightened by his appearance, but I managed to control my reaction so as not to wound him. I recalled Anas, the son of one of the farmers in al-Yam-ama: he had been similarly colorless, as if washed clean. The other children refused to play with him, and called him "leper." They said the Devil had urinated on him because he had gone to bed without washing himself or praying, so he had lost his color, although they all knew full well that he had been born this way, and was a decent and well-mannered boy capable of outstripping them in a footrace. Still, they insisted on mocking and making fun of him, especially as he preferred to sit in dark, cool rooms because his skin and eyes were irritated by the sunlight. "He prefers the dark," the boys whispered, "so that he can be alone with his father, the Devil."

God help you, al-Yamama of Najd—how cruel you are! Anas died young. At his funeral, his mother wept and said, "Heaven forgive you all! My son died of the malice and spite with which the boys of al-Yamama beleaguered him!"

In low, polite tones, the boy at the door said, "There is no one at home."

"What of Yunis?"

"He is out too, with my master," he said, "and they have not yet returned."

I was overcome with apprehension: where was I going? What lay behind the walls of this house of mystery? Where could Kahramana be? Had she gone with them?

I withdrew. When I was nearly at the door to my house, I heard footsteps hurrying behind me and a voice saying, "Doctor! Doctor!"

The albino boy, his face bright red from running after me, said, "My mistress, the mother of the children, wishes to speak with you." I made my hesitant way back. I almost made some flimsy excuse to protect me from delving deeper into this bizarre family, but the albino boy said to me, "She says it is of the utmost importance."

It was important, so important that it confirmed my suspicions: the mother of the children told me that it was her husband who had written these pamphlets, spending the nights copying them out, and whenever he ran out of paper and ink, he yelled to the household to bring him what he needed from a storeroom on the other side of the house. When the morning came, he rolled them up into scrolls and placed them in his bag, then went to scatter them throughout Cairo. He added that he planned to distribute them throughout Fustat and al-Qatai to foment revolution, so people would challenge the rule of the tyrant on the throne of Egypt.

She bowed her head and half covered her face with her veil, overcome with sobs. "You know that the streets are filled with spies and informers: any whisper of betrayal in the ear of the wild boy"—she meant the caliph—"could have him beheaded. Not only that: they will seize and confiscate his properties, and annex them to the treasury." Slyly, she added, "His vengeance may even reach you. You are, after all, the one who told him of the benefits of grapes."

Was she trying to frighten me, or win me over to her side? In any case, she was overcome with distress and despair. "Since he drank the raisin water, he has been improving, especially because in this season, no farmer in Egypt dares grow grapes, not after last year's harvest was thrown in its entirety into the Nile, and the vineyards all set alight, on suspicion that wine was being prepared there. The caliph cared nothing for the protests of the growers, and never repaid them for their losses."

Suddenly the albino boy spoke from where he stood by the door: I had forgotten he was there. "Also, mistress," he said, "in the market yesterday, I found that they were no longer selling *mulukhiya* leaves or catfish, on the caliph's orders."

She dusted off her hands in a gesture of astonishment. "Good heavens! Lord, have you set this ruler above us to expiate our sins? Why, he passed by a women's bathhouse, and when he heard them laughing within, he had the door to the bathhouse bricked up with the women trapped inside." I recalled hearing this story from Hassan the Egyptian when we were in Baghdad. How I missed him! I wished he were here with me in his homeland: things would be clearer and make more sense in his presence.

The mother of the children looked down and fell silent; now she broke into loud sobbing. "O God, what shall I do?" Through her sobs, she told me that her cousin and her young daughter had been among the women in the bathhouse. "I had to go to offer my condolences in secret," she confessed, "dressed as a servant woman, for the caliph has forbidden free women to walk in the streets."

I froze, remembering the eggplant woman at the police headquarters. What did the Egyptians eat, then, when the caliph took it upon himself to select what should be placed upon their tables? The mother of the children had stopped sobbing: she raised her head, contemplating the colored light pouring in from one of the windows onto her face. It made her beautiful, despite her kohl smudged from weeping. Distractedly, she whispered, "After the death of his slave girl Lamis, who was bearing his child, his health has deteriorated. I have often guided slave girls into his bed, telling him that they are Lamis's sisters; he will not believe it, and remains steadfastly searching for her. When he is himself," she continued, "and in his own mind, he speaks with a wisdom that the greatest sheikhs could not match. In a moment of clarity, he copied out the grape pamphlets, secreted them in his clothing, and went out at dawn, waiting for no man. His previous distracted air has returned after the slight improvement in his condition brought on by the raisin water you brought."

This was the side of the story told to me by the mother of the children. But the tale told to me by Kahramana a few nights later, as she lay in my arms, the bed around us bursting into flame and subsiding to ash, then bursting into flame again, was quite different. Or was it Kahramana's sweetness that made it more palatable?

"Lamis," she said, "was Master's favorite slave. Al-Hakim bi-Amr Allah presented her to him in this very house when Master arrived in Egypt in obedience to his summons. The caliph, you see, sought to bring more Shiites into Cairo to bolster his power and advise him. Even now, the servants and the household speak in wonder about Lamis the nymph, with her swaying gait and her melodious lute. Our master fell passionately in love with her, and spent long hours in her company, missing the dawn prayers and arriving late to mosque on Friday. In the evening, she would prepare a couch for him upon the roof and start to play. Silence fell and a hush came over the city, all listening to her. Cairo would await the nights when the slave girl Lamis played her lute. All the while, my master's passion for her only increased."

She went on: "Lamis had a strange habit: she plucked the petals of irises and placed them in her mouth, using them as a whistle to produce a sweet sound. The mother of the children said she used them to summon the demons who had captivated the mind of our master. They did indeed, for he was captivated with love for her. When the old harridan, the mother of the children, saw how enamored my master was of her, she was careful to make her drink neem with barley every night, to keep her from becoming pregnant and bearing an heir that might share her sons' inheritance.

"When my master found she was slow to become pregnant, he swore a holy pact to take her on a pilgrimage to Mecca and pray to the Prophet Muhammad, the best of all men, to unlock her womb. When the season of pilgrimage arrived, the clarion call to Mecca sounded and the caravans formed. The mother of the children was insistent on going with them, but my master refused, on the pretext that the pilgrimage was unsafe, and that she must stay behind with their children. The Arabs were split between Sunni and Shiite, and he knew not for whom the preacher in Mecca would pray that year in his sermon: with so many people there, it might well devolve into chaos. Well, when Lamis ceased drinking the neem with barley, she returned from Mecca pregnant, as the reward for her pilgrimage. The mother of the children lost her senses: her pregnancy meant that there would be a brother to vie with her sons and share their birthright. So she made the poppet.

"Mabrouk says that they are poppets made by the mother of the children from scraps of cloth and remnants of wool. At midnight, she brought out the poppet and pricked it with pins, calling down maledictions on Lamis without cease. Lamis contracted smallpox. Some said she caught it on her pilgrimage to Mecca; some said she had drunk polluted water. But Mabrouk says that the smallpox pustules on Lamis's body were the same in number as the pinpricks on the poppet. She rotted away and died, and they buried her in a faraway grave after covering her body with ashes.

"They left the house and stayed in one of my master's estates outside Cairo, a day and a night's journey away, until the house was cleansed of the remnants of smallpox. Mabrouk and Yunis stayed behind, burning mugwort and purifying the house with its smoke, washing the floors with Nile water, and setting the furnishings out in the sun; they also burned all of Lamis's clothes, until the house was cleansed. All came back to the caliph's Cairo, but my master's sanity never returned. He was a body without a soul, the shell of a man. He heard nothing but the music of Lamis, her lute and her poetry. He saw nothing but her shadow all about him. At first, he would sit at the door as if in a trance, refusing to bathe or perform ablutions. Afterward, he took to walking through the streets and alleyways, refusing to stay at home.

"My mistress was obliged to send Yunis to Andalusia and the Maghreb to find girls to entertain him and quench his passion. They bought a slave girl for a thousand dinars, but all she found was the shell of a man: he would not touch her unless she braided her hair into four braids and put on a turban with silver dinars, letting its end hang over her brow as Lamis had done. In the dark, she pressed close to him, whispering, 'My master, light of my heart,' which was what Lamis used to call him. Whereupon he would pat her on the shoulder, kiss her on the cheek, and fall into a deep sleep, hoping to meet Lamis in some passageway of his mind." She sighed. "The mother of the children insisted on the drink of neem and barley, and the red kerchief."

I was astounded. Was she speaking of herself? I was overcome with the desire to hold her closely and hide her beneath my ribs, far from the drinks they forced her to consume, and from the mother of the children and the pins and the small-pox. But Kahramana, mischievous girl, wanted more. She wanted to play, and laugh, and drag the stallion to the river.

## The Skinned Wolves and the Tales of the Quraysh

I regularly attended the gatherings Rashid ibn Ali held behind his shop, for every scrap of news passed through it, if it did not actually originate there. The men who frequented it called it the Saqifa, after Saqifat Bani Saida, the place where the Prophet's disciples congregated, and where they had pledged allegiance to Abu Bakr to rule after Muhammad's death; the name embarrassed him, though, and he entreated them not to use it in case it should find its way back to the caliph, who might think the Quraysh were raising the flags of war against his rule.

That day, they were speaking about the skinned corpses of wolves that they had started to find strewn about al-Qatai, a terrifying spectacle. Who was it that skinned them, took the heads and skin, and left the corpses? It was clear that the per-petrator, whoever it was, was performing some kind of dark demonic rite, like the rites performed to vanquish their ene-mies by the idolaters who lived in southern Egypt.

I sometimes glimpsed the idolaters of Egypt in the road: dark-complexioned and tall, they walked through the streets of Fustat, barefoot and naked but for a loincloth, bizarre turbans on their heads formed of shells or animal skins or birds' feathers. The folk of Fustat whispered fearfully that the caliph hosted them in his palace, where he had signed a pact of brotherhood with the Devil under their guidance. It was he that the caliph went to meet every night on the summit of Muqattam, wearing the head of a wolf or lion on the recom-mendation of sorcerers from Sudan, who promised him the courage of a leopard, the cunning of a fox, and the submis-siveness of his subjects.

Such was the gossip abroad in the streets; and here it was, come to the house of Rashid ibn Ali. When the man himself felt that it had gone beyond the bounds of reason and common sense, he changed the subject and asked me to recite some poetry.

Rashid ibn Ali had not indicated any book buyers to me so far: should I await him, or commence my own search for purchasers?

## When He Loves, He Becomes More Pleasant

Ever since Kahramana had started creeping into my room, I had become a regular at the neighboring bathhouse, careful to emerge with my nails trimmed and my hair combed. I completed my finery with new clothing, which Mabrouk pledged to wash and care for. Nothing tames a wild man like the seduction of a beautiful woman. My grandfather always quoted the desert Arab who, it is recounted, was told "Your son is in love." "What of it?" the desert Arab said. "When he loves, he becomes cleaner and more pleasant." I swear, O Arab, you spoke only truth.

I now returned home eagerly. The stranger's shyness had left me. My breast had absorbed the Egyptian air and my blood had mingled with its Nile. I no longer merged two prayers together, or prayed fleetingly like a passing traveler, and I swear if the bugle call had sounded to defend that country, I would have gone out to fight with her people!

Ataa and I attended one of the mosque's discussion circles together. The sheikh who held it was teaching from the book of Islamic history by al-Tabari. Whenever mention was made in the book of al-Hassan and al-Husayn, or any of the line of Umaya, he cursed them, following up his curses with "Upon them and all who follow them," and a hard stare into my face and Ataa's, lips pursed. So as not to permit him to drag us into an argument, we would remain steadfastly silent. Perhaps the constant company I kept with Ataa made the sheikh think I was one of the Nawasib: the clan of Rashid ibn Ali was one of the well-established merchant families in Egypt. Their great-grandfather had come to Egypt with Ibn Tulun as the captain of a military company; Ibn Tulun had made him a gift of a plot of land, where he had settled and set up a business that was later passed on to his descendants.

The sheikh of the circle continued, digressing and expanding and nodding and winking at us, until he came to the story of the monk and the bird. "The great astrologer Ibn Yunis says: One day we were visited by an old monk who had been in the city of Silvan, and told us that he had abided in a monk's cell in his youth. One foggy day, a bird alighted where he could see it, bearing a piece of meat in its beak. The bird left it there, and returned with another, until he had returned with many pieces that came together in the shape of a man. Then the bird came up to him and pecked at him and tore him up and ate him, as he cried for help. Said the monk, 'When I saw him, I cried out to him, "What is your story, O man? What is this I see befalling you?" And he responded, "I am Abd al-Rahman ibn Muljim, who murdered Ali ibn Abu Talib, peace be upon him, and the Lord has set this bird upon me to exact the vengeance you see, moving me from place to place."' The monk said that when he saw what had befallen the man, he left his cell and converted to Islam."

The sheikh was telling the story with great confidence, describing the pieces of meat that came together in the air with his hands. At this juncture, Ataa began whispering jovially in my ear, "It's lunchtime, and I can see somebody who wants meat for lunch! He probably made the whole thing up to get a stray hand or shoulder from this Ibn Muljim!" When we felt that our giggles might start to become audible and disturb those around us, we slipped away quietly, as Ataa said, "Let's go before he finishes off what's left of our sanity."

*

The house of the madman formed part of the eastern wing of the palace. My daily rounds rarely deviated from the house and the mosque, while Ataa's constant company kept me in contact with Rashid ibn Ali, who still warned me against selling my books in al-Azhar, as it was, he said, full of spies.

However, these spies remained unaware of a Persian sheikh of al-Azhar by the name of Dia al-Din al-Karamani, who taught the fundamentals of Qur'an recitation using al-Farabi's book on music. He talked freely and expansively, while his circle grew ever larger. Perhaps al-Farabi had only been declared an infidel and a heretic in Baghdad. We were astounded: who had given al-Karamani permission to teach in the hallowed halls of al-Azhar? He was not old in the least, the blood of youth surging through his veins. He had the eyes of a hawk and an aquiline nose. Despite his foreign origins, his proficiency in Arabic was matchless. His words flowed, as he said: "There can be no recitation without a musical ear, and music is divided into notes and pauses. It is like the colors you see with your eyes. You recognize red, blue, and white. Musical keys are the same. You cannot recognize them without listening to them and knowing their character." He then read from al-Farabi's book: "Rhythm is moving from note to note in strictly calculated time." He tapped the armrest of his seat, saying, "The lighter version of the verse meter *al-raml* is composed of two light beats, *ta, ta-tum, ta, ta-tum*: one strong beat, *ta*, then merge the letter *n* with the letter before or after it, and emphasize it, then a light *ta, ta-tum* after it." Then he burst into a recitation of the Sura of al-Rahman, pointing out the pauses and beats of silence, while the mosque settled into an awed hush, listening.

Although it was now fall, Cairo still had days when it was hot and stifling, making for sleepy, sticky discussion circles in the mosque: you could see nothing but the fly whisks waved about by the sheikhs of the circles to flick away the flies and keep away sleep. Then Ataa and I would go to the banks of the Nile, to a place close by the island in its center, where there was some farmland owned by his family, the clan of Ali. When the fisherfolk glimpsed Ataa, they would cheer joyously and hurry to prepare a seating area for us. They spread out a carpet, two boys would hold up sunshades, and the fisherman's wife would bring us stalks of sugarcane, washed and cut up.

No one went swimming on that side of the river, for there were whirlpools and crocodiles. However, they gave us ropes to tie around our waists, and we paddled and took a quick plunge into the river to cool our bodies from the sweltering weather. When we came out, they would have grilled fish ready for us from their baskets, while our wet clothes would have us shivering with cold, forgetting the heat.

We were refreshed and fed, and that is ever the moment when humankind starts to turn its nose up at its own good fortune, delving into a discussion of truths and certainties, and chatter that verges on heresy. Ataa and I whispered about his great love for the knowledge of the Greeks. "Do you recall," he said, "Theaetetus's dialogue with Plato in which he denies fixed knowledge?"

"If you remind me," I said, "I shall recall it."

"He said, 'Does it not occur that the same breeze will make one man shiver, but the other not? That one man will perceive the wind as violent, and the other not? What is that breeze in itself? Are we to say that it is cold, or that it is not cold? Or shall we admit that it is cold for the one who shivers, but not for the other?' If that is so," he went on, his voice dropping, "there is nothing that is One, in and of itself."

"Perhaps," I said, "that is why Eastern philosophers have called it Subjectivism, denying fixed realities and saying that things are to me as they appear to me, but to you as they appear to you."

*

The scents of the thick and intertwining plants; the cries of migrating birds; the storks and pike in the river; the flocks of cranes; the croaking of the frogs as they leapt about; the clouds above our heads, each with its own story; the cloud above me thick and white, but not weeping as yet. He was holding the rope, sometimes pulling me close, sometimes letting me go far, the water rocking me—I splashed it away, and it rushed back playfully. The rope that bound me to the shore, I thought, was like myself. It kept me from being swept away by the currents of thought. No sooner did I quit Aristotle's heresy than I ran to prayer, pressing my forehead to the dusty ground in the hands of my Creator. Perhaps I was, after all, a coward: I could not swim without a rope.

Ataa was lying on his back on the mat, looking at the running water. "Look at the river!" he called to me from the bank. "Heraclitus says you cannot go into the same river twice."

I emerged, dripping. "Times change, nothing is eternal. It's a river, after all."

"Did you hear what al-Karamani said today in the recitation lesson about al-Farabi? I feel he is a heretic. He is trying to worm al-Farabi's sayings into his teachings whether they belong there or not. He jumped from music to al-Farabi, saying, 'God is One, there is no difference between Himself and His intellect. He is the Mind, He is Sanity and Reason, he is Knowledge, He is the All-Knowing and the Known."

I sat down, crossing my legs. "But, let me tell you, Ataa. He gave me an answer to something that had been giving me sleepless nights. Namely, that God is eternal, but the world is changeable; and what is changeable cannot be created by what is unchanging."

He sat up. "Do you mean the issue resolved by al-Farabi by the idea of Divine Inspiration and Godly Light?"

"Yes." I frowned. "That could be an answer, but I fear that talk of divine inspiration is nothing but the heresy and blasphemy of foreigners and Persians. When I was in Baghdad, they dared not speak of such topics unless it be in whispers."

He craned his neck toward me, eyes shining. "It is not heresy! It protects you from heresy, it urges you to *think*. Al-Farabi says that the existence of things for God is not the same as their existence for us: things appeared from Him because He Himself is Knowledge, He is the impulse of goodness in the world. Therefore, ten intellects emerged from Him, the last of which is our human intellect. And now I find that a great many sheikhs of al-Azhar are speaking of the Ten Minds."

"I don't know." I felt that his speech was too pat and readymade an answer. It might be enough for this young boy, secure in his certainty, with a great urge for contention and winning an argument. Or it might be the world seen through the eyes of a pampered boy who had never known hunger or fear. According to the fifth commandment of the Voyagers, each one finds monotheism "through his mind according to his ability." That is when it becomes a sacred journey: no one can give you the map of the way. You must take the path alone, guided by the lantern of your mind and the whispers of your heart.

On rare occasions, Ataa and I would take a boat to the opposite bank of the river, then walk until we were nearly at a collection of great stone structures, larger than mountains, which the Egyptians called the Pyramids of Giza. I felt heavyhearted at the knowledge that they were tombs of their bygone kings. We climbed their stones and sat there, looking at the caliph's Cairo, Fustat, and the Nile from above, as seen by the gods. With the sunset, we would make our way back, the sky filling with birds. Great flocks passed over our heads, coming from the north, calling out among themselves as they headed southward.

Ataa said that the change of seasons was their time: they came from the north, bringing the cool air in their beaks.

"They seem to me," I said, "to be pained and frightened."

He smiled. "Have you read the tale of the Greek monarch and the cranes?"

"I think I may have seen something of the sort. Remind me of it."

"They say that one of the Greek monarchs asked the poet Quintus to supply him with a store of philosophy books. Quintus packed his books into a crate and set off for the king. However, a band of robbers lay in wait for him and made to kill him. He entreated them to take his money and spare his life, but they refused. At a loss, he looked right and left, seeking assistance, but found none. He lifted his head to the sky and saw cranes circling high overhead. 'O cranes!' he cried, 'the Almighty has abandoned me! I call on you to avenge me!'

"'This is a feebleminded man indeed,' said the robbers. They murdered him and took his money, then divided it up and returned to the city. When the news reached the folk of his city, they were sad and outraged: they followed the tracks of his murderers, but it came to nothing. The nation of Greece all came together at his funeral—including the murdering bandits, who mingled with the other folk and feigned sadness at his death. The cranes flew overhead, crying out to each other. The thieves raised their eyes and faces to the sky: the cranes screamed, flew, and blocked the horizon. They laughed and said to one another, 'They are calling for the blood of the ignorant Quintus,' and took to mocking him. Those close by heard them. News reached the monarch: he took them and questioned them. They confessed to his murder, so he had them executed, and thus the cranes avenged the poet."

The evening fell like sobs. My heart was still heavy and my chest tight, here by the tombs of the god-kings and the snorting of exhausted camels. The place was desolate, echoing with the tale of the murdered poet avenged by the storks.

On many occasions, Lady Justice comes too late. But she always comes. I still did not know then that she might come to betray the murderers in the shape of a fairy with enchanting beauty.

I went to Fustat when I was in the mood for loaves with syrup on hot iron plates, or sometimes baked in ovens built into walls by the women who made the bread. They pulled out the hot loaves, steam rising, poured dark syrup over them, rolled them up, and handed them to you with a merry smile. Their flirtatiousness had struck Amr ibn al-Aas speechless; but I had never found anything to turn my head like Kahramana's body. She blossomed and opened like a lily over the darkness of my soul.

The folk of Fustat were more cheerful and friendlier than the military men in Cairo. Although there was still worry and disquiet in the streets, watching and waiting for the commands of the Caliph Who Can Do No Wrong to settle upon their heads like a renewed bolt from the blue—or, more accurately, from the royal palace east of Cairo—the people in Fustat sang, laughed, gossiped, and secretly named their four-footed animals after their ruler and his men.

Ataa sometimes chafed at his father's and uncles' insistence on remaining in al-Qatai: its eastern half had been in ruins for nearly a hundred years, destroyed by the Abbasid wali, Muhammad ibn Sulayman, who had demolished and sabotaged it until it was nothing but ruins inhabited by robbers and stray animals. Still, a great many of its buildings were still standing on the western side of the city. According to Ataa, "The estates and mansions of my family are built around the mosque of Ibn Tulun. That is why they are still standing, along with some paved plazas, bathhouses, and shops. They say," he went on, "that they survived thanks to a clever stratagem on the part of my grandfather against the army of Muhammad ibn Sulayman. When the Abbasid army besieged al-Qatai, one of my grandfather's slaves, disobedient filth, slipped out under cover of night and betrayed his masters. He told the enemies the locations of the gates, the number of guards, and even the locations of the women's quarters! But," he added, "God punished him for his treachery by afflicting him with whooping cough on the way back, and they found him dead outside the gate at dawn. However, my grandfather saved the day. He held a banquet for the Abbasid army, and all and sundry ate their fill. This saved the family from the demolition. After that, the family motto became, 'Be careful the company you keep: in times of trouble, you find out a man's true mettle.'"

We arrived at the houses of the clan of Ali from the western side. They were like great locked fortresses, but they flung open their gates when they saw us coming at the end of the road. The gates parted to reveal orchards of orange trees with a long stone wall the height of four men.

Everything in Egypt was generously and readily available. Rashid ibn Ali finally asked me to write down a list of the books I possessed, and start showing them to those I trusted, or to people he recommended to me. There was no need for anyone to know, he said, where the books were kept in my house, lest the fires of suspicion turn them to ash.

Still, when I saw the library of his house, and examined its contents and titles, I learned that my feeble crate was but one shelf of his library. It was a library that I would not have believed could be amassed by a single person: generations, it appeared to me, had handed down these rows of books and set them out by subject: sciences, translations, biographies, books of quotations, and poetry. I began to see things with more clarity: Rashid ibn Ali insisted on keeping the knowledge of the Voyagers alive between the lines, seeing to the spread of their books, and attracting followers; he had no interest in my books. I must pass on the great secret to someone in every city in which I alighted, and plant the seeds of rationality in darkened minds. I had not found someone to select as a disciple until now. In Jerusalem, it had been Hamilcar. But what about Cairo?

On occasion, I met some Andalusians at the assembly of Rashid ibn Ali whom I had previously seen at the carpet store; they had not only bought the most expensive and best of the carpets, but they became regular visitors to Saqi-fat Bani Saida, paying special attention to knowledge and the sciences. When Rashid spoke, they craned their necks toward him, listening reverently. Only these were highly recommended to me by Rashid ibn Ali as suitable buyers: they held science in high esteem and thirsted for knowledge. The books would travel with them to Andalusia. One Fri-day, therefore, I showed them the lists of the books I had. Before they made their decisions, they gathered around their portly master, stealing glances at me from time to time, until I began to worry. My palms sweated; I thought to slip away. Then, a boy with them, who appeared to be their servant, came and whispered in my ear, "My master wishes to acquire the original manuscript of Galen of Pergamon, a copy of *Ikhwan al-Safa*, a copy of Ibn Wahshiya's *Nabatean Agriculture*, and al-Kindi's *A Treatise against Alchemy.*"

They agreed to the exorbitant price I demanded: a thou-sand dinars for each book, the price of a young slave from the slave market. I rushed home and came back with them tucked into the folds of my clothing. I watched them leafing through the books I had brought with curiosity and interest. They had large, round, fair faces and thick necks, and their clothes were perfumed. I compared them with the pitiable booksellers of Fustat: lean, dark-skinned, smelling of alley sweat. The sol-diers and guards had not been kind to the people of Fustat, keeping all of Egypt's riches for themselves and leaving the common people nothing but scraps.

Most of the Andalusians' interest and eagerness lay in the Greek translations. They were insistent that they be the originals, scrutinizing them and examining them carefully, as copies and bastardizations had proliferated among the booksellers of Baghdad and Cairo.

The assembly that day was discussing predestination. The portly master of the Andalusians patted his stomach as he chuckled to Rashid ibn Ali. "Away with you! We are only following what is written; or else what would make us pay such exorbitant sums for books and carpets?" He frowned in concentration. "And you say you have nothing other than free will, when your choice has alighted upon these books, with full awareness and true desire? If you cared nothing for them, you would have passed them by, as you pass by pebbles and cow pies. Men of Andalusia, you came here to exchange your darkness for light. The believers in predestination are the meek, those who bow their heads, the fuel of tyrants who use their bent backs as a step to ascend their thrones."

As they made to leave, the portly Andalusian, the one who appeared to be the master, approached me. "These books are enough for us now," he said, "but perhaps you will bring the rest to us in Cordoba, Mazid."

That phrase was the trap that drew me in and remained within me until, one day, I found myself on my camel, with my crate of books, on my way to Andalusia. Was I predestined, or was it my choice? Or did I lie in a status between two statuses? Each of these answers bore a measure of right and a measure of wrong: our fates merely knock upon the doors, and we choose to open the door to them or reject them.

## Lo! We Have Given Thee Abundance

Kahramana still crept in to me, and I drowned in my desire for her. How terrifying were the pleasures contained within that body! I would spend my days in a trance, remembering our nights together. At the discussion circles, I felt her breath around my face and her lute with its melancholy strains would mingle with her luscious moans in my ear. Ataa noticed. He asked, "Why are you sometimes so distracted? Do you eat too many figs? They say that eating figs softens the heart. Or do you listen to music habitually? Music not only pleases the ear, but fills the heart with melancholy. Your sighs are weighty as rocks." He added with a sly grin. "What is it? Are you burdened with something . . . or are you in love?"

I was so taken aback with his question that I could not take up the cheery thread. My flustered mutterings must have confirmed his suspicions. "Who?" he asked. "And where?"

I evaded his question. "Did you believe that? Who could capture the heart of Mazid al-Hanafi? Why, I am a Voyager in the Flock of Cranes!"

How had the terms "Voyager" and "Cranes" slipped out? Had love made me loose-lipped? But Ataa did not react at my reference, although he was sharp-witted and missed nothing. It seemed that it was he whom I would choose to carry the torch of the Voyagers in Egypt. But I must introduce him to it quietly and smoothly: the boy's heart was still buffeted by high winds, and his ship had not yet settled on the shores of certainty.

That day, as soon as our discussion circle was over, he repeated his debauched desire to visit Shaaban, the slave trader in Fustat. "He is a shrewd trader," he said. "In front of his house is a courtyard where he displays his slaves, but he keeps a garden behind his house with rooms in it, and in every room there is a slave girl like a hidden jewel." He took to describing them like a hungry man dreaming of a banquet. "There is an Indian woman with a lovely figure and great beauty, with clear creamy skin, a wonderful flavor, and a pliant disposition . . ."

I raised an eyebrow. "You have tasted her?"

He replied airily, "Lord, forgive us the venial sins." He went on: "There are women from Kandahar, who are always virgins no matter how many times they make love. There is a woman from Sindh, small-waisted, incredibly beautiful with long hair . . ." He trailed off as though he had recalled something. "Oh! He has a girl who says she is from Medina, bringing together sweetness of speech, fullness of figure, beauty, and coquetry." He slapped his forehead. "And the girl from Mecca! She is a nymph with her broken speech and her soft wrists. She is white with tanned skin, voluptuous and shapely. The slave girls of Shaaban the slave trader have pure, cool mouths and soft, drowsy eyes . . ."

"Enough, Ataa!" I cried. "I am not myself with your talk! Look above you! We are beneath the dome of the mosque."

He bowed his head in mock modesty. "Heaven forgive me!" The corners of his mouth turned up. "Lord, forgive us the venial sins."

Kahramana's visits were irregular: she made them when she was not being watched. If Yunis or her mistress were not monitoring her, and her master asleep, she crept out to me. Sometimes she would come three nights in succession, reducing my soul to a ruin in her hands, but sometimes it would be a long time between visits, filling me with overpowering desire for her. Cairo would fall asleep, and only I would remain awake, alongside the brass pots of beans simmering in the coals to provide breakfast for the city. When morning came, I would almost go to the madman's house to catch a glimpse of her. I tried to learn of her from Mabrouk, but he was tight-lipped and careful not to let out the secrets of his master's house. "In winter," she said, "it will be hard to slip out to you." This was because her master slept in the eastern room giving onto the roof. Sometimes I would wake at dawn to find that she had placed a plate in my room with three apples bearing the marks of her teeth: I would tear into them, enjoying her apples.

We lived like this for a long time. I was unmade, and had no desire to leave Cairo for more cities to distribute the books of the Cranes. There I stayed, desiring to remain by her side, until we quarreled and the thread between us was broken. I had teased her the previous week, saying, "How many hands have plucked this low-hanging fruit, and how many thirsty men have drunk at this spring before me?" She was clearly adept, knowing where to guide my hands, and laughing at my inexperience on some occasions. That night, despite the still and reverent darkness, she sat up in the bed as though stung, and slapped my face.

"I thought you respected this gift and the risk I am taking," she wept. "I have always preserved my virtue, and that through the slave markets where girls and boys are sold. Covetous eyes, wandering hands, depraved words—I resist them all, only to come to you and have you describe me as a debauched strumpet? Your eyes betrayed your overwhelming desire, so I sought to give you the ultimate in pleasure, that your desires might not stand in the way of my path to your heart. I refused to play the coquette and pretend to rebuff you in order to heighten your longing, as is the way of all the women of the world. I wished to cut short this eternal dance and lie in your arms until dawn. There is nothing between us but two souls that have clung together; I have placed no traps or snares in our path in the form of false rejection. It was my wish to smash the urn that springs with desire between a man and a woman, to traverse that field between mare and stallion!"

She was gasping, tears pouring down her face, her chest rising and falling so violently that I thought she might choke. I made to hold her and comfort her. I swore that I should not touch her that night, only recite the poems of Imru al-Qays or the line "Have you left me to punish me, or out of tedium?"

But she shoved me away from her and disappeared into the curtain of the night. When I heard her footsteps on the roof, leaping over the wall of mugwort and sweet basil, I felt such a desolation and a longing for her that my heart constricted with grief as it had the day of Grandfather's death.

A week passed in which I did not see her or even hear her playing. Was she still incensed?

It appeared that my trouble was not with Kahramana, but with myself. I was even now unable to translate the feelings of love into words. And was what I felt for her love, or a flood of desire and the snare of youth? In al-Yamama there was nothing more than a ripple of flirtatious laughter quickly hidden behind a burka; in Baghdad, I had only thought of Zahira, who was a shining star to be seen and not touched ere she disappeared on the horizon. I rejected all the offers of Hassan the Egyptian to go with him to the tavern for fear it be said that Sheikh al-Tamimi's scribe frequented bars. In Jerusalem, the beautiful Surianese women had tempted me, as had the freshness of Elissar and the meekness of Hanna, Hamilcar's sisters, who were so soft that it seemed a spring had just flowed into their faces. But that charm was like lightning that flashed and disappeared with storm clouds that briefly appear over desert dunes. Kahramana, though, was like a fever that had overtaken me and eaten me up. She had introduced me to worlds suffused with rainwater, perfume, and melody. The texture of her tight, hot body; the wellspring within her . . . she was a kind of madness, a fairy who had taken me by the reins like a lost camel and led me to a fertile field where couples roamed joyously. Kahramana! With her, I seemed to be rolling atop a mountain made of butter.

I did not know what was happening, but she had been silent for days and not returned. She had given up playing the lute.

At night, I blundered between the balcony and the door. In the end, I prepared the sage drink and took it to the madman, although I had vowed to myself never to visit him again after the grape pamphlet incident, as I had taken to calling it. But longing drove me to his house like a sheep.

I found him lying on a couch, staring at nothing, running a *miswak* around his teeth. Whenever he saw me, he brightened, and this time was no different. He drank what I brought him straight away, and asked me to recite some verses of the Qur'an to him, or the epic poem of al-Asha. Then he asked me, "Who is the caliph who says, 'I have had so many women that I no longer care who comes or goes; I have eaten delicacies until I can no longer tell sweet from sour; I have no pleasure left but knowledge and the company of learned men?' One tires of everything but knowledge: the more there is, the sweeter to the soul. Keep me company, learned man."

"You have spoken nothing but truth, wise man," I responded, thinking, "But who will tell this to Kahramana's body, bubbling and boiling over like a pit of flame!"

I glimpsed her coming and going and bringing this and that. I was careful not to let our eyes meet, for a lover's eyes betray him, and Yunis was extremely observant. He availed himself of my visit to sit on the couch with his turban pushed back, his belt undone, and his paunch hanging free, even dozing off from time to time as I entertained his master, knowing he was in no need of direct attention and was tamed by my presence.

I had not known that Yunis was a eunuch until Kahramana told me. He always sat with me and the madman, and appeared a man of full virility: his voice, his aspect, his firm handshake, none of these evidenced the softness, effeminacy, or cunning of eunuchs. One day, with the beginnings of dawn, when Kahramana had been readying herself to leave, and taking up two dishes of sweetmeats she had brought, she had said, "I must leave now before the eunuch comes to wake my master." I thought she meant Mabrouk. But she winked. "No. The old one. Yunis, the foreigner who has accompanied my master since the dawn of his youth. But I do not know when they castrated him."

I pulled her to me hard, jokingly, not wishing her to leave. "How do you know he is a eunuch?" I asked. "Did you go to him seeking something and not find it?"

She playfully batted at me with her fists. "Ah, you desert Arabs! Always thinking the worst!"

She had ever been cheerful, with a ready wit: she had always joked along with me. Why had she left me and gone away?

The madman asked me to recite some of the Qur'an, but no sooner had I recited the first few words of a verse than he finished it for me. I turned to the Prophet's sayings, and he recited these one after the other, without missing a word. Indeed, he took me down twists and turns of interpretation of which I had not been aware. As though sharing great news, he said, "Did you know, Mazid, that there are seven ways of reciting the Qur'an? There is Sheikh Tamim's method of *kashkasha*, as when, in verse twenty-four of the Sura of Mary, instead of, *'your Lord has provided beneath you a stream,'* he says, *'your Lord hash provided beneath you a shtream.'* Or the *istintaa* of the tribe of Hadheel, who, instead of, *'Lo! We have given thee Abundance,'* say, *'No! We have given thee Abundance.'"*

His Qur'anic recitations baffled me—he was dragging me to a place I knew nothing of, and in which I knew not what was safe and what was dangerous. "Yes," I said, feigning knowledge, "also, we are from Hanifa and we and the people of Tamim use *kaskasa*, which is changing the letter *k* to the letter *s* when speaking to a woman."

What I said appeared to please him: he nodded and talked on until I was dizzy. He was trying to gather the threads of his memory, now speaking of the position of judge he'd rejected, now of some new pamphlets he wished to distribute in secret by way of rebellion over the caliph's injustices. When I announced my wish to go to the mosque, he kept me back. "Where would you go, in unjust Egypt? Have you not heard al-Mutanabbi's verse: 'Egypt's guards sleep; the foxes hunt their fill; / But still her vines hang heavy, bountiful'?"

I pleaded with him not to distribute the benefits of grapes again in secret. He laughed at me and said, "We shall see."

My heart beat fast and my eyes remained glued to his face. At that moment, I realized that this man would not cease to distribute writings against the ruler.

## The Doctor Who Heals

The books of Hippocrates and his student Galen of Pergamon had passed the scepter of medicine on to me in Egypt: I became a false physician to whom people constantly came for treatment. I know not who put it about, but in all probability it was the garrulous mother of the children. My fame slowly began to spread: some students at al-Azhar came to me complaining of a change in their innards, or a weakness in their bodies, or flatulence. I would tell them to boil their drinking water and purify it with slices of lemon, and clean their pots and steam them with mastic before storing water in them, "to cleanse your liver and return the color to your faces." Sometimes the sheikhs of the circles would come to me complaining of joint pain from long hours sitting with their knees bent: I would tell them to heat castor oil and rub it into the afflicted joints, then crush fenugreek into a powder and make a poultice to wrap around their knees, "which will heal you with God's help." I was careful to conclude all my advice with verse seventy-six of the Sura of Noah: "*Over every possessor of knowledge, there is One more knowing.*" This, I felt, preserved a face-saving escape when they discovered that I was a pretend doctor, an interloper.

However, with God's help, their bodies responded. When they took the medicine with the intention to recover, recover they did, and their afflictions disappeared. Our bodies are created to recover, to cast aside their poisons and pollutions. If the humors are in balance, we eventually achieve what Galen of Pergamon called "well-being." Most of the mumbo jumbo I prescribed, which I enjoyed and in which I indulged until I almost believed it, was the law of resemblance. The Greeks said that every ailment had a cure of the same genus, or something similar to it; therefore, if someone came to me complaining of a headache or poor memory, I prescribed walnuts, because they resemble a brain. If someone came to me complaining of a pale or sallow complexion, I prescribed beetroot to strengthen the blood. Ear complaints received a prescription of broad beans, because they resembled an ear. Then I would nod, feigning wisdom, and say, "Resemblance and similarity are half the cure, as the father of medicine, Hippocrates, tells us."

But my greatest surprise as a false physician was when Ataa's mother—the wife of Rashid ibn Ali—called me in to cure her. I was visiting Ataa, when he said without shame, "My mother wants to see you, O great physician."

I paled. He had never spoken to me of a mother: I had never seen nor heard the women of the household on my visits, except for a slave girl who saw to our hospitality. I fell silent. What if that lady had a serious illness that I could not cure? I tried to think of a way to avoid the summons, but he had already stood and was saying, "Come with me and I shall take you to her visiting room."

We exited the library and walked around the house, heading for the southern gate that led to the rest of the orchards and gardens that adjoined their fields and lands. In a colonnade inside sat a luminous woman, a slave sitting below her rubbing her feet with oil. She had removed her face veil and was looking to the ceiling, in obvious pain. Her face lit up to see Ataa. Seeing me behind him, she said, "Come closer! You are like my son, Ataa, and I need not wear a veil in front of you!"

She had a strong foreign accent. When I drew near, I realized why Ataa had not mentioned her: a woman with this many sons, at such an age, and still possessed of such radiant beauty, must not be spoken of lightly to strangers for fear of the Evil Eye. She was bright and smiling, with parted blond hair, a shadow of Ataa on her features while the rest of her face was pure Byzantium. No sooner had I stood before her than she began to complain to me of the attacks of mosquitoes upon her body, whose bites sometimes became enflamed and occasionally afflicted her with fever. "Twenty-five years in Egypt," she said, "and her mosquitoes have not had their fill of my blood yet!"

She was clearly Circassian, or perhaps of the *saqaliba*. I had not seen among the Surianese such whiteness—so pale the veins showed beneath—and such transparent blue eyes. I bowed my head without daring to stare at her. "My lady, your blood is sweet. The bites go beneath the skin to create inflammation. Your cure lies in a paste of basil and marjoram leaves with rosewater, applied to the exposed areas of your body."

To tell the truth, this was what I used myself. This was no recipe of Galen's, but the recipe of Shammaa of the House of Wael, with which I had resisted the fierce mosquitoes of the Nile. When Kahramana had expressed her approval of that scent on my bed and my clothing, I put it on every night. I turned to Ataa, addressing myself to him out of modesty rather than speaking to his mother: "I shall make some of it and bring it to you. If it pleases you, I shall tell you the quantities for the recipe that you may yourselves make the mosquito paste."

Ataa laughed. "Use Mazid's paste, Mother, and if it doesn't work, I'll feed him to the crocodiles."

The fall passed. Egypt and her people were busy with the harvest and preparing the fields for the new season. The days were starting to grow shorter, while the flocks of birds migrating from the north filled the air with the deafening din of their cries, spreading their longing over the rooftops. I ached, remembering the rooftops of the houses of al-Yamama. By now they would be laden with bunches of dates in preparation for pressing, so that the syrup would drip out. There was a special tower of our house dedicated to preserving dates. It smelled sweet, like honey, all year long.

I recited the verses of the desert Arab Maysoon, daughter of Bahdal, of the clan of Kalb, when she left her childhood haunts in the Arabian Peninsula and moved to the Levant as Muawiya's wife:

> What is the fault of a desert Arab
> Cast into a place she never knew?
> Her only wish: sheep's milk and a tent in Najd,
> But that wish was not to come true.
> She cried out in pain to recall the sweet water
> Of Uzayb, and its cool gravel at night's end;
> But for her cries of pain, this Arab daughter
> Of the desert would go mad and never mend.

Homesickness scatters you. It divides your soul between two places. Egypt was generous as its Nile . . . until the Day of the Doll.

## The Day of the Doll

The Day of the Doll has been told in many different fashions, and different historians set it down differently. Later, I found out that in the history of Egypt in the era of al-Hakim, there was not one doll but many, for the people had made many dolls demanding their rights.

When I visited Ataa's family home, we almost always sat in one of two places: we either haunted his father's library late into the night, or, in the daytime, enjoyed the garden that lay between their house and the northern wall. This appeared to be the private garden for their house, separate from the adjoining gardens of his paternal uncles. If I stayed up late enough at Ataa's, he asked me to spend the night, as the way to Cairo could be dangerous after dark, and the Zuweila Gate was closed and guarded by the worst and most belligerent guards. Sometimes I insisted on going home, afraid that

Kahramana might creep in and I could miss a night with her; other times I spent the night in the house of Rashid ibn Ali, Ataa tempting me with a new book his father had acquired or with some of the exquisite sweetmeats they made. Still, I missed Kahramana. I felt that I should not spend too many nights there, as I did not know Rashid's feelings about it. Did it please him, or was he secretly put out and only acquiesced because of his son's persuasions? Therefore, quite often, I would put on my turban and walk through the streets leading to the western gate, ignoring Ataa's pleas to stay and play a game of chess. In Baghdad, they were leery of the game, calling the pieces "the Devil's soldiers." But here, strangely enough, although grapes and raisins were forbidden, I often glimpsed chessboards in people's hands and in the windows of some shops.

"I do not wish to spend our time in frivolous pursuits," I said one night. "Have you not heard Galen say, 'Enjoy nothing that is not useful to others'?"

I said this in hopes that he would invite me into his father's library, for I never tired of sitting in it and smelling the Chinese paper and Khorasan leather, softened with the scent of papyrus. But it seemed that he had found an irresistible way to keep me there that night: as I moved away, he called after me, "Do you want to see the Devil?"

Although Ataa's insistence could be relentless, this time he had given me pause. I turned. "What do you mean?"

He muttered in a low voice, to draw me nearer, "Our Caliph Who Can Do No Wrong often passes this way on his journey up the Muqattam Mountain. He goes through the winding mountain paths on his gray donkey to the summit to practice magic and theurgy, and observe the planets. If tonight the star he awaits has risen, you will see him riding by the wall with his retinue."

Sensing my curiosity and seeing my eyes widen, he said, "One of the western rooms of the house overlooks his accustomed path. We often see him through the windows on his way to his spot on the mountaintop. They say that he has a high degree of accuracy in astrology." He made his voice tempting. "A dark night; a new moon; the Devil is expected to show up any minute. Let us wait in the western room, play chess, and wait for him to pass."

I recalled my long talks with Father Samaan by the orange tree, Samaan trying to convert me. When the perfume-laden breeze sprang up, he would say, "When the angels flutter around us, you are surrounded by peace and the scent of flowers. When demons come, they announce their presence with a repulsive smell, and you hear the clopping of hooves."

That night, waiting for the Devil, I heard and smelled nothing. Just before midnight, when sleep was beginning to play around my eyelids, the sense of a presence came over me strongly, and Ataa lifted his eyes from the chessboard, listening. We heard the clopping of hooves and the neighing of horses in the distance, followed by the clangor of weapons. Ataa grasped my shoulder powerfully and whispered in triumph, "Shh! It seems the Devil has arrived."

My stomach seized in fear. We put out the lantern that had stood between us. We hung the feeble, fading light on the wall, and crouched behind the carved shutters.

A loud procession was approaching, four soldiers walking before it, each bearing a blazing torch like the flames of Hell (I never would have imagined at the time that those tongues of flame would one day burn Cairo to ash), their silken abayas shining with the fire's glow. Behind these were a group of mounted horsemen, helmets gleaming and horses whinnying. On their horses, they seemed like stone statues, never moving their necks or their bodies. When they drew level with the wall, we managed to make out their features, lit by the flames. They were definitely soldiers from the tribe of Kutama. Then we glimpsed him in their midst.

He rode a great gray donkey with tall, erect ears and large hooves, moving haltingly amid the group of tall, neighing horses. Why had he, the leader of the caliphate, chosen this irritable mount? As he passed close by, we held our breath. I trembled to see him surrounded by blackness, lit only by the torches. Upon his head, he had placed the head of a tiger, jaws agape. Its skin fell down his back all the way to his donkey's haunches. I know not whether some demon had whispered to him of our presence or if we had made some movement that drew his attention, but he suddenly raised his face to us and fixed his eyes on the window where we were hiding. When the guards slowed their pace in response to their caliph's pause, he motioned to them with the scepter in his hand to resume. His face shone among the light of the torches: a young, healthy face with round eyes and thin lips, incongruous with the jaws of the tiger upon his head. But there was a savage, fearsome glitter in his eyes, telling you that nothing, *nothing*, could stand in their way.

That fleeting glimpse of his face froze the blood in my veins, and made me realize that he was the descendant of some strange inhuman line. He quickly forged ahead into the darkness, the saddle of his donkey bulging with scrolls and papers. The horsemen with their torches kept pace with him, lighting his way. We froze, limbs stiff, watching him as he moved toward the mountain. When he reached the foot, he raised his scepter in a command for his men to turn back. Alone, he ascended into the shadows of the paths leading up into the Muqattam Mountain.

I spent the night in perplexed contemplation, turning the matter this way and that. It refused to make sense. What had raised this man up to sit on the throne of Egypt? Egypt, with all its learned men, clerics, and theologians bowing their heads under the wings of this boy who wore a tiger's head for a turban and spent his time in a cave in the Muqattam Mountain.

I found the answer spread out on Rashid ibn Ali's breakfast table the following morning in a brief phrase: "Tyranny, the ecstasy of sovereignty, and a winner's power."

"Is it true," Ataa whispered as he scooped up some honey with a piece of bread, "that he had the teacher Bragon, who raised him, executed?"

Rashid raised his head and stared into space. "Bragon was a noble Copt, the regent, and he was a man of plain and honest speech, but careful with his words. None could have served this caliph but a debauched dissembler, a man who achieves his ends through dishonesty and escapes his wrath through obsequious flattery—or else a fool who could arouse the envy of no one."

Rashid ibn Ali was not alone in bearing the answer to my questions: the weeks that followed also provided some answer, in the form of new taxes being levied on the harvests of wheat, barley, and corn, which inspired a great wave of public discontent that started in the alleyways of Fustat and culminated in setting up the doll.

It was a gigantic doll, fashioned of the remnants of old clothing and papers, and it resembled the scarecrows of the field. They set it up in the path of the Caliph Who Can Do No Wrong on his nightly trek to Muqattam. They hung a sheet of paper on its hand bearing curses against the caliph, his ancestors, and his rule, shaming him for his Christian mother and accusing him of being illegitimate: such behavior, they said, such injustice, and such tyranny could only come from a bastard. It concluded by saying that they would soon storm his palace, tear him to pieces, and scatter them to the lions and birds.

People hurried past the doll, fearing to approach it for fear of the obscenity of the words on the sheet. Yet, by evening, every limb of the doll had some complaint affixed to it. Its hair was a long scroll of goatskin hung there by the Coptic Christians, split into two, half bearing the names of their demolished churches, and half bearing a list of the Copts killed and dismissed from their professions after their churches had been torn down. The scroll was so long it reached the ground.

Fearfully, I recalled the grape scrolls. Had the madman done it again, and set up this doll?

I left my discussion circle: we had all been told to leave early that day, and vacate the interior halls of the mosque, because the sultana, the caliph's sister, called Sitt al-Mulk or the Lady on the Throne, was to be there that evening to award prizes and rewards to the women graduating from the discussion circles of al-Azhar. If only she could, with her power and authority, lift the caliph's sentence of women's perpetual imprisonment in their homes. By now, no shoemaker was permitted to make women's shoes in Cairo. And yet the women's discussion circles were alive and well in al-Azhar. How did they get there? Did they wrap their feet in fabric? Or perhaps they took refuge in the power of Sitt al-Mulk, whom it was said the caliph revered. There were discussion circles for women here, which I had not seen in Baghdad or Jerusalem. Even in al-Yamama, where my mother adored learning, she was only permitted to listen in secret to my grandfather's circle and learn from him, proudly repeating what she had learned among the other women.

I left the mosque and hurried to the madman's house. He was not there. "He's out," Mabrouk said shortly. Kahramana would definitely know whether he had something to do with the doll. If only she would come tonight and repair the rends in my heart!

The madman's house had experience in making dolls. I always found small poppets in colored costumes with staring eyes, lying on shelves and scattered around. The mother of the children told me that she made them for her little girls to play with, but Kahramana gave the lie to her words, saying, "She's an old witch. She makes them to bring calamity down on her enemies. She repeats the names of her enemies while breathing into her poppets, poking pins and needles into them until her enemy dies."

By evening, the doll of the Zuweila Gate had been plucked from where it stood and brought to the Caliph Who Can Do No Wrong. The guards not only brought it to him, but copied out some of what was written on the sheet to show to their superiors. I knew full well that the guards of Cairo eagerly awaited the day that the caliph would give them permission to do their worst to the folk of Fustat for what they saw as their unruly and insubordinate nature, their mutinous responses to the guards, and the way they named their beasts of burden after them.

The mysterious scrolls extolling the virtues of grapes—the fruit banned by the caliph—flooded Cairo once more. All this was a few days before the great horror that broke out on a Wednesday night.

Those who witnessed it say that the caliph himself, on his way to Muqattam, returned the doll to its spot and set it alight. Some say that he had the commander of the armies do it. The moon was in its first quarter when the Caliph Who Can Do No Wrong instructed his soldiers to set fire to the alley opposite the place where the doll had been planted, and the alleys around it. He told them to make a list of all those who could write in those alleys, and cut off their fingers.

Everyone cowered in their houses like the tribe of Thamud after God's punishment of them for hamstringing the Prophet Salih's camel. On the wind, there came the smell of roasting flesh and the sounds of screaming, wailing, roaring, and howls barely recognizable as human.

By dawn, everyone had fallen silent, all except the muezzin of al-Azhar calling out for the dawn prayers. No sooner had the

madman heard him than he burst out into the street, screaming the verse: "Yazid! Cry, threaten as you might, / Your
threats and taunts give me no fright!"

Everyone cowered in their homes for three days, unable
to pluck up the courage to go out even to bury their dead. I
stayed in my room, shaking with the beginnings of a fever, and
when I managed to gather myself and rise, I pulled out my
compass and astrolabe and turned them in my hands all night,
attempting to calculate the location of the stars, obscured now
by a great pall of smoke that had hung over Cairo since the
night of the fire. The human remains remained by the western gate, no one daring to approach them but the madman,
who sought out any door that was ajar to slip through and
scream, "Yazid! Cry, threaten as you might, / Your threats
and taunts give me no fright!"

Ataa said to me that Egypt remained silent, afraid to
move, until his clan, the clan of Ali, came out with buckets
and pots of water and challenged the guards by putting out
the fire, on the pretext that it might spread to their estates
and fields. At the sight of this family, other people plucked
up the courage to leave their houses with utensils and gourds
of water to put out the fire. When everyone looked into
each other's faces and saw the toll taken by terror, panic,
and sleeplessness, a number of Egypt's notables resolved to
go to the caliph and beg his permission to bury the human
remains and dismembered corpses so that Cairo might not
be overrun with rats and plagues. They promised him that
they would investigate the matter of the doll and find out
who had dared so to disrespect the majesty of the throne.
They must be, they said, some of the riffraff from Fustat, not
members of the inner circle.

When the burials started, it was said that there were 1,300
dead Christians and 1,500 dead Muslims; however, a great
many of the corpses were unidentifiable because they had
been scalped.

*

The Agate Cities: cities steeped in blood and screaming. All that remained to me was to spend days and nights in prayer and contemplation of the stars. I no longer heard the lamentations of the lute or the cries of the cranes and the storks over the Nile. Occasionally, someone knocked, but I never answered. I never knew whether it was one fleeing persecution from the soldiers and knocking at any door for sanctuary, a patient looking for the pretend doctor, or the police, for the killing had spread to "suspicious characters" and itinerant vendors from Fustat.

If only Kahramana were here! I used to reproach her for her daring in coming to me; now I wished to catch even a glimpse of her. Why was she absent? I no longer saw her in the madman's company, only Yunis. His master called him "harbinger of joy" and thought him a bringer of good fortune, for it was Yunis who had led him to the slave trader who had sold him Lamis. But I recalled Kahramana telling me brokenly that they called her "harbinger of doom" because when she had arrived, her master had lost what remained of his sanity and taken to wandering in the streets. Her defeated demeanor and her breath, which smelled of apples, made me melancholy: I embraced her and drank of every part of her—even her face, which they thought to be a harbinger of doom.

It took the caliph's Cairo months to lick its wounds and gather itself together. The blood dried in the streets and doorways, and dried up in the veins of the dead. The sheikhs of al-Azhar, in their Friday prayers and the discussion circles, warned us ceaselessly against the seditiousness of disobeying the ruler, and impressed upon us the importance of obeying him, to prevent bloodshed and violation.

After the burning of the doll, the Royal Palace acquired a new habit: before the noon prayers, four Nubian slaves would arrive from the eastern palace bearing a great pot filled with rice and lentils, and every student or one of the faithful leaving the mosque would receive a ladleful. Most people took to bringing a bowl with them in anticipation of the ladleful of rice: those not in the know lifted their garments and received their portion of rice therein, then left praying for long life for the caliph.

Was it time for me to depart? I had spent a year and three months in Egypt, and sold a small number of books. Many people in this land appeared to have no desire for reading: they were confused, distracted, as though awaiting the parting of the clouds of misery. But could I bear to leave Kahramana?

I remained silent and pensive that day. I had no wish to pass through the gate of lentils and rice, scattered into people's stomachs as folk scatter seed for hungry birds to fight over.

Ataa told me that his father wished to see me. I went to him immediately: I had not seen him since the incident of the doll, and I wished to inform him that my sojourn in Egypt had drawn to a close. I must leave for Cordoba.

But it remained to hand the lantern of the Voyagers over to Ataa. His dissolute urges notwithstanding, aptitude and intelligence lay behind his bright brow. My final, important need, which I could not leave Egypt without accomplishing, was to meet Ibn al-Haytham, who remained imprisoned in his own house, by order of the Caliph Who Can Do No Wrong. If I left Egypt without meeting him, speaking with him, and learning from him, it would leave a mark upon me, and my knowledge would be the poorer for it.

Perhaps Rashid ibn Ali might find some way to let me see him. But all these preparations aside, could I endure parting with Kahramana, who had disappeared into the darkness of the balcony never to return?

We exited through the Zuweila Gate, heading for al-Qatai. The guards still subjected all who entered and exited to suspicious scrutiny. I searched their eyes for gloating and the hubris of triumph, but found nothing but fatigue and tedium. They were leaning back against the wall by the gate, which was still sooty and half demolished by the flames, polishing their shields with dirty rags they handed to each other.

Beyond the walls, the fishermen had slipped back again to the banks of the Nile, glancing about them cautiously. Some itinerant vendors had resumed pushing their handcarts with cautious steps. They no longer cried their wares in light-hearted, melodious tones, but wandered aimlessly with their carts as though at a great funeral.

I had never seen Rashid ibn Ali's face as dark and grim as I did that day. He was alone in his reception hall but for two of his sons, his bookkeeper, and Yakout, who worked in his shop. He was not holding a book, as was his wont; his head was not held high as though he were about to impart some great news. He was merely looking about at those around him. Drawing closer, you could make out red lines in the depths of his eyes, which reflected the shattering blow.

He was not wearing a turban, and I kissed his bare head. He began to mutter, "They said only a descendant of the Prophet could be caliph, even if he burned the city down around our heads. Is this caliph, this imam, the only way to manifest Divine Will on Earth and prevent *fitna*? And is there any greater *fitna* in the world than the horrors that Egypt has witnessed, leaving behind burned houses, bereaved mothers, and orphans?" He drew in a shuddering breath. "The soldiers he set upon the folk of Cairo wreaked havoc upon everyone. Everyone. They sought to punish the Copts for the crime of being Copts—"

"What of it?" the bookkeeper on his right burst out. "What crime did they commit? They are only dhimmi, after all."

"Do not say dhimmi!" Rashid ibn Ali burst out. "That only demeans them, makes them ever inferior and subordinate. They are human, nothing more. God has granted them dignity on land and sea." He shook his head unhappily. "Al-Basti writes,

You who ask me of my creed,
Ask my methods and my deeds.
Justice, self-control: my vow.
Would you my method disallow?

Rashid ibn Ali turned to me, his head seemingly too heavy for his shoulders. "Do you recall the porter who brought your things and ended up in prison?"

I nodded.

"They killed him."

I gasped.

He went on, "He used to be a priest in Alexandria. They pulled down his church, and he refused to leave for Byzantium: he stayed on in Egypt, reluctant to leave the land where his ancestors had lived for hundreds of years. He worked in the basest jobs, accepting the lowest payment, so that none would find out that he and his family were now mendicants. Most of them live as day laborers, or by what skills they have, now that their churches are demolished."

Ataa went on in a low voice, respecting his father's sorrow. "This garden of ours, which you have long admired, is kept by a Coptic gardener and his family. They care for its plants and birds with contentment and all they say is, 'Happy are they who know their way to the Lord.'"

To reassure him, and to keep up my end of the conversation, I said, "There is something similar even in Baghdad. When the people revolted against the Christians in Baghdad, they looted their church in Qatiyat al-Daqiq, and then burned it down. It fell on some people and they died."

There was a guest of Rashid ibn Ali, an older man with two pendulous double chins, whom I always saw but knew not his identity. "They say that the Coptic women have a great deal of freedom," he said in a seeming attempt to smooth out the atmosphere. "Some say it is because when the men drowned with Pharaoh, there were none left but the slaves and the day laborers. The women had no patience for a world without husbands: each woman freed her slave, then married him, with the stipulation that none of them could do anything without his wife's permission. They agreed, and thus Egypt's men obeyed the commands of their womenfolk."

This light anecdote fell flat. Yakout, the shop attendant, said, "Textile manufacture in the Nile Delta is a cottage industry. The Coptic women spin linen thread, and the men weave it. The fabric merchants pay them daily. But they can only sell to the middlemen appointed by the government, and a weaver makes very little, no more than half a dirham, not enough for the bread they eat; but the price of a piece of fabric is high due to levies and taxes. They never see any of it; it is swallowed up by the middlemen."

I know not why, at that moment, I sensed that Yakout was a Copt, for his words were heavy with great trouble. I recalled what Amr al-Qaysi had always said to me: "If you wish to gauge the sweetness and lightness of the water of a land, go to the fabric sellers and the spice traders and look them in the face. If you see the freshness of the water in them, know that it is as sweet as they are fresh. If you find them like the faces of the dead, with bowed heads, make haste and hurry away." Now there were only the faces of the dead left in Egypt.

When the tray of food was laid out, it was sparse, unlike the opulent banquets that Rashid ibn Ali had offered to reflect upon his generosity and hospitality. Bread with butter and molasses of the type sold in Fustat, and milk with black seeds, plus some slices of watermelon. Everyone muttered, "We should not fill our gullets, I swear, now that there is a bereaved mother or an orphan in every house."

After the afternoon prayers, the mood of the gathering began to change. The chief cleric at al-Azhar arrived and gave a sermon on the benefits of charity and zakat. A group of merchants and nobles began to arrive, pledging to take up a collection to rebuild houses, cure the injured, and feed the hungry. Ataa whispered in my ear, as the servants came and went to prepare the sheikh's circle, "They say that one of the reasons the ruler was angry is that he sent a letter to Mahmoud, the ruler of Ghazni, to annex his land; but Mahmoud tore up the letter and spat on it, then sent it to the Abbasid caliph, which drove our Fatimid caliph out of his mind."

"Bless the ruler of Ghazni!" I smiled.

The Azharite sheikh began to clear his throat and quote the Qur'an and hadith that urged Muslims to be charitable so as to allay the wrath of God. He ranted and raved, and spoke without end, but still, the basket that Rashid had brought to collect his guests' charity was less than half full.

When evening came and I prepared to return home, I divined that this was the best time to confide in Rashid ibn Ali that I intended to leave Egypt. No sooner had I told him this than he asked me to take a seat by his side. "Do you know," he said, "that before you leave Egypt, you must prepare a disciple to ascend the path of the Voyagers?"

"I have found him," I said.

He tilted his head questioningly. "Oh?"

"And who better than the son of a noble house?" I made a discreet gesture to where Ataa sat.

He lowered his head. The ghost of a smile played upon his face in tacit agreement.

The world around me was packing its bags. I must leave. But not before I passed the torch to Ataa. He had a lightness and impulsiveness about him that might have disqualified him from the Voyagers' vocation, which required discretion and patience. It would be no easy task to convey the commandments and instructions to him, so he must absorb them by degrees. He had a good knowledge of philosophy, logic, and history; I would not impress him with my knowledge of these subjects.

In any event, despite the difficulty of the task, it would not be harder than the task of Abu Abbas the Persian blacksmith, may he rest in peace, who had first called me, all unwitting, to the path of the Voyagers. How often had I made light of him! How careless I had been, to the point of derision! I imagined his great head, severed and rolling on the floor of his shop like the severed animal's head around which the flies had swarmed in Basra. That head had been as a mirror reflecting the Unseen to me. I should have thought to be cautious and circumspect then. But the mirrors of my soul had been dark: they could not see, nor could my soul comprehend. I must not only enlist Ataa, but swear him to secrecy as a member of a secret society of which some aspects would always remain mysterious. Even its members did not know one another. A great body it was, extending over deserts and different lands, its head indistinguishable from its corpus.

My grandfather always used to say, "Wisdom is like an antidote. If you take it all at once, it will kill you. Wisdom is best imbibed drop by drop. Examples, inferences, and metaphors must be carefully chosen according to the listener. If he be a tailor, speak to him of needle and thread, the needle's eye, and the scissors. If he be a shepherd, speak of his staff and his flock." Ataa was keenly intelligent. How should I introduce the subject to him?

When Ataa invited me to stay at his house that night, I accepted without hesitation. A conversation in the library would open up many paths to us. I refused his offer to lie in wait for the Devil's procession, saying instead, "He will definitely be bent on evil and vengeance now that Cairo has burned, and be prepared to do away with anyone whose face he sees in passing. He sees in the dark like an owl. He still rides that donkey with the gilded saddle up to Muqattam."

"My father always says that a gilded saddle will not make a horse of a donkey," Ataa whispered mockingly.

And, because wonders always take us by surprise without asking our permission, forcing us to call them "strange coincidences" or "fate"—or perhaps it is the will of the universe that manifests in glances and gestures—Ataa whispered, staring at me, "If only we could see him without him seeing us! If we only had the camera obscura of Ibn al-Haytham, we could see him without moving from our spot."

I turned to face him. "What is the camera obscura of Ibn al-Haytham?"

"They say that he has a darkened room from which light spills out. The demons permit him to see what lies outside it."

I swallowed, seeking to conceal my overwhelming eagerness to be introduced to Ibn al-Haytham. He spoke of him so lightly, like one speaking of a lunatic. "What do you mean?" I pressed.

"I heard them speaking at my father's assembly of his dark room filled with demons. They claim that he is mad. This is why there are guards around his house and he may not set foot outside without the permission of the caliph."

Feigning apprehension, I said, "But what if he is in fact a lunatic and murders those who visit him?"

Ataa pouted pityingly. "No. He is a poor unfortunate, like a bird fallen into a dragon's claws. The donkey driver on the throne brought him in from Baghdad when he said he had a solution for the annual flooding of the Nile. But when he had spent several months here and built several wooden dams and waterwheels, through which he tried to divert the Nile waters, he failed at preventing the flooding. Fearing the vengeance of the ruler, especially as he had spent the annual revenue from Damascus for that year on his projects, he feigned madness, and now makes his living copying books. It is said that he received seventy-five dirhams for the copy he made of Euclid's *Optics*, a sum that could sustain him for six months."

I caught Ataa's wrist. "Is there a way to see him?"

"What has come over you?" Ataa burst out. "I tell you the man feigns madness! He is heavily guarded! And you ask to see him?"

In a low voice, I said, "If we can convince the guards that we are students from al-Azhar sent to recite some Qur'anic verses to cure his madness, we may be permitted to see him."

How wonderful it is to have an impulsive friend who looks not before he leaps. He will respond immediately to all your ill-considered ideas. Ataa smiled immediately and said, "We shall see."

And so I took to dreaming of the camera obscura of Ibn al-Haytham. The proverb says, "He who hath a need must find it." And he who is addicted to knocking at doors must enter.

The path to Ibn al-Haytham was not as simple as my dreams desired, especially now that we were moving in the tense space between the caliph's men and the populace. The people were resentful and the soldiers were angry. It was no longer confined to sour insults where the townsfolk named their donkeys, mules, and dogs after the caliph's men; the soldiers now found their animals poisoned, or human waste strewn outside their head-quarters. The tradesmen in the stores refused to sell to them, on the pretext that their goods were old. If forced, they hid away their best wares. As for the tyrannical chief of police, whom all of Egypt feared, he woke one morning to find a dead donkey tied to the door of his house.

In this space filled with suspicion, vitriol, and insults, how were we to reach Ibn al-Haytham? Ataa said to me flip-pantly, strutting along as he always did and picking up the hem of his garment from the dust of the road, "Never you mind! Perhaps this rift between the people and the guards will create gaps through which we can slip and reach Ibn al-Haytham."

I had not chosen wrong in selecting Ataa as the next Voy-ager. I found out in that moment that my jealousy of him lay not in his intelligence, his bright face, or his noble family, but precisely in this free spirit that soared above all cares and obstacles, and this recklessness that made a falcon of him, flying high above the problem, then diving to snatch it up with great skill and ease.

That was exactly the case when I saw him the next day in the mosque. His eyes were sparkling. He motioned to me slyly with his head that he had something in mind. This resourceful young man—nothing could stand in his way!

The sheikh's circle broke up early that day because the sheikh was afflicted with a sudden cough. Sheikh Abd al-Wahid was teaching us *The Mufaddaliyat*, a collection of poems compiled by al-Mufaddal from the golden age of Arabic poetry. Our Azharite sheikh was not possessed of eloquence: the words did not trip smoothly off his tongue. His pronunciation was too melodious, more like the Qur'an than poetry, and he made errors in meter. He had the halting tongue of a country boy, his lips stiff despite the spittle that flew from them. We were rescued from him by the cough that came over him, and only ceased with the call to the noon prayers. As we walked out through the place for ablutions, Ataa whispered to me, "Before the caliph placed Ibn al-Haytham under house arrest and seized his fortune, he worked in the treasury. The man who has taken over his job is named al-Manqari. Do you remember him from my father's gatherings?"

"Your father's gatherings are always packed. How should I remember him?"

"The tall, thin man like an ibis. He is always at my father's house. He has a cunning face and wears odd, colorful turbans." I pretended to remember the man so as not to dampen Ataa's enthusiasm. He went on, "We will go to him and borrow some files from the treasury, and tell him that we are training to organize them on my father's orders. These files bear the stamp of the treasury and the seal of the caliph. Then, posing as employees of the treasury, we will take them to the house where Ibn al-Haytham is imprisoned. We will say we wish to revise some records we found dealing with mansions that were his domain when he worked there."

He was speaking quickly, his eyes darting this way and that for fear of being overheard. His plan appeared to be in place: there was nothing for me but to nod in acquiescence. I was willing to accept any path he devised that would lead to Ibn al-Haytham. "The ignorant, illiterate guards at his door will doubtless be impressed by the stamps and seals and open the door forthwith. They will not concern themselves with examining the details within."

I was overcome with fear. "And if they suspect us?" I asked, hoping he had prepared an avenue of retreat.

But as usual, the impetuous Ataa said, "Let us try. We have nothing to lose. We wish only to know that his mind is still intact: they say they hear his ramblings as he chases his shadow through the passageways of his home, or his prison. They also hear him in the middle of the night shouting that he is turning the grinding mill."

We stood in a row for the noon prayers. Ataa said, "I will finish the prayers and run straight to Mr. Manqari the Ibis. If he gives me the files, we can head directly for Ibn al-Haytham's house tomorrow."

It appeared that divine will was on our side: the doors opened to us, one after another. The next day at sunset, when our shadows were disappearing, we stood before the house—or the prison—where Ibn al-Haytham was under house arrest.

We had disagreed before we arrived: should we tell him our real names, or merely that we were students? "Patience," I said. "It is the state we find him in that will dictate how we speak."

As luck would have it, the guard at the gate was sleepy and lethargic. He turned the files over in his hands without looking too hard at them, then asked us to wait. Listlessly, he pulled a bellpull that hung by him, and we heard a ringing in the bowels of the house. Moments later, the creak of the wooden door opening reached our ears, and the guard was motioning with his head for us to enter.

We ascended three stone steps. The door opened, revealing a man in his fifties with a pointed gray beard, his face pale with astonishment, his eyes fixed on our faces. He didn't step aside to let us in. Ataa stood straight like a nobleman. "Is Hassan in?"

The man nodded. He wore a light cotton garment and a broad belt around his waist, nothing like the garments of the men of Egypt, but more like the garb of the servants I used to see in Jerusalem and Bosra. Affecting the same supercilious air, Ataa said, "Tell him that we are from the treasury."

Good lord! What was Ataa doing? He sounded like one of the forty thieves at the mouth of the treasure trove! The man swung the door wide open. "Come in." He gestured to straw seats in a row in the inner hallway of the house, then disappeared down the corridor.

We were in a wide colonnade surrounded by a pleasant passageway. This must have been the house of some notable or nobleman, but now it was lonely, the hall deserted. Strewn about in the corners were rolls of rope, pieces of wood, and linen bags filled with odd-looking stones, in addition to hammers and nails of various shapes and sizes. It was an oppressive, abandoned place, not lightened by friezes of swaying ladies and leaping children on its walls. "What are we to say to him?" I asked Ataa. "How are we to earn his trust, he who it is said feigned madness to evade retribution?"

"Nothing," Ataa responded. "We will await what he says. Then we'll see how to enter the madman's cell. They say his awareness has left him and he raves incomprehensibly; but my father swears his mind is intact, and he is but protecting himself from vengeance."

We fell silent, discovering that our voices were echoing loudly in the stone arches above us. We heard murmurings and approaching footsteps before two men appeared at the end of the passageway. One was the older man who had opened the door, and the other approached us slowly enough for me to contemplate him as he paced among the columns of the colonnade, between light and shadow. He was slight of build, in a green cotton garment with a red silk abaya atop it, which completely swallowed up his small figure. When he drew near, we stood and smiled at him. He slowed his steps, perhaps disquieted by the mention of the treasury. He jammed his turban onto his head: it was slightly squashed, forming three parallel lines on his forehead over thick eyebrows and reddened eyes. Their depths glimmered with that light of genius that is but a pace from the land of madness—a light not dissimilar to that in the eyes of the madman. How many fugitives in Egypt had fled the land of tyranny for the land of insanity?

He paused roughly five paces from us, ignoring both of our hands extended to shake his. He only raised a hand in greeting and said, "The sun does not shine with the light of a lamp."

This told me that our task would not be easy, and that the man was wandering down the paths of madness. Ataa, with his Egyptian tact and smoothness, overcame the awkward moment. "Good evening, al-Hassan ibn al-Haytham, our revered inventor and the author of *Model of the Motions*." When he received no answer, Ataa said, "We are here from the treasury, from al-Manqari. We wish to ask you about certain details." Ibn al-Haytham did not move; he merely muttered and looked down. "Be at your leisure, eminent scholar," Ataa continued. "My master Mr. Manqari is in no rush. Here is the ledger. We shall return in three days to see what has transpired."

I had slipped a note into the book in my finest hand, in black ink, with the following:

My Dear Sir, Eminent Scientist, Learned Inventor,

Peace be upon you. We would be delighted to enter the
gardens of your knowledge, drink of the fount of your
science, and learn of your wide reading, may the Lord
always guide your words and your path.

Allow me, sir, to introduce myself: I am Mazid of Najd,
a bookseller, and possessed of an abiding curiosity to
contemplate God's creation. It is He who has given
humans intellect and set us apart on land and sea, and
made us stewards.

Sir, I shall not waste your time. I am now in a status
between two statuses: either to enjoy your company, or
to return disappointed and empty-handed.

Best and warmest greetings,

Mazid al-Najdi al-Hanafi

I know not what mad impulse drove me to write this letter, which
I had set down the day before and slipped between the covers of
the ledger. I had left Ataa out of it so as not to involve him: this
letter would either grant me an audience with Ibn al-Haytham
or lead him to betray me to the guards and so to severe repercussions from which even my powerful mentor, Rashid ibn Ali,
would not manage to liberate me, for I had seen his helplessness
in the face of the ruler's vengeance in the matter of the doll.
Not only this, but I had mentioned the password of the Voyagers in the message, assuming that he was one of them. Even
if he were, he might suspect me, for Voyagers usually had their
own discreet passageways, never bursting into others' dwellings
so rashly. I knew not; I simply thought it the only path to Ibn
al-Haytham's magical, supernatural world, floating between
the ships of light and the rivers of darkness.

Three days and nights I spent in a state of perturbation, moving from the circles of the mosque to my house and back again.
I had not even seen Ataa since we parted at Ibn al-Haytham's

gate. The letter that I had slipped into the treasury ledger completely stole my thinking: would it open the secret, magical cavern of Ibn al-Haytham to me? Or would it send my head rolling into the Nile to feed the crocodiles?

The morning of the fourth day, I washed and dressed, and was preparing to go out to the mosque, when I heard a fierce knocking on the door. "Coming!" I called. "Coming!" I tried to calm my fears, telling myself it was probably the mosque attendant, whom the sheikh often sent to rebuke the students who had been late for the dawn prayers. But I heard Mabrouk calling me. I hurried down to the door, and when I opened it, a policeman stood there, his shiny helmet obscuring his eyes.

I leaned on the doorframe for fear I should fall. The police had arrived. Should I step back or flee? But where to, when "Egypt's guards sleep / The foxes hunt their fill"?

In his slow, slightly stupid way, Mabrouk said, "This guard says that the chief of police is ill, and he requires your services, doctor."

I sighed with relief, as though the Muqattam Mountain itself had just been lifted off my chest. "I shall accompany you forthwith," I said. The truth was, I required some time to calm my breathing and subdue my trembling. I took a few gulps of citron water, it being good to clear the liver, as Galen, the great physician, says to Mazid, the pretend physician.

We moved through the paths and alleyways. People on their way to their daily labors stared curiously at the man walking alongside the soldier. Eventually, we arrived at the eastern wall. There was a great house surrounded with palm trees, two guards at the gate. They motioned to me to enter. In a corner of the house's courtyard sat a weak, thin man like a starved cat, propped up on worn velvet cushions and pillows. I only recognized him when he stood up to greet me: it was none other than the rude bull-headed fellow who had seized my possessions and had the Coptic porter thrown into prison because the cross around his neck did not make the weight or size decreed by the Caliph Who Can Do No Wrong—an arm span long, as I recalled, and five pounds in weight, and stamped with lead.

Mr. Bull's Head, who had afflicted every one of Egypt's homes with a calamity, had been consumed by illness. His face was pale, his shoulders drooping. He had a pot of water in his hand, and was drinking from it and complaining, "My thirst is never quenched. I am always parched. My tongue is dry as a bone. It is as though pins and needles are pricking at my extremities. I am weak."

Was it divine vengeance, high time for the Lord to scourge him with disease? But this was no time for naive gloating. This thin face staring at me was expecting a cure: although it was much faded, cruelty and savagery could still be seen there. Every symptom he had mentioned matched what the priest Samaan—and Galen—had described of the illness of sugar in the blood, which eats at the body and shrivels it up, robbing it of freshness and vitality. I approached him and took his hand. His pulse was regular and he was free from fever. Softly, with some hesitation, I said, "Is there an anthill here?"

They looked about them oddly, thinking that this was the esoteric request of a charlatan. But I repeated it to them in a tone I attempted to keep steady. The chief of police jerked his head at a boy next to him and said, "Do as you are commanded."

The boy disappeared briefly, then returned, gesturing to the roof. The chief of police leaned on his shoulder and we mounted the stairs to the roof. It was spacious, surrounded by chicken coops and dovecotes. We stopped at a mound of sand in which ants dwelt. When I asked the chief of police to urinate on it, he glanced about it and quoted from the Sura of al-Naml, "*O Ants! Enter your dwellings.*" I almost burst out laughing. Was he shy?

Commandingly—for I had discovered that the medical profession had granted me some power before this ox—I said, "Cease addressing the ants! Only urinate upon it."

We let him have what remained of his dignity and retreated to the other end of the roof until he had finished. Hearing his returning footsteps, I looked up. Seeing him weak and thirsty, almost falling, I asked his boy to take him downstairs, while I went to investigate the anthill. Sure enough, circles of ants had started to form around the damp sand. I thanked God that it was the sugar sickness: at the very least, if I prescribed some cure, it would heal him.

I descended the stairs, proclaiming confidently, "It is sugar in the blood. If he does not follow a strict regimen, it will consume him. Diet is his only cure. Your food shall be your medicine: eat little. The origins of this disease lie in too much eating. Also, worry weakens the body. Citron water will purify your blood and cleanse it of impurities."

He appeared comforted, as though my visit in itself had resolved his condition and snatched him back from the brink of death. I could see the blood returning to his cheeks. I asked his boy to prepare him a soup of Egyptian pulses: they are sacred, mentioned in the Qur'an. I then recited verse sixty-one of the Sura of al-Baqara: "*So call upon your Lord to bring forth for us from the earth its green herbs and its cucumbers and its garlic and its lentils and its onions.*" Feigning erudition, I added a passage from *Nabatean Agriculture*, which I felt would confer an air of the knowledgeable physician: "Do not mix fish and pulses. They weaken the mind and spoil the humor of the stomach. Do not eat too many pulses: Hippocrates says, 'Less of what is harmful is better than more of what is good.'" At the exit, the guard gave me a small bag of coins, which I did not open or even look at, merely taking it while appearing above such sordid matters as money.

Some soldiers stopped me as I exited. One of them showed me an open sore on his wrist, within which worms could clearly be seen squirming about. "There is nothing for it but cautery," I said. "Find someone to cauterize it and you shall heal, with God's blessing." Another showed me his swollen stomach; I could see yellow in the whites of his eyes. I could see that it was the laziness of the liver that was so common among the folk of Egypt. I knew of no permanent cure for it, so I advised him to drink citron water. I knew that the latter helped to enhance virility, and it was my guess that lust is one of the most prominent signs of health, and returns the desire for life and procreation to a man, so that if it did him no good, it would at least do no harm. I liberated myself from their company before they could discover the false physician, and headed back before the afternoon prayers, fearing that the entire population of the alleyway might come out to stand before me with their ailments. Today was the day Ataa and I were due to go to Ibn al-Haytham, and I would not have anyone exhaust my vigor and concentration. Much would happen there.

The house where Ibn al-Haytham lived sat alone on a hill not far from the center of Cairo. When we approached, my heart started to beat faster, and I told myself that what I had done had been reckless in the extreme, a step that might disrupt the fabric of the Voyagers and betray them. They had strict rules of secrecy, after all. However, I calmed myself with the thought that if Ibn al-Haytham was not one of them, he would not understand my meaning, and if he was, he would use his head and appreciate the desire of a student thirsty for his knowledge and erudition.

When the guard saw us coming, he shook his head mockingly. "Your comrade disturbed our sleep yesterday asking about you, and asking me to bring you to him. He pretends he has the ability to see in the dark." Then, showing a row of yellowed teeth, he added mockingly, "He is nothing but a charlatan."

"They spoke truth when they said not to cast pearls before swine," I whispered to Ataa through gritted teeth. "He knows nothing of the mind of that great man who lives inside."

Before we reached the three stone steps leading up to the house, the door swung open and his servant came out, holding three books. But when he saw us, he stopped short and looked inquiringly at us. We told him of our wish to see his master. He said not a word, merely retreating into the interior and closing the door. After a while he returned and said, "Wait here. He wishes to see you as well."

A book lover like myself could not miss the titles of the books in his hands: Euclid's *The Elements* on geometry—I had wished to give him the same book, and I knew not if this were the translation of Hanin ibn Ishaq or another copy—Ptolemy's *Almagest*, and the third I had not managed to see, but the leather cover was that of the House of Knowledge library in al-Azhar. What was it doing here, in the home of this imprisoned native of Basra?

The library of al-Azhar was, to say the least, magnificent. It was open to all freely, on condition that no book, manuscript, or even a sheet of paper should be borrowed unless they were absolutely certain it would be returned to its shelves safe and sound. It maintained its dignity and position, untouched by fire or sabotage. Their demon had occupied himself with women's shoes, dolls, and banning jute leaves, and left the theologians to their silent study in the House of Knowledge, far from his interest or attention.

The servant returned and opened the door for us. "I was on my way to the library of al-Azhar to return these books my master borrowed," he said. "He devours books in a most extraordinary fashion. He is forever sending books back and receiving others, but in all the days I have served him, I have not seen him so cheerful as with your arrival. I am almost certain he will ask you to stay for dinner, and I must return quickly to prepare it for you."

I might have said to the servant, "We did not ask you for all this information, and we did not ask you to make us dinner," but we saw the imprisoned man hurrying toward us with both hands extended to shake ours. I was waiting for my eyes to meet his: the first glance would tell me everything about where he stood, his madness, and whether or not he knew about the Voyagers. But he was careful not to meet my eyes. He only said quickly, "Welcome to you both! Come upstairs, for I have prepared the ledger of the salaries for the treasury and gone over it."

We said nothing. We now knew that he had divined our intent, and was complicit with us. No sooner were we halfway down the colonnade than he turned to us, whispering, "Leave the ledger with me tonight: it will give you an excuse to come tomorrow morning. I will show you the ghosts of the camera obscura then, as the sun has now set."

With that, we took our leave.

## The Ghosts of the Camera Obscura

The next morning, we encountered virtually no difficulty in entering the home of Ibn al-Haytham. Instead of casting pearls before swine, Ataa placed two dirhams in the hand of the guard. He bestowed a smile upon us and opened the door. It appears that everything loses its rough edges when tamed by familiarity and custom.

The morning had lifted some of the gloom from the colonnade: the smell of fresh bread filled the room. The bread was set out on a low table with dishes of honey and butter and some radishes and Armenian cucumbers. Hassan was still glad, all but jumping for joy at our company. His vivacity returned as we shared his breakfast. "You do not seem like an Egyptian," he said, "although your accent is close to Baghdad. Where are you from?"

"I am Mazid. Mazid al-Hanafi from Najd, a student of knowledge."

He kept staring at me until I could see the red veins in his eyes. "Knowledge? Ah, the flames of thirst for knowledge, which cannot be quenched by all the rivers of the world, driving their owner almost to ruin." Leaning over the table, he whispered, "Come with me: I will show you wonders."

Why had he not mentioned a status between two statuses? Was he not aware of what it meant? Or was this warm welcome inspired by that phrase?

He walked with us to the end of the corridor and opened one of the doors leading onto it. His voice trembled slightly as he said, "The guards made a hole in this room to watch me as I slept, for fear I might feign sleep and escape over the rooftops." He patted the hole. "From this hole, the cone of light forms." His thin, veined hand indicated the opposite wall. "It expands to form a circle of light, bearing its secrets within.

"In the early days of my imprisonment, I was terrified, jumping at every sound. One morning, I sat for a long while contemplating the line of light. It was my only link to the outside world, before I discovered that it had had pity upon me, and conveyed to me the images of the things that passed in the street, only inverted."

His eyes bulged with a kind of triumph. He swallowed and continued like a prophet recounting his revelations. "It was here that my journey started, as I followed the light through thick mediums and thin." His room was dark, lit only by the sharp spark of his eyes tinged with a kind of mania. My skin crawled. I was overcome with a sense that the room was filled with mysterious spirits and an awe-inspiring presence, although there were only the three of us there. He closed the door, whispering, "Welcome, Voyagers."

I trembled. It was as I had suspected: he too was a Voyager. I feared that Ataa would ask him what it meant, but he had not noticed. Ataa, for all his keen intelligence, was as usual occupied with the best way to impress Ibn al-Haytham with his knowledge and prowess.

"Have a seat," Ibn al-Haytham said, indicating a mat on the floor of the dark room with the covered windows. He laid a finger to his lips: now the demons would appear. I trembled and pulled my knees up to my chest, and sat waiting. Silence fell, and three men watched in stunned wonder as a thin thread of light came in through the hole and expanded on the wall.

At first, I saw nothing but specks of dust swirling lazily in the beam of light. However, before long I saw tiny things flickering, like a mirage; then their details became clearer, resolving into images, until we saw the blurred image of a cart, a donkey, and two men. We sat there, staring at the wall, until we discovered that this was none other than the shadows of the old servant with the green turban, who had gone out into the street and was standing at the cart of a vegetable seller: it was his cart and donkey that we could see, and he appeared to be haggling with the vendor over price. They waved their hands about for some time before the servant took what he had bought and went on his way home.

Suddenly, Ibn al-Haytham leapt up from his seat like a courageous cat, ripping the covering off the window and flinging open the door. We saw the servant coming in through the main door, carrying Armenian cucumbers and other vegetables. Ibn al-Haytham's turban had slipped back halfway over his head: he was openmouthed, a look of bewildered triumph on his face. I was terrified that his madness had chosen this moment to return, but he only hissed, "Do you see what light bears within? The world entire. It bears every shadow that passes through it. Only prepare a space for it, and permit it to pour the world onto your wall." Then he added, nodding, "Only this interplay of light and shadow has lightened the burden of imprisonment and the pain of being in a foreign land."

I was jumping for joy with him, seized by a strange ecstasy. When we left the dark room, he took up a stick and drew in the dust of his courtyard a cone with the lens of an eye at its top. "Look," he said. "This, thus, is the light in the books of the Greeks."

Impressed, I asked him, "But this is what the Surianese translated into Arabic, and what they, in their turn, copied from the Greeks: the Surianese stand between us and the Greeks. What say you of meanings that have changed in translation from the ancient Greek language that has long been dead, and its folk extinct, and all those gone who used to speak it?"

Ibn al-Haytham straightened with alacrity. "We have minds that think, better than they. Our eyes do not emit light, as they imagined. The proof is that we cannot see in the dark. There is no light emanating from us."

Ataa, who was a great defender of the Greeks, responded, "Although Greece and its language are extinct, translation has preserved its aims and conveyed its meanings and remained true to the facts."

"True," Ibn al-Haytham conceded. "Although, you see, the Greeks were in error when they claimed that the source of light was the eye. Knowledge and translation are like a torch. If there is a torch lighting the caravans of those who travel through history, every caravan will fear that it may burn out: whatever the source of the oil that will keep it burning, whenever the torch passes by a people or a group, they will pour some of their own oil onto the torch to keep it alight." He nodded. "Yes. The main thing is for it to remain lit, lighting up the paths of the caravan of humanity.

"The Greeks spoke of things in their science; I built upon what they said, and added what was missing in their work with what intellect God gave me; there will come after me those who will add to what I have said and build up the earth. Why, then, do we concern ourselves with the kingdom of the heavens, when before us lies the kingdom of the earth? There lie injustice, tyranny, bloodshed, and absolute power wielded by the rulers over all!"

This last line appeared to have exhausted him and summoned his fears anew. He sat down and fell silent. He did not speak after that.

\*

We kissed his head and left. I said to Ataa, "What that great man from Basra said is the sum of all: he summarized everything, and he spoke truth. This is the wisdom of the Voyagers."

On the way home, I was overcome with a strange ecstasy. Was it the wonder of learning that shook us to the core, or because I had learned that the Voyagers were only joined by the rare great men, and God had given me the honor of being one of them alongside the master of light and shadow, Ibn al-Haytham?

Ataa was as stunned as I. He had quite abandoned his flighty manner and seemed deep in thought. This would make it easier for me. He asked me to walk awhile toward the river. I walked by his side, the universe opening doors. No sooner had I said to him, "Ibn al-Haytham's torch does not belong to him alone; it belongs to all the Just Monotheists, to those who have purified their minds of endless quotations from the ancients, and think for themselves."

Ataa smiled slyly. "Do you mean the Voyagers, who are in a status between two statuses?"

I stopped walking, like a man caught naked. Ataa patted my shoulder, having burst into a wide grin. "Oh, Arab of the desert! You exchange the secrets and affairs of the Voyagers with my father, when they are always at my father's gatherings. You jealously guard your books as though they are your infant daughters. And you expect me to remain like an ignorant babe, knowing nothing?"

I only stared. He went on, "You were not the first, and will not be the last, of the Voyagers who have passed through our house, Mazid. But what brought us together is friendship and familiarity, the blandishments of youth and the thirst for knowledge. You are my friend and companion and a bright mind in the darkness of my questions and my confusion." He laughed out loud and started walking again, causing me to scurry after him from where I stood openmouthed. "No matter, Mazid. I shall be the disciple you bring into the secret society. It is not a thing I would wish to happen soon, however, because that would mean that you shall leave us."

I shook my head in wonder, breaking into a smile of my own. A flock of cranes flew over our heads.

Just then, I missed Kahramana intensely. I wished to hold her until she broke down and the wall between us disintegrated.

I took a sheet of paper and inscribed upon it the verses of al-Mutanabbi:

> Love makes tongues silent and broken;
> The sweetest love remains unspoken.
> If only my love would stick as close
> as the frailty I feel in absence's throes!

She had gone too far in being distant. I would storm her gates, which she had always warned me against doing for fear of prying eyes, but she must know that I would shadow her and follow her wherever she went. I boiled some sage and other herbs the spice trader had told me were efficacious against headaches, poured them into the pot I used for Turkish coffee, and hurried to the madman's house.

The boy, Mabrouk, met me at the door and told me that his master was not at home. He might be listening to one of the mosque's circles; he might be roaming the streets of Cairo; he might be standing at the Zuweila Gate watching the comings and goings. Mabrouk added, "Yunis has gone out to find him. They will surely be here after the evening prayers, when Master goes to bed."

Out of politeness, Mabrouk invited me in, but I was honor bound to refuse, for it is not done to enter a house whose master is absent. I hoped that the mother of the children would hear my voice and invite me in to chatter with her or perhaps convey to her some feminine recipes for beauty, but it did not come to pass.

Before I left, I was overcome with the sensation of being watched. I looked about me; then I heard the wood of the upper window creaking above the door to the house.

Mabrouk brought a cup into which I poured the sage for his master. When I made to leave, I lingered, sipping the remnants of the sage in the coffeepot, stealing glances at the window above me. I saw nothing but shadows, and heard nothing but the creaking of wood.

I went back from the alley to my house, my chest pierced with longing. I had lost the delight of the demons moving on Ibn al-Haytham's wall. Had the realization finally dawned that I had always deferred and buried in the dust of deliberate disregard? Was this the end with Kahramana? Had she decided to disappear? How should the air make its way into my breast without her flirtations, her laugh, her perfume? I had thought her available, always there, like a spring that never runs dry. But why had she closed her window in my face and plunged into darkness?

How lonely Cairo was! I began to smell dead bodies and blood all about!

That day also, they kept us out of the mosque. Sitt al-Mulk, the caliph's sister, was holding a mass funeral for the dead, and would hold a banquet for all the inhabitants of Cairo. I sometimes caught a glimpse of her close by, veiled, exiting her sedan that came from the Eastern Palace; but the few who had had the honor of being in the mosque in her presence said that when she revealed her face, the radiance of her beauty spilled out among the pillars and domes like a tree of light. She paid no heed to the laws banning women from going out at night or revealing their faces at funerals.

According to Ataa, she was the only one who kept the scales balanced for the ruling family. "She sent her ministers and criers to the nobles and notables of Egypt to tempt them with promises and bequests. She pressed her Christian uncles to remain close to the Copts, mended their pride, salved their

375

wounds by granting them high positions and gifts, and spread glad tidings that the dark cloud was soon to be dispelled. If not for her promises that something would soon change, a violent revolution would have broken out." He added slyly, "It is said that she is the lover of one of the ministers of the state, and that she has allowed him into her bed. He is her hidden hand, and they rule Egypt together."

That evening, after Sitt al-Mulk had left the mosque, I watched the crowds of women and children leaving the mosque in her wake, as they do on feast days, their hands full of silver dirhams and almonds and apple slices dipped in honey. The scroll of al-Mutanabbi's poems was still in my pocket, and loneliness was eating away at me. I remained in the library downstairs, for I feared the upper floor, where the pillows and couches lay in wait for me, teasing me with what remained of Kahramana's scent. I could not bear it; my heart would break. I needed to seek out the books by Ptolemy and Euclid on vision, which included their theories about vision and how it comes about as a result of a ray of light from the eye to the object of vision. I wished to follow Ibn al-Haytham's theories disproving this, and examine it tomorrow at the House of Knowledge in al-Azhar. But where could I find light in the painful darkness of my heart? I would invite Ataa to my house tomorrow and show him my book collection. He could see what he wished to acquire and what he wished to add to it before I left.

But what if Kahramana saw him while he was there; saw his fair face, fell in love with him, and redoubled her absence? He would place 1,500 gold pieces in a silken bag and she would be his. The madman did not notice her presence around him, and the mother of the children would not hesitate to sell her. She would cover their expenses for a year, including a pilgrimage to Mecca and rebuilding the water tower in their house.

I broke out of my thoughts, discovering that love can take you to the brink of folly. I would let jealousy eat away at my breast, and bear it as stoically as a lion bears the bites of a jackal, never showing my suffering. Jealousy is unbecoming of a Voyager; at any rate, that was what I would attempt to show in front of Ataa.

Egypt is forgiving, and washes itself clean of its sorrows. A light drizzle was falling, and the sky had more lying in wait, so that we were obliged to perform the evening prayers in the inner colonnade—an early winter. In al-Yamama, these early clouds were called the Wasm Storm. In Egypt, the rain fell on the alleys where blood and terror had spilled, washing them clean.

I went to my house with Ataa. I had planned to go and buy dinner for us, but Mabrouk had appeared at the door, bearing bowls, saying, "This is a gift from the mother of the children: rice and lentils, which she is giving out to the neighbors in celebration of the rain. To you alone, she has also sent fig jam and sugared meat with rice, or *jawazib*."

I was pleased. Was this a prelude to a visit from Kahramana tonight? I did not like to ask him. I asked Mabrouk to prepare our seating area, and lit the lanterns, letting Ataa look over the shelves. I said to him in a jab at the Greeks, hoping to hear some of his brilliance, "This is mostly Greek work, translated by the House of Wisdom. But Greek metaphysics are atheist in nature, believing in the death of the individual and the eternity of the genus."

"Do you mean," he asked, "what our sheikh said about al-Farabi?"

"Well, no," I said. "Al-Farabi speaks of divine inspiration and the ten intellects of the universe. But the Greeks exchanged heaven on high for well-being."

He smiled slyly. "Each of us cleaves to the tale that suits him best."

Ataa needed no companion or guide, for he ascended the path of the Voyagers like a brilliant steed. I was leaving him in Egypt in the company of three pyramids: Ibn al-Haytham,

Rashid ibn Ali, and his father's library. All that remained now was for me to slip him a copy of the seven commandments.

## The Amber Bird's Lament

Ataa left when the rain ceased. I could not keep myself from the childish disappointment that seized me when Kahramana failed to creep in. I wanted to show her off to Ataa: "Look, my flighty friend! This beauty loves me!"

I went up to the roof to find that the carpets on the balcony were wet and the pillows soaked with rainwater, making the entire roof smell of straw. I gazed at the wall over which she used to leap, coming toward me filled with longing; it looked back mockingly. Only the gutters dripped the last of their water into the street.

We stole another visit to Ibn al-Haytham, but he was in a foul humor, and showed us none of the welcome he had given us previously. He might have been working on a new invention and not been in the mood for interruptions, like an eagle on a mountaintop listening to the universe breathing around him.

Ataa and I now spent a great deal of time at my house, but Kahramana never appeared. Had she slipped through my unlucky fingers?

My longing made me so brave in my questioning as to be foolish. One evening, keeping my face down, I asked Mabrouk as he was clearing away the dinner dishes, "How is Kahramana?"

A sly smile crept across his face, mixed with surprise. "Who is Kahramana?"

Was he concealing her from me or was I starting to imagine things?

I recalled that she had never told me that her name was Kahramana. It was her amber eyes that had made me call her that. Kahramana, her eyes like a tiger's, and her essence like grapes with honey, the red kerchief in the folds of my bedding. My astonishment drove Mabrouk to lay a solicitous hand on my shoulder. "Sir, are you well?"

"Is your master's slave girl called Kahramana?" I whispered.

The veils fell as he spoke. They disappeared and faded, and the tale took on another complexion. My knees gave way as I listened. I sat and asked question after question, while Mabrouk took off his turban and scratched his head, his mocking smile never leaving him. But he did say in surprise, "The woman you are describing is none other than Lamis, may she rest in peace. There is no one with my master now but the mother of the children."

Was Lamis–Kahramana the manifestation of a call for vengeance which never dies, like the cranes that flew above the murdered man in the story, to avenge him? But how could this be? Kahramana, the fountain of sugar, the scent of her dew dissolved in lust, the perfume in my bed . . . none of this could belong to a ghost or a spirit. Was it possible that she could come to me across the isthmus, then depart once more? I fumbled at my body. Was I really here? Had the mother of the children slit her throat and thrown her down the well of the house, and threatened the servants that they would meet her fate if they betrayed her secret? Where was she?

I must leave. I knew not who would be the next one thrown into the well—the well of sweet water in the center of the madman's house. The fourth commandment commands me to consult my heart and mind, and both of these call on me to depart. It had been no hallucination. Who had opened the isthmus and brought Lamis crying out to me like a flock of storks, betraying her murderers?

So as not to be accused of seeing things, or madness, or communing with spirits, I must remain silent and hold the burning coal tight, as they used to say in the early days of Islam, and quell my longings. Our inner kingdom is what we experience, and we contemplate it, our souls saturated with the pain of loneliness. They enjoy being chosen, like a beautiful dream that is ruined on contact with light. But where had Kahramana gone?

It required several visits to say goodbye to Rashid ibn Ali in order to gradually loosen and dislodge the bonds of affection and friendship from within myself and depart for Andalusia, leaving behind the pains of separation. At the door, I would make many promises to return. I would definitely be back; I might even settle in Egypt . . . all the promises customarily made by those on the thresholds of parting, usually never kept.

On my last visit, I slipped Ataa a copy of the seven commandments, while Rashid ibn Ali passed me a letter written in an elegant hand on Samarqand paper, secured in a shiny, ornamented cylinder of brass, and told me briefly, "Hand this to Bahaa al-Zaman in the Great Mosque in Cordoba."

The books that Rashid gave me were not many, but they were valuable, the most important among them being Thabit ibn Qurra's translation of Ptolemy's *Almagest*. As to Ataa, he would certainly find a guide. His father was pleased with my performance in Egypt: I had sold thirty books and saved forty more from burning at the booksellers' stalls in Fustat. With the chaos brought on by the fire, the soldiers had threatened to burn the "books of heresy," which had "brought sin and evil down upon Egypt." On the strength of this, I had managed to acquire a complete collection of Hippocrates from the paper traders in Fustat, which I had secreted in a greengrocer's cart beneath the onions, cucumbers, and bunches of mint, and smuggled into my library in Cairo. My treatment of the chief of police had granted me some power, which allowed me to free some of the unfortunates who were rounded up in groups and thrown into prison for no crime other than living next to the wall where the doll had been erected. From the sheikhs of al-Azhar, I had earned degrees in Qur'an recitation, elocution, Arabic language, and Arabic literature. I had no desire to stay until the end of the year, at which time it was said that the Caliph Who Can Do No Wrong would hold a ceremony for the graduates and bestow gifts upon them. Remembering his face and the tiger's head he had worn on his way up to Muqattam, I recognized that leaving was my only salvation.

I went home that day to find the place like a tomb, as though I were only now discovering how small the rooms were, how low the ceilings, and how uneven the staircase. Only Kahramana had spilled her soul into the rooms and lit them up. The caravan was leaving at dawn, and there was one last thing I needed to do: the coward's note, penned as usual with my left hand. It read:

If you wish for justice to be done in Egypt, search the madman's well that lies in the center of his house, and ask the mother of the children about the sorcery that killed Lamis.

Then I rolled it up carefully to the size of my ring finger and stuffed it into the seam between the outer gate and the stones of the wall.

Egypt now lay behind me. I moved forward, with my beasts of burden and my crates of books. I no longer parted with them, feeling they were part of me, like a hump on my back.

Each morning, the caliph's Cairo opened its gates to admit the folk of Fustat and the peasants from the surrounding hamlets to toil and strive among its opulent streets, letting the city absorb their essence and energy, expelling them in the evenings and closing the doors against them. Egypt was still washing itself of its wounds. Its skies glowed crimson. Its monarch still went up the Muqattam Mountain to consult the stars. The demons of Ibn al-Haytham danced on the walls each night; the lethal dolls were there; Rashid ibn

Ali stood firm like one of the pyramids, keeping Egypt from sinking; and in a well in the house of the madman, a girl of gold had drowned because she knew too much. Egypt was receding behind me, leaving only the glow of amber.

# 5

# Kairouan,
# 15 Rajab, AH 404; January 20, AD 1014

I KNOW NOT IF IT was good or bad luck that I joined a caravan so great that it was feared by thieves and bandits, but it was unjust and cruel, comprising merchants and pilgrims on their return journey to Andalusia. It was guarded by ten mounted guards and twenty more on foot. It would eventually split into two groups: one would go to al-Mahdiya, then embark upon a boat for Andalusia, while the other would go on to Morocco. Al-Muizz li-Din Allah had appointed the Berber tribe of Sanhaja to rule over Tunisia. My heart ached to recall Kahramana–Lamis and her Berber origins, her perfume and her laughter and the gold dust that scattered from her skin. The arrogant mind attempted to tell me that she had been an illusion, like the dreams of the morning mists; but I paid it no heed. She had been real—as real as the blood that pumped through my veins and the taste of water in my mouth.

**He Who Conceals His Illness Heals with Difficulty**
Hanin ibn Ishaq tells us that Galen's ring was engraved with the inscription "He who conceals his illness heals with difficulty." I imagined that I had left Egypt behind me, never knowing that it walked alongside me. Trouble is lethal to the organs of the body, and feeds on the luster of youth.

I had joined the branch of the caravan headed for al-Mahdiya so as to ride upon the sea to Almería, in Andalusia. Ere sunset on the fifteenth day, we reached Kairouan; no sooner were we on the outskirts than I was struck by a terrible fever. It crept up on me at first in the form of weakness and nausea, quickly subsuming my whole body and leaving me shaking. I was no longer able to ride my camel, and lay upon the ground raving, unaware of those around me. My innards were burning with fire. I could see one of the servant boys of the caravan passing a damp cloth over my lips and attempting to feed me watered-down oatmeal with honey, but I could not let a drop of anything pass my lips. I withered and would have died, and at dawn, between sleeping and waking, I saw Canopus looking down at me in pain. In my ravings, I recited a poem of Ibn al-Rayb's, which he had penned as he lay dying:

> If only poetry would grant another night,
> Suffering and fever-racked, the world above to see!
> I tell my friends to lift me up. I see the light
> Of Canopus, and it is joy enough for me.

But no friend lifted me up. On the contrary: the members of the caravan took my raving and moaning as an ill omen, and moved away from me. I heard them discussing if they should bury me facing Mecca now, or wait until the following day. "It appears he is dying," said one helpful soul. "Let us dig his grave."

"We cannot go into Kairouan with him in this state," said another. "They will stop us, thinking we bring the plague."

I trembled. I did not want to die here in this desert: I wanted to go back. I started to scream at the top of my lungs, or thought I did: "I want to go back!" But it appeared they did not hear me, for they did not so much as turn to me, even though they stood at my head. In the end, they settled upon digging a pit beneath a large acacia tree, placing me in it, and putting food and water and a bag of flour next to me, and flint to start a fire. If I recovered from the fever, I would wake and follow them; if not, I would be buried beneath the acacia tree, as the winds would eventually pile the sand up on me.

Who would tell Shammaa of my death? Who would distribute the books? I sobbed until I lost consciousness.

In my dreams, I saw Shammaa at my head, dabbing at my fevered brow and washing me with water from the well of al-Yamama, whispering, "God of all, banish this affliction, heal this sickness. Heal it, for you are the All-Healing." Shammaa kept washing me until a great lion appeared beneath the acacia. I was terrified, and took it for Death. But instead, it crouched at my feet, guarding me, while Mazid's heretical tongue muttered Aristotle's words on theology: "I may be alone with myself, take off my body, and become pure bodiless essence; I may be within myself, outside all things, and see in myself such beauty and brilliance that I stand speechless and admiring, and thus know that I am part of the ideal higher world."

I know not how much time passed, but when I came to myself, I glimpsed in my grave the shadows of my mule shaking its head and my camel ruminating, both tied up next to me. The caravan had left. I fell into another deep slumber.

I awoke to a woman in a burka circling me and looking at me. I gathered my strength about me and climbed out of my grave, sitting on the edge and looking into it with revulsion. She seemed to pluck up her courage, and approached me. She was a Bedouin shepherdess, who lived close by, with a small pot in her hand. "May you recover soon," she said. "Drink from this pot and it shall heal you. You will return to full health, God willing. It is from the Spring of Brouta, which they call the Zamzam of Kairouan, because its wellsprings are connected to those of Zamzam in Mecca; and as you know, Zamzam's water becomes a cure for any affliction for which it is taken."

Stunned, I looked up at this shepherdess: had she too been sent by Shammaa of the House of Wael? When I lost consciousness, the air around me had smelled strongly of the flowers that covered our hillsides in spring. I washed myself and prayed. I examined my effects and my crates of books.

They were covered in dust, but still unopened, the keys hanging at my chest. I went back to sleep.

When I woke again, the sun was high in the sky. I was overcome with a great hunger for everything: food, motion, and life.

## The Helper

I entered Kairouan, wasted with illness, lack of nourishment, and the fatigue of travel. Curious eyes scoured me as I walked, but the dirhams around my waist secured me a room where I could remain until I had fully recovered.

On the afternoon of the first day, a tall boy with a fair face and fine features knocked at my door. He had wide-set eyes, almost on opposite sides of his head, and protruding teeth: the whole reminded me a little of a rabbit. "I am Mu'in," he said, which means Helper.

"Mu'in?" I sighed, still weak. "And whom are you going to help?"

"One of the members of the caravan you were with," he said, "decided to act like a God-fearing man, pricked by conscience because they dug a grave for you while you were still alive. He told me where you were and asked me to take care of you, feed you, and bring you water. He gave me a gold dinar as payment. He told me that you were a learned man coming from the Arabian Peninsula, and that your head was filled with knowledge and your boxes with books. If I took good care of you and nursed you diligently, I might be apprenticed to you and earn a shade of your glory, and you might take me to Andalusia as your servant or your assistant, and—"

"Come in," I said, hoping to shut him up. He seemed delighted. "But where were you?" I questioned him. "Why did you not come?"

"The man only told me of you last night. I went immediately to the acacia tree, but you were not there. I did find a shepherdess who told me that you had recovered and mounted your animals and come into Kairouan. I returned to Kairouan and asked after you until I found you."

His genuine demeanor eased my worries. I made him welcome. He had a ringing, refreshing laugh that drove me to ask him, "Is your name *Mu*-een, for assistance, or *Ma*-een, which means a spring of water?"

He grinned. "Call me what you will, Arab. You yourself are the spring." It was then that I realized he knew something about me. "But my name is Ma'in al-Sanhaji." He told me of a woman at the far end of the market who kept a chicken coop, selling birds and eggs, who also had goat's milk and dates. "These foods are just what you require for your convalescence. You are obviously much weakened."

He came and went away for short periods, which I passed lying upon my bed; the final time, he entered bearing fruit and cooked chicken. "Fruit and flesh of fowl that ye enjoy," he half quoted from the Qur'an, "to regain your strength. Come, why still abed? Much awaits you outside."

The fruit and the chicken were not the only things to return my energy to me; I also had the water of youth in my veins. Youth is the best antidote humanity has known against illness and feebleness.

I have seen no lower forms of humanity than caravan leaders. The leader of the caravan would have sought any method to rid himself of me for fear I had some infectious disease that would sweep his caravan and keep him from coming into Kairouan; and ship's captains are no better. They are careful in selecting their passengers, I have heard, and do not hesitate to cast anyone struck with fever into the sea. What a world of many veils! Each time she rips off a veil, she shows us a face uglier than the last.

Shammaa of the House of Wael brought me into the world once again by that graveside. I came back to life with the grief of an old man and the skin of a young one. I left my cares behind in that grave, and came out thin and light, thirsty for wellsprings. To my shock, I emerged from it completely cleansed of the sorrow of leaving Egypt, my longing for Kahramana, and the talk of the cranes. I had shed my skin and left it in the bottom of the grave, slowly being covered up by the sands. It was an exhausting rebirth, of which I had been in dire need so as to remove myself from Egypt, and to remove Egypt from myself.

The first time I left the house was to go to the mosque for Friday prayers. Ma'in took to calling me "the Arab doctor"; I lost the title of "the man with the fever" and acquired the title of "the doctor." The folk of Kairouan took to examining me, finding in my face neither the wisdom of age nor the gravity of a learned man. They saw only a young man from Arabia whose eyes sharpened under his long lashes when a woman passed by.

The call to prayer mentioned Ali ibn Abu Talib, this part of the world being Shiite, and from the pulpit they prayed for the Fatimid caliph and the Sanhaji wali he had appointed. Apart from this, though, I could see no signs of their sect. After prayers, some of them stayed at the mosque of Kairouan, and the circle began to expand around a sheikh they called Abu Ishaq Ibrahim ibn Ali al-Hosari al-Kairouani. Many people appeared to revere him, most of them young men who carefully took down every word he said. He was speaking of the science of Arabic meter and the modifications to it that appear in verse in practice. I did not stay long at his circle, for there was nothing there that I had not already studied at al-Azhar, so I went out to investigate the affairs of Kairouan. I found that most of those who had left the mosque after prayer had gone to the tomb of Abu Zamaa al-Balawi, said to be one of the Prophet's men.

The tomb was close to the Great Mosque with its breathtaking blue dome. The grave itself was inlaid with mosaics and decorated with birds wearing crowns of gold. Once they left the

Friday prayers, people visited the tomb to pay their respects and pray to the saint to lighten their loads, banish their cares, and give them their daily bread: he was a saint and an intercessor, said to have kept three hairs of the Prophet Muhammad, whose barber he had supposedly been. I recalled the mausoleum of al-Qarmati and the Pyramids. Why do people leave the living and seek out the dead to intercede for them and solve their problems? Is death a just adjudicator?

Why did Kairouan captivate me? I had been seeking the port of al-Mahdiya. What was the message it wished to convey to me? It had given me Ma'in. Its folk spoke the same foreign tongue of the soldiers of Cairo, who were from the tribe of Kutama. However, if I met someone who spoke Arabic, it was always with a fluency and eloquence that amazed me. I knew no Voyagers in this city. Its air was as sweet as date jam. I would tour its mosques and libraries, and spend a few days in the discussion circles of its imams, until I had regained my full health, whereupon I would resume my journey.

Their books were not for everyone. They stored them in the mosque in closets with ornamented façades, but locked with a padlock. They were not arranged on shelves, except some books of historical anecdotes and biographies of the prophets.

I spent nearly a month in Kairouan. Then I told Ma'in to start looking at caravans and find one that would, for a reasonable price, convey us to al-Mahdiya. In truth, Ma'in did everything he could to convince me of his usefulness. He was polite and attentive and spoke only when spoken to. If he did speak, his speech was concise and indicated intelligence and perceptiveness beyond his years. He did not ask me about the boxes of books, although he observed my care when I opened them and looked through their contents. He believed that speaking to a desert Arab from the Peninsula would help him diminish his Berber accent. In truth, his presence provided companionship and comfort now, in my convalescence, but what about taking him on as a permanent assistant and companion? I had always enjoyed my solitude.

In any event, Ma'in was not a disturbance, except for one thing: he always recounted his dreams and visions. He told me of the many people who had watched me in my sleep after my illness; of the lion who had crouched at my feet, or the bald man holding a drum who looked in on me from a door that stood ajar, or the woman he had glimpsed walking back and forth the length of the room wearing a yellow veil embroidered with flowers and spreading the scent of their blossoms everywhere. When he saw my eyes glinting with mockery, he said, "It is well known here, a kind of miracle in the Sanhaji tribes." I felt that Ma'in had a great many of these tales hidden away, but I carefully held my peace. I had no need of more storks alighting on the roof of my house.

Ma'in arranged with a caravan to bring us to the port of al-Mahdiya, from where we would travel by sea to Almería. How I wished for a caravan with which to travel overland to Gibraltar, to cut short the time we spent on the water. I feared the days between al-Mahdiya and Almería, on this blue, rippling, treacherous terrain. I am a son of the desert. Only sand embraces and warms my feet. But it appeared that Ma'in thought differently. "It is faster and cheaper to travel by sea," he said.

When we arrived in al-Mahdiya, we found the city silent and grim as a bereaved mother. The sea embraced it on three sides, only an isthmus linking it to the land on the western side. Over its streets spilled a veil of the grief of abandoned women, despite the commotion of sailors, travelers, and store owners surrounding Almería.

The ship we were to take to Almería was called *al-Nagiya*. Most of the passengers were merchants. It was a large ship, used for transporting goods and supplies. I stood on the docks watching Ma'in move our things onto the deck of the ship, along with sacks of wheat, hemp, and cinnamon being stacked and piled into the ship's storerooms. My heart beat in terror: how would this great beast take to the sea with all this baggage in its belly?

When Ma'in had reassured himself that our things had been safely conveyed into the ship, and had secured us a room, he returned, out of breath. "We shall set sail tomorrow at dawn."

### al-Nagiya

I left al-Mahdiya, still silent and grim. When the sea swallows up the four directions of the compass, staring you arrogantly in the face, lying in wait, a desert Arab must be frightened and greatly disturbed.

The rivers of Baghdad and Cairo had flowed between two banks: they rippled like a refreshing breeze between two lovers, bearing small craft, greeting people, listening to their woes, and washing away the sorrows of the day with fresh air. Cities on the river are friendlier, always thirsty for affection, fertilized with hot silt like the first life God breathed into humankind. But this was the sea. I had not befriended it, and did not think I should. We sailed upon it like a band of terrified dwarves walking upon the body of a giant djinn, rippling and blue, not knowing when he would wake to swallow us all.

Our room on the boat had a window onto the deck. We would spend five days to a week on board between al-Mahdiya and Andalusia, depending on the humor of the sea, stopping at a few cities. We might take on new passengers, or some of ours might alight; in any case, we would remain in the hands of this scowling, salty creature for entire days and nights. I stood on deck, greeting the sea and contemplating it: it slapped me in the face outright, with a salty wave that soaked me to the gills and drenched every hair on my head.

On the second night, sleep did not come easily: the sound of the waves was so loud that it drew me out of my room.

Outside, the moon was playing its favorite game of laying bare the graves of grief and bringing forth longings. It had attracted other travelers besides me, including two Andalusian merchants who were in the habit of traveling with a great store of musk, ouds, and Chinese cinnamon. Their wares exceeded the limit for each traveler on the boat, and the fierce captain had threatened to throw the excess into the sea, saying that all he cared for was the safety of the boat. Every day, he placed a dish of fat and rice on deck to feed the angels that watched over the boat. Faced with the haplessness of the merchants and the captain's ire, we had hit upon a solution. Our room had enough space for some of their goods, and we willingly let them use it. Although our room was packed with their additional crates before we set sail, the gratitude they showed was worth the sacrifice. In addition, they now called me "honorable Arab," which filled me with pride, reassuring me. In a strange land, it is wise to have an abundance of brethren and men you call friend, for you never know when you shall need them.

The moon broke up on the surface of the water. I examined my compass and astrolabe in an attempt to map the stars and follow their directions. Meanwhile, the two merchants had taken to insulting the cruel and grasping captain and swearing that they would never more ride with him. Then we heard women wailing.

I looked about me, frightened, seeking the source of the sound. Then I saw them. They appeared on the surface of the water, bareheaded, their long, thick hair glinting in the moonlight, waving their arms and screaming for help. Their voices were strange, echoing like the cries of gulls. There were three of them, bobbing up and down in the waves, bare-chested, their long hair floating all about them. They approached the boat, so close that I could make out their features. Whence had they come? "Stop! Stop!" I screamed at the top of my lungs. "There are people drowning!"

The Andalusian merchants laughed, looking at the sea where the three women were. Calm yourself," they said, "these are the sirens, the demons of the sea. They signal to lonely mariners who have been months at sea without women, making them think they are shipwrecked, and when they lure them in, they drag them to the depths of the sea and take them to the merfolk."

I shuddered. I recalled the succubi of al-Yamama, who chose a boy to love, then flew him on the trunk of a palm tree to Amman. But the witches of the tree trunks only showed themselves to those who had forgotten to perform the evening prayers, while the sirens could be seen by everyone.

One of the traders approached the edge of the deck and mocked their voices, making obscene gestures at them with his fingers and spitting on them. One of the sirens retaliated, hitting him in the face with a well-aimed, sticky jellyfish. At this juncture, one of the sailors approached from the other end of the boat, crying, "Do not jest with them or provoke them. They are demons of the sea: their ire might affect the boat and all those in it."

Since I am gentle and not accustomed to harming any creature, I took to going out on deck every night to look at them, meaning to ask them secretly what had become of Kahramana. But when any of the sailors saw me, they would tell me to stop my ears with cotton, because their song was tempting, stealing your sanity and causing sailors to fling themselves to the sirens. So they floated on, with pert breasts and long hair that glittered, shapely arms and wide eyes glinting with lust.

How many dangers and wonders does the sea hold in store for us, and ordeals too! On the fourth day after we set sail, we encountered high winds laden thickly with rain. The boat listed, and our things were scattered all around. I exited my room, nauseated, my feet stumbling on the deck as I walked, and so terrified I feared I should faint clean away. The sailors were nonchalant, I found, while the captain had a tight grip on one of the poles. He had large, strong hands. His lips muttered prayers. He was in his forties, with narrow, frowning eyes set deep in wrinkled skin tanned by the sun. I approached him, questioning him in terror. He looked at me for a moment, then told me in a high-pitched voice, struggling to be heard over the wind and the rain, "Fear not! We are merely passing over the grave of the good man buried at sea: we must simply call down God's mercies on his soul and pray for him. His name is Sari al-Saqati, a Sufi saint, and the best man of all his time. The world came to him in the shape of an old woman, swept his house, and brought him two loaves of bread every day. One of his miracles is that when he died on a boat, they prepared his body, prayed for him, and would have thrown him into the sea, but the sea dried up suddenly, and the ship sank to the bottom. They dug a grave for him in the seabed and buried him, whereupon the waters rose again and the ship sailed once more."

The waves had started to calm, and the rain ceased. The travelers' heads popped out of their rooms, pale with terror. The captain called loudly, "We are now past the grave of the good saint and his miracles, but the greatest miracle humankind can enjoy is for the Lord to replace one of their execrable attributes with a wholesome one. None can hold back a blessing the Lord grants you, and none can grant you what the Lord has withheld."

The captain's aphorism echoed through my head all day. It was like a pearl he had pressed into my hand. Wisdom is what every believer seeks, even from this primitive and savage captain with his burning eyes. But what was the attribute within me that I must pray to God to modify? Was it disobedience?

# 6

## The Mirror of Almería

AFTER THE DAWN PRAYERS, THE first sign of the land of Andalusia appeared. The lookout in the crow's nest called, "Bless all those who say '*Allahu akbar!*' Land!"

The sailors and the travelers all took up a joyous cheer of "*Allahu akbar*," sharing the good news and embracing, and some burst into tears. As we approached the land, we saw a bright light shining from a tower that craned its neck over a hill beside Almería. It was like two great pieces of flint struck together. One of the sailors whispered to us, "The port is Muslim. They announce incoming ships by reflecting light off mirrors. Two flashes for merchant carriers, and four for a threatening or enemy ship; two flashes, then a pause, then two more, is a suspicious vessel, to alert the guards. If the light is a long unbroken beam, then the Norman fire worshippers are attacking, so the soldiers beat the drums and light the fires."

The port lay between two mountains flanking a fertile valley. We went inland to Almería before we docked. Its houses and streets and date palms were all reflected on the sea, lying beneath us with the appearance of a great mirror. Coming into it, one saw its streets and minarets, down to the beasts of burden in the street, reflected upon the surface of the water.

We stayed on board as we were instructed, until some soldiers from the land could come to search the vessel and ensure we were not carrying any weapons or infectious diseases. No one came all morning. The port was crowded with ships. We remained on board until after the afternoon prayers, when two boats bearing groups of soldiers approached, the late-afternoon sun glinting off their spears. They rowed so smoothly and manipulated the ropes leading up to our boat so skillfully that it was clear that they were experienced sons of the sea. I feared they would search us violently and levy exorbitant taxes, for the boat was from al-Mahdiya, and the scars of the Fatimids and their sustained attacks on Almería were still fresh in the soldiers' memories. Anyone coming from that shore was suspicious.

My heart beat violently. The books! Would they be destroyed, or subject to suspicion? I had stacked the two merchants' crates on top of them, one filled with valuable Indian incense, the other with poorly made wooden boxes filled with raisins. Whoever found these would not think of books. Andalusian tax was one-half of one-tenth the value of the goods, and one-tenth for liquor: but what of books?

As luck would have it, because Almería was so crowded, with so many ships arriving at once, the soldiers were exhausted. Most of them were white-skinned, red-bearded *saqaliba* wearing pointed helmets and green scarves. When they had finished their inspection, they paused for the treasury official to collect the taxes, and their leader called to them, "Fall in!" They fell into line on deck, shoulders erect and chins high, then filed off the boat by means of the rope ladders, while their physician sat on a box in the boat next to the ropes, taking the pulse and temperature of each passenger alighting from the boat, and smelling his breath, then stamping the back of his hand with ink. At that juncture, they would be allowed onto the smaller vessel that would take them to land.

When the soldiers were some distance from the boat, most of the passengers came out on deck. The sails were furled, and dozens of small boats set out toward us, manned with bare-chested, muscular sailors in loose white pantaloons and hastily wrapped turbans. They rowed quickly, racing toward us. When they began to toss their chains and ropes onto our boat, the captain roared at them, "Soft! To each his turn! None of you will move any goods unless he waits his turn!"

The captain had changed out of the humble clothing he had worn at sea, and now sported a silken *gallabiya* topped with a long abaya of ribbed silk. He stood erect, commanding his sailors to keep the chaos of porters under control—they had swarmed the ship by now—and telling us, "These are the ones who will transfer your things to shore. We shall commence emptying the ship with the smaller loads. Since most of you are merchants with more than ten crates, we will defer those until tomorrow. Under ten crates, please step forward for unloading."

Ma'in darted forward, and I saw him standing by the captain and whispering into his ear. The captain looked at him askance through his narrow eyes, then, amazingly, motioned to one of the sailors and whistled. The boatmen began to climb up the rope ladders that surrounded the ship. No sooner had their heads popped over the railing than Ma'in was negotiating with them, before they had ever set foot on deck. He started by speaking to them in his foreign tongue; when they were unable to comprehend him, he spoke in Arabic, and finally rushed to me bursting with enthusiasm. "They all charge ten dinars for bringing down the boxes—five for each box," he panted.

I was too proud to bargain, for I was now a master with a servant, and I must act like the nobles. Two young men approached us with bare feet, completely shaved heads— their bald pates shone with the greenish tint of hair sprouting under the skin—and bulging muscles with prominent veins. They were like marine creatures just emerged from a seashell. With enthusiasm untainted by the suspicion of strangers, they asked, "Are you from al-Mahdiya?"

"Yes," said Ma'in, "but my master is from the Arabian Peninsula."

Their eyes shone. "Where in the Peninsula?"

"I am from al-Yamama."

They welcomed me with words that leapt from them like the neighing of stallions. "We are from the tribes of Qudaa, in Yemen. It is they whom the Umayyads entrusted with guarding this region and its architecture, thanks to our long history of seamanship in the East. That is why this port is dubbed 'the land of the folk of Yemen'—their province and their home." As they spoke, they were tying our things with ropes, with great alacrity and skill, and sliding them across the wooden gangplank that extended from the ship's deck to their boat. When the boxes were all in place, Ma'in and I followed them, climbing down the rope ladders. The shore was not far from the ship, although the water made it seem so; the sea air was still sticky and salty against my skin. I was not accustomed to it, nor did I intend to become so.

We left behind the rushing of the waves, the scent of rain and gathering clouds over our heads, and the cries of the boatmen and the seabirds. We arrived on land as the sunset was purpling the sky above the happy homes of Almería. The houses rose up unevenly upon the sides of two hills, built of white stone with windows the color of the waves. I turned to Ma'in, only to find him haggling with a seller of shoes and slippers. Then he hurried to me. "Master, we must purchase two new pairs of shoes for good luck in the new ground upon which we tread." Ma'in was always finding a way to loosen my money belt.

With my first step into the city, a sweet and pleasant humor had come over me like the embrace of some beauty, and I was captivated, turning my face this way and that in exhilaration. I saw Ma'in's face turned toward mine, as if to say "What now?"

Now that I had Ma'in, things were different. All my life, I had picked my way along the outer edges of the world, not bursting in, and not making a decision, allowing the days to buffet me this way and that. But now that he was with me, it became necessary to make a decision—a correct and convincing decision worthy of a master of men. I had no desire to tackle this task. I wanted young Mazid of Najd, free flying on high, to watch and maneuver warily in the sky before taking the plunge. But Ma'in's questioning eyes, fixed on my face, drove me to say, "We must find lodgings. We shall stop awhile in Almería before going on to Cordoba."

In the end, we resolved to rent a cart to carry our things, and go to the market, where unfamiliar doors might open to us. Evening fell upon Almería with strange docility, like the hand of a father playing with a little daughter who has waited for him all day. As colors clashed and voices babbled, I found no trace of Mazid of Najd, and knew not when I should find him again.

The clouds gathered thickly about us. Thunder rolled and lightning flashed, driving Ma'in to redouble his efforts to find someone to carry our things as the rain began to fall. I looked at the faces of the porters around us: they did not inspire confidence. They were like a group of vultures circling their prey and seeking a way to swoop down. Finally, Ma'in found a battered old cart pulled by an aging and exhausted mule. I pitied his aged head, bowed with eternal servitude, with no liberation in sight but the grave. Why did I feel sorry for the mule? I had tried hard on my travels to form only a fleeting attachment to all I encountered, granting only a small part of my heart, fearing that it might break and scatter over the paths and thresholds of the cities I visited.

No sooner did the cart begin to climb through the paths of Almería than the palm trees began to sing. The carter asked us, "Are you travelers just passing through or merchants here to stay?"

I was circumspect in my answer, because it would dictate the lodgings he would find for us—he would receive his commission from the owner for me and my heavy and suspicious boxes and my smartly dressed servant whose head was always held high. "We are seeking temporary lodgings. We have family and friends waiting for us in the great market," I said, trying to give him to understand that we had many people to spring to our defense.

The cart rocked this way and that on its way up, the rain drizzling onto our heads, until we reached a great plaza, part of which was set aside for a well and a great trough for beasts of burden to drink, and some shops on the other side that were closing their doors and carrying their goods inside, out of the rain. We continued on our upward journey. We hoped that the rain would weaken; instead, there were great flashes of lightning and rumbles of thunder, and a downpour commenced, pouring through the streets. I had an irrational fear that the cart would slip straight back down to the bottom of the sea, but the carter cracked his whip at the poor mule, who moved forward and sought shelter under an overhanging balcony, where we stayed awaiting clearer weather. The driver looked at us and smiled. "The port has not had enough rain this year. It appears you brought the storm clouds in your abayas. Good fortune!"

But I was preoccupied with my crates, hoping no water had made its way through any crack. The path before us was blocked by the stone wall of a house, beneath which a cheerful garden sprouted. To continue on our journey to the market, we must turn around at the garden gate, and return to the broader path leading up from Almería. However, the carter had made the decision to shelter under the balcony from the rain.

The great changes in our fates flash like lightning, without wasting time asking our permission. The door of the house opposite the balcony opened and a woman peered out, her face covered with a blue veil, looking warily this way and that in the road, before lifting her veil to protect her head from the rain. She walked quickly toward us. "Ah! At last you are here! I have been waiting long, strangers!"

We looked around, thinking she must be addressing someone else. But when she was level with us, she cried loudly, "Why are you late?"

I raised my eyes to her questioningly. She was not young. There was a green tattoo on her chin with three lines like a pigeon's foot, or perhaps it was her wrinkles that made it look so. Why was she waiting for us to arrive at her house? I turned to the carter, only to find him unconcerned, examining the saddle of his mule and waiting for the rain to cease. Taken aback, I was torn with questions, plunged into perplexity, and unable to find any answers—there was nothing for it but to shrink beneath a polite silence. Fearing that Ma'in might respond with something unbecoming, I responded quickly: "Are we not all strangers? Life in this world is but a passageway, we are only here for a while."

As though she had not heard me, she cried out, "I have a room for rent in my house if you require it." She came closer and craned her neck toward us, letting us see her smile as she went on. "In addition to my bright and cheerful room, with its own water tower and basin, you can pluck oranges and lemons from the garden of the house, and drink from the well, and you can have two glasses of cow's milk every morning. Twenty dinars a week."

In the caliph's Cairo, the new and lush city, my room had cost only seven dinars. What had this elderly tattooed woman to offer worth such a price? I had been told in Egypt that it was expensive in Andalusia, that her people loved beauty and decorating their houses and clothes, perfuming their hair, and bathing with soap mixed with musk. Twenty dinars was an exorbitant price for a single week. But it was the only week I would spend in Almería: why should I not live in luxury for a while?

I was happy to be on dry land once more. My joints felt loose. I was overcome with the desire to lie upon a bed that was solid beneath me and not buffeted by the waves, and drink the milk of this woman's cow. I wished to sleep an entire night, from sunset to dawn, without bolting up in fright thinking the sea had swallowed us up, or that I was in a whale's belly. I would go through this door that had opened itself to me. I did not yet know that this door would lead into a labyrinth from which I would never be free.

With our first steps into the room, I understood the exorbitant rent. There was a main room to the left of the entrance, comfortable and like a reception hall, connected to a smaller room for sleeping, complete with a narrow staircase in one corner leading up to the servant's or companion's room. The roof was wood inlaid with mother-of-pearl. There were two windows, one onto the rear garden of the house, and one onto the streets. There were fresh white curtains over them, their folds filled with something like joy. The floor was covered with sturdy wool carpets from Sindh, made from the hair of mountain goats. As for the couches swathed in green silk, they encircled the room, which, together with the throws and carvings, created an impression I had only seen before in palaces.

My slumber in that room poured essence of lavender into my limbs. It slipped even into my dreams that night, gifting me a calm, sprightly morning and steps that longed to explore every corner of Almería. I must go forth and discover the city. I left Ma'in to unpack and organize our things in the room, and went out walking alongside what clouds remained from the day before. The street was fresh and flowering after the rain; the brass that ornamented the doorway gleamed; and my heart was singing like the gypsies' brass castanets.

The streets of the city were paved with stone, and the water-wheels by them were free of any refuse or dirt from the buildings they passed. There was hardly a house without a balcony. It was a feature of every house, like the doors and windows, and most of the balconies were laden with pots of flowers and sweet basil. In the center of Almería was the market: it was not gigantic with streets branching off it like those in Baghdad or Fustat, but it was crowded with shops, most of them fabric traders selling silk. I bought a suit from one of them, and took it with me to the bathhouse. As usual, in the darkness and steam of the bath, I listened to the chatter of the patrons, for this held the keys to the city. In the bath, caution, wariness, and modesty all fall away with one's clothing.

At the main gate, I was welcomed by a boy who examined me, saying, "There are two tubs in the bath: one for two dirhams and one for two dinars. Which will you choose?"

He asked it as if he was asking "Are you a nobleman or one of the common folk?" Naturally, I said, "Two dinars." After all, I had no wish to bathe with folk who blew their noses and spat into the tub.

Still, it appeared that the folk of Almería were refined and pampered. The clothing of those who passed by me was spotless and elegant; none walked with bare feet; in fact, they lifted the hems of their clothing fastidiously as they went by. When I removed my old clothes, the boy in the bathhouse did not set them aside as was the custom of every land I had been in; here, they burned them in the oven along with the coals that heated the water.

I went into the steam, timid but all ears. I was not there long until I found that everyone was speaking of Khayran al-Amiri and Aflah al-Saqlibi.

## Khayran al-Amiri

The news of Chamberlain al-Amiri was but a more detailed account of what Rashid ibn Ali's guests had spoken of in Egypt. He had been one of Caliph al-Hakam's men for close to a quarter of a century; he had been a chamberlain before becoming regent of the throne of Hisham ibn al-Hakam of the Umayyads, also known as al-Muayyad, after the death of al-Hakam. Al-Amiri had managed the affairs of state well at the start, with a group of his best *saqaliba* soldiers. In summer and winter he had led campaigns to protect the gaps in their defenses from the attacks of the Normans. But after he was overcome with the lust for power, he seized the reins of the caliphate and strangled it like a voracious lion. He sent huge numbers of Andalusian men to their deaths, brought the Umayyads low, and kept their descendants away from positions of power, causing the collapse of the state upon his death. His opulent palace, known as al-Zahir, was looted, and his generals and his servants were dismissed. One of his generals was Khayran al-Amiri, who had fled Cordoba for Almería and declared its independence, becoming its prince. He ran it well and prudently, and defended it efficiently from the attacks of the fire worshippers who came from the high seas.

In the bath, everyone plunges into the mists of hot steam, the smell of soap, and a heavy herbal perfume with which they anoint their hair when finished. Whispers of dark subjects: the sinking of a boat of Khayran's fleet on its way to Sicily. "He will be none the worse off for the sinking of one ship," I heard someone say, "for he possesses a great fleet and his ships traverse the entire world."

Another voice whispered tremulously, "With the revenue from the trade of his fleet, he strengthens and betters his kingdom, and buys the consciences of those who would not have a *saqaliba* slave as their prince."

A suspicious silence followed. Then the conversation resumed, only this time it held a note of deep gratitude and oblique respect for Khayran. Were it not for his adroit management and intelligent political maneuvering, Almería would not have prospered nor its trade flourished. "It would not have grown in this fashion," the speaker continued. "Nor would its people have felt so safe in their person and possessions." I guessed that the man chattering so was the owner of a ship.

The bath attendant was turning me this way and that, scrubbing and washing. I could not make out the speakers' faces. But later in the colonnade, where we cooled ourselves after the steam and they gave us glasses of mint tea with basil, my intuition proved correct—the speaker was the captain of a merchant vessel that transported silks between Almería and Constantinople. He looked like a pirate, with the strength of a man proud of his Yemeni Qudai origins. His ancestors had moved to Andalusia with the first conquests. "You, too, are from Qudaa?" I asked.

As though stating an eternal truth, he intoned, "What is Qudaa but Yemen? It is named Almería."

His name was Abu Nasr. His eyes had a piercing glint, like jade, and he had a broad brow. But his black and broken teeth gave him the air of a jackal. When I told him I was a bookseller, he replied with a half mocking laugh, "Ha ha! A seller of papers. But paper fades, and is swallowed up by the earth, and ruined by water."

Eager to enter into more conversation with him, I ignored his derision. "If what is in the head becomes vapor, that which remains is what's set on paper," I said, quoting the proverb, surprised that he made so light of my profession. Was it merely his habit with strangers, to denigrate them so as to test their mettle, or did he really think so little of booksellers?

When I tried to obtain more information from him about Almería and Khayran al-Amiri, he cried, "Beware! *Fitna* is at a fever pitch between the Amiris and the Berbers, and there are eyes and ears everywhere. If you confine yourself to selling books, however, you are safe."

Annoyed by his superior, reproving tone, and his unsolicited advice, I said mockingly, "Is it permitted to discuss trade, then?" And I went on, "How are your journeys to Constantinople, when you must traverse the Byzantine Sea?"

"You are a shrewd man!" he cried. "You have touched upon the one thing that is the talk of all Almería: the textile trade. Almería is the most important center in the world for spinning silk." He looked about him as though calling upon all to bear witness. "It is said that the tax collectors counted 5,800 looms. The most eminent merchants here all trade in silk, and in fact it is said that one of them in times gone by hosted Chamberlain Mansour ibn Abu Amir and his army in Almería, comprising thousands of men, for fourteen days!"

I knew nothing of the veracity of this man's tales, or lack thereof. But he seemed to be a charlatan: his stories were many and confused, now praying for Khayran, now whispering that Almería had been safer and cheaper in the time of its previous ruler, Aflah. It appeared that he had grown up in the back alleys, and no amount of living could tame the prickly and wild nature that comes with being raised in the streets.

I took my leave of Captain Abu Nasr with promises to meet again. He said that he could always be found in his store inside an industrial complex built next to the port of Almería and mainly used for shipbuilding and manufacture of weapons. The Umayyads had wanted it to supply their armies with ships and arms to repel the fire-worshipping Normans. "I sell not only some marine weapons in my shop," he said, "but bows and arrows and other hunting equipment. The *saqaliba* soldiers are fond of hunting, and everyone who comes to Almería for trade comes to me, although I am not in the store for long stretches of the year because of my long sea voyages. But my sons and those who work for me do the job." Abu Nasr, talkative and full of himself, was my best window onto Almería. I must visit him at his store.

After my bath, the fall breeze was refreshing, despite a chill in the air. The scent of the sea penetrated every wall and alleyway; the farther north we went in Almería, leaving the sea behind, we saw the roofs of the houses below us, with gardens where children chased each other around, women running from house to house with dishes to share, and pleasing girls hanging out their washing, which danced in the breeze.

My return to the boardinghouse of the woman who sold silk took a long time: I lost myself in the intertwining, interconnected paths of the market, and knew not which passageway or street to take. I was obliged to return to the port and start from there. When I returned, I found that Ma'in had made friends with most of the inhabitants of the boardinghouse. Seaside dwellers are skilled at starting conversations with passing travelers and opening the windows of friendliness and the doors of familiarity to strangers.

## Hamdouna's Boardinghouse

On my return journey, I found that it did not require much asking, for everyone in Almería knew Hamdouna's Boardinghouse, where I was staying. It was a great house on the outskirts of the Almería marketplace, and they say she inherited it from one of many husbands who had entered and exited her life, either disappearing down the roads of life or being conveyed into a coffin and thence the ground. When her beauty had faded and her attractiveness waned, and she found no rich husband to support her, she had divided her house into two: half a luxurious place to stay for merchants, containing a stable for their mounts, and the other half a silk factory and a tailor's for luxurious garments.

I arrived at Hamdouna's Boardinghouse with the stars of Almería twinkling brightly above and my head swimming as though I were still on the boat. Ma'in had set out some food for me: figs, honey, and oatcakes. I slept until the next day, more deeply than I had in ages. I planted my head into the linen pillows perfumed with bitter orange blossom, while climbing jasmine looked in on me from the window and stood guard at the gates of the night, standing between me and the nightmares that always haunt me when I am in a new land.

I only woke to hear the dawn prayer call. It was a Sunni call: the Andalusians have nothing of the Shiite in their call to prayer, nor do they pray to Ali's descendants from the pulpit. They are the descendants of Marwan, who made the caliphate strong. I heard them repeating "*Allahu akbar*" only three times, instead of four, at the dawn prayers, as is the custom of soldiers in barracks and dwellers in battle zones. I remained abed, listening to the footfall of the men going to the mosque. Then I performed my ablutions in the stone basin with a brass spigot above it, located in the corner of the room, and prayed. All the while, I was listening to the bustle of activity behind the house that came to me from a high window above the room.

I ascended the steps leading up to Ma'in's room softly, not wishing to wake him: I wanted to be alone with Mazid. I had barely reached the window and looked out onto the back garden when I saw long wooden tables laid out adjoining each other, and in the corner of the garden a row of seven massive brass cauldrons, with circular shapes like eggs boiling in them. A young woman in a yellow scarf was stirring the shapes and peering down at them. I drew back quickly lest she think I was peeping, and dressed quickly to go out.

In the center of the courtyard was a fountain of worn and cracked mosaic. There were small mint plants around it, leaning passionately and flirtatiously into the water. The columns at the side were still violet with the light of dawn, but some of the doors had opened and there were footsteps gently padding along the marble of the colonnade. I put in my sleeve a book by Abu Hazil al-Allaf al-Mutazili, and resolved to seek out the booksellers in this city. There was nothing wrong with seeking out book lovers and booksellers during my fleeting stay here. Who knew but that I might sell some in Almería? I would not wait until I reached Cordoba. I knew that the people of Andalusia were hungering for a book such as *Arguments and*

*Molds* by Abu Hazil, for it held many of the arguments of the Just Monotheists in response to other sects, and many of these lived in Cordoba.

On my way out, I spied Hamdouna sitting in a corner of the passage on a long wooden bench surrounded by pillows of green silk like those in my room. She was craning her neck as though waiting for me to go out: I must go to her and greet her and speak with her awhile, even if it meant being a little late for the discussion circle after the dawn prayers at the mosque, which was usually the most important and the richest. At the dawn circle, I usually found the keys to the city's knowledge, and learned the names of its learned men and clerics, and who was the Mecca of its intellect. The side conversations and whispers would lead me to men, and the men would lead me to the pathways of the Voyagers. I felt the joy of a man holding the stars in his hand, about to scatter them across the Earth. I was filled with the ecstasy of planting fields with seeds: embryonic doubts and questions that blocked the paths of the preachers of fixed ideas and empty words. Still, tensions appeared rife in Almería. When swords clash, the circles of logic and poetry and speech dwindle and disappear, moving to sound loudly on the battlefield.

Next to Hamdouna stood an effete boy, swaying this way and that, batting his lashes and lisping. He was handing her walnuts and rubbing her shoulders, speaking to her in whispers that bespoke gossip of some kind. She looked fresher and younger in the morning, not at all the aged crone who had clung to our cart that day beneath the rain. As soon as she saw me, she motioned to me to come. Her enthusiasm made me more certain that she had been waiting there for me. She pushed out a chair furnished with pillows. "Have a seat."

Her effete boy rushed off, his braids hanging over his shoulders, like an energetic nanny goat. He brought a glass of milk and a plate of dried figs by way of breakfast for me. I was embarrassed: what should I call her? "Madam," or by her name? Some women dislike being called "Aunt" or "Mother" or the like, which offends their fleeing youth and lays bare an old age that can no longer be concealed with paint or makeup. "What do they call you, my lady?" I asked her.

As though resolving an inconsequential matter, she said, "Call me only Hamdouna—Hamdouna of Almería." She looked at me. "Do you recall the moment of your arrival, when I said I had been expecting you?"

"Yes, yes." I nodded. "I was about to disillusion you."

She answered with a broad smile, "It was because I knew the law of parallels and resemblances would bring you to me."

I knitted my brows, a little mockingly, and tilted my head as though to ask her to continue. "A few days before you arrived," she said, "I planted a green banner and a spear by the wall of my house. And here it is, today, the standard of the East, the Arab of the Peninsula, sitting here with me."

I was charmed by the pleasant nature of the Andalusians. She had made a flag of me, when she would not have found a guest to cough up twenty dinars for a room, with Almería full of boardinghouses with vacancies. The city was but a first step for those who disembarked there, seeking to journey on into Andalusia. She smiled, showing a row of good teeth untouched by time. Her hair was bound up with a crimson scarf with silver dinars hanging from it. Playfully, I raised my glass of milk and asked her, "And what will this milk bring me, according to your law of parallels and resemblances?"

She gave me a sunny smile. "It will only bring the purest of spotless hearts."

I rose and excused myself. But I asked her, I knew not why, "Why do the date palms sing in Almería, Hamdouna?"

She lowered her head. "They sing?"

I nodded.

Clearly fearful of losing her role of wise seer, she volunteered, "Perhaps because they are the closest to an animal.

There are male and female date palms; and if you cut their heads off, they die."

How did Hamdouna know what al-Jahiz had said about date palms? Truly, you learn something new each day you pass in the company of strangers.

I returned from my first day fruitless. I passed by a man who sold jars of honey in the market, and another who sold great round honeycombs; desiring to taste it, I bought a jar. On my way, I began to think what the honey pot would bring me according to Hamdouna's law of parallels and resemblances.

That night in my room, I froze to hear the mulberry tree behind the house starting to sing along with the date palms. I placed the honey pot on a gesso shelf set into the wall, never realizing what had begun to take shape on the walls of my room. Hamdouna's law of parallels and resemblances applied not only to her, but to those who lived in her house.

I no longer saw much of Ma'in: he was occupied with many new friends, which he appeared to make easily. I did not seek him out, but I asked him for discretion's sake not to divulge that he was a Sanhaji: that Berber tribe was not welcome among the Andalusians because of their loyalty to the Fatim-ids in Tunisia.

Making light of my fears, Ma'in answered, "Fear not, sir. There are many Sanhajis in Andalusia. Some Berber chiefs and tribes were such skilled warriors that the late Mansour al-Amiri called upon them to come here. But now, there is no distinction between the Berber tribes, as the *fitna* is between the Umayyads and the Amiris. As long as you are prudent and do not draw your sword, none shall pay you heed."

Ma'in, as was his habit, had begun to announce proudly that I was a doctor. I had no desire to stop him—I did not ask him to and it did not displease me—for while it might attract unwanted attention, I could not resist that false distinction. Tomorrow, I would go again to the Great Mosque. I would listen to the sheikhs and investigate the discussion circles and seek a place to distribute or sell my books in Almería. Rashid of Egypt had only told me of al-Bahaa, who awaited me in Cordoba in a status between two statuses, not guessing that I would stop in Kairouan and Almería. I recited verse nine of the Sura of Yasin so that God would protect my boxes of books: "*And We have put before them a barrier and behind them a barrier and covered them, so they do not see.*" Then I smartened up my appearance, put my book up my sleeve, and headed out to the discussion circles in Almería, where I found a surprise.

Despite the mosque's eight imposing doors, its marble columns, and its colonnades with ornamented roofs, there were only two discussion circles within it. One was devoted to reciting the Qur'an, where the sheikh would recite the Sura of al-Alaq and his students would repeat after him; the other, completely the reverse, was immense, with nearly ten semi-circular rows around the sheikh. Other than this, there were some individuals scattered around the mosque, absorbed in their books.

I approached the crowded circle. The sheikh was portly, sitting with the many folds of his stomach plainly visible, with a nasal voice and a whistle in his speech more suited to a carter than a venerable holy man. He was saying, "The philosophers and the heretics and the blasphemers—God curse them!—only listened to their own minds and opinions. Furthermore, they spoke of what they thought without regard for the prophets."

I shrank into myself. Had he been waiting for me to enter the mosque to pour this into my ear? I pushed the notion away, lest I be like the thief who acted so suspiciously it was as though he were begging the police to clap him in irons. But where was the Andalusia they had told me of, that celebrated the arts of rhetoric, wisdom, and philosophy, and venerated its sheikhs? Apparently, when soldiers enter by the door, philosophy leaves through the window. For almost a quarter of a century, al-Mansour al-Amiri had controlled the affairs of state, ridding it of the philosophers and theologians, and humiliating the Umayyad Dynasty, and now here was his boy Khayran al-Amiri finishing what al-Mansour had started.

Philosophy is a shy bird, retiring, formed of fearful and pensive clouds. It circles and never lands, for it knows that no sooner has it looked through the window of the mosque to convey its crop of minds to the lands of wonder than the hammers of heresy and debauchery will be raised in its face, and the knives of "infidel" sharpened. I tucked the book well into my belt that none might glimpse it, and started a short prayer in honor of the mosque. When I knelt, the windows brought the sounds of the trees to me. They were still singing.

I finished my prayer and rose, heading for the exit. I had no desire to stay, for I did not think I would find any buyers for my books here. I would try the Citadel of Alcazaba—if Khayran was a *saqalibi* foreigner, his scribes and companions must have some men who had been touched by the craft of literature.

## The Ships of Silk

Long travel and journeying have taught me that every city has not only an essence, but a center around which the rest of it revolves, springing thence and returning, obeying its orders, following its laws, and colored with its rainbow. In Baghdad, it had been the Circular City, and the Rusafa Bridge over the river linking the caliph's palaces to the common people. The heart of Jerusalem had been the tombs of her prophets, interwoven with their prophecies and the valiant deeds of her saints, and a timeless sorrow for a face chipped away at by myths, each banner seeking to snatch a piece. The Nile is Egypt: how close or far you are from its banks is what tells your fortune in Egypt. Illness had kept me from Kairouan. Here, there were only Khayran and his citadel as the heart of Almería.

Alcazaba, the Citadel of Khayran, is surrounded by the city on all sides. Almería flows from it and into it, bringing news of trade ships, battles with the Normans, and skirmishes with the remnants of the Umayyads. Khayran controls the security of Almería with an iron fist: his men walk about the markets, inspect the goods, and look into people's faces. Last night, after midnight, I observed the shadows of two guards bearing torches passing beneath my window, walking with a slow, measured tread. Had they learned of the stranger coming to Almería, sending spies to investigate him? Or were they only patrolling the odd boardinghouse that draws in its boarders by means of parallels and resemblances?

I woke to the sound of women whispering, like a mist that slipped beneath my bedcovers. Twitterings, chatterings, high-pitched voices, sprightly and spirited. When women are speaking, fields blossom and a sweet smell spreads around: there are soft fingers, delicious hot food, shining courtyards, and pots of sweet basil keeping the secrets of private rooms, while the clouds of narcissus betray and spread those selfsame secrets.

I was weary of the deep voices of men, and the implicit command that always lurked in their depths. Always in the conversation of men there is an imperative: "Speak that I may see you and gauge your worth: spread out your plumage and preen and show me what you have." Within every man, a warrior lurks, awaiting the opportunity to duel with you. When he passes, he will display his knowledge, his riches, or his physical prowess, and he will display them from the first round, so you must be ready to duel. Last night, the captain who told tales of his victories at sea and his trading triumphs without being asked had been spreading his wings, like a male bustard intimidating its enemies in the desert. His strange face and drooping eyelids were still engraved on my mind. His wide circle of acquaintances might be some use to me in selling a few books, but it might also do me harm, for he was not only garrulous, but pretentious and eager to seize on others' mistakes.

The water that flowed from the tap in my room was sweet and delicious. I had let myself believe Hamdouna's heretical babbling that made no sense, and bought a jar of honey to await her laws of parallels and resemblances. My conversation with her filled me with a motherly warmth I could neither deny nor resist. We should meet, she and I, in the middle of the road between superstition and good sense. After all, Aristotle says that virtue is a status between two statuses. And here were the bright white pillows, the cushions and carpets strewn about my room, driving me to dress elegantly and perfume my mustache before I went out.

Ma'in brought me breakfast—honey, seeds, milk, and disks of flat bread—and wrapped my turban around my head for me. I must sell some of the books in my possession. I had been warned of going up to Alcazaba, and I knew nothing of how Khayran felt with regard to books. He was but a foreigner, one of Mansour ibn Abu Amir's *saqaliba* who had climbed to power and declared Almería's independence. But there must be some in his court and retinue, not to mention his scribes and the court's clerics, who held books in high esteem.

I preferred not to appear like a begging salesman hawking his wares. I wished to raise my craft above such meanness: I would not be like the folk with boxes of peaches who come down from the farms and villages to Khayran's Citadel every morning. This gave me much pause, and I turned the matter about on all sides until I finally made a decision. I pulled out a sheet of heavy parchment from my store of paper and wrote upon it:

*In the name of God, the Merciful, the Compassionate, He who granteth bounty and assistance,*

Prayers and peace upon the Prophet Muhammad, the best of all prophets,

To the Victorious, Just, Bountiful, and Noble Prince of Almería, Khayran al-Saqalibi al-Amiri, may God grant him long life and power on earth and victory over his enemies and frustrate those who envy him,

I am your servant Mazid ibn Abdullah al-Hanafi. I have alighted in your great city with a collection of rare and valuable books in my possession, most of which are from the House of Wisdom in Baghdad. If you wish to do me the honor of looking through them, your servant may be found praying at the Mosque of Almería at the customary times.

I rolled it up carefully, tied it with silk thread, and tucked it into my pocket. Then I prepared to go out.

Hamdouna was sitting in her customary seat, a table before her with a pitcher and glasses set out. She offered me a fragrant beverage, saying, "Water yourself in the morning with orange blossom water, that your moments may bear flower and fruit."

"He who stays at your house," I replied, "drinks the nectar of blessings."

"When God decides to give you his bounty," she said, "open your hands to receive it."

I stilled, staring. I recalled having heard this before. Then she asked me, "What are your family's roots?"

"I am from Bani Hanifa," I told her.

"Welcome," she said in the traditional response. "I am a desert Arab like yourself. But many lands have mingled in my blood. My maternal grandmother is Berber, and my mother is a Basque. Look!" And she showed me a tattoo on the back of her hand that looked like intersecting circles. "It is the mark of my grandmother's Berber tribe."

Suddenly, at the gate, there was a clamor: men shouting, horses whinnying, and the clatter of cartwheels coming to a halt. Hamdouna craned her neck and called to her household, "Come out! The cocoons have arrived!"

From an inner door at the far end of the colonnade, a group of demure girls emerged, hurrying to the gates. I guessed that they had come from the rear garden, as one of them was the young woman with the yellow scarf I had seen stirring the great pot. Hamdouna's effete boy came after them with hurried steps. They only stayed outside a little while before returning, carrying on their heads things like great wooden coffins, with gleaming white balls atop them like jealously guarded eggs.

"These are the cocoons of the silkworm," Hamdouna explained with the air of an expert. The great coffins borne on their heads glided in through the door to the back garden, one after the other. It was then that I realized the massive brass cauldrons had been awaiting the cocoons to be emptied out into them, the sticks in the girls' hands stirring them delicately in the boiling water. Hamdouna saw my raised eyebrows and absorbed stare. "From here, the journey of silk begins," she said. "It starts when the cocoons are bought from the folk who raise the silkworms on the mulberry farms, all the way to when the silk unfurls over the body of some lovely girl, or forms a shirt over the shoulders of some handsome young man like yourself."

Well pleased by her praise, I accepted her invitation to view more. I leapt up and she walked before me with a sprightly tread. I followed her. Once through the wooden door at the end of the colonnade, we entered a dark, damp corridor with water dripping from the ceiling. It opened onto the back garden I had been watching from the window of my room. It was not large, but it had high walls. Its air was heavy with burning wood and the steam rising from the great cauldrons.

The young women working redoubled their efforts at Hamdouna's arrival, especially with a stranger visiting. One of them was watching the cauldrons and stirring delicately with a wooden stick. Another was moving what looked like a straw broom over the surface of the boiling cauldron with great care. Strands of silk, tangled and intertwined, clung to it; these she released over a great wooden table. The rest of the girls picked up the threads carefully. Then, as the women in al-Yamama do when weaving sheep's wool, Hamdouna's girls sat at spindles beneath the wall and from the tangled bunches of silk drew single shining threads, wrapping them around large spindles with two wheels and a great many heads and protrusions. In the end, out of these spindles would emerge a shining skein of silk, collected by Hamdouna's boy in a hefty basket for dyeing, after which the skeins were placed on the looms for weaving.

After we had been there for a while, the girls' shyness was transformed into laughter and smiles as they whispered among themselves. The silk girls are playing with your heart, Mazid! Their faces, bedewed with steam; their eyes, ravishing with black lashes; Heaven alone must have helped me restrain myself from smiling and winking at them.

With a note of pride in her voice, Hamdouna said, "Although this is one of hundreds of factories in Almería, our work is in high demand. We even receive orders from Cordoba itself, specifically the Umayyad princesses, especially after the gown we made for Wallada bint al-Mustakfi, the poetess of Andalusia." She shook her head and laughed. "What a story behind that gown! That was what made Hamdouna's silks the talk of every caravan. Princess Wallada asked us to embroider some verses of poetry on her gown. Because she did not specify which, I asked a debauched poet—who was clearly an enemy of the al-Amiri and held a hatred for the Umayyads—for some lines on her beauty. The poet presented me with some lines he claimed were written by Wallada herself, which ran:

Highborn am I; I lift my garment's hem in pride at this.
I give my love my favor, and each passerby a kiss.

I selected only the first line, describing her garment of pride. But the women doing the embroidery, whether out of malice or misprision, added the second as well. The gown was wrapped in damask and sent off to Cordoba without my knowledge of the extra line. Thanks be to God, Wallada did not take offense; not only that, amused, she wore it out in public, and continued ordering her gowns from our workshop. The silk caravan leaves from here to Cordoba twice a year, once in summer and once in winter. Saffron-tinted abayas; scarves the hue of apricots early in season; caftans the shade of sunlight behind a cloud; belts like the iridescent pigeon's neck . . . no workshop in Almería can match Hamdouna's silks! We received orders after that from all the princesses of the House of Marwan, each princess with a verse of poetry praising her beauty and noble lineage."

She laid a hand upon her head. "But I am wiser now! I no longer allow any abaya or silk garment to leave my workshop without looking at it and carefully inspecting its verse." As we made our exit through the dark passage between the boardinghouse and the rear garden, she said, "And thank heaven, the two lines of poetry passed without repercussions, although someone did teach the lines to the cheap tavern songstresses, and they are now sung in drunken dance to humiliate the House of Marwan. I did not suffer for it, though. It is the law of parallels and resemblances: souls are moved by passion through the selves and minds they inhabit. I work in silk, so everything that reaches me is attracted by smoothness, luster, and luxury. I cause it to shine in every corner of my domain, eschewing the roughness of wool and linen, and I keep my hands clear of ill-gotten gains."

I left Hamdouna's house swathed in talk of silk. The threads of the sun were just starting to climb the walls of its courtyard, and the street outside was beginning to vibrate with the sound of carts and pedestrians. I went to the Great Mosque, still turning over in my mind the law of parallels and resemblances, now pushing it away as mere mumbo jumbo, now remembering Aristotle's dictum "Nothing comes of nothing." According to him, attributes do not inhere in the observer, but in the matter, or subject itself, which is then said to participate in the attribute. It then changes because of manifestation. The image is forcibly present in its ideal form, whether or not it is manifested in the real world; it becomes tangible once it is manifested. Well! I would bring this law into my life, then, and see what the pot of honey in my room would bring.

The outer courtyard of the mosque was thickly planted with tangerine and bitter orange, in rows of pots nearly equal in size, in a manner I had never seen in any other mosque. Today as well, there was nothing but circles for teaching the Qur'an to little boys. They repeated the verses after a scowling and distracted sheikh, who stopped them occasionally to explain details of enunciation specific to the Qur'an, then went back to staring into space. Where was everyone? Had they dispersed after the dawn prayers, or did the theologians and clerics of Almería have specific days when they held their circles? In times of battles and armies, the mind is shunted aside, replaced by fatwas that sound the bugle to fight. I hoped that this was not the case in Cordoba, for my books were valuable and only for the brightest: Aristotle's *Ethics* and *History of Animals*, a revised copy of *Ikhwan al-Safa*, and the book of Abu Hazil al-Allaf al-Mutazili— books good enough only for the libraries of Cordoba. Was it Hamdouna's comfortable and well-loved boardinghouse that made me linger in Almería? In a city ruled by a military commander, the most I could ask for was safe roads, well-lit streets, and guards coming and going, looking into men's faces and opening men's hands to see if they held a dagger or a purse or a book.

## The Captain

Almería was small, with winding streets that all opened onto each other. You saw the same faces several times a day. Despite the plethora of ships and boats docking every day, it remained a bridge between those just arrived in Andalusia and their various paths leading on to Murcia, Granada, or Seville. I often ran into the Qudai captain. I espied him at the market gates, with his drooping eyelids and stained teeth like a jackal's. He wore a black silk turban and an opulent caftan, but his elegant attire did nothing to improve the mysterious air in his face, which indicated that he had been raised in the back alleys. He was bargaining with a potter over a receptacle, holding it high and turning it in his hands. He did not appear serious in his negotiations, for his eyes were neither on the seller nor on the goods, but idly looking at the passersby, coming to rest on me. He soon approached me with good cheer. "Welcome to al-Hanafi from the Arabian Peninsula!"

His loud voice made all heads turn toward me. My circumspect nature was mortified, and my fear was compounded by the books tucked in my sleeve, already driving me to walk in the shadows and avoid the light. "How is your time in Almería?" he boomed. "Are you enjoying the air here?"

I disliked this man. I did not wish to become familiar with him. There was something about him that repelled me: perhaps it was his tiresome nature and constant posturing. Or was it his drooping eyes, which concealed a great deal of cunning? Therefore, I did not stop, merely saying over my shoulder, "It is as beautiful as its name, bless it and all who live here!"

I tried to keep walking with a casual wave, but he gripped my hand powerfully and whispered, "How goes it with the books? Have you found buyers?" Then he came closer and lowered his voice. "Beware. These days, they care nothing for books. Most of their time is spent in training and sparring. It is said that many bookstores in Cordoba were looted and robbed."

Oh, how I regretted having told this posturing fool that I was a bookseller, and bringing him into my business! A Voyager is circumspect and builds walls of mystery between himself and others. It was the madness of the hot, perfumed bath, which lets us drop our guard along with our clothes. In vain did I try to mend matters. "In any event," I said, "I do not have many books, only richly covered manuscripts in Fatimid calligraphy, and some Ibn Hisham biographies and works of the great poets." Too late, I realized I had fallen into a grave error in mentioning the Fatimids: the Almerians had not yet forgotten their resentment of that dynasty. There was nothing for it but to make my excuses to the captain and hurry on to the mosque.

I went into the mosque and performed the afternoon prayers. Then I waited for the discussion circles to form, as is the custom in any Great Mosque. But it remained vacant but for a few sheikhs sitting beneath the columns with no students. I looked around the shelves and walls in search of the closets of books. Suddenly I heard the sound of loud laughter, the clatter of weapons, and a great ruckus at the eastern gate of the mosque. Then, in ones and twos, young men in military uniform, with red faces and yellow hair, began to filter through the colonnades. I asked one of the mosque attendants about them. Carelessly, he said, "They are *saqaliba*, soldiers belonging to Khayran. Some are Christian slaves newly converted to Islam. They are brought here that they may become fluent in Arabic by means of reciting the Qur'an with Sheikh Muafa."

Their number multiplied rapidly until they filled the courtyard of the mosque, and formed circles around Sheikh Muafa sluggishly and without much enthusiasm. They did not appear to have any particular passion for the sheikh's recitations and his low nasal voice. The duration of their lesson, between the afternoon and sunset prayers, was passed in whispering and confidences and laughter and examining their weapons, while I combed through scattered manuscripts on the shelves comprising parts of the Qur'an and segments of the *Life of the Prophet* by Ibn Hisham.

I was overcome with disappointment. It occurred to me that there might indeed be none in Almería who wished to acquire my books. When the *saqaliba* were done with the sunset prayers, they hurried to the marketplace opposite the mosque and took to fencing, shouting, guffawing, and boasting of their exploits with shield, sword, and spear. They played with the wares of the itinerant vendors, showing their skill at marksmanship by shooting arrows at store displays. They stopped a seller of Armenian cucumbers, walking heavily at the end of the day, and asked him to place one atop his head that they might shoot at it. Although they paid him for his goods at the end, their effrontery and recklessness were plain to see, as though their aim was to terrify any watching passersby. "Fall in!" their commander cried, whereupon they made a long double line, side by side, straight-backed, chests out, and made their way back up to the Citadel of Khayran in the north of the city on the edge of the Gador Mountains. It was an impregnable structure, spreading like the nest of the mythical al-Anqaa bird, overlooking the city.

The air was congested with tension, the soldiers' swords and shields glittering above it, like the smell of Baghdad's markets when the Bouhi soldiers pushed through the marketplace, looking into every face with belligerent impudence, engendering a feeling that an attack could come at any moment.

The soldiers' recklessness and carelessness had dissipated my awe of them and emboldened me. I would not waste this rare opportunity and must seize it before it slipped through my fingers. I hurried after the ranks of soldiers, their eyes raking me derisively, until I reached their leader with his great brass helmet and congested red face. I pulled out my message to Khayran, presented it to him, and entreated him to convey it. He showed no surprise at my action, but appeared to preen as though he had achieved some special status in front of his soldiers. Paper correspondence between Khayran and his subjects seemed to be a familiar sight in Almería.

I stood at the bottom of the path to the Citadel, watching the regiment ascend to the summit.

On my way back, I took the seaward path by the port, the line of the horizon still filled with ships and the last threads of sunlight. Some of the ships had docked; others awaited permission. The mirrors on the mountains still flashed according to the type of ship. But everyone was speaking with trepidation of the fleets of godless Normans, claiming that the year of their attack was nigh, although the Almerían fleet had become almost an armada, comprising hundreds of ships. Still, the Normans never ceased their attacks on the ports. They had great strength, and the shores always cleared of people once there was news of their coming. They only raided every six or seven years, vanquishing and enslaving all they encountered, usually with a fleet of forty-five to a hundred ships, killing, burning, and laying waste to any port they passed through, and taking captives with them as slaves.

Passersby were not permitted to approach the great shipyard where the ships were built: it was a great basin of water surrounded by a high stone wall. I feared to draw near lest I be taken for a spy. None was there but the workers and sailors entering and exiting, and some vendors selling sweet barley cakes and dried figs to those just arrived from the port. But the winds of doubt were blowing in my breast, and I was overcome with worry. Had I done right in sending my message to Khayran?

**The Honey Pot**
Suspended between despair and hope, I waited to hear from the Citadel. I prayed sometimes at the Great Mosque, and waited. Nothing had come of it until now. Had the scroll been

delivered? Had it reached Khayran, or fallen into the hands of some clerk who had discarded it, mocking the ambition of what he considered some mendicant salesman begging at the doors of kings?

On my way home that evening, the workmen had begun to recede from the shore gradually, the sounds of hammering in the shipyard dying down. The fishermen returned from the depths of the sea, followed by flocks of seagulls eagerly awaiting what might fall from their baskets. The city began to embrace the feet of men and distribute them among her houses. I walked along the streets of Almería, the intimate perfume of home emanating from the windows: wives preparing hot meals and perfumed pillows for the weary shoulders of men. I was overcome with loneliness and homesickness, smelling in my fancy the air of al-Yamama, the white flowers of the waterwheels that close their petals in sleep of an evening, and the whispering of the palm fronds to the first stars in the night.

The breeze from the Almería hills tasted of dried plums. The trees still sang in loud, ringing tones. This time it was a gentle, swaying melody that drove me to snap my fingers and bob my head along to its music. Should I buy my food from the market or content myself with whatever Ma'in had prepared for our dinner?

I resolved that when I arrived at my room I would take down the pot of honey and devour its contents. Enjoy it, Mazid of Najd, and stop pining after it without tasting on the orders of some superstitious fancy of parallels and resemblances, like the desert Arabs before Islam who made a god of dates and then, when they were hungry, ate it. Cast aside myths and fancies, for a Voyager has nothing but his good sense.

I had found a shortcut to the boardinghouse that went around the Almería marketplace and led directly to the gates of Hamdouna's. But when I approached, I found a great hullabaloo, and a group of men standing by a princely carriage, with sturdy wheels and plush seats. It had a roof held up on poles, from which hung great green shining curtains. There were two Ethiopian grooms, and the carriage was drawn by two powerful mules with big heads. I thought at the outset that it belonged to one of the Umayyad princesses or perhaps a silk merchant, as the men standing by the carriage were muscular, with expensive embellished clothing and mustaches waxed and turned up at the ends like the dandies of Baghdad. I had the sense of having seen them before. Were they new tenants at Hamdouna's boardinghouse? Were they the retinue of one of the Marwani princesses who had sent for her silk garments?

I went into the passageway. My room was the first door on the left. My curiosity tempted me to walk a few paces down the corridor to peek around the corner of the inner colonnade, but at the last moment I refrained. No matter: if I opened the door to my room fully, it would show me a great deal of the inner courtyard, the fountain, and the columns of the colonnade, and also Hamdouna's usual seat. Ma'in would definitely bring me news of the prestigious visitors who had turned the street upside down. No sooner had I taken my first steps into the passageway than I heard Hamdouna's voice arguing with someone in a loud, commanding tone. When she heard the door to my room, she cried, "Come here, Mazid! We need an impartial judge! Come and hear us both out!"

I adjusted my turban and nervously went to where she usually sat. She was stiff and straight in her seat, a thin older man by her side, two women seated on the couch by them. Swatches of silk lay by them, purple, sea blue, crimson, and gold, rippling and bright.

Times and places converged. For a moment, I was stolen away from the place, and was forced to clutch at the doorknob. Hair like the curtains of night, shining daggers, a neck like an urn of silver . . . could it be? Was it really Zahira?

# The Fleeting Scent of the Dog Rose

It was none other. I could never mistake her, not in a thousand years away from Baghdad. Was I now seeing her in all the beauties of the world, or was it her shade that had revealed itself to me?

When Hamdouna saw that I had stilled, standing fixedly at the end of the corridor like an idiot, she became insistent. "Come, smartly dressed Arab, and tell us your opinion of what you think is best! This man"—she gestured to the thin man—"insists that blue suits the complexion of this fair lady."

Zahira was sitting there in all her alluring glory, having divested herself of her veils, and her hair hung loose and free as she perched on the edge of the seat. There was an old woman with her, watching her mistress's face and gauging what colors best suited her, while Hamdouna's effete boy was rushing hither and yon, bringing more swatches. There were not only pieces of silk, but shining caftans, attractive women's slippers in colors matching the caftans, scarves, belts, and head wraps. I moved toward them with faltering steps, trying to keep some semblance of composure. Everyone looked toward me, but I could not tear my eyes away from her. She gave me a fleeting glance, then looked a little closer, as though remembering my visage. Then she waved her hand carelessly, with the air of one who drew glances like flies wherever she went, and shooed them away lightly. I know not how I seemed, although I must have given the impression of some lunatic or fool, a far cry from the self-possessed young man who had recited his poetry at the house of al-Hashimi. Did she recall me at all?

I drew the curtains of pretended learning over my perturbation, putting on the airs and graces of an intellectual. I managed to catch my breath and said in a shaking voice, "The devout monk, Miskin al-Darimi, in Medina, recited poetry on the Lady of the Black Veil:

Go, ask the sweet beauty who wears the black veil,

O what have you done to the monk so ascetic?
He did his ablutions in peace, yea, until
You walked by the mosque and thus turned him heretic!
By the faith of the Prophet, O please do not kill
Your worshipper, with his great love so frenetic.

I made my tone deliberately musical on the last verse, in hopes that she might cast her memory back some years to Baghdad, when I had recited the poem of al-Asha. She contemplated me with the shadow of a smile on her face. It melted my heart. I said, "The one who wears the garment is the one who chooses the color. The dignity of the self, it is said, is its pleasure. Therefore, let the one who shall wear it decide."

Zahira straightened in her seat. She seemed about to speak, then thought better of it and fell silent. I recalled the face of the thin old man sitting at Hamdouna's side: it was the same grim-faced fellow who had ridden by her side on his mule. He stared at me and quirked his lips derisively. "God forbid we be guided by fancy."

Hamdouna cried out, "How lovely! Would you write down for us, O fair-faced gentleman, your verses on paper that I might give them to the girls to embroider onto black silk abayas?"

Still breathless, I added, "There are a great many fine verses to embroider, including those that accompany Zahira's appearance before her audience:

You are the full moon of the house,
The musk that perfumes the halls;
The fleeting scent of the dog rose,
The flowers on the trees so tall;
With heels like ivory, you are
Like a tanbur breaking hearts all;
You are the throne of Solomon,
Full of wisdom both great and small;

You are the Holy Kaaba with
Its pilgrims, curtains, and its wall;
For love of you I am adrift:
In Paradise, or Hell to fall?

Zahira's smile broadened, while her companion murmured the last line with me and asked, "Are you from
Baghdad?" Zahira merely fluttered her lashes, glancing at me
from beneath them.

The older man seemed annoyed by their lack of formality
and their loud laughter. With a frown, he said, "There are
dozens of silk factories in Almería. Perhaps we came to you in
particular, Hamdouna, knowing the quality of your fabric and
the art of your design. But recall that when your garments are
wrapped around the figure of Zahira, news of you shall fly
about the caravans. Let us therefore have prices that are easy
on the purse."

"The silks and caftans of Hamdouna are worn by the
princesses of the Umayyad house," she responded with asper-
ity, in the tone of one who does not need to cast about for
an answer. "I have no need of caravans, God grant you long
life." Her tone turned respectful. "That said, you hold a special place in my heart and my mind, and now that you are in
the house of Hamdouna, I will not allow it but that you leave
well-pleased and satisfied."

They took to turning over each piece of silk and each garment and holding it up to Zahira's face and arms to gauge the
color against her complexion. I retreated to my room, staring
bemused at the honey pot. "Did you bring Zahira?" I asked it.
"Did you tear her from the depths of Baghdad and transport
her to Hamdouna's house? Will she settle in Almería, or is she
merely passing through?"

It appeared that she was still practicing her old profession. The grim-faced old man was with her, and the Ethiopian
grooms, and the slave girl musicians. I had not known that the

hateful old man poked his nose even into the colors of her clothing. Was he a jeweler polishing his gem?

She had sat gracefully enough on the seat. Still, she had seemed lackluster, unhappy. Was she jaded? Where was the bubbly coquetry that had stormed the room of al-Hashimi like a meteor shower?

I collapsed onto my bed, trying to get my breath back. Suddenly I heard a knocking on the door. Ma'in poked his head around it. "Shall I bring you your meal, master?"

"I want no meal tonight," I managed to say.

My disturbed demeanor and pale face appearing to worry him, he said, "Master, are you well?"

"Very well," I responded dismissively. "Just close the door after you."

He withdrew, still looking at me curiously. When he was gone, the room was a little dimmer. Its ghosts emerged in full force, pacing slowly toward the honey pot, chanting,

You are the full moon of the house,
The musk that perfumes the halls;
The fleeting scent of the dog rose,
The flowers on the trees so tall;
With heels like ivory, you are
Like a tanbur breaking hearts all;
You are the throne of Solomon,
Full of wisdom both great and small;
You are the Holy Kaaba with
Its pilgrims, curtains, and its wall;
For love of you I am adrift:
In Paradise, or Hell to fall?

## An Implicit Invitation

How deep within my breast was this woman ensconced! My infatuation with the girls of Jerusalem, or my affair with the ethereal Kahramana: what were these but variations on my painful passion for her? Shame on you, Mazid al-Hanafi, Voyager! You have been seduced by a strumpet who displays her charms to fleece men of their dinars. I was but one of hundreds who had fallen in love with her beauty. Or was it the Eternal Tempter who made her so fair in my sight? But I swear that just now, I glimpsed an implicit invitation in her eyes. The attraction of souls is a divine secret that exists in the world of astral bodies.

What should I do? Should I buy a padlock and place it next to the pot of honey to bring her to me? But my path might lead me to her. What was I to do? Should I consult Hamdouna? Had I started to fall into superstition, consulting fortune-tellers and magicians and charlatans? What befalls us when love overcomes us and steals our sanity, making us not only commit sins but excuse them? What was the name of this thing clamoring deep within me?

A Voyager is a falcon, only inhabiting the most forbidding peaks, never stooping to meat previously tasted by other predators. But this was Zahira, a mountain peak: who should have her? Had not Hassan the Egyptian in Baghdad told me that she had refused to join the harem of the palace of al-Qadir bi-Allah, and that she had withheld her favors from al-Bouhi and entered into a sham marriage with one of her musicians to keep away the men who desired her? When I had seen her at the house of al-Hashimi, she had been in her full splendor, her beauty painful. But today, when I approached her, she was merely a beauty, not a thunderbolt. There was a shadow beneath her eyes and her face was darkened by the sun; her chin was long and slightly pointed; her shoulders were sagging. Had it been my imagination that fabricated her? Paradoxically, this only increased my ardor. She now resembled the housewives you might see in the courtyard of their houses, cooking and clattering about in the company of their small children. What kind of house would Zahira run through with her children around her?

I stilled when I thought this. I was a Voyager. I could not be lured by a woman who cavorts in the arms of men. I started to calm down when I called Zahira such names, as though I were throwing mud at her! How else could I heal of the beauty of this woman who has but to pass by the trees to make them sing?

I waited out the night alone in my room, fearing the press of questions about my silence and pale face. But I resolved to ask after her, come the dawn.

In the morning, I waited in my room until I heard Hamdouna instructing the men bringing the cocoons to enter. I emerged and greeted her, standing at the door of my room and expecting her to invite me for a glass of milk and some conversation. "May your morning be of silk that always brings freshness and beauty to the house of Hamdouna!"

"Good morning, desert Arab enamored of the lady of the black veil!"

I froze. Was she referring to yesterday's incident, or merely extrapolating? I did not evade her, for this was a woman with whom feigning indifference and pretending sagacity would gain nothing. With a gusty sigh, I said, "Do you know that the woman sliding over that seat yesterday is the loveliest songstress in Baghdad? She captivated all who lived there with the sweetness of her voice and her beauty."

In her proud way, she said, "Yes, I know. This is the first factory she came to in Almería. Our fame has reached Baghdad." Then she added slyly, the tattoo flashing on her chin, "And I know that Zahira has stolen the hearts of many men." Ah! Here it was. It was no use. I would come to the point. There was no way to be indirect with her.

"Silk brought Zahira," I said. "The flag brought me to your house. What is the thing that may keep someone in my life without disappearing? Is it a padlock?"

She raised her eyebrows, wisdom flitting across her face. "It has nothing to do with the image of what brought her.

Rather, it has to do with the intention within your heart. If you bring a padlock and lock it with the intent to stay, it will do what you brought it to do. The world around you is a set of messages, hints, indications. Those who read them and use their intellect to interpret them are saved." She bowed her head slightly. The sunlight had crept into the hallway, and I could see her wrinkles and the depths of her eyes, shining a sharp blue among the traces of her kohl. "Arab of the fair face," she said, "before locking the padlock, wait and think fully. You might bring a devil or a jackal into your house, making your life a misery, and ending you. Be patient. Wisdom dictates that you think well on it, for the law of parallels and resemblances is an obedient servant that only brings what you command, without asking if it is good or bad for you." If only I had listened to what Hamdouna had said that morning within the walls of her house, and waited.

Hamdouna did not chatter as was her wont, but excused herself to go to the silk workshop inside, leaving me standing there without my glass of milk.

The smell of Almería's sea was spilling over Zahira's breast even now. I breathed the same air as she, in a city whose walls were the color of bolts of silk. I went to the mosque, not expecting to find many people there, only the cries of the little boys going from one discussion circle to the next until they had learned a set portion of the Qur'an. My destination was the libraries of the "jewel of the world," Cordoba. I had been told that the caliph al-Hakam al-Marwani had had four hundred thousand books in his library; were they still there? He had paid a thousand gold dinars for the *Aghani* of al-Isfahani!

Whenever I made to leave Almería, I was held back by some new occurrence. Should I go to the market and buy a padlock? Why are you keeping me here, Almería? I am the crane who circles on high! Why do cities always set traps for me? Every time, a temptation more shameless than the last to keep me there? I should have been in Cordoba days ago! What was I doing here?

Still, perhaps it was a good thing that I had been kept here to avoid some evil that awaited me in Cordoba. I had heard its people described as "like a camel—screaming if you lighten its load, screaming if you weigh it down, so inconsistent that you never know what will please them or what will upset them." The captain had told me that entire markets had sprung up and stores opened in Almería—indeed, all over Andalusia— selling the merchandise looted by the common people and the thieves from the Umayyad city of al-Zahraa and the Amiri city of Zahira: carpets, silver, cushions . . . even the windows and the lanterns had been uprooted from homes and sold, for during the Fitna of Cordoba, everything had been looted. Heaven preserve the books.

I must tell Ma'in to prepare for our visit to Cordoba and arrange for a large caravan whose owner enjoyed a good reputation, for the road to Cordoba was perilous and set about with *fitna* and spies. Sulayman ibn al-Hakam, or al-Musta'in bi-Allah, the Umayyad caliph, could not abide those who came to him from Khayran's Almería, especially now that there were rumors of Khayran being in contact with the exiled Prince "al-Muayyad" Hisham II, and corresponding with him as well. The Berbers in Cordoba were also feared by the common folk, and two horses had only to neigh belligerently at each other for the matter to devolve into an uprising against them, so set against them were the people; but the Berbers exerted admirable self-control and forbade the rash members of their community and their slaves from raising a hand to any Andalusian.

I would tell Ma'in to seek without delay a caravan heading to Cordoba the following week, and I would have to find some way to deal with the passions in my breast. I must wake from this amorous stupor of the mind, and save Mazid al-Hanafi

434

from drowning in a honey pot. This was what I intended: but Fate had other plans.

The imam had called for the start of prayer when the captain turned to me from where he stood in the front. Quickly, he hurried back several rows to stand beside me and whisper, "I have found someone who wants your books."

I was still repulsed by his drooping eyelids and his unevenly pigmented cheeks, with hair growing out of some places and not others. When my silence lengthened, he pressed, "Do you still have them?"

Heavens! Was he still speaking of the matter? I said curtly, "Only a few, and those I use. Most have departed with the caravans."

Before the imam could start the prayers, he blurted, "The Citadel wants your books."

He must have seen me blink and swallow. Had my message reached Khayran al-Amiri?

I was grateful that the imam lingered over the prayers, which allowed me to collect myself somewhat and think over what the captain had suggested. But at the doors of the Great Mosque, I found the captain lying in wait for me again. I promised to meet him the next day, never knowing that the Fates were laughing at me, for at that very moment, new chapters of my journey were being inscribed on the Preserved Tablet.

I left the captain behind and elected to go to the sea through the Almería marketplace, the road being shorter and easier. Had the captain's invitation been due to the message I had given to the captain of the guard? What was his relation to the inhabitants of the Citadel? Could I trust him, or was he a gossip and spiller of secrets?

I had no answers to these questions. Still, I looked carefully at all the stores, as was my wont, hoping to find booksellers in some hidden corner I had not seen before. I parried the insistent invitations of the shopkeepers to come and view their wares, and their stares at this young man traversing their market, one with a false smile, another with a nod that might have been a greeting. Suddenly a soft but piercing voice came to my ears. "O Miskin al-Darimi! Lover of the Lady with the Black Veil!"

I immediately recognized one of the veiled women as Zahira. My heart saw her before my eyes did, and I approached her like one compelled. She stood there in a blue veil that showed no scrap of her: she did well, for if she walked through this marketplace unveiled, she would start a riot that would rival the Fitna of Cordoba. As for her slave girl, whom she called Bustan, she only wore a scrap of fabric about her cheeks. Coyly, Zahira went on, "O desert Arab, you trader in the city who has sold his goods, what of al-Darimi? Is he still consumed by ardor?"

Mazid al-Hanafi! Is this the oft-spoken-of moment the goshawk sights its prey? Should I seize the moment? Pleasure is only had by the brave! Something ran wild in my head. I no longer saw her face beneath its veil, but her long, delicate fingers as she danced with the silver daggers. I stepped closer to breathe in her scent. She pushed back her veil a little, showing part of her face. "I ask God never to torment this face in fire," I blurted, then rushed on, "Never hold daggers in your hands as you dance, for your glance is a dagger, your figure is a spear, your silence is speech, and your song is a choir of angels." I could not go on, for the words stopped in my throat. I felt I had laid myself bare before her.

Coyly, she drew her veil over her face again. Fearing she would leave and take the honey pot out of my sight, I babbled, "Do you want pure honey? I know a man who sells the best honey this side of . . ." I trailed off, biting my lip. I took a few steps forward through the marketplace. To my astonishment, the women followed me without hesitation. I had entered the market alone, and was leaving with the most beautiful woman ever to tread the earth of Almería and her slave girl. Bustan seemed displeased and never left off whispering angrily in her ear, but Zahira paid her no heed, tripping behind me with her blue veil fluttering in the breeze, the trees singing around us.

"What brings you to Almería?" she whispered, following my footsteps.

"What brings you?" I asked her, avoiding any mention of love or passion. What is parallel comes together, and parallels and resemblances, and every whit of mumbo jumbo to make me into a great fool in front of her.

"Oh," she sighed, "there is no living in Baghdad any longer, what with the Ayyarin gangs, and the soldiers, and the Rajilat al-Hanabila. The caliph can do nothing against them. He merely waves his al-Qadir document, which none heed." She was silent, walking on. "But I am only here for a space. I am going on to Cordoba, for it is said that the Umayyad caliph has secured the city well."

"I too am only in the market seeking a caravan to Cordoba," I said quickly. "If only I could be with you in the same caravan, I would hear the song of the trees . . ."

"And my song as well," she smiled.

It was as though the gates of Heaven had opened. "I saw you playing with the silver daggers and was stabbed withal. I heard you singing at the Ashmuni Festival in Baghdad, and it touched my soul—"

Her slave girl elbowed her nervously. "On the soul of the daughter of the Prophet, Fatima al-Zahraa," she said, "stop speaking with him!"

*Zahraa* means "flower," and so I replied, "There is no flower in the universe but you."

At the honey store, the shopkeeper took to spinning bizarre yarns about the honey he sold: that he had brought it from the wild mountains around Granada, where a monk lived among the rocks and would recite verse sixty-eight of the

Sura of al-Nahl—"*And thy Lord inspired the bee, saying: Choose thou habitations in the hills and in the trees and in that which men thatch*"—whereupon a beehive would appear, filled with bees, nectar, and honey. "Do you want jar honey or reed honey?" he asked.

"I know jar honey," I said, "but what is reed honey?"

"It is honey heated in the sun," he said, "then poured into hollow reeds, which are stored for days in a cool place until it is hard once again. Then the mouth of the reed is stoppered, and if you wish to set it out at a table, the reed is beaten against the ground to free a reedlike pole made of honey, which can be cut with knives over a pastry or loaf."

I said, puffing out my chest, "We'll take it all."

A male never spares anything to make a display before his female, which includes dinars. I bought her four pots of honey and two reeds of honey, swallowing my protests at the greed of the shopkeeper, who charged me an exorbitant price upon seeing the way I stared at Zahira and obeyed her every whim. I undid my money belt and paid handsomely, while Zahira, accustomed to the gifts of monarchs and of the highborn, looked about her unaffected. I remained captivated, with some of that lightheadedness and impulsiveness that comes to lovers in the presence of their beloved. I made the excuse of carrying the honey to her house to spend more time by her side, and to find out where she was staying. I was reckless and unstoppable: this time nothing would hold me back, and I would not close my hands to the heavenly spring pouring into them. All the while, Bustan was worried, looking around nervously and whispering in her ear, "We must go back. We must not be late."

I carried two pots and the honey seller's boy took the other two. Because he was a native of Almería, he guided us to the house she had rented upon her arrival, only two streets away from Hamdouna's. When we were almost at her lodgings, and I saw her opulent carriage with the green curtains at the door, she touched my hand with her fingertips. "This is far enough."

She added, "I will come to Hamdouna's in a few days to try on some silk abayas. We may see you there." Then, without any expression on her face, she left with hurried footsteps, followed by Bustan, who seemed mollified by the pots of honey. Was Zahira attempting to get rid of me, or was she making me a promise? But I was no longer seeking a caravan to take me out of Almería, for she was still holding me captive.

I spent my time wandering between the house and the mosque, passing the street where she lived in hopes of seeing her or seeing someone who saw her. I would not let her go this time, even if I had to kidnap her.

Ma'in could sense that I was changed, but said nothing. However, I began to see a conspiratorial gleam in his eye. He disappeared a great deal these days, for I regularly dismissed him from the room. I always warned him not to show his Berber origins before the Amiri guards. But he said, "Fear not, master! The Sanhaji are powerful now and have taken the city of Elvira by order of the caliph."

I understood nothing of what he said and cared not a whit for it. I would ask him later. I needed to be alone and gather myself. I closed the door and opened the crate, looking for a book to take me away from myself. I decided on *Ikhwan al-Safa*, but read one line and only stared at the rest.

"Let us go to the Alcazaba of my lord Khayran," said the captain the next morning, in a commanding tone, standing before Hamdouna's boardinghouse.

I trembled: what did he want? "Now?" I whispered.

He appeared not to have heard me. "Come," he said. "You appear distracted and not yourself. Did you not sleep well last night?" Then he asked, "Do you have any of your bits of paper with you now?"

The way he made light of my books irritated me. Perhaps this was what made me tell him, staring him hard in the eye, "Bits of paper are what we feed the cows. What I have are called books and manuscripts that are beyond the ignorant and the witless, and if the kings knew their value, they would fight us for them with swords. They contain knowledge and facts with the power to take hold of a man's heart, turn it this way and that as though within two fingers, and change it in the twinkling of an eye." I quoted from the Sura of al-Nahl: "*Be! And it is.*"

He made no answer to my tirade, merely waving his hand and staring into the road. "Give me some time," I added. "I shall bring some of them before we ascend to the Citadel."

I knelt before the crate, confused. What should I take, and what would be the humor of the recipients? I must avoid any book that touched upon anything heretical, lest it be burned to ash, and anything tasteless and uninspiring, which would make my buyer think less of me. I settled upon Ibn al-Haytham, the poetry collection *Hamasah*, compiled by Abu Tammam, and a manuscript I had bought in Fustat attributed to al-Farabi. I emerged to meet the captain, who was visibly irked and tired of waiting. Before I could reach him, he hurried ahead of me onto the path parallel to the port, which led upward and northward to the Citadel of Khayran.

The path led us to a wooden bridge on tall supports. Then we moved upward to a path of oddly colored stone with a reddish hue, different from the route taken by the *saqaliba* soldiers. Alongside us were many farmers' carts, pulled by donkeys and mules, some laden with pumpkins, some with pulses, and some with jars of milk and baskets of eggs. The captain told me that the farmers brought the first choice of everything to the Alcazaba of Khayran; after the Citadel had selected the best of it, they returned to sell the rest at the Almería market.

Our hurrying steps and smart clothing piqued the curiosity of the farmers and the guards. Most of the guards were soldiers I had seen in the discussion circles of the mosque—tall, powerfully built men with blue-black eyes like a cat's, which they narrowed at us when we passed. I drew the books into my chest warily, but I was not only fearful and apprehensive. The books had only brought me good things since I had encountered them, and here I was going to two good things—for *khayran* is the Arabic for "two good things."

In a great room, almost a hall, we found him sitting with a bowed head, an old man with a pale face that seemed never to have seen the sun and had remained youthful. His blue-black eyes still bore the recklessness of youth. But over his white-haired head, still with traces of his original red hair, there hung a pall of sorrow. When we stood before him, he first looked at the captain curiously, then back at me, before motioning to us both to be seated. I bowed respectfully. "Good morning to my lord Khayran."

"This is not your lord Khayran," the captain whispered.

I sat, silent with awe. This haughty hand motion was only for kings and sultans. Even my lord al-Hashimi had not gestured so. I was overcome with fear. Who was this man, scowling like an abandoned palace? He was not alone. Behind one shoulder, head lowered respectfully, was a clean-shaven old man with white hair and blue eyes, like his guardian angel.

The man asked me, expressionless, "What books and manuscripts have you? Have you reliable books, or are you one of the traders who have sullied manuscripts with the additions and anecdotes of the riffraff and the common people, who have copied them in this way and that?" He turned to the old man behind him. "Nowadays, we find foreigners copying books without understanding the language, resulting in truly bizarre things—you find one line with the proper diacritics and one without. It ruins the enjoyment of a book." Then he lowered his head again, never losing his noble mien. "I care nothing for being the descendant of the Umayyads. Our ancestors are the fathers of our bodies but the philosophers are the fathers of our souls, which makes me a son of the philosophers."

The captain, still standing with his hands clasped, volunteered to hand him the books in my possession. He took to leafing through them. Then he motioned us to go, muttering, "I shall surely call upon you at a later date. Go now."

He shooed us away as you shoo cats from a banquet. I dared not ask the captain who he was, but realized this man had definitely been a monarch for a long time.

Zahira only came to try on her clothing after a week had passed. I had taken to leaving the door to my room open after the afternoon prayers, waiting for her. I no longer found great joy in leafing through Aristotle. I would read one line, then a great wave would crash behind me, sweeping me and tossing me to the hem of Zahira's veil. What had she done to me? Distracted, scattered, unable to speak, abandoning my habit of reading books or going over the poetry I had memorized to be of use to me at gatherings and on paper. Instead, I now went to Hamdouna on the pretext of showing her Arab poetry to embroider on silk abayas and caftans. When I went to her for the fourth time, Hamdouna said, "What is the matter with you, Mazid? What ails you? You are like a man possessed."

Hamdouna, who had seen as many lovers as there were white hairs on her head, whispered slyly to me, like one telling a secret, "Zahira of Baghdad will come today to try on the garments she ordered. My girls work on weaving and sewing them every day from dawn to midnight, as she is in a hurry and seems to be leaving for Cordoba soon."

I don't know what stole my words at that moment—the rashness they attribute to youth, or the madness they attribute to love, or perhaps the softness of Shammaa of the House of Wael that I saw in Hamdouna—but I said, "I pray you, Hamdouna, make her stay."

Hamdouna laughed sadly. "Mazid! I swear, I see only that your love for her has addled your senses!"

Zahira arrived when it was nearly sunset, accompanied by Bustan and the scowling old man instead of her entire retinue. I glimpsed him hurrying after her, looking around him curiously at the courtyard of Hamdouna's house. When he drew level with Zahira beneath the orange tree, he appeared disgusting and shriveled, for her imposing figure was a handspan taller than he. Was this the moment that God had decided to make her mine?

"If Zahira comes to you," I had entreated, "tell her that the young Arab man, the bookseller, is pining for you." That was the last thing I had said to Hamdouna. I had not imagined that Hamdouna would rush with girlish glee to work toward our engagement. I never stopped her. If the days had chosen to bring us together, it was a consummation devoutly to be wished.

This was before events unfolded before me like a runaway horse, twisting and turning and throwing me and Zahira into one room and locking the door, while outside, the rest of the guests in the boardinghouse celebrated our wedding.

## Youth and Zahira

What happened after that I only remember in flashes. The thundering of my heart in my breast, my chest heaving with labored breaths. I recall that the ireful old man raised his eyebrows in stunned mockery, while Zahira threw her head back with a ringing laugh before sitting back upon her seat and appearing to gather herself. She wiped away the tears of laughter on her face and put on a serious expression. "I accept." She did not wait for her companion, the old man, to respond; she merely continued, "My bride price is four pots of honey, already paid."

At that moment, stunned, looking from one face to another, I discovered that the man with her was only an empty abaya, with no real man inside it. He was akin to a fly whisk with which Zahira dismissed the men who clustered around her, when I had thought him a jeweler polishing his gem. "There is no time for foolery!" he cried. "The caravan leaves on Tuesday, and today is Thursday. When will you get married?"

That was when Hamdouna (or perhaps it was Ma'in) cried, "Let the wedding be on Saturday!"

But Zahira, still pressing her lips together to hide her laughter, said, "No, tomorrow. It is Friday, a blessed day." The horse was galloping over the gravel and the thorns and my passions and the fields of violets. I could not forget that Zahira looked at me coyly and said in a firm, unwavering voice, "My marriage will be in the style of Kairouan and Andalusia, and I shall be like the women of Andalusia." This meant that she had the right to part with me, divorce me, and dismiss me from her life at any moment.

I cared not. I never stopped. I did not understand the import of what she said. The runaway horse gave me no opportunity to catch my breath. I remember that Hamdouna cried out, "Congratulations on your wedding!" and let out an ululation. Everything else is a blur and fragments of images: laughter, anger, disapproval, sleepy eyes, Ma'in and the effete boy dancing with joy in the courtyard, and Hamdouna's girls clapping in time to the music. Zahira disappeared from sight: the Lord had put before me a barrier and behind me a barrier and above me a barrier. Truly, nothing drew me in but my fate, for much occurred after that.

The dawn of my wedding day I took to muttering, "I am Mazid al-Hanafi of Najd, the secret crane, who follows the imam of his intellect. What will I do tonight?" What should I do now that I had been chosen as a Voyager, as one of those who hold in their breast the torch of this nation and of their intellect, hiding it in the cage of their ribs for fear of those who follow texts literally, a bearer of books as the Jews bore their tablets?

I, the guardian of the books of the Voyagers, must plant them in every mosque and in every library and with every learned and knowledgeable person so they become not extinct. What would the Voyagers do to me, I who was sworn to secrecy and circumspection, to avoiding noise and attention, suspicion and interest, and to seeking the shadows, but had instead brought a ball of flame and silver into my very lap? This woman whose presence is announced by the singing trees, who is watched by every eye with gasps at her loveliness, who is followed by a cloud of distracted and captivated minds, who slices at heartstrings with her silver daggers. What was I doing? What was I about to do? I, al-Hanafi, the silent and mysterious man, whose face Shammaa of the House of Wael covered with a veil for fear of the evil eye, had invited every eye to my garden. Was there still time to flee?

All these questions clamored in my head like low whispers from behind a wall, part of which I could see and most of which I could not. I could barely hear them any more.

My grandfather used to say, "If something perplexes you, give it time, and wait before making a decision." But the runaway horse was galloping and stopped for nobody. Where would it fling me?

I rushed toward her, my soul a little resentful of the past and the lonely nights without a companion. I wanted to drink her in, wholly, making her mine and part of me. I should hide her away from prying eyes and wrap her in my abaya. No one, no matter who, could glimpse a hair of her henceforward.

## The Moon That Lights the Dusk, and the Spice Trader's Musk

I did not have to think about choosing my woman, nor the time or place of the wedding: Fate brought her to me. Is making things easy the sign of divine benediction? An overpowering flood that carries everything with it, with no way to resist? Or did they lead me to it like a sheep to the slaughter?

Hamdouna took over the arrangements like a step she was duty-bound to complete after mediating my engagement to Zahira. "You can get married here in my boardinghouse," she said. "Let it ring out with the joy it has not seen since the last time I was married! We will sing and dance with the wind and the trees, for there has been no music in this place for a long time. Next to this fountain, surrounded by jasmine and sweet basil, you will be married, so that your life together may remain as fertile as a spring."

I hurried to her and kissed her head, then gave her some gold dinars to pay for the necessary arrangements. She feigned reluctance at first, but soon placed the coins in a box around her waist. "Tomorrow, after the dawn prayers," she instructed, "go to a bathhouse and prepare yourself. I advise you to go to a luxury bathhouse. If you leave the boardinghouse and go to the right, you'll find one on this very street. It will lead onto the square where the farmers arrive when they come down from the Citadel of Khayran. Buy sweet basil from them to put in your bathwater, and buy walnuts. They polish the teeth. Also, buy apples for yourself." She gave me a sly glance. "Your marriage to this wild mare is tomorrow and you must be a virile stallion."

Then, she added, "Ask for the bathhouse of Nuzhat al-Mushtaq, and tell the owner, 'I come from Hamdouna, and my wedding is tonight,' and he will take care of you. Then, when you are done, and have performed the Friday prayers, go to the gold market. Seek out the Jewish gold merchant Yaaqoub, purchase a bracelet and a ring, and make sure they are costly. Do not make much of what she said yesterday about jars of honey: jewelry wraps itself around women's hearts before it winds about their necks. After all this, come back to me, and you shall find everything ready and waiting for the fair-faced Arab."

446

How could love make me so friendly and docile, like a lamb trotting by its mother's udder? That night I spent in the company of Shammaa of the House of Wael, who stayed with me until dawn, speaking with me, but never looked me in the face the way she had when I insisted on her blessing to go to Baghdad. Was she unhappy with me? I also saw Grandfather, but he was blurred, like a cloud of light appearing in a dream, then disappearing. He was still bent over his papers, writing and making notes. I approached him as usual, spying on what he was writing. It was a letter to Khayran; however, he did not call him al-Saqalibi, but "the Umayyad." Grandfather only left me with the break of dawn. When I woke, my eyes remained fixed on the ceiling. Why was he writing a letter to Khayran and calling him "the Umayyad," when there is no love lost between Khayran and Umayyad House of Marawan?

Early the next morning, I wrapped my new clothes in a bundle and headed for the square in the center of western Almería. The farmers had returned from the Citadel and had formed a circle, the bleating of their sheep filling the square. They were displaying their harvests upon wooden carts spread out with straw, on which were piled early apricots and apples, jars of fresh milk, and earthenware pots for butter and buttermilk. The peasant women were cheerful, giving you their fruit with a smile, the children on their breasts also smiling at the buyers. The men contented themselves with yelling and crying their wares with musical chants.

In the sprightly, joyous morning, I bought the sweet basil, walnuts, and apples in the square, and brought them to the Nuzhat al-Mushtaq bathhouse. In the steam and the scent of soap, I went over my dream of yesterday. Was Shammaa upset at my marriage? I had rejected all the women of al-Yamama, slim and stunted and sweet, whom she presented to me. What could I see in them but a fetter tying me to her? I had to escape the ropes of fear that tied me to her as a little boy. She feared I would roam too far and play with the older boys who would pluck the roses from my cheeks—and now here was Zahira of Persia, who had plucked me entire.

I knew Zahira was not the woman mothers normally want for their sons, perpetually surrounded by a clamor, possessed of great charms and freely displayed assets, so strikingly fair of face that she prolonged the life of all who looked upon her, with hands of pure butter made only for being painted with henna and dancing, not for kneading dough or carrying children.

The Friday sermon for that day was about the sedition of made-up, flighty women who tempted men. "Whom does he mean by that?" I muttered. I had not seen anyone in the market but exhausted peasant women with chapped hands. Whom did he mean by "the swaying women," who bore sin with them? Had Zahira passed by him, or was the Devil starting to play his games in my head?

The gold market was behind the bathhouse, not far away. It was made up of several stores in a row, in a street branching off from the marketplace. Only two of these sold jewelry, while the other sold perfumes, bolts of silk, and soaps, scrubs, and other bath paraphernalia, in addition to gold and ornaments. Hamdouna's Jewish friend brought out a bracelet for me to look at, scrutinizing me before setting the price. He seemed an experienced shopkeeper, with whom you feel familiar after exchanging a few words, and who speaks to you like an old friend. He gave me a small chair of straw and a glass of rose-water, and brought out a piece of silk with a valuable bracelet inside, inscribed with the words "Nothing Is Eternal but God" and two snakes with intertwined heads. "It's for a bride," I said. "I won't give her snakes and a line usually said at funerals."

He took the bracelet back, realizing I was buying a present for a woman I had already captured. "I have just the thing for your bride," he said, "but I don't know if you can afford it."

Ah, the usual traps set by a trader for his prey! "Let's see it," I said airily.

He ascended a wooden staircase leading to an opening in the ceiling of his store. I heard his footsteps above me; then his thin legs descended once more. He had a blue silken bag in his hand. He pushed the door slightly to, lit a lantern, and lifted it. With his other hand, he untied the strings of the bag. He pulled out a magnificent necklace, in the shape of a crown, but to be worn around the neck. It was studded with dark red rubies, worked in gold, edged with pearls that glittered like tears. My eyes had never seen the like, not even at the gold-smiths of Baghdad.

The goldsmith watched my expression; then, with the fire of a man describing a pampered daughter to an amorous suitor, he said, "These stones are brought from Persia, rare rubies scattered around a cave with a shrine whose fire never dies. It is guarded by a great snake. If anyone dares approach the fire, it attacks him and squeezes the life out of him. The drops of blood of these men turn into rubies and are scattered on the mountainside, and only the brave can acquire them, those who take their hearts in their hands for courage, as we say, and creep up the mountainside in the scant moments between the dawning of the light and the rising of the sun. That is the time when the snake drowses for a while. They collect these stones and sell them to jewelers for exorbitant sums."

"Are we back to snakes again?" I mocked, trying to belittle the necklace and reduce the price, confronted with this bizarre tale concocted by the jeweler.

"These rubies pulse with life," he said. "They feel and hear, and bring good fortune."

He did not tell me that they also brought ill luck and ruin, for they were drops of the blood of the men whose dreams and adventures had turned to stone, transformed into a necklace to be wound around the neck of some beauty. I willingly paid the price he asked of me, for all I could see was the necklace around Zahira's neck, and the surprise and excitement on her face. I longed to see her without the usual abstracted, careless air that made you feel she was only passing through, burdened with thoughts that stole her away and left her barely connected to the material world.

I made my way back to the boardinghouse. As soon as I turned onto the street, there was a welcoming hullabaloo, people I had never seen before coming and going at the gate. When they caught sight of me, they smiled broadly and set to whispering. The street outside the gate was covered with reed mats; the ground beneath the inner colonnade was covered with rich Indian carpets. Beneath the orange trees were couches furnished with brightly colored pillows, and before every couch was a low table bearing dishes of nuts and dried fruit. Around the fountain were set pitchers of water flavored with mint and lime and rose. There were earthenware pitchers of milk as well, covered with silk kerchiefs with beaded edges.

No sooner had I taken my first step inside the door than Hamdouna's girls swarmed me, singing and ululating and clicking wooden castanets. They were singing foreign songs. I knew not if they were *saqaliba* songs or Berber, but they filled my heart with gladness. In the room, Ma'in and the effete boy had opened the windows, aired the carpets in the sun, polished the mother-of-pearl furniture, shined the mirrors, filled the pitchers with rosewater, and prepared new bedcovers and a quilt perfumed with bitter oranges. I felt the desire to run away from all this to meet Mazid al-Hanafi and ask him, "Are you serious in this undertaking? The husband of a strumpet who might kick you out of her tent at any moment?" Was this truly the room I would share with Zahira this night?

After the afternoon prayers, the guests began to troop in: friends of Hamdouna's, the girls from the workshop, and the neighbors. Even the bathhouse owner, some of his boys, and the Jewish goldsmith had accepted Hamdouna's invitation. However, there was no sign of Zahira or her people. She had not even sent her things on to my room. Was she making a mockery of me and Hamdouna, and the Jewish goldsmith, and everybody, even now on her way to Granada, laughing her fill with the frowning old man? To tell the truth, this fancy did not frighten me as much as the voice in my depths that wished it would come to pass, rescuing me from the cocoon of silk. But before I could think too much on it, I heard the sound of the musicians singing from the end of the street:

You are the full moon of the house,
The musk that perfumes the halls;
The fleeting scent of the dog rose,
The flowers on the trees so tall;
With heels like ivory, you are
Like a tanbur breaking hearts all;
You are the throne of Solomon,
Full of wisdom both great and small.

Curse them! Could they find no other song than this, the one they used to introduce Zahira to be devoured by the eyes of men? I ran out, shouting, "Stop your music immediately! The sheikh who is to marry us is here! Shut your mouths out of respect to him!" With loud, brazen laughter, they came inside.

Zahira was dressed in ribbed red silk from head to toe, and I could not see her face. I took her hand and pressed it to know if it was she. She whispered, "I am afraid. I am nervous." I wanted to ask her, "Is it your first time? Have you done this before?" Was she a virgin or not? Was she a slave or a free woman? But the sheikh who married us took care of these questions. When we signed the marriage contract, I found out that Zahira was free, but not a virgin, and was twenty-six years of age. I soon found myself signing the Andalusian marriage contract, with a note on the bottom,

The husband, Mazid ibn Abdullah al-Thaqif al-Hanafi, pledges to his wife Anahid bint Nadir Shah al-Karamani, now that he is her lawful husband, seeking her affection and to gladden her heart, not to marry another while she remains his wife, not to couple with a slave woman while she remains his wife, and not to take another slave woman as the mother of his son. If he should do any of this, the new woman taken either as a wife or through remarriage is forthwith divorced, while the slave woman or the mother of the son are forthwith free women. He pledges not to injure her in her person or take any of her possessions, nor be absent from her for more than six months unless it be on the pilgrimage to Mecca, not to move her from place to place without her consent, and not to prevent her from visiting her family, and if he were to do any of the aforementioned, she is forthwith freed from this contract and all of its obligations.

The only thing I paid attention to in all of the previous was that Zahira's real name was Anahid. When I had signed and sealed the bottom of the contract, they slipped it beneath Zahira's veil to put her fingerprint on it and keep it. Was I a ram that Zahira had bought, and she kept the contract? Before the demons of suspicion could take over my head, the musicians began to ululate, beat the drums, play the castanets, and sing, "Highborn am I; I lift my garment's hem in pride at this. / I give my love my favor, and each passerby a kiss!"

When we lifted our heads, the place was packed. The company was all present, enthused at the promise of food and song, caring nothing for a desert Arab married to a Persian strumpet who he had thought was named Zahira, but was in truth Anahid.

There was a corner prepared for us: two neighboring seats surrounded by pillows and baskets of apples, and with strings of sweet basil and jasmine set over the seats like a canopy. No sooner had Zahira sat on her seat than the women called upon her to come and dance. My blood froze as the questions I had discarded came flooding back. She would dance? She would show her charms through the slits in her clothing? Her upper thighs would appear, smooth and shining? I felt myself grow pale, and my breathing grew labored like a rat in the sights of a cat. Although the colors of my face changed, she did not hold back. Instead, she was laying down her first law: she was no blushing virgin wrapped in her garments sitting docilely at my feet.

She danced, but did not sway overmuch: she merely rose, wearing her respectable garment, and took a turn with quick steps around the fountain, approaching me and hanging a necklace of jasmine around my neck as the musicians sang in their feminine voices,

O lovely one, O pampered love
Rebuff me not, withhold you naught;
Have mercy on my loving heart,
Let coldness ne'er enter your thought.

With the evening prayer call, the guests began to disperse. Hamdouna asked us to circle the fountain seven times as if it were the Holy Kaaba, in anticipation of the pilgrimage to Mecca that she said we would undertake together the next year. We did so, ecstasy filling my limbs. An entire year with Zahira, a year with its four seasons, to be concluded in Mecca, thanking my Lord for His blessings, in which I would hand out the Voyagers' books to the pilgrims, whence they would spread like the light of the sun to every nook and cranny.

When we had finished the circling, we went to my room and closed the door on us, the honey pot and I. I wanted to spend my first night contemplating her. She lay down exhausted on the bed, spread out her hair on the pillow, and said, "Recite poetry to me." I touched her mouth, which led down to her pointed chin, kissed her forehead, pressed my head into her neck, and slept.

## The Chick

When I woke, she was still sleeping, wearing a shift of white silk, hair lying in waves on the pillow. I brought my mouth close to her nostrils and plucked her breaths. They were regular, but hot. The water in the basin in the corner of the room was mixed with jasmine and orange blossoms. I poured the cold water over my body and dressed, staggering as I did so. I needed to perform a prolonged prayer of thanks. I needed a long conversation with my God and with Mazid.

I laid the expensive necklace by her head on the pillow and left the room quietly, leaving the door ajar. Ma'in waylaid me by the door: he had clearly been lying in wait for me. "Good morning, full of joys!"

"A thousand years of blessings upon you, Ma'in," I said.

"A man has been standing at the gate since the dawn prayers," he told me, "and says he wants to see you for an important matter."

It was only the captain, as I had guessed. "Citadel wants you," he said shortly, falling silent without giving details.

Oh no! Not on the morning after my wedding, the Citadel of Khayran! Had I come too close to the lion's den? I doubted that whoever passed there could escape unscathed. Too rashly had I sought a buyer in the Citadel of Khayran, and become like the man al-Mutanabbi describes:

> He who seeks to hunt the lion one day
> Becomes himself anon the lion's prey.

The captain took the road up to the palace, grim-faced. I tried to draw him out as to the reason for the summons, but he was sunk in a deep silence. Where was this hateful man taking me? Had they found out the heresy in the books, and wanted me as kindling? What bad luck! I had only spent one night with Zahira. We entered without being stopped by the guards, for they seemed to be familiar with my face. I looked around apprehensively. Would I walk out of here?

I found the mysterious nobleman in his hall, waiting for us. He was not sitting this time, but was pacing to and fro, bare-headed in a blue silk garment, with a ribbed belt around his waist that emphasized the shortness of his legs. No sooner did I approach with a greeting and a bow than he said, without returning my greeting, "I wanted to ask you, Mazid. It is said that Ali ibn Yahya, the astrologer, also known as Abu Mashar, had a great closet filled with books in his meeting room, which he named the Closet of Wisdom. People went there to learn from it, all paid for by Ali ibn Yahya. Do you know what became of that closet?"

I recalled the library of my lord al-Hashimi, which was a similar thing. "Do you mean," I ventured, "the library of the Hashimi Endowment in Baghdad?"

"No," he said. "That one we have heard of. I mean the library of Abu Mashar the astrologer. He was about to set off for Mecca, but knew nothing of the stars, so he stopped in the library and refrained from the pilgrimage, and learned the science of the stars, getting so deep into it that he lost his faith and turned atheist. That was the last of Abu Mashar's belief in Islam."

"We have heard nothing of this, my lord," I said truthfully, "but we do know that entering a library is like entering a land filled with lions and jackals. You must draw the sword of your intellect and fight them, and duel with every truth that approaches, or else you become the captive of a single truth and end up in the belly of the lions."

His eyes narrowed as he looked at me. Perhaps what I had said pleased him. He plucked Abu Tammam's *Hamasah* from a shelf, and said to me, "Do you know the story of Abu Tammam and Caliph al-Mutasim?"

I searched for the details in the corridors of my mind, which had been echoing since yesterday with the wooden castanets in the women's hands. "The poet Abu Tammam," I stammered, "was the pioneer innovator in poetry—"

He stopped me with a gesture of his hand. "I did not ask for his biography. I wanted his story in al-Mutasim's court, when he indited the following verse in praise of his son:

> He hath the courage of Amr al-Zubaydi—Knight of the
>     Arabs he;
> The munificence of Hatim al-Tai, the paragon of
>     generosity;
> He is like unto the meek Ahnaf ibn Qays in kindness
>     and docility;
> And hath th'intellect of Judge Ayas al-Mazini, known
>     for his sagacity.

Whereupon one of the ministers of al-Mutasim said, 'You have likened the Prince of the Faithful to a collection of Arab boors!'"

It appeared that he knew the story of Abu Tammam, but enjoyed hearing it and repeating it among his guests, as is the wont of the powerful and respected. I responded, "Yes! I recall the lines composed by Abu Tammam at that moment, with stunning presence of mind, there in the court of the caliph, in the same rhyme, in response to the envious minister:

> Blame me not for likening the prince's affability
> And courage and intellect to those lesser than he.
> The Lord hath likened Himself to a lantern in a
>     simile,
> And that hath not a fraction of His luminosity."

The mysterious nobleman nodded, well pleased. "Yes. You are correct. Abu Tammam is here referring to verse thirty-five of the Sura of al-Nur, '*Allah is the Light of the heavens and the earth. The Parable of His Light is as if there were a Niche and within it a Lamp: the Lamp enclosed in Glass: the glass as it were a brilliant star: Lit from a blessed Tree, an Olive, neither of the east nor of the west, whose oil is well-nigh luminous, though fire scarce touched it: Light upon Light! Allah doth guide whom He will to His Light.*'"

Who was this elderly man who knew so much and presumed to act like a theologian? Before I could give free rein to my imaginings and suspicions, the white-haired man with the piercing blue eyes who was always in his company and stood behind his shoulder turned to him and said, "Pay him for the books."

In his words and his gestures were the dignity of a sultan's lineage. Would the fierce, mysterious captain tell me who he was? I should find no better repository for *Ikhwan al-Safa* and al-Kindi.

I descended alone from the Citadel of Khayran with gold coins in my pockets bearing the inscription "Caliph Hisham al-Muayyad, AH 396." Money that had been coined in the era of the young caliph whose throne had been usurped. They called him "the chick" for his weakness and powerlessness. In his absence, wars and *fitna*s had broken out between the Marwanis and the Amiri Berber. Some said that Caliph al-Musta'in had had his throat slit, while others said he had escaped in disguise to Algeciras, and some said that he had fled to Almería and sought protection with Khayran al-Amiri. Could it be . . . ?

I trembled. What shores are you on, Mazid?

At home, Zahira had put on her makeup and appeared like a nymph who had just crept out of her sedan chair. "Would you like to take a turn about the streets of Almería?"

I took her hand. Let us see how the streets would receive me walking alongside my wife.

The old man was at the gate, the color of his eyes iridescent like a fly's wing. They narrowed, joining his big nose. He ignored me, only saying to Zahira, "Don't be late, Anahid."

It irritated me that he was acting as though I was not there. "Why does he call you by your Persian name?"

With a coy and meek glance, she said, "Anahid is my real name, but I call myself Zahira to call down the blessings of Fatima al-Zahraa, the daughter of the Prophet, that his house may protect me. It has kept so many calamities from striking me, and covered me with the veil of her protection. The Ayyarin would be facing me, about to kidnap me, but a veil would fall between us and they would not see me." She pulled her veil down over her face and leaned her head on my shoulder. "Al-Zahraa brought you to me."

She was wearing a gown of green silk the color of her delicate slippers, her face covered with a silken scarf that matched her dress. Her forehead was bound with another scarf worked with pearls. I was discovering the world of women between the hands of this nymph! Her kohl applicator, her combs, her perfume bottles, a receptacle filled with a pearlescent paste that she rubbed on her hands and brow to make them shine.

When you walk with a woman you love, you don't care that she pauses without cease to look at the store windows or that she is constantly complaining of her new slippers or wishes to taste of every sweet shop we pass, then thirsts after and asks for water. All you desire is that the birds of happiness should not cease their song in her voice. At the perfumer's, the shopkeeper showed us a scent that he said was a mixture of thirty flowers, one of which only grew behind a fountain among the rocks that separated it from the mountain, and bloomed only two weeks out of the year. There is nothing more fertile than the imagination of a lying salesman. She put some of it in her palm. "I want to lick it from beneath your ear," I said.

The trees still sang when she passed them by.

The morning of the next day, I gathered the scattered pieces of myself from her fields of jasmine with difficulty, and prepared to go out. But she was displeased with my sudden disappearance every time. I pressed my face into her collarbone. "I will soon be back," I said, and added, "'I leave you all in hesitation, / Like one off to his execution.' There is a man waiting for me by the mosque, and I must sell him some books."

The captain was waiting by the mosque with a cart and carter. "I knew you would bring more of your books and scraps of paper," he said.

I no longer minded his provoking words. I joked, "Do you know what Christ says? Do not cast pearls before swine. Also, al-Mutanabbi says, 'The thinking man suffers in the midst of luxury, / While the ignorant enjoy life in their penury.'"

It appeared that I had succeeded in disturbing him, for he took a step back. "Forgive me. I meant no offense. That is the way of the ignorant and the small-minded; we say what we do not understand. I have resolved to spend this year reading Ibn Abd Rabbu's *The Unique Necklace.*"

I ignored him. He was a pretender; he did not even dare to sit in the nobleman's company, only stand with his head down. I had brought Ikhwan al-Safa, al-Kindi, Abu al-Allaf al-Mutazili, and *The Book of Animals* by al-Jahiz. "We have no need of your cart," I said. "I bear that which, as the saying goes, is light in weight and dear in price."

The fountains as we climbed to the Citadel of Khayran were making an unusual hoarse sound like gasping, while the young *saqaliba* men were training and sparring with loud shouts and clashes. We went, as usual, to the western wing of the Citadel.

Unlike the previous occasions, the noble master smiled happily to see us. He approached me, taking the books eagerly. "Do you have anything by Abu al-Alaa al-Maari?"

I shook my head regretfully. "He visited Baghdad and spent some time there, but I never met him or acquired any books or collections of his."

"It is said that he and Abu Hayan al-Tawhidi delved so deeply into science that they turned heretic."

I trembled. What response should I make? "My lord," I said, "if we lent our ear to every piece of gossip, a *fitna* would start that would never be extinguished."

When I handed him the book by al-Jahiz, he took it with both hands, almost embracing it. "Amr ibn Bahr al-Jahiz! *Bahr* means the sea, and I swear he is a sea of knowledge! But," he added, "they say he copied much from the Greeks, especially his *Book of Animals*, which is adapted from Aristotle."

"They say so, my lord," I responded. "However, he says that meanings can be found everywhere in the public street, but in literature what is noteworthy is eloquence, a well-turned phrase, clarity of meaning, and smoothness and elegance. And this is what al-Jahiz possesses in all his books. As for booksellers, they have nothing but talk."

Suddenly he pursed his lips and looked at me with blazing eyes. "Are you going on to Cordoba? The Qudai captain says that you were seeking a caravan to that city."

Hesitantly, I nodded. "Yes, my lord."

He motioned to his guardian angel, who was standing at his shoulder, and said commandingly, "Have you finished what you commenced?"

At that moment, I heard a racket at the door and a pounding of feet and a clattering of weapons. A servant called out, "My lord Khayran al-Amiri, God bless him, is at the door!"

My eyes remained fixed on the door as I saw Khayran moving toward the descendant of sultans. He was tall, with a big head and white eyebrows knitted in a frown over alert green eyes that passed swiftly over our faces, never settling in one place. He bowed and said, "Good morning, Your Majesty."

The man of noble lineage did not stand in respect, but merely responded, "Good morning to you, Khayran."

I goggled. Who was this who spoke to Khayran without a single title, when Almería spoke of nothing but his revered status day and night? Who was this who raised his soft, smooth hand for silence when Khayran made to speak, and commanded him to be silent and sit, making Khayran al-Saqalibi, the leader of Almería, sit docilely at his command? The nobleman looked at me. "What do you wish with Cordoba, where *fitna* is blazing and swords are drawn? Gone are the Umayyad soldiers who were the flower of the land and the pride of the armies, and there are none left in the army but butchers and street sweepers. The libraries in Cordoba in the time of Caliph al-Mustansir, may he rest in peace, numbered in the dozens: where are they now?"

Khayran appeared taken aback and embarrassed at the nobleman's expansiveness with me. "Your Majesty—"

The nobleman silenced him with a wave of the hand. "Mazid is a stranger in this land. No one knows him. His soul has been groomed and polished by reading books; a reader of books cannot be low nor treasonous—he knows the meaning of dignity and honor." He fell silent, looking into my eyes. "I shall send with him the message to the Umayyad princes in Cordoba that I am alive and well, not dead; that those who claimed I was dead lied; and that the one they prayed over with al-Musta'in was a Jew who resembles me almost perfectly, so that the Umayyad princes may unite in ousting that feckless Umayyad boy who has amassed himself an army, half of bakers, builders, and smiths, and the other half of Berbers. There he is, ruling Cordoba, running wild, dividing up the surrounding land among his Berber commanders—the land that the clan of Umayya sacrificed their lives and their blood to conquer! That is not all: he calls himself al-Musta'in bi-Allah,

461

which means 'the one whose only support is God,' as a means of saying that he needs none of them, and can rule alone!"

He stared at me again. His reddish beard was sweating with the vehemence of his emotion. "When you arrive in Cordoba, you will seek out Tammam al-Saqalibi, and assure yourself that is it he. Then you will give him the letter, and your reward will be great. Perhaps I will appoint you wali if I regain rule over one of the states—but beware! Let no one fool you and say they will convey it to him, for if Tammam has left Cordoba or died, you must burn the letter immediately, and let it not linger in your possession."

"Your Majesty," said Khayran, "what makes you trust that this man will convey the message and not betray you? And why not send it with one of our men?"

"Your men are so imprudent and precipitate that they are immediately recognizable by the people of Cordoba." He turned to me with a threatening air. "And if this Hanafite betrays us, I shall find him out and bring him back, and his head shall roll out of the window of Alcazaba."

I staggered out of the meeting with Hisham al-Muayyad, the ousted caliph, with a thousand dinars in gold in my pocket, and a letter in my sleeve from a dethroned king to a reigning one, and I between them like Tarafa, the Arabian poet who conveyed to the governor of Bahrain the orders for his own execution. The missive bore in red sealing wax: "Hisham ibn al-Hakam bi-Allah seeks salvation, vanquished and with no sway."

What are these paths of burning coals wherein you walk, Mazid? The Umayyad princes had roped me into their wars and their feudal conflicts. The sixth commandment appeared before me:

Sixth Commandment
Beware! Never become the enemy of the wise sciences, never be tribal or feudal or bias yourself toward one

creed or knowledge: he who hateth any of the sciences remaineth ignorant of it.

I did not listen at that time, as is the way of the reckless.

# 7

# The Caravan of Bani Murrah

THE CARAVAN THAT WE ACCOMPANIED to Cordoba had camels whose backs were yellow with the ginger and saffron they bore from the cities of Tlemcen and Fez, and most of its travelers were from Bani Murrah. They said that they had arrived after a long journey from the depths of the Arabian Peninsula, after which they had scattered. Some had settled in Egypt, some had gone to Kairouan, and the remainder had continued on to Andalusia. The owner of the caravan would be obliged to hire more guards to protect the caravan, and asked me when he saw my boxes, weighty on the backs of three mules, "What do you want with Cordoba? Her folk are departed from her."

I said vaguely, to stop his questioning but not sever the bonds of friendship, "'What is large starts with what is small; / Seas built on seas were naught at all.'"

In Granada, my main concern was keeping the old man who had traveled with Zahira, and whose name was Dirbas, away from me and from Zahira. I approached her sedan chair to find her slumbering, almost supine. When she saw me, she reached out to embrace me: I would ask to lift her up onto my strong camel that she might sleep on my shoulder. When a shooting star decided to fall, we lagged behind the caravan, and canoodled between the murmurings of the demons and the springs with glittering stones.

Many times I asked her about herself, her family, her past, her childhood; her responses were usually short and she was clearly reluctant to expand. But this never dissuaded me from excavating the days and years of her life. I desired to grasp every inch of her, even the mysterious gaps in her memory, leaving no part of her behind a veil.

She told me of her father, the lute player, and her family that trained their girls to dance from an early age. The men learned to play and manufacture the lute, while the women learned to dance and sing. "My ancestors were priests of an old sect that served the temple of Zarathustra down the ages, but the Lord blessed us with Islam, and Fatima al-Zahraa, the Prophet's daughter, took our clan under her wing and forgave us our slips and sins." She smiled coyly. "It was Zahraa who sent me my fair-faced Arab boy who loves me with runaway ardor, an ardor I have never seen in the eyes of all those who came before him."

I knew not whether to be pleased at what she said, or be dismayed at the "all" she had known, and mentioned so casually. Who? How? How many? Woe unto you, Mazid! How long can you withstand your frustration, and the flood of questions?

At the Albaicín market in Granada, she bought an anklet and a face veil embroidered with silver dirhams. I did not ask her what she would do with it in Granada, or whether Zahira would rekindle her old glory by placing a pearl in her navel and displaying it before the eyes of men. I would not ask her, for we might quarrel, and I could not part from her, at least not now. Old Fly Eye, Dirbas, watched us constantly, but I cared not. I knew that it was the cost of the war I had embarked upon to win the heart of a songstress: a war unbecoming of a Voyager, but still, I would keep sipping at her, and preserve the thick curtain that separated her from my books. When we arrived in Cordoba, I would rent a house and make my own rules. I would not permit Zahira to put herself on display once more before the lusts of men.

Rashid ibn Ali of Egypt had told me that the Andalusians were Sunnis, followers of the imam Malik, not inclined to follow the path of the Just Monotheists, and that their caliph, al-Mansour ibn Abu Amir, had banned Mutazilite thought, but that it remained a region bustling with libraries, discussion circles, and some lush oases; and it would not be exempt from the thinking of the Just Monotheists. He had given me the name of their man in Cordoba, Bahaa al-Zaman, and perhaps we might be blessed enough to be able to place a book in every library.

## Lovers Suffer, but They Sing

I had expected from Zahira the brazen, high-pitched laughter of a temptress; I had expected seduction, coquetry, melting moments; I had expected debauched words and depraved actions, winks and raised eyebrows and bold looks and a bed burning with all the arts of lovemaking known to whores; but so far, all that had been shown to me was a housebound girl, shy and wary, as though I had asked for her hand from a family home outside of which she had never set foot. Was she concealing her true nature from her horned husband?

Her silence in the presence of men, her shy, nibbling way of eating, her reticence—for she only allowed me to touch her in the dark—the way she listened to me when I spoke, her eyes clinging to me like a young girl touched by love for the first time. The way she was fascinated at everything I said, even impossible things or the heresy of philosophers; the way she deliberately sat close to me and drew near me, and ignored the other passengers in the caravan who urged us to walk faster. She was disturbed by everything that called on her to part from me, and was slow to leave my side. If I recited explicit poetry to her, she blushed and covered her face with her hands, begging me to cease: "I swear I only fell in love with the chaste, pensive Arab who recites poems as though they were psalms, and sells books as though they were pearls—who buries his face in the pages of a book and ignores all women around him!"

The paths to Cordoba lengthened, especially as the caravan driver sent spies ahead of us to investigate the safe paths free of any remnants of soldiers or bandits, returning with bad news of highwaymen and military encampments. Therefore, the caravan moved haltingly along the bank of a river or beneath mountain outcroppings, and when the inhabitants of those regions saw the caravan passing, they descended the mountain paths and displayed dried fruit, flatbread, milk, and delicious butter. We stayed there for days, resting our bodies, plucking and eating from the walnut trees and rubbing our teeth with their leaves to make them white and shining, and lighting fires upon which we grilled small goats wrapped in leaves and stuffed with walnuts, figs, and apricots. Zahira and I might take ourselves off to some cave in the mountainside that looked down upon us from above.

One day, the old man Dirbas was at the mouth of the cave, waiting for us. Incensed, I cried, determined to subdue him this time, "What seek you here? I swear you will see something that will displease you, for you bring together ignorance and ill-breeding as you come to disturb us in the cave, much as the infidels sought to find the Prophet and Abu Bakr hiding in their cavern."

He fixed me with a hateful glare. "I only wished to reassure myself of Zahira's well-being. She was absent from the caravan for a while," he said.

He was still speaking of her independently of me! "Zahira has a husband to take care of her now," I retorted, "and you had better depart now before I roll you down the mountaintop."

"Poor thing!" Zahira said, placating me. "He only wished to reassure himself."

"This cur has gone too far," I said between gritted teeth. I divined then that getting rid of this man would not be easy.

Zahira stuck close to me, reading over my shoulder out of the book to which I devoted a portion of my day. I gave her the *Aghani* to occupy herself, but she said, "Take it away: it was written for the palaces of the sultans and their company, and I have wasted my days going over its poems to recite them to drunken men and in the gatherings of nobles. Give me one of the books that make you speak like a wise man a hundred years old."

I gave her al-Farabi's *The Virtuous City*, hoping that it might be too much for her understanding and thus gain me some solitude; I knew not that it would shake the foundations of her world and rub the lantern that would let out the genie lurking inside her, leading her sweetly to the paths of utopias she could never abandon. She took to reading it and reciting it over and over, her long lashes fluttering as she contemplated its passages, completely absorbed by every line. When Dirbas passed by her, he muttered mockingly, "'Great staffs shall small sticks surely make; / A snake can only spawn a snake.'"

His interference and intrusion galled me; I was waiting for a chance to pluck his white beard.

But Zahira did not mind, and was undisturbed by his passage, instead asking me insistently about the Essential City of al-Farabi, and whether its inhabitants could survive only on necessities such as food, water, and whatever they could come together to acquire. She then described the city of Kerman, where she had grown up, as "the Low City," which epithet al-Farabi had used for the city where people only enjoyed sensory pleasures of food, drink, joking, and all manner of amusement. Her lips twisted in derision, making her pointed chin protrude. "In all the cities I passed through on my path from Baghdad to here," she said, "I never found what al-Farabi calls 'the City of Dignity,' whose inhabitants cooperate to ensure dignity and fame, honor and renown, in word and deed."

Mournfully I responded, "On this path you shall only see the Agate Cities, pulsing with blood and wounds. They are cities of conflict, whose monarchs seek only power."

The thing that made us burst into laughter with such abandon that all eyes stared at us was her admiration of the idea al-Farabi had adapted from Plato in comparing a city to a human body. Just as in a complete and healthy body whose every organ cooperates, in their difference and integration, to preserve the life of a person, there is a main organ, the heart—so the city's sections are different in form, integrated in function, and it has a person who is the leader. Just as in the body there are organs that serve and wait upon each other, in a city there are people who serve one another.

We divided the parts of our body into the forms of the city's institutions. "The right hand," she said, "is for the planters, the farmers who plant our food."

"And the left," I said, "is for the police, who drive off those who would usurp the planters' efforts."

"The head for the wise folk."

"The tongue for the poets." Then I would put my hand on her breast. "And what is the role of this?"

She would lift my hand, blushing. "This is a silo of wheat. The other is honey."

Lewdly I asked, referencing the Qur'anic rivers of milk and honey, "Is it good to drink from?"

She gave me a reproving glance. "Only for the devout."

Still, this mischievous talk never stopped her asking me more and more questions, especially about the reason al-Farabi gave the keys of the Virtuous City to the philosophers and wise folk, leaving mimesis and representation to the common people. I opened the book to the page where he mentions that attributes are based on natural inclination— that is, the instinct we are born with—and kept on reading to show her the twelve attributes with which a leader is born.

Thus, a leader is chosen by a city for his positive attributes, not out of power or by dint of being a descendant of any royal family. I never knew then that I was planting a seed, in parched and fertile land, from which would sprout a field of questions.

## Crimson Winds

My head was turned by the singing of the trees whenever Zahira passed them. She still had the eyes of a virgin raised in a walled garden. I sought out chances for the caravan to stop in order to hold and kiss her and smell the scent of her hair, and slip my hand into the folds of her clothing. She had finished al-Farabi's book and asked for another to fill the long hours of journeying within the silken curtains of her sedan chair. "Would you like a book by al-Farabi's teacher?" I asked her. "For al-Farabi is but the Second Teacher."

Still enamored of al-Farabi, she said, "I doubt that one so great could have a teacher. Who could be better than him in this world?"

Tenderly, I said, "I fear for this beautiful little head to be stolen away by delusions and heresies."

She leaned on my shoulder lovingly. "I fear nothing. Fatima al-Zahraa is with me, and so are you. Every day the wings grow that will bear me above the paths of debauchery."

Was she saying this to grant me the illusion that she had abandoned her old habits? I knew not, but I had no desire to tell her that the path in my company was not as secure as she thought: the birds of confusion and suspicion pecked at me too. I had never told her that I was Shiite, for I knew not if I still was. I had left al-Yamama; should I keep the religion of its monarchs? Nor had I told her that I was a Voyager, bearing my seven commandments to spread throughout many lands, nor that I had in my possession a letter from a dethroned king seeking to regain his power. What heavy burdens! But no matter; perhaps she would know some day.

Half a day's journey from Cordoba, we stopped in a field among the mountains known as the Valley of the Walnuts. We were told that there was a waterfall close to the valley, but that reaching it required circumnavigating the mountain over uneven, rocky paths. The caravan driver gave us directions, as a special privilege for two newlyweds thrust onto the path of travel, who had not enjoyed the safety of a roof over their heads.

The treacherous path took a long time to traverse, and when we arrived, the sun was high in the sky. When we found it, it was not as full as had been described to us, but it emptied into a pellucid stream with small stones glistening on the bottom. The stream was surrounded by lavender and wild mugwort. We plunged into it, washing off the strain and fatigue of the mountain, and rubbed ourselves with lavender. Zahira collected handfuls of a tiny insect with red wings that she said was good for making henna paste.

At that moment, we heard two lions fighting savagely atop a nearby mountain. Around us, great winds stormed, of a strange crimson color. They moaned as if telling a story. As we hurried back to the caravan, I said to Zahira, "Do you hear the wind?"

She replied, "I swear, O wise Solomon, you who hear the song of the trees and the wind, I only heard the sound of two lions fighting, and it struck fear into my heart."

Cordoba is surrounded by fighting lions and ravaged by crimson winds. When the evening star rose, we had reached the outskirts of the city.

## An Alabaster Bridge and a Burning City
### Safar 29, AH 405 / August 29, AD 1014

That was the night we awaited the sighting of the new moon for the month of Rabi al-Awwal, while the folk of the caravan cheered, "May God fill the new month with good fortune, gladness, and blessings!" I have traversed the universe to reach you, Cordoba: what lurks for me behind your gates and closed doors?

I looked down at the city from a hill on the outskirts, separated from the city by a river and a bridge. The bridge had been built by the Romans, though not with the intention to divide Cordoba; the city had sprung up on either bank. Evening was falling, and the lanterns had begun to twinkle upon the garment of night. As usual, I was wary of entering a new city in the evening. We would not be able to see its streets; we would arouse the suspicions of the inhabitants and might lose our way. Better to remain by the caravan until the morning, which always bears good news on its wings.

There were great crowds of people traversing the bridge, exiting from Cordoba to the surrounding hamlets. They seemed to be servants and slaves, with tattered clothing and exhausted, dismal faces. The paths leading away from Cordoba divided them into streams, flowing to their miserable mud-brick houses alongside some dhimmi and gypsy tribes. I was laden with gifts for Cordoba. The books of the Voyagers and their commandments, silken garments we were conveying for Hamdouna to the princesses of the Umayyad house, and a letter from their ousted king. All this in the company of a blossoming woman who bore all the women of the world within her person. I wished to provide a suitable and safe dwelling for her, especially because Ma'in had been frank with me from the start of the journey, and said he would not be able to come with me to Cordoba, but would join a Sanhaji tribe in Elvira.

Ma'in's departure had left me unbalanced: there was no prop for me to support myself and shoo away my enemies, especially old Dirbas, who kept popping up with eyes reddened with hatred, as though lurking in wait to ambush me. Whenever I wished to get at him, Zahira told me to beware of him. "He makes a bad enemy. He only agreed to our marriage when he assured himself that it was a Kairouan

473

contract, which allows me to divorce you at any time." Her voice always dropped beseechingly. "He has kept me company these past ten years, like a tent that sheltered me from the vicissitudes of time and the vagaries of fate, and they were many. It is his right to be dismissed with the dignity befitting his advanced age."

I had no wish to start an interrogation: who was he? Why did she hold him in such respect? Why did he circle us like an expectant jackal? I had no desire to hear things that would dismay or anger me, so I remained silent. I would handle these matters in due time. Most importantly, now I must separate from Zahira's troupe, from their music and drums and dancers and mules and the cunning old man, and draw her away alone to some small, quiet home, far from prying eyes and nosy neighbors.

With the morning light, Cordoba dawned bright and appetizing, like a spring of silver. I crossed the bridge and entered by the door facing Mecca, topped with a statue of the Virgin Mary. It is said that its inhabitants, the first Christians, had erected it there, where it still stood. How I wished for Ma'in then! He was wily and observant, and always found the shortest route to his goal. The tales of ordeals and battles between the Berber and the Umayyads he had heard in Almería had made him wary of entering Cordoba, although he had made light of the matter at first. In vain had I attempted to persuade him to accompany me. I had told him that all in the caravan were confident that there was no more danger for the Berbers. "The swords are no longer drawn in their faces," I said, trying to convince them, "but are in their hands, and they draw them when they please, now that the Umayyad caliph al-Musta'in has enlisted their help and given them entire villages and estates in recompense for his predecessor al-Mahdi's mistreatment of them." But these reassurances fell on deaf ears, and Ma'in insisted on leaving, promising to visit me soon.

Zahira and her slave girl Bustan walked alongside me in silence, looking at the balconies and passageways and into the Khoudariya, the Jewish quarter near the Great Mosque. They found a women's bathhouse with a great doorway surrounded by mosaics of crouching lions facing each other as though set there to protect the women bathing. The scent of perfumes and soap drew them inside, and they asked to spend the afternoon there; I would return after arranging our affairs.

Hassan the Egyptian had always jokingly explained away his reluctance to marry by saying, "A married man gradually becomes a beast of burden, a hired man groaning under baggage and weighed down with cares!" Should I search my back for a hump? My grandfather always repeated the words of Imam Ali: "Marriage is cowardice and miserliness." He explained it as having a woman who eats and drinks with you, forcing you to be the lion who protects her from the misfortunes that befall her, an early doom inconsistent with the Voyager Mazid al-Hanafi who had emerged from Najd, from the depths of the desert, and was now perched high on the shoulder of the world in Cordoba. Were these merely excuses that I might escape from Zahira, the charming Persian Anahid, in whose dark eyes lay all the enchantments and all the demons of Persia? But she was still a woman, a burden, an interference in life—indeed, she opened the boxes of books with curious ardor and took out the volumes that pleased her, and spent her time discussing them and arguing about them.

Were these the imaginings of a man still under the spell of his woman's ecstasy, in an attempt to save himself from her power over his heart? A bid to dry the sticky river of perfumes from his wings, to soar once more?

I escaped from my imaginings and set out to find a house for us to rent. It was not the best house, but the rooms were sunny and the air refreshing. It had a courtyard with a fountain in the center ringed with rooms with bright blue doors, prominent sunshades above its windows that resembled balconies, and a tiled floor. The agent, in an attempt to make it more attractive, said, "This is a benefit. Most houses in Cordoba are floored with arsenic, not tile." And because it had a stable and a trough for beasts wide enough for two camels and four stubborn mules, I did not haggle overmuch with the agent about its rental.

I returned to the caravan to bring Zahira and her slave girl only, and to announce a clean break with the rest of the chorus who had accompanied her from Baghdad. The old man Dirbas no longer spoke to me after I had rebuked him, and I avoided looking at him. I paid him no heed, collecting our things and separating the beasts in silence, my brow furrowed. One of the Ethiopian boys accompanying her said in a placating, submissive tone, "Where are my lady Zahira and Bustan?"

I gave him a menacing glare. "She is now in her home. When she needs any of you, she will send for you." I dragged the beasts and their burdens over the bridge, accompanied by a boy from the caravan. I feared that this decision might not suit Zahira, or that she might take some action that would make me appear green and idiotic in their eyes. No matter. It appeared that we would pass the first few months in a soft battle and many skirmishes until we had established the features of our life to come.

There was a great waterwheel by the bridge that lifted the water from one side and poured it out into the other. These are the days of our lives. We think they belong to us, but time comes and makes them slip through our fingers, pouring them into the river that reclaims them. The universe is changing about me and shedding its garment: who is the green, naive Mazid al-Hanafi who left al-Yamama on a caravan to Mecca to me now?

Wisdom comes, but it steals innocence and carelessness with it. I awaited the afternoon prayers to go to the Great Mosque and search for Bahaa to pay him the greeting of the Just Monotheists.

# The Light That Never Dies

Zahira was almost mad with books. None knew better than I that there is no antidote that can cure one bitten by the asp of knowledge.

I had thought previously that women had sweet little minds, incapable of ascending the plateaus of wisdom and the towers of philosophy, kept from this by menstruation and ovulation. But this tigress fairly devoured books, even staying away from my bed for many nights in favor of reading by candlelight! It did not disturb me: first, it would make her forget the melodies of the tanbur and the beats of the drum, or at the very least defer her decision about such things; second, it would make her care for the crates of books like precious gems, finding them a place away from the damp, polishing the brass fittings and dusting the dross of travel from their pages.

She was currently immersed in reading books on theology and wisdom, and the writings of al-Kindi and Allaf al-Mutazili and Ikhwan al-Safa. She said petulantly, "Instead of giving me answers, they have given me noise."

I told her, "Let your only guiding imam be your intellect."

"What is my intellect? My intellect is marred by the madness of my emotions, my past, my changing moods, and my homesickness for Baghdad. How will I find it?"

I laughed out loud. "Bless you! You have instinctually hit upon the Law of Circumstance, which the Mutazilites of Basra made a condition of passing just judgment. We must respond to the change of circumstance from one era and one place to another. Still, your mind will remain your light on the path, and your guide to the Valley of the Virtues."

"What is virtue?" she asked. "For instance, if a man marries a widow in addition to his wife in order to protect her and raise her children, are we to consider it a virtue? It is the greatest curse and vice to the first wife. There is no such thing as absolute virtue."

I snatched at Aristotle's response to relieve me of her contentiousness. "Virtue is the mean between two vices." Then I escaped her argument, for I knew no more than she. "When is Bustan going to present the silken garments to the princesses?"

"Perhaps tomorrow," she said carelessly. "The women in the bath told her that the princesses no longer live in Zahraa since it has been destroyed, and most have returned to Cordoba. Their palaces are surrounded by a private wall of palm trees adjoining the wall of the Great Mosque, and its gate faces west, opposite the prince's stables, surrounded by high palms revered by the folk of Cordoba. They say that they are planted from the pits of the first conquerors' dates."

I called on Bustan and told her to go to the palaces tomorrow, and when she was there, to ask discreetly and circumspectly about a man named Tammam al-Saqalibi.

Hisham ibn Hakam al-Marwani's missive was still in my sleeve, hardly ever leaving me. Even when I undressed, I placed it in a box and locked it with a padlock I wore around my neck in anticipation of what Bustan would tell me, that I might pass it to Tammam or else burn it. I had told Zahira nothing of the message, although she had become addicted to leafing through the crates of books and disturbing their contents. This remained a darkness between us.

They say that a man must keep some mysterious things away from his woman, by which he can arrange his affairs and rearrange his armies before a world that keeps him in a constant state of battle. I did not know her intentions yet: would she return to dancing and song, which was the reason she had left Baghdad? I know nothing of you, full moon of the house, musk that perfumes the halls.

## Bahaa al-Zaman

The Great Mosque was the soul of Cordoba and the center of its glory. The tenderness of its flagstones was embraced by flirtatious gilded mosaics, awe-inspiring arches, and stucco so well wrought that it seemed to move, with circles of plaster branches endlessly chasing bunches of grapes. Outside, the water in the fountains of the mosque lapped in a golden sea at the bases of the date palms and poured gold onto the orange trees.

The inner doors of the mosque all stood open, most of the faithful bearing a book or a scroll under their sleeves. I performed my ablutions and entered. The columns towered above me like a cohort of noble giants, rising and joining hands to protect the people praying: their arches were formed of palm fronds providing shade. It went on and on, and I could scarcely see the pulpit from where I stood. The scent of Indian incense permeated the atmosphere.

When I finished my prayers, I looked around for a discussion circle to take refuge in and ask the students about Bahaa al-Zaman. The closest was the circle of a sheikh telling an anecdote he thought was funny. I recalled having read it in al-Hamazani: the story of a young man whose father furnished him with money to go into business, and warned him against the blandishments of the self. But the boy fell in love with learning and spent his money on seeking it, and returned to his father penniless. "Father," the boy said, "I come to you with the power of history, and the riches of history, and eternal life: the Qur'an with all its interpretations, and the Prophet's Tradition with all its references, and religious jurisprudence with all its permutations, and rhetoric with its arts, and poetry with its oddities, and grammar with its conjugations, and language and its origins."

The father, it is said, took him to the moneychanger, the tailor, the spice trader, the baker, and the butcher, ending with the grocery store. He asked for some groceries, whereupon the grocer said, "We accept the coin of the nation, not coinage and interpretation."

Then the father scooped up dust and heaped it on his son's head, saying, "Son of misfortune! You set out with cash, and came back with trash, myths that none with a brain in his head will give you groceries in their stead."

Was dust on the head Cordoba's measure for sciences and arts? What a dismal and depressing reception committee from the circles of the Great Mosque. Groceries were now superior to knowledge! Those who repeat old tales of biographies and parrot quotations filled the mosque, and the circles of learning and jurisprudence had lost their luster. I slipped away from the circle and moved through the pillars of the mosque to find out where the books that had captivated the world were hidden, but could not find them.

The first Friday prayers at the Great Mosque, I glimpsed two of the mosque attendants helping each other carry a massive copy of the Qur'an between them, a man with a candle walking ahead of them, head held high. They said it was the Qur'an of Uthman, the ancestor of the Umayyad Dynasty. Had his copy arrived here, too? Did they too pretend that upon its pages there were droplets of Uthman's blood, the Umayyad claim to a vendetta that was even now alive and well?

The copy had a beautiful silver cover with verses of the Qur'an and ornaments in relief. It was placed on a chair and the imam read some verses from it. Then the attendants smoothly and carefully returned it to its place in the closet. I looked around the pillars. There were two men I must find today. The first was al-Qadi Abu Mutrif, who, I had been told, held a circle in the mosque after Friday prayers, and had amassed a collection of books in Cordoba greater than that of any Andalusian in his era. It was said that he kept six copyists permanently in his employ, and when he learned of a new book, bought it forthwith, even if the seller charged an exorbitant price. The other was Bahaa al-Zaman, a Voyager of Cordoba, who would give me its keys and its maps.

The pathways of Cordoba were crowded with soldiers and beggars, but its great mosque was still filled with Arab students and those white-faced, red-bearded foreigners.

I had no need to ask after the circle of al-Qadi Abu Mutrif: it was opposite the pulpit, with ten semicircular rows about it, and everyone headed there. I sat at the outer edges. The first thing that came to my hearing was "He who quotes the First Teacher, Aristotle, is an atheist!"

O God! Why was Andalusia set against the philosophers? First Almería, and now Cordoba!

Abu Mutrif fell silent, staring into the people's faces. Then, in an apparent access of energy, he burst out, "Atheists!" He swallowed, waiting to observe the effect of his words on the assembled faces. "That means the philosophers. From their first teacher, Aristotle, to their second, al-Farabi, who followed his predecessor's path into atheism and disbelief in Almighty God and His angels and prophets and the Judgment Day. If philosophy, in essence, is based on liberating the mind and using the unfettered intellect, according to clerics and theologians, any deviation or doubt is caused by the use of the mind. The Devil's doubt, may the Devil be cursed, lay in his privileging of his own opinion over the text, and following his own judgment in disobeying God."

I stared. After all these books you have read, O Sheikh Abu Mutrif, are you nothing but a copy of my sheikh Muhammad al-Tamimi, who sees the mind as the source of all deviation? I swear, Cordoba, you are nothing but a burning coal pulsing with rage and blood, one of the Agate Cities.

I took to gazing at the ceiling, ignoring Abu Mutrif's ramblings. I gave myself over to the melancholy columns that shaded us, shaped by the first conquerors into the form of palm fronds. Longing crowded my breast: I sighed and rose, seeking a pathway to the storehouse of books in the Great Mosque—if one even existed.

A woman's voice in the mosque! Yes, a woman's voice, slightly nasal but with the characteristic pronunciation that is unique to clerics. "Thanks be to God," she said. "We thank Him and return to Him, and invoke prayers and peace upon the Prophet Muhammad. There are two forms of devotion: religious jurisprudence and politics. Religious jurisprudence fulfills devotions; politics peoples the earth and builds nations."

I headed, stunned, for the source of the voice. I had heard that there were female clerics in the Haraam Mosque of Mecca, and in the Umayyad Mosque in Damascus, but I had not known that the mosques of Andalusia opened their doors to female clerics. I kept my footsteps light, fearing that the voice might be coming to me from beyond the barrier separating the women's section of the mosque from ours, but I glimpsed her among the columns, erect on a chair, surrounded by her students and disciples. "The *fitna* of the creation of the Qur'an is a great *fitna* to whom many lost their lives and their faith. Some attribute it to philosophers and heretics; some attribute it to the Just Monotheists, sometimes called Mutazilites." She glanced around with self-possession before continuing. "This *fitna* goes back to the concept that 'nothing comes of nothing,' which indicates that the world is eternal and was not newly created. Even the philosophers themselves have debated this. Al-Kindi affirmed the pillars of our religion, such as the creation of all creatures and the natural world, and that everything that the Prophet Muhammad says, prayers and peace be upon him, does not go against reason. Al-Kindi, therefore, confirms things that neither blaspheme nor transgress."

I was filled with an overwhelming ecstasy. I was not accustomed to hearing such shining logical arguments from any other than a rough male throat, but here the words were flowing in a soft feminine lilt, like the sound of the waterwheel over the Great Valley. She was sitting in the southern corner of the mosque, at the end of the corner parallel to al-Qadi Abu Mutrif, separated from him by a forest of columns. On her right was a latticed, ornamented window running the length of the wall and overlooking a garden by the mosque. At the end of it shone the waters of the Great Valley.

She sat tall, straight-backed, kneeling as though finishing her prayers. Before her was a chair bearing a large book at which she glanced, a piece of embroidered silk beneath it hanging down to the ground. Her features were delicate and her skin clear. Her beauty was not overweening, but soft like a star's. The gentleness of her features did not keep a slight frown from her forehead—the mark of a serious scholar. Her head was covered with a red silk cap from which a saffron-colored veil descended, matching the color of her caftan, which fell respectably over her slight shoulders and pooled about her in carefully arranged folds. As she looked at the book, she appeared absorbed and ecstatic, with a hint of pain. She soon raised her eyes. "The absolute infallibility of Almighty God means there is nothing whatever like unto Him, nothing similar nor any embodiment, which elevates God above all earthly things. As for the interpretation of verse twenty-seven of the Sura of al-Rahman, '*There remaineth but the Countenance of thy Lord of Might and Glory*,' the evident meaning of *countenance* is 'face,' and we say here that 'face' is not literal, but signifies 'essence.'"

I slipped into her circle, captivated by what I was hearing, the words of the Voyagers and the Just Monotheists, with which this woman was singing like the birds with eloquence and powerful proofs. I whispered to the young man next to me, "Who is this cleric?"

He answered without turning, eyes fixed on her, "Bahaa al-Zaman al-Mrouzia."

## Garments of Umayyad Silk

"If the mirror is distorted, and depicts physical forms falsely—also if a mirror is stained—then nothing can be seen in it." That was what Zahira said to me as I came in through the door.

I kissed her and inhaled the scent of her hair. "Abandon the heresies of the philosophers! I have seen a wonder in the mosque. There is an eminent female cleric at the Great Mosque."

"Where?" she asked.

"At a discussion circle in the mosque."

"You mean in the women's section?" asked Bustan, as though trying to find an explanation.

"No," I said. "When they finished the Friday prayer, men and women sat at her circle." I turned to Bustan, "And what of you? Did you find Tammam al-Saqalibi when you took the caftans to the Umayyad palace?"

Bemused, she responded, "They said they knew him not, and I could seek him in the Great Palace."

"What great palace?"

"The one," she said, "where the Umayyad caliph resides, Sulayman al-Musta'in bi-Allah."

I slumped. Sulayman al-Musta'in? It was said that he was a lover of books and a writer of poetry, but was currently occupied with his own affairs, attempting to rule in the face of the revolt of the people of Cordoba. The Berbers had taken over all the surrounding hamlets, leaving him only with Cordoba.

"Dirbas came to visit today," said Zahira seriously.

I felt the veins pounding in my temple. "Old Fly Eye? What brought him here in my absence?"

"Dirbas is a lifelong companion," Zahira said, trying to calm matters. "Oft has he defended me and protected me. How can a person abandon his life's companions and shut the door in their faces? Betray once, and you shall grow accustomed to it."

I choked on my irritation, for she was imparting a moral lesson and reminding me that she was older than I, and that I was a green ignoramus who as yet knew little of the world—and that she still expected Dirbas to protect her. I screamed, spittle flying from my mouth, "He protected your thighs and your buttocks that you put on display for the drunkards, and lived off your labor! He did not protect you as a revered lady of the house! He dragged you out of men's arms only to send you back naked unto them, time after time!"

I had not realized the cruelty of these words until her face turned blue, and she began to sob before me with a sound like wailing. Never before had I spoken to her with such harshness and obscenity.

I stormed out, slamming the door hard enough to make the hinges rattle, intending to find Dirbas and threaten him with all forms of harm if he visited again. But I did not know where he lived. The streets of Cordoba were bursting with soldiers, and the gates were mostly barred, and you had to avoid asking too many questions so as not to draw curious eyes. The city's hearts were still broken, its wounds still raw: the stores only displayed some dried fruit, wheat, and jars of olive oil, for food and supplies were bought by the soldiers, who devoured it like locusts before it ever reached Cordoba, leaving nothing but scraps for the folk of the city.

Despite this, Cordoba rebelled against the rule of the soldiers, putting on her finery every morning: her windows still bore pots of flowers, her fountains sang as they watered flocks of birds accustomed to bathing in their spray, her streets were paved with shining flagstones, and her bathhouses' doors were filled with the steam of perfume and soap. I walked aimlessly until I reached the gate that faced Mecca, and exited to the bank of the Great Valley to look at the waterwheel scooping up my life and pouring it away. I found the people of Cordoba, men, women, and children, out for holiday excursions on the banks of the river. The riverbank was planted with silks and perfumes and filled with the laughter of young girls. Their veils fluttered in the river breeze, showing their hair, and they let them fly in the wind with heart-melting coquetry.

Would Zahira forgive my impugning her honor and insulting her? Would I find her there when I came back home? Or would I find that the Kairouan contract between us had been severed? My soul would bleed dry if this woman left me, but I must stand firm. Now I was setting the terms of our life together. I would rekindle her passion for books and the words of the philosophers, the madness that had captivated her mind: that was the only way to bury her past.

I passed by the Great Mosque. I asked one of the attendants when the circle of Bahaa al-Zaman was held. "Tuesdays, Thursdays, Fridays, and Saturdays," he said, "after the noon prayers."

Zahira would not be comforted nor her grief dissipated until she sat in the circle of Bahaa al-Zaman.

We came early and sat together, Zahira and I, in her circle, which made Bahaa al-Zaman notice us. She nodded to us pleasantly in welcome. We sat close to Bahaa al-Zaman. Zahira was stunned, looking around at the columns of the mosque, the ornaments on the ceiling, and the people around her. I drew near to her until I heard the sighs that followed long weeping, rending my heart. She looked at Bahaa al-Zaman awhile, fascinated by this female cleric whose face shone like the flame of a lantern, and she stole a glance at my eyes, then sighed again. I pressed her fingers gently to let her know she was mine, next to whom all the women of the world were nothing.

Bahaa al-Zaman was speaking pleasantly of the origins of the Just Monotheists, careful of the curious eyes and inquisitive would-be hecklers. "Islam is a structure built on the Five Pillars. What lies within this structure is yours: you have the free will to build and establish your life with whatever choices you may take. Al-Qadi Abd al-Jabbar has divided those who preach virtue and admonish vice into two categories: one only to be performed by imams, such as enacting lawful punishment and preserving Islam and blocking gaps and building armies and the like, while the other is to be performed by all and sundry, such as admonishing the drinking of alcohol, fornication, theft, and so on. However, if there is an imam to be obeyed, it is most prudent to consult them."

What a calamity! Bahaa al-Zaman was quoting the great Mutazilite, al-Qadi Abd al-Jabbar, before witnesses, before the guardians of the credo of Imam ibn Malik? Either Abd al-Jabbar was not known here in Andalusia, or they ignored the fatwas he issued, which had him branded a heretic. I was seeking an opening in her speech that might allow me to produce the key phrase of the Cranes. The circle was expanding around her, more and more rows forming.

I had no experience with speaking to women beyond the confines of closed doors. How was I to address this female cleric, who looked at our faces with such majesty, as though looking down from on high? Not only this, but I must tell her that one of the Voyagers had journeyed far to see her and kneel at her discussion circle. I whispered to Zahira, "Ask her of the ruling over those who commit venial sins—who should preach virtue and admonish vice to them?"

Like a child eager to prove its prowess to its parents, she burst out, "What of those who commit venial sins, Sheikh Bahaa al-Zaman?"

I seized the golden opportunity to say, enunciating clearly, "They are in a status between two statuses."

Although Bahaa al-Zaman retained her seriousness and fixed expression, she looked fleetingly up at me with the ghost of a conspiratorial smile. "That is the fourth pillar of the Just Monotheists," she said, "and it is the pillar we discussed in a previous circle. Today, our discussion revolves around the origins of preaching virtue and admonishing vice."

On our way home, Zahira was twittering with happiness, virtually floating, clinging to me, her hand wrapped around mine. "What am I in comparison to all this knowledge and learning!" she gushed. "I swear, if my family had taught me anything other than shaking my hips, I would have been a cleric like Bahaa al-Zaman!"

"And they would call you Zahirat al-Zaman," I teased.

"No," she insisted. "I would keep my name as Zahira, to recall the blessings of Our Lady Fatima al-Zahraa, the Prophet's daughter, who shades me in her love and care." She went on with sweet melancholy, "I remember back home in Karman—I must have been no older than four, but I remember that my grandparents kept their old religion. When the folk of Karman began to embrace Islam in great numbers, many people fled to India to preserve their faith, and settled there. My grandparents never ceased praying to Zarathustra, and kept his image in the house. You could not imagine how similar that religion is to Islam. They pray five times a day, wash themselves exactly like Muslim ablutions, and believe in resurrection and the straight path; even Zarathustra himself had the experience of the two angels that split open his chest and pulled out the evils of the Self, just like our prophet Muhammad, prayers and peace be upon him!"

"Truly?" I asked, surprised. "Who do you mean? Zarathustra or Mani?" I recalled the poor water carrier of Baghdad, when they burned the image of Mani in front of him.

"I do not recall," she said thoughtfully, "but they had the picture of a bright-faced and cheerful-seeming man, with great eyes and an imposing squared-off beard."

"And when did you become a Muslim?"

"When I was born," she said. "My parents were already Muslim—Shiite, believing in the family of the Prophet, and Ali—so I was born thus."

"But the Just Monotheists," I said, "are ruled by their minds, and do not turn Shiite nor privilege one Muslim over another. We know of no great differences between them, after all. My grandfather says that in his time, the only difference between Sunni and Shiite was the preference of Ali over Uthman—but just look how it has become in Baghdad."

She turned to me curiously, mischief dancing in her eyes. "Who are the Just Monotheists?"

I had slipped! I murmured, "Perhaps I will tell you of them one day."

What if I passed on the torch of justice and monotheism in Cordoba to Zahira? There would be none more passionate and loving and eager to gallop through the paths of knowledge than she. But now I must hold back: it must be love that veiled my mind and made me confused in passing the wisdom of the Voyagers to this crane who excelled in waggling her hips. I would wait and see.

But what of Bahaa al-Zaman? Did she menstruate and ovulate? I swear, if her wisdom and knowledge were spread out over Cordoba and its outskirts and the neighboring hamlets, they would overflow.

We arrived at the house. I had sent Bustan to discreetly ask after Tammam al-Saqalibi around the Great Palace. When we entered, we found her in the courtyard of the house, pale and crying. "There is a snake in a hole under the fountain!" she wailed.

Zahira stood rooted to the spot and refused to go farther inside. I rushed forward, drawing my dagger and scrabbling under the fountain. "Are you certain?" I snapped at Bustan.

"Yes. A long silvery snake, slithering up the pots of basil. It drank from the fountain, then slipped back into its hole. Here," she said, pointing to a crack in the basin. I dug in it with the handle of the dagger. "Leave it, sir," Bustan said. "This may be its home, and we intruders. If we kill it, we shall bring great misfortune down upon ourselves!"

"What do you want, foolish woman?" cried Zahira from the doorway. "That we should be neighbors with the snake?"

"No," said Bustan, "but we could beg it to go. I heard tell in Baghdad that if you see such creatures in your house, you should not kill them until you beg them thrice in the name of the Lord, saying, 'I beg you thrice in the name of the Lord to leave this place if you be a demon!'"

"Do it, then," I said.

"I cannot, not I," she said, "for you are the master of the house."

I fell silent, and refrained from uttering the words. It would injure my dignity in their eyes and make me appear less of a rational man. Should I seem like a madman, talking to the things that creep and crawl and fly upon this earth? Enough that they already knew I listened to the voice of the wind and the song of the trees. Instead, I begged Zahira to come inside, and told her, "I will deal with the snake tomorrow." Now I would go to market to buy food, for the snake had distracted the slave girl Bustan from preparing our meal.

I glimpsed old Fly Eye Dirbas standing at a butcher's stall. I saw him observing me with his cunning gaze, with an overtone of gloating that disquieted me. Should I go to him and threaten him? But now my anger had cooled, and I would not attack him as long as the women assured me that he hadn't visited the house again. A few paces before I reached our home, I recalled Hamdouna's law of parallels and resemblances. Was I back to superstitious mumbo jumbo? But then again, what was that snake doing in our house?

I stormed into the house, calling on Bustan. "Has anyone visited the house in my absence? Did that damned Dirbas come here?"

Despite her vehement denials, her bloodless face and trembling hands only increased my suspicions.

We spent a long time laughing and leaping about, entreating the snake to leave. Even Zahira lost her fear and offered to dance for him if he came out, but he did not.

Bustan suggested a bizarre stratagem to get him out, used, she said, in royal palaces to kill unwanted animal guests. Diamond dust pounded into a paste and mixed in with food near the hole would kill it, she said: diamond was not a poison in itself, but due to its extreme hardness and its sharp edges that never rounded off like other stones, it would stick to the walls of the stomach and intestines if ingested, puncture them when food pressed against the innards, and kill instantly. No other stone adhered like diamond.

This recipe disturbed me. It was an innocent poison that none could discover. What was the mystery held by Bustan that drove her to lower her eyes when I spoke to her? What did she not want me to see?

"Do you expect us to waste diamonds on a snake's innards?" Zahira burst out. "Heavens, what a silly goose!"

All this time, I had been seeking a suitable location for my two crates of books to keep them safe. Zahira suggested a space in the cellar I suspected had been used for grain storage, and was designed in such a manner as to allow an upper and lower current of air to pass through it by means of two windows, one easterly and one westerly, that let in the light and thus would keep them from rotting. I liked her suggestion. She said, "I think it the ideal spot for them. On the one hand, it will keep them safe and away from prying eyes, and on the other, they will remain close to me whenever I require a book from them."

At that, I held her and kissed her, and embraced her so tightly that she cried out. How delicious she was! How amazing the world in her eyes! At that moment, she felt the letter to Hisham al-Muayyad in my sleeve that I brought with me everywhere I went. "What is this?"

I said immediately, "Contracts of sale between myself and the booksellers."

I decided then and there to slip it into the bottom of one of the boxes next to the commandments of the Just

Monotheists, for it was dangerous to keep it with me in my comings and goings. It was no collection of theological quotations, after all, but a message from a vanquished king seeking to reclaim his throne.

A little while before the sunset prayers, there was a gentle knocking on the door, so soft we thought it was merely the wind moving it this way and that. When we listened carefully, we heard a continual, shy knocking. I leapt to the door, bristling, thinking it was Dirbas, and meaning to destroy him. I wrenched the door open violently. At the door was a young woman who took several steps back at my stormy approach. She had a soft voice and was dewy as the dawn, with shining blue eyes and golden braids wrapped in a blue veil the color of her eyes. She seemed hurried and wary, looking about her. In a sweet voice, she said, "My lady Bahaa al-Zaman, may God grant her long life, invites you both to the discussion circle held in her house tomorrow after the afternoon prayers."

I stood transfixed at the girl's beauty and the speed of Sheikh Bahaa al-Zaman's response to my sign in the mosque, and the path that had opened up. The girl disappeared down a side street before I could ask her where her mistress's house was. No matter; we whould find it.

As I was asking the mosque attendants the location of her house, it became clear to me that Bahaa al-Zaman was a person of some status and esteem in Cordoba: she had studied for seven years in Mecca, then returned to become the teacher for the princesses of the Umayyad palace, all while continuing her studies. She had never married, and had many students and adherents. The palace had conferred upon her a space in the Great Mosque. Still, Zahira and I spent a long time circling the streets of Cordoba in search of her house. Finally, a small boy volunteered to take us there. It was a house with white walls, on the corner of two streets, with a great barred wooden gate guarded by an elderly man. He opened a smaller door set into the great gate to admit us. "Is this the house of Bahaa?" we asked.

He nodded, welcoming as though he was used to receiving strangers. He looked into the street behind us, turning his head this way and that. "You have arrived."

There was a great gulf between her house and the street, as though you were stepping into Paradise and the angel Radwan closed the heavenly gates behind you. The roof of the passage leading inside was a wooden trellis, wound about with a climbing plant whose astonishing purple flowers hung in garlands, their scent filling the path. After this, we entered a wide courtyard surrounded by a colonnade with marble pillars, likewise with the flowering plants wound around them. The basin of the fountain in the center was covered with the petals and leaves of the flowers.

"To see her glow and beauty and the splendor of her clothing, and the details in that woman's appearance," gasped Zahira, "you would know that she comes from a place such as this before she ever reached the mosque."

Bahaa was sitting in a corner of the courtyard of her home, a book in her lap, upon a small stone platform covered with carpets, apparently prepared especially for her to teach. A curtain of silk hung between two columns on either side of her. Beneath her feet sat a cat with thick fur looking down at the guests haughtily—after all, it was only he who had attained the privilege of sitting at the feet of Bahaa.

When Bahaa saw us enter, overwhelmed and hesitant, she nodded pleasantly and motioned to us to sit on one of the seats scattered. There were no more than twenty people in attendance, including two women. My mind was set at rest to see them, as I had not wished for Zahira to be the odd one out.

Bahaa went on with what she appeared to have been saying. "Al-Ashaari is said to have numbered many women among the prophets, and the clerics say they are six: Eve, Sarah, Hagar,

Moses's mother, Asiya, and Mary. The Lord sent His message to Mary, mother of Jesus, for it says in verse nineteen of the Sura of Maryam, '*I am only a messenger from thy Lord, to announce to thee the gift of a holy son.*' This is a genuine prophecy, with genuine inspiration: a message from the Lord God to her.

"Some," she went on, "disputed this, saying that prophecy must comprise the prophet preaching the message of right and disputing those who stand against it; but this is not a position for women but for men. Our response is that what they mention is the message and not the status of prophet: a prophet is any person whom God has inspired with His message. What Mary heard was not an illusion nor a divination—it is known that demons may whisper into a diviner's ear, and divination ended with the Prophet Muhammad, peace be upon him. What Mary heard was not a vision, which might be true or false, but a direct communication from God, which makes her a prophet."

Bahaa appeared more comfortable and expansive in her own home than she had been in the mosque. She read from a book on her lap, while the attendees listened silently, in awe. I noticed that most of the attendees were young men. There were a smaller number of older men in expensive caftans and costly turbans, of dignified mien. The lesson ended a little before the sunset prayers, and everyone headed to the door, while bright-faced slave girls moved about, bearing glasses of ginger with honey. Parodying verse twenty-five of the Sura of al-Mutaffifin, "*They are given to drink of a pure wine, sealed,*" I winked at Zahira and said, "They are given to drink of ginger, honeyed!"

She bit her lip. "You seem impressed. You have not taken your eyes off this woman. But when we get home, things will be different. Spend the night here, for you will not be sleeping in my bed tonight."

I was delighted at her jealousy, and would have teased her further, but spied Bahaa coming toward us. Her feminine lilt and nasal, musical cadence could not conceal the strong, unyielding soul behind that voice, lending coherence to her phrases and clarity to her words. Her handshake was firm, and her eyes met mine steadily. Her presence overpowered all around her and overflowed, luminous and dignified. Before I could say a word, she said, "Whence come you?"

"I am from Najd, and she is from Baghdad. We came together in Almería in marriage, and found shelter in the garden of your company." She appeared nonplussed: she was clearly accustomed to being approached by cranes singly, not in pairs. I reassured her. "I have a collection of books, some original translations from the House of Wisdom, and others that I have collected on my journeys from Baghdad to Cordoba, according to the precepts of the Just Monotheists. Rashid ibn Ali in Cairo sends you a letter with his greetings."

Her face split into a gentle smile. "How does Egypt? Is there still suspicion between the folk of Cairo and of Fustat? Are the swords of the soldiers still drawn in the streets?"

"Egypt is licking its wounds," I told her, "but it is still a rare and precious gem. It bleeds like an agate."

Zahira's silence piqued Bahaa's curiosity. "Welcome to the society of the Cranes," she told her. "Whenever a woman steps into a discussion circle, a window of light opens in the city."

Zahira stammered and blushed in a manner I had never seen before, she who had no qualms about swaying and dancing at a gathering surrounded by dozens of lustful eyes! Perhaps she saw in Bahaa al-Zaman another type of woman, one who had no need of flirtations and coquetry and the usual tricks when speaking to men. Bahaa added, "In Cordoba, times have changed. You must both be careful here and walk with measured steps. The wounds are still bleeding. There are a vanquished monarch and a usurper, and some preachers lined up behind the victor. The streets are lurking in wait and the houses of learning are silent, every head turning this way and that in an attempt to divine whence disaster will strike. Did you observe," she asked, "how many spies were watching the entrance to my house?"

I shook my head. "No."

Nodding, she went on. "I know them well. Sometimes they wear a beggar's disguise; sometimes that of a water carrier; sometimes they even come in uniform, staring curiously at those who enter my house." She sighed. "I may have to cease these lectures until the situation is resolved."

"I am sorry to hear it," I said with sincere distress.

She adjusted her veil. "In any event, I shall send for you both when we find a suitable place for the books. Although the libraries have been burned and looted, there are many who would like to acquire them, and seek them out, most importantly the Jews of Cordoba." She then went inside, her garment spreading about her and rippling around her firm steps.

## The Air of Cordoba

The Great Valley wakes Cordoba early, blowing the gentle breezes of the field through it and sending the neighing of the horses across the bridge. Its air suited me and filled me with familiarity and comfort, but its streets disquieted me. I was still fettered by my wariness, ignited further by Bahaa al-Zaman and the soldiers' scrutiny of my face. It was enough for me to attend her circle and search through the market and the paper traders' stalls for books, careful not to chatter or talk too long. Zahira occasionally came with me on my tours, for a man out with his wife is less suspicious than a stranger inspecting stores and sitting at lessons in mosques.

One day, we happened to encounter the lute player from Zahira's old troupe. A woman from Sindh of about fifty, with an imposing presence, she still retained some of the freshness of her old beauty. She told us that Dirbas had rented a house for them in Rusafa, on the other side of the Great Valley. They had started to receive invitations to entertain at weddings and circumcisions. She hesitated awhile before saying, "But everyone is asking about Zahira."

Out of pity for her and respect for her age, I refrained from cursing her all the way back to Rusafa. I merely turned on my heel and left without a word, letting Zahira stumble after me, barely able to keep up with my strides. I knew that I could not erase her past as one removes an eggshell, for it had merged with her consciousness early, and mingled with her essence. Even if the sciences of the Greek philosophers poured into her, and she read them day and night without pause, she was nothing but a whore. Mazid al-Hanafi, you are the first person who should know this. Today you met the lute player; tomorrow it will be the one who beats the tambourine, and the day after the tambour. But I had satisfied her heart with affection and compliments, warmed her bed with a young man in love with her, furnished her home with the best carpets and covers, and filled her coffers with good things and spices . . . what more could a woman want?

I breathed in the good air of Cordoba: it did away with displeasure and cured heaviness of heart. I had not found Tammam al-Saqalibi, which meant I must burn the letter with all haste. Still, Bustan returned every time with an answer that left a thread of hope still connected. First they would say he was gone to Elvira and would return in a week; another time they told her the odd news that he had become a monk and retreated to a cave close to Cordoba to get away from the Berbers and Sulayman al-Musta'in. And still the letter remained unburned. The second new moon had risen on Cordoba and I had not yet burned the letter.

Are you keeping the letter, Mazid, out of some greedy hope that Muayyad may return to his throne and appoint you to a position or give you a bounty to last you all the days of your life? This world is nothing but temptation: its demons never cease dancing, and they arrive incessantly, in the ever-changing garments of seduction. I was still overcome with the desire to get to the library of the surgeon al-Zahrawi. I had been told by a paper merchant that his heirs refused to sell it. His *al-Tasrif*, or *The Method of Medicine*, comprised thirty volumes of every miracle of this field.

Although we had dismissed Dirbas, he had not forgotten us: and, as Zahira said, he made a bad enemy, slow to retreat. One day, I returned home to find Bustan presenting me with a package. "One of Dirbas's boys brought it for you."

I took it, hands shaking with rage, and unwrapped it to find the book *Why Dogs Are Better Than a Great Many Men* by Ibn Mirziban. Should I go to his house in Rusafa and whip him until he vomited his mother's milk? He had not left us alone, and would not—not until I made him eat dirt. But my life in Cordoba was on a crumbling cliffside: my books, my letter, the commandments of the Voyagers, a woman whose discussion circles I must attend, and another, a beauty bitten by the seduction of knowledge. Was this what they called prudence, or wisdom? Or was it cowardice, the fear of teaching a lesson to one who called you a dog?

I would refrain. But I would not forget my vengeance on that dog, Dirbas.

A brave knight chooses his enemies with care, as he chooses his friends. Dirbas was unworthy of my enmity. Where you set your horizons, there are your aims and your kingdom. My quarrel with Dirbas was no more than two house cats squabbling over a dish, while the horizon glimmered with winged creatures and adorned stallions. What did you have in store for me, Cordoba, pomegranate tree with fruits full of rubies?

I am Mazid al-Najdi. I have ridden long and hard to find you, from the heart of Najd. But all I have found in you is another Agate City, lit with vendettas, blood, and fights over power. What lies within you, Cordoba, for a young man who always rises from the depths to soar on high? What city should I go to after you, you who perch on the shoulder of the world?

Cordoba did not wait long to respond.

# Fling Him into the Depths of the Pit

> Lord, Companion of every stranger, friend of every lonely man, refuge of all the fearful, You who dismiss every affliction, know every solitary prayer, hear every complaint, and are everywhere, Ever-living, Self-subsisting Sustainer of All, I ask You to fill my heart with faith in You, so that I have no concern but You. Let there be an end and salvation to my affliction, for You are capable of everything.

This was the prayer that never ceased to fall from the lips of my companion in this solid stone dungeon, as though he imagined it as a saw that could cut away the bars of our cell. As if this was not enough, he asked me to repeat it with him: it was, he said, the prayer that had liberated Joseph from his prison, ended his captivity, lightened his affliction, dismissed his fears, and given him dominion over the treasures of the earth.

But I was not afraid. Nor was I reassured, sad, stricken, or despairing. My heart was only empty, like the site of some great battle after the armies have withdrawn, leaving broken arrows and shattered swords in severed hands that had been readying themselves to embrace a lover, and turbans for heads that were filled with dreams, and shoes with feet in them that had been seeking a way to return. I was not afraid or grieved or lonely or anything at all. Is this what the dead feel at the taste of dust? I know not how long I have been in this place. The days are circles within which I turn, unable to grasp a beginning or an end. Perhaps I can make out some of the seasons through the window at the top of the cell, through which a great tree can be seen, extending its branches and leaves to dance with the sky and inform me of the succession of the seasons in its foliage. When I am tired of looking at the tree, I open the windows of my soul to see what has become of the boy from Najd who bears such a heavy burden upon his soul that it has brought him to his knees.

I no longer dare to remember my time in the house in Cordoba, for the pain might destroy me.

When the soldiers came to take me thence, Zahira was wailing and shrieking, clawing at her face and chest, Bustan trying to calm her. It was as though I glimpsed old Fly Eye Dirbas at the gate; then everything slipped from around me and became part of the past.

The soldiers said they had been watching me since I arrived in Cordoba, and told me that those who spread the books of the heretics receive a terrible punishment; but how could they have known that my crates contained books of heresy? Who had betrayed me? Dirbas? Bustan? Or perhaps Zahira? Had she only been a flight of fancy, or had I been a fool, transported by love, the victim of a troupe of conjurers and dancers whose mission was to capture the minds—and money—of men? Or had they seen me frequenting the circles, and home, of Bahaa al-Zaman? Two days before my arrest, I had gone to her house, where the old guard at the door had told me, in tears, that the caliph's soldiers had come and taken her away, along with all the books in her library. But the crates of books were still there in my cellar. What had Zahira done with them? Had she betrayed me? Had she given them to Dirbas to sell at the paper market for next to nothing? Or had she kept them?

No one had visited me as yet in my cell. One desolate day in the freezing dead of winter, my companion in the cell had died, and since then, I had spent long months without speaking to anyone. When the Berber guard told me, "There is a man asking to see you," I trembled with fear—not of the person arriving, but for fear that I had lost the capacity to speak.

It was my boy, Ma'in. When he saw my tattered clothing and emaciated body, my bones sticking out, he wept, and I with him. We did not speak long, sobbing the length of his visit. Before he left, he told me that he had come to Cordoba and searched far and wide for me, following the news of me until he found out that I was here; if the warden of the prison, he said, had not been a Sanhaji from his tribe, he would not have been permitted to see me. On the way out, he murmured, "With hardship there shall be ease," and "The Lord's deliverance is nigh," and told me that the Hammudid Dynasty ruled Cordoba now, and that they were descendants of the Prophet's house and known for justice and wisdom. "At their hands, you shall be released, God willing." He left, looking back at me and weeping.

Ma'in kept visiting, bringing me the food I loved, and small books to which the Sanhaji guard turned a blind eye, and papers and pens and inks with which to gather my life that had been wasted on the wandering roads and in the Agate Cities. This was my torch, my antidote, my lantern in the depths of my cell. Without these, I would have died.

There is not much left in my empty heart but the seventh commandment of the Voyagers.

Seventh Commandment
Burn all these commandments, that they may not become a parallel religion to entrap you in bars of their own. Life is greater than instructions and commandments. Life is ever-changing and nothing remaineth the same. Time floweth on and taketh all withal. Everything leaveth its place; nothing remaineth forever.

The desire for learning is the mother of all virtues. Burn these commandments and start anew.

I am Mazid al-Hanafi, and I come from Najd. It is a land of plenty, filled with lush vegetation, rich herds, freely flowing springs, and great blessings. I am the secret crane, for whom the nets of darkness have lain in wait and taken me to a cell whose ponderous stones lament every night as they recount the sorrows of those who have passed through.

I must burn everything, and rise again from the ashes.

I am the embryo in the darkness, trapped in eternal labor, passing my time and history lying in wait for the game of light and shadow, awaiting the breath of morning, through the narrow window at the top of my dungeon.

SELECTED HOOPOE TITLES

*My First and Only Love*
by Sahar Khalifeh, translated by Aida Bamia

*The Girl with Braided Hair*
by Rasha Adly, translated by Sarah Enany

*The Magnificent Conman of Cairo*
By Adel Kamel, translated by Waleed Almusharaf

\*

**hoopoe** is an imprint for engaged, open-minded readers hungry for outstanding fiction that challenges headlines, re-imagines histories, and celebrates original storytelling. Through elegant paperback and digital editions, **hoopoe** champions bold, contemporary writers from across the Middle East alongside some of the finest, groundbreaking authors of earlier generations.

At hoopoefiction.com, curious and adventurous readers from around the world will find new writing, interviews, and criticism from our authors, translators, and editors.